KING

OF

CHRISTMAS

A CHOOSE YOUR OWN PATH
PSYCHOLOGICAL THRILLER

JE ROWNEY

LITTLE FOX
PUBLISHING

Also by JE Rowney
I Can't Sleep
The Woman in the Woods
Other People's Lives
The Book Swap
Gaslight
The House Sitter
The Work Retreat
The Other Passenger
Waking Up In Vegas
Xmas Break
Where No One Can Hear You
Wish You Were Her
Red Flags

For further information, please visit the author's website.
http://jerowney.com/

Disclaimer:
This novel is a work of fiction. All characters, places, and businesses within this story are entirely fictitious. They are not representative of any real persons, places, or organisations. Any resemblance to actual persons, living or dead, or actual events, is purely coincidental. If any names of persons, places, or organisations within this novel coincide with real-world entities, it is by chance, and no inference should be made regarding their connection to the real world.

HOW TO READ THIS BOOK

This is not a story you simply read. It's a story you enter.

In King of Christmas, you decide what happens next.

At the end of many sections, you'll face a choice: sometimes small, sometimes life-changing – or life-ending. Each option will send you to a different numbered or titled section.

Follow the instructions at the end of the passage (for example, "Go to The Pine Hollow Inn" or "Turn to page 42") to continue your version of the story.

There are no wrong turns—only different truths.

Some paths will bring Jenny closer to the answers she's sought for decades.

Others will lead her into darkness, to endings you may not see coming.

Every decision reveals a new layer of Pine Hollow's secrets and the people who have kept them buried.

When you reach an ending, you may begin again.

Start over from the beginning, or from any earlier decision, and follow a different path.

Each route uncovers new clues, new betrayals, and new parts of the solution.

You control the investigation.

You decide who to trust.

And you determine whether Jenny Matthews will uncover the truth...

or join the list of the missing.

Choose carefully. The King of Christmas is always watching.

THEN - CHRISTMAS EVE 1986

You've never liked the way the Frost Mountains loom over Pine Hollow, especially at dusk in winter when the snow makes everything too bright and too dark at the same time. The jagged peaks cut into the grey December sky like teeth, and sometimes, when the wind blows just right, the sound reminds you of bells - the kind that might hang from a sleigh, or from something worse.

Your family moved to Pine Hollow three years ago, in 1983, when Dad got the job at the lumber mill. You were seven then, about to turn eight, Sarah almost six, and neither of you understood why the realtor seemed so relieved to finally sell the house on Evergreen Lane, or why you got it for such a good price. You didn't know about Tommy Wilson yet, or about the other children who had disappeared before him. All you knew was that your new bedroom had a window seat overlooking the mountains, and that Sarah's room, right next to yours, had pink flowered wallpaper she adored.

The house itself is one of those big old Victorians that seem to collect shadows in its corners. Dad says it was built during the logging boom, back when Pine Hollow was a prosperous town instead of a place people end up when they have nowhere left to go. The porch wraps around three sides, its gingerbread trim and sagging steps giving it the air of a tired old lady who used to be beautiful. In summer, Mom grows geraniums in the window boxes. In winter, she hangs evergreen garlands and red ribbons, trying to make it look like something from a Christmas card.

You're eleven now, and you know things you didn't know when you first moved here. You know that Tommy Wilson vanished on Christmas Eve, 1981, leaving nothing but footprints in the snow that led to the woods and then stopped. You know his older sister found a note the next morning, confessing to breaking their mother's favourite vase - a crime Tommy had been punished for the week before. You know he was the fourth child to disappear this way, all on Christmas Eve, all leaving similar notes about things they hadn't actually done.

These are the kinds of stories people in Pine Hollow only whisper about, usually at the Snowed Inn Café where your mother works part time. They talk about the King of Christmas, a figure that's somewhere between Santa Claus and the Bogeyman. They say he knows which children have been naughty and which have been nice. They say he doesn't make mistakes. They say he leaves the good children and takes the bad ones away to his castle in the mountains, where the endless winter wind rings with the sound of silver bells.

Sarah, your nine-year-old sister, doesn't know any of these stories. Mom and Dad have made sure of that. They've made sure she stays innocent, perfect Sarah, who never gets in trouble, who always does her homework, who helps old Mrs Craig across the street with her groceries. Sarah, who right now is sitting by the fireplace writing her letter to Santa, her tongue poking out slightly as she concentrates on making her handwriting extra neat.

You're supposed to be helping with the Christmas cookies, but you're upstairs in your room, sitting in your window seat, turning Barbara's silver charm bracelet over and over in your hands. You stole it from her locker three days ago, the last day of school before Christmas break. The plan had seemed so perfect then - take the bracelet, plant it in Sarah's backpack, watch for once as she gets in trouble instead of you.

The guilt sits in your stomach like a stone, but not enough to make you change your mind. Not after the parent-teacher conference last week, when your teacher spent twenty minutes comparing your behaviour to Sarah's. Not after Sunday school, when Sarah got to play Mary in the nativity scene while you were stuck being one of the shepherds. Not after years of *"Why can't you be more like your sister?"*

Outside your window, the Christmas lights Dad strung along the eaves are starting to twinkle on, little coloured stars against the early darkness. The snow is falling harder now, big flakes that muffle the world like a blanket. Down the street, you can see the Clegg house, where Barbara is probably crying about her lost bracelet. Beyond that, the other Victorian houses of Pine Hollow fade into the growing gloom, their windows warm with holiday lights, their chimneys puffing wood smoke into the steel-grey sky.

And behind it all, always, the mountains. Even now, you can see the highest peaks catching the last of the sunset, turning them the colour of old blood.

"Jenny!" Sarah's voice floats up the stairs. "Mom says you have to come help with the cookies!"

You slip the bracelet into your sock drawer. The charms - a ballerina, a tiny silver book, a heart - clink against each other like miniature bells.

What you don't know yet is that in exactly forty-seven minutes, Sarah will disappear.

What you don't know yet is that her footprints will stop at the edge of the woods, just like Tommy Wilson's did.

What you don't know yet is that this will be the last time you hear her call your name.

What do you do now?

Go downstairs to help with the cookies Turn to page 8
Stay in your room a little longer Turn to page 9
Look out the window at the mountains Turn to page 10
Call Sarah up to your room to talk Turn to page 11

GO DOWNSTAIRS TO HELP

You go downstairs, but Sarah's already racing to the back door in her new red mittens. "It's snowing harder!" she calls out. By the time you reach the kitchen window, she's already at the tree line, reaching toward something you can't quite see.

Head to the back door Turn to page 12

STAY IN YOUR ROOM

You're still holding the bracelet when you hear Sarah's delighted gasp from downstairs. "Look at the snow!" Through your window, you see her running into the backyard, red mittens bright against the white. You're halfway down the stairs when she reaches the tree line.

Head to the back door Turn to page 12

LOOK OUT OF THE WINDOW

You're still at the window when Sarah bursts into the yard below, spinning in the snow in her red mittens. You start to turn away, but something makes you look back - a flash of darker red at the edge of the woods. Sarah's already running toward it.

Head to the back door Turn to page 12

CALL SARAH UP TO YOUR ROOM

"Sarah! Come up here!" you call, suddenly wanting to confess everything about the bracelet. Maybe if you tell her first, she can help you make it right.

But Sarah never makes it upstairs. "Just a minute!" she calls back. "I want to see if it's still snowing!" The back door creaks open, and through your window you see her red mittens catching the last light as she runs toward the trees.

Head to the back door Turn to page 12

YOU HEAD TO THE BACK DOOR

No matter what you do next, you're too late. By the time you reach the back door, there's nothing but Sarah's footprints in the snow, stopping abruptly at the tree line. Beyond that point: nothing. No drag marks, no signs of struggle, just the sudden end of her path as if she'd simply ceased to exist.

You call her name until your throat is raw. Your parents join you, then the neighbours, then half the town. The police arrive with dogs that circle the tree line, whining, refusing to go further. They search the woods all night, flashlights bobbing through the darkness like fallen stars.

They never find her red mittens.

They never find a single trace.

What you don't know yet, and what you won't discover until next Christmas morning when your father opens the front door, is that this disappearance is only the beginning. That there will be a bell waiting on the porch, silver and perfect, its bright chime marking the start of an annual ritual of terror. One bell the first year, then another, then another, each one a reminder that whoever took Sarah is still out there. Still watching. Still waiting.

But tonight, in this moment, all you know is that your sister ran into the snow wearing red mittens, and she never came back.

And that somewhere in those mountains, the King of Christmas is satisfied with his choice.

Turn to the next page to begin your journey.

The Frost Mountains haven't changed since you left town at eighteen years old. They still loom over Pine Hollow like teeth against the winter sky, hungry and waiting. You're fifty now, but something about driving down Main Street makes you feel like a kid again, clutching a stolen silver charm bracelet in your sweating palm.

Not that anyone back in Boston cares about Pine Hollow. At *The Beacon*—the newspaper you've poured most of your life into—they're talking about cutting staff again. Ad revenue's down, subscriptions are falling, and online readers want *viral outrage,* not careful investigative features. You know your editor is running out of patience.

You've made a career reporting on missing children, cold cases, disappearances that never made the national news. You've kept your distance, never once pointing your lens back toward Pine Hollow. Not toward Sarah. Not toward the night she vanished.

But if you're honest, you've been circling it all along. Every missing child you've written about was really just a shadow of her.

Now, when you pitched the story about the *"King of Christmas,"* your editor leaned in for the first time in months.

"That urban legend upstate? Missing kids, creepy Santa angle? It's seasonal, it'll sell. If you can nail it, Matthews, we run it front page."

That's all the permission you need. You've broken stories the police gave up on. You've found leads in cases three decades cold. Pine Hollow's mystery won't be any different—just smaller, more personal. You know how to work a source. You know how to find the thread no one else sees.

That's why you're here. Not because of the paper alone. Not because of your slipping career. But because the story has always been waiting for you.

The Snowed Inn Café is still here, though the sign is different. The lumber mill where Dad worked is closed, its skeleton rusting against the mountainside. The logging camp up in the mountains had already shut down by the early seventies; the ski resort took over that land. By the time you moved here in '83, the mill was limping along on timber from elsewhere, a ghost operation that finally died in '85. And your parents' house on Evergreen Lane stands exactly as you remember it: the gingerbread trim, the sagging porch steps, the evergreen garlands and red ribbons your mother has hung every December without fail.

You park across the street, engine idling, staring at the windows. You know what waits inside. Since 1987, every Christmas Eve, your parents have received a silver bell on their doorstep.

They never left Pine Hollow. They never stopped opening the door on Christmas morning to find another bell. They never told you, not at first. You only learned years later, when the bells had filled a wooden chest in the hallway, mocking every attempt your family made to move on.

Even so, they stayed.

Three more children have disappeared since Sarah - all on Christmas Eve, all leaving nothing but footprints in the snow. The most recent was just last year: Amy Crawford, age eight.

The local papers still call him the King of Christmas. The stories have grown over the decades: he lives in an ice castle, he keeps the children in glass cases, he only takes the guilty.

But you know better. Sarah wasn't guilty. Sarah was perfect.

For almost forty years you've imagined this moment, and now you're here. No longer a child, but still trembling like one.

You've brought your notebook. Your recorder. Your press badge that doesn't carry as much weight as it used to.

This time, you've also brought the questions no one else has dared ask.

You've booked a room at the Pine Hollow Inn. Your excuse to yourself was that you'd need a base of operations, somewhere to lay out notes and equipment. The truth is simpler: you weren't sure you could face your parents the moment you got here.

The house across the street is just a short walk away, yet the distance feels unbearable. How do you knock on a door you've avoided for almost four decades? How do you look your mother in the eye knowing she's carried every single one of those bells? She's got a reminder of every single year that's passed. Maybe you're not ready to tell her that you bear the burden too.

Maybe you'll never be ready.

Part of you wants to go straight to Amy Crawford's family instead. The Crawfords are strangers, and strangers are easier. You could slide into your role as a journalist, ask your questions, keep it professional. Pretend this is just another case file instead of your own sister's ghost.

Another part of you is pulled toward the old ski resort in the mountains. You've read the case files, stared at the grainy photos — you know the story begins there: the first child taken from the lodge built upon those slopes. If this nightmare has a beginning, maybe it will have an end.

Snowflakes streak across the windshield, sticking and melting in uneven trails. The Frost Mountains loom in the rearview mirror.

You can almost hear your editor's voice: *Get the angle. Get the hook. Make them read again.*

But before you can write anything, you have to decide where to begin.

What do you do?
Check into the Pine Hollow Inn. Turn to page 33
Visit Amy Crawford's family Turn to page 23
Go across to your parents' house Turn to page 27
Drive to the old ski resort Turn to page 16

DRIVE TO THE SKI RESORT

You shift the car into drive, hands tight on the wheel. The ski resort. If you're going to understand this, you need to see where it began.

But as you pull away from your parents' house, the sky is already deepening to indigo. The streetlights flicker on, one by one, casting yellow pools across the snow. You check the dashboard clock: 6:43pm. The sun set twenty minutes ago.

The mountain road will be worse than the highway. No streetlights up there, just miles of switchbacks and black ice. You remember what it was like as a kid, riding in the backseat while your father navigated those curves, how the headlights would catch nothing but snow and more snow, how the trees seemed to lean in like they were trying to grab the car.

And even the maintained road into town was icy.

You loosen your grip on the wheel slightly, feeling the ache in your knuckles. You've been driving all day. Seven hours from Boston, fighting holiday traffic and your own mounting dread. Your eyes burn with fatigue. Your neck is stiff. The coffee you downed at the last rest stop has left you jittery and hollow.

Going up that mountain tonight, alone, in the dark, exhausted? That's not determination. That's recklessness.

The journalist in you knows better. You don't chase a story when you're not thinking clearly. You don't put yourself at risk when you're already compromised. How many times have you told younger reporters to wait, to regroup, to approach a source when they're sharp, not when they're running on fumes?

The ski resort will still be there tomorrow. In daylight. When you're rested. When you can see the road, and what's on either side of it.

Tomorrow. You'll go tomorrow. You tell yourself it's the smart choice. You try not to think about how it feels like retreat.

You take the next right, heading back toward Main Street. Toward the Pine Hollow Inn. Turn to page 33

SNAP BACK AT KATIE

Something in you snaps.

"You think Sarah is just another headline for me?" Your voice comes out sharper than you intended, too loud for the too-quiet lobby. "I've carried her every damn day since she vanished. Every case I've ever worked, every child I've ever written about—it's all been her. Don't stand there and tell me I don't know what it's like to lose someone."

Katie flinches, but only for a second. Then her mouth twists into a bitter smile. "Carrying isn't the same as staying."

The words land like a blade. She doesn't have to explain them; you already know. You left. She didn't. That's the difference, the wound between you.

"I stayed in this town," Katie goes on, her voice rising, her hand flat on the counter like she's holding herself upright. "Me and my sister, watching my mother put out a stocking for Tommy every Christmas until the year she died. I stayed. She stayed. I walked these streets, listened to the whispers, saw the woods every day. You got to run, Jenny. You got to bury yourself in bylines and deadlines and *pretend* that distance was healing."

"I wasn't pretending," you shoot back. "You think writing about those kids was easy? Talking to their parents, seeing the photographs, hearing their voices on home videos, knowing that every single one of them looked like Sarah to me? You think that was some kind of escape?"

Katie studies you for a long moment, her jaw tight. Then she shakes her head slowly. "You wrote about other people's children because it was safer than writing about your own sister."

The heat drains from your anger, leaving only the hollow weight beneath. She's not wrong.

The radiator hums in the corner, the only sound between you. Outside, snow lashes against the old glass panes.

Katie finally breaks eye contact, busying herself with the guest book. "You've got your room. Sleep there. See if the nightmares follow you."

You close your fist around the key, the edges digging into your palm. The entire building seems to groan around you, tired wood settling, as if the Inn itself resents having to keep your secrets too.

Your throat burns with words you can't decide whether to swallow or spit out.

Do you:
Say nothing more and head upstairs to Room 12 Turn to page 31
Press Katie about the bells Turn to page 34
Ask why the police never helped Turn to page 29

HEAD TO THE BAR

The Timberline sits two blocks down from the Inn, squeezed between a shuttered hardware store and the post office. You remember it from when you were a kid, though it was called something else then. The Old Mill Tavern, maybe? Your father used to stop in after his shifts at the lumber mill, come home smelling of sawdust and beer, too tired to talk.

The exterior is dark wood and river rock, with a hanging sign creaking in the wind. Through the front window you can see warm light, the glow of beer signs, and the shapes of people at the bar.

People. Other human beings who aren't your parents, aren't Katie Wilson, aren't ghosts.

You push through the door.

The warmth hits first, then the smell: fryer grease, beer, old wood, and something piney that might be cleaner or might just be Pine Hollow itself. The bar runs along the left wall, bottles backlit in amber and green. A few booths line the right side. A jukebox sits silent in the corner, its lights cycling through colours no one's watching.

There are maybe a dozen people inside. A couple in one of the booths, bent over their phones. Three men at the bar, spread out with empty stools between them like they're not together but have been coming here long enough that being alone together is its own kind of company. A woman shooting pool in the back, her movements economical, bored.

Every single one of them looks up when you enter.

The conversation doesn't stop, exactly. But it quiets. Shifts. The bartender, a woman around your age with short grey hair and reading glasses hanging from a chain, glances at you once, then away. You try to place her. You must have been at school together, but you come up short.

You've walked into a hundred bars in a hundred towns chasing a hundred stories. You know how to read a room. This one is reading you right back, and it doesn't like what it sees.

But you're here now. Leaving would be worse than staying.

You cross to the bar, take a stool near the end, away from the three men but not so far that you're making a statement about it. The bartender moves down to you, no hurry, wiping her hands on a towel.

"What can I get you?"

Her tone isn't rude. But it isn't warm either. It's the voice you use for outsiders. If she recognises you, she doesn't show it.

"Bourbon," you say. "Neat. Whatever you pour."

She nods, turns away. The conversation around you hasn't resumed. You can feel eyes on your back. The man closest to you, white beard, flannel shirt, nursing what looks like whisky, is definitely watching you.

The bartender returns with your drink. Sets it down without ceremony. "Eight dollars."

You hand her a ten, tell her to keep it. She takes it, still no smile, and moves away.

The bourbon burns going down, cheap and sharp, but you welcome it. You've had worse. You've drunk in worse places, asked harder questions, faced down more hostile sources.

But somehow this feels different. This feels personal.

"They don't like outsiders much around here."

The voice comes from beside you. The bearded man. His eyes are pale blue, rheumy with age, but sharp underneath. He's not looking at you, just staring into his whisky like it might have answers.

You turn slightly. "I'm not an outsider. My parents have lived here for over forty years. I grew up here."

"Is that right?" He takes a sip, slow, deliberate. Still not looking at you. "And where are you now?"

"Boston. But I'm back because…"

"Boston." He says it like it's a foreign country. "So, you left."

"Yes, but that doesn't mean…"

"Who's your people?"

You hesitate, then realise he's asking who your parents are. "Bill and Anne Matthews. Evergreen Lane."

Something flickers in his eyes. Recognition. He finally turns to look at you, really look at you, and you can see him doing the math. The timeline. The name.

"Matthews," he repeats quietly. Then, after a pause that feels like a held breath: "Shame about your sister."

The words land like stones. Polite. Expected. Empty.

"Thank you," you manage.

He nods, looking back at his glass. For a moment you think the conversation is over, that being Bill Matthews' daughter means something here.

Then he says, "Doesn't matter though."

You blink. "What doesn't?"

"You're not *FROM* here." Now he turns, fixes you with those pale eyes. "Not you, not your parents. Not your sister neither, God rest her. Comer-inners, all of you."

Around you, the bar has gone completely silent. The couple in the booth are watching. The woman by the pool table has stopped playing. Even the bartender is paying attention now, wiping the same spot on the bar over and over.

He leans in slightly. "And now you show up after thirty years. Here to start asking questions about things that are none of your business anymore, stirring up pain for folks who've learned to live with it. That about sum it up?"

Your jaw tightens. "I'm trying to find out what happened to Sarah. And to the others."

"The others." He shakes his head. "You mean our kids. Our neighbours' kids. Our town's grief. Not yours. Not anymore. You left that behind when you got on that bus to Boston."

The bartender is watching you now, expression unreadable. The three men at the bar might as well be a wall of flannel and judgment. The couple in the booth have their phones down, waiting to see what you'll do.

You could argue. You could defend yourself, explain about your career, about how every missing child you've written about has been Sarah's shadow, about how you've never stopped carrying this.

But they don't care. And more importantly, they won't listen.

Because you're not *FROM* here.

You down the rest of your bourbon in one burning swallow. Set the glass on the bar harder than you meant to. The sound echoes in the silence.

"Thanks for the drink," you say to the bartender.

She nods. Still no expression.

You slide off the stool, button your coat. The walk to the door feels like miles, every eye in the place tracking your movement. No one says goodbye. No one tells you to come back.

The door closes behind you, and the cold hits like a wall, but you're grateful for it. Grateful for the darkness, for the empty street, for the snow that's started falling again, erasing your footprints almost as soon as you make them.

You return to the Pine Hollow Inn, where Katie Wilson is still waiting at the front desk. **Do you:**

Tell Katie why you're back Turn to page 25
Ask Katie about the bells Turn to page 34
Go straight up to your room Turn to page 31

VISIT AMY CRAWFORD'S FAMILY

The Crawfords. Amy's family. The most recent loss, raw and bleeding in a way the others have had decades to scar over. They'll remember details the older families have buried or forgotten. They might even talk to you.

You pull out your phone, thumb hovering over your notes. You have the address. It's only a ten-minute drive from here.

But it's also 6:43pm on December 23rd.

Christmas Eve is tomorrow. Right now, they're probably trying to hold themselves together for Amy's younger sibling, the one who's still here. You know this from the reports, from the case files. Trying to make tonight feel normal, or as close to normal as it can ever be again when you're missing a child. Wrapping presents, maybe. Baking cookies. Going through the motions because what else can you do?

You know, because your parents did the same for you after Sarah…

And you want to show up on their doorstep? A stranger with a notebook and a recorder, asking them to relive the worst night of their lives?

You've done this before. You've knocked on doors, asked the hard questions, pushed sources when you needed to. But you always called first. You always gave them the choice. You always approached with the respect their grief deserved.

Showing up unannounced, at night, the day before Christmas Eve? That's not journalism. That's an ambush. That's using their pain for your story without giving them any agency in how it's told.

Sarah deserves better than that. Amy deserves better than that.

So do you, if you're honest. You're not ready. Not tonight. Not after the drive, after seeing your parents' house, after feeling Pine Hollow's weight settle back onto your shoulders like it never left.

You need to think. You need to plan. You need to figure out your approach, your questions, what you're actually asking them to give you.

The Crawfords aren't going anywhere. You can call tomorrow, ask for an interview properly. Do this right.

You lower your phone and put the car back in drive. The Inn, then. Check in, get your thoughts in order, come at this like the professional you've spent thirty years becoming.

Not like the desperate eleven-year-old you're terrified you still are.

You head for the Pine Hollow Inn. **Turn to page 33**

TELL KATIE WHY YOU'RE BACK

You clear your throat. The words feel heavy, but you push them out anyway.

"I'm here about Sarah," you say. "And the others. I'm writing a story."

Katie's lips press into a line, her gaze sharp. "The others? They have names, *Jenny*. Rachel. David. Claire. Tommy. Sarah. Daniel. Emily. Amy. Eight children." Her voice catches only once—on her brother's name—but she steadies herself quickly. "Don't make them sound like statistics in one of your articles."

Heat creeps up your neck.

You know the names. You know all the names. You've repeated them so many times that they have become a mantra.

"That's not what I meant."

"Isn't it?" She leans her elbows on the desk, eyes glittering. "Jenny Matthews, the big-shot journalist. I've read your bylines. You made it out of this place, didn't you? Went off to college, got yourself a career. Meanwhile, the rest of us stayed here, trying to build lives in the shadow of those mountains."

You want to argue, to tell her she's wrong, that you've been carrying Sarah's ghost every day since you left. But Katie's right: you did run.

Katie straightens, smoothing her sweater sleeves the way she used to when she was nervous in class. "You want a room, you got it. But if you're here for answers, Jenny… don't expect anyone in this town to start talking to you just because you're writing a story."

Writing a story. As if that's all this is. Katie doesn't understand: journalism isn't just recording events. It's excavation. It's reconstruction. It's taking fragments and building truth. You've given voices to families who'd been silenced. You've forced cold cases back into the light. That's not "just writing a story." That's justice.

She slides a brass key across the counter. Room 12. The number tag is worn smooth with age. The inn is more boarding house than hotel, really. The town isn't known for its tourist attractions. The wallpaper is faded holly print, edges peeling at the seams, as though even the walls have grown tired of keeping up appearances.

You take the key, your throat tight.

Do you:
Ask about the bells Turn to page 39
Snap back at Katie Turn to page 17
Retreat upstairs to your room Turn to page 31

GO TO YOUR PARENTS' HOUSE

Your hands won't move. They're still gripping the steering wheel, knuckles white, even though the engine is off and your parents' house is right there, fifty feet away across the street. Close enough to see the wreath on the door, the lights in the windows, the same gingerbread trim that's been slowly rotting for forty years.

Your mother is probably in the kitchen. It's almost seven. She'll be starting dinner, moving through the same routines she's moved through every December since 1986. Your father will be in his chair with the newspaper, or pretending to read it while he stares at nothing.

They know you're coming. You called yesterday, told them you'd be here today. They said they'd leave the porch light on.

And there it is. Glowing warm and yellow, the same way it did when Sarah used to wait for you to come home from school.

Your throat closes.

You can't do this. Not yet. Not like this.

You've spent thirty-nine years building distance. Not just miles, but layers of professional detachment, of other people's tragedies, of stories you could control because they weren't yours. You became the journalist who could stare down grieving parents and ask the questions no one else would ask, who could chase leads into dark places and come out with the truth.

But that was someone else's truth. Someone else's dark places.

This is yours. This is Sarah. This is the lie you told and the sister you lost and the bells that have been coming every Christmas morning while you were safely in Boston, pretending distance made it hurt less.

How do you walk through that door? How do you look your mother in the eye when she's carried every one of those bells? How do you face your father's quiet grief, the way he never blamed you even though you blamed yourself enough for both of you?

You need time. You need to prepare. You need to have something to offer them besides your presence and your guilt.

You need one night to remember how to breathe in this town before you can face what you left behind.

Your hands finally move. You turn the key. The engine coughs back to life.

In your rearview mirror, you watch your parents' house shrink away. The porch light stays on. They'll wait up for a call that isn't coming tonight.

Tomorrow. You'll face them tomorrow. When you're stronger. When you have a plan. When you can walk through that door as the journalist you've become instead of the child you were.

The Pine Hollow Inn rises ahead, its Victorian trim strung with tired lights, and you tell yourself this isn't running away.

You tell yourself this is strategy.

You tell yourself you're allowed one more night before you confront the ghost that's been waiting thirty-nine years.

Sarah can wait one more night too.

Can't she?

You head for the Pine Hollow Inn Turn to page 33

You tighten your grip on the key, but you can't stop yourself.

"All these years. Eight kids. Why the hell didn't the police ever do a stakeout? If he comes back every Christmas Eve to leave a bell, they've had decades of chances to catch him at it."

Katie lets out a sharp laugh that has no humour in it. "You think they didn't talk about it? Of course they did. Back in the early days, after Tommy, after Sarah, the idea came up plenty."

Katie's fingers drum restlessly on the desk. "Claire Henderson was taken in 1980. Her family didn't find a bell until the Christmas after, 1981. Just sitting there on the porch. They kept quiet at first. I mean, it was just a bell. It didn't mean anything."

Her throat works, and for a moment her voice goes thin. "That was the year Tommy was taken. My parents found our first bell the following Christmas, in '82. By then the Hendersons already had two."

She shakes her head. "By 1983, the Hendersons had three, and we'd had our second. That's when they finally mentioned it—quietly, carefully, like they were afraid saying it out loud might make it worse. One was nothing. Two was strange. Three? Three was deliberate. Three was a pattern."

You picture your parents that first Christmas after Sarah, opening the door and finding a bell glinting on the porch. The start of your family's tally. The start of your own obsession.

Katie continues, "That was enough to start the whispers. Church basements, school parking lots, late-night phone calls. People started putting it together. And from then on, the bells just kept coming. Every single Christmas."

"Every single Christmas," you whisper, though your voice barely makes a sound.

"Anyway, when Sarah... when your family started to get the bells too, there was some action. Patrol cars parked near our houses, deputies sitting in their cruisers with thermoses of coffee. But no one wanted to sit out all night in the freezing dark on Christmas Eve. Not when they had families of their own. Families they were scared to leave unprotected."

You know this already, from the case notes. By the time the police finally acknowledged the pattern in the '80s, they already had years of missed opportunities behind them.

Katie leans forward, elbows on the desk, eyes glittering with old fury. "Not that they'd ever admit it. No, they wrote it off. Said the bells were just toys from the dollar store. Said there wasn't enough manpower. Said the trail was too cold. Excuses stacked on excuses until nobody expected them to try anymore."

"And then after Sarah…" Katie exhales, almost laughs. "Nothing. Nine years without another child taken. People let themselves believe he'd stopped."

Your jaw tightens. "But the bells never stopped."

Katie nods once, hard. "Every damn year. My mom would find one on the porch before she'd even had her coffee. No prints, they said. No DNA. Just another cheap trinket anyone could buy in December. Never the same twice, so they couldn't even trace where they came from. The cops shrugged, said there was nothing to go on. And we were left to open the door every Christmas morning, wondering if this was the year he came back for another child."

You press your lips together, the weight of her words sinking into your chest. Four decades of bells. Four decades of inaction.

Katie's voice cuts back in, quieter now. "Don't think for a second the police will help you, Jenny. If you're really here to stir this up, you're on your own."

You study her face. She has softened since you first walked in, but only just. When she said she'd help, you hoped she meant it, because it feels like you're going to need every ally you can get.

Head up to your room Turn to page 31

ROOM 12, PINE HOLLOW INN

The key is cold in your hand as you leave the desk behind. Katie doesn't speak again, and you don't look back. The lobby smells of radiator heat and pine cleaner, the sagging tree blinking weakly in the corner like it's tired of keeping watch.

You climb the staircase, boots creaking against old wood. Each step seems to groan beneath your weight, a sound too loud in the hush of the Inn. At the landing, the hallway stretches narrow and dim, wallpaper a faded holly print, curling at the seams. Shadows cling to the edges like dust.

Room 12 waits at the far end. The brass number plate is worn smooth; the lock stiff when you turn the key.

Inside: a narrow bed dressed in quilted patchwork, a dresser scarred with cigarette burns, a single chair pushed under the window. The radiator ticks faintly, not quite keeping up with the cold. You close the door behind you, and the silence settles heavy.

You drop your bag on the bed and sit. The mattress dips under your weight, groaning like it resents the intrusion. You press your hands to your face, but it doesn't block out the thoughts echoing in your head.

You dig through your bag, pulling free the leather notebook that's followed you from case to case. Pages crammed with names, dates, notes scribbled at 2am when sleep wouldn't come. But this time you don't need to write. The list already lives within you:

- Rachel, 1976.
- David, 1978.
- Claire, 1980.
- Tommy, 1981.
- Sarah, 1986.
- Daniel, 1995.
- Emily, 2009.
- Amy, 2024.

Eight children. Gone.

Taken.

The radiator clanks suddenly, and you flinch. The shadows in the corners feel deeper now, thickening with the cold. You stand, cross to the window. The glass is old, warped slightly, but you can see down into the street. Snow drifts across the lamplight. For a moment, you think you see movement near the treeline, a flicker of red against the white. But when you blink, it's gone.

You rest your forehead against the cold glass, breath fogging it faintly. You told Katie you weren't here for headlines. That you were here because it's time. But now, alone in Room 12, you admit the truth: you don't know if you're ready.

You think of Sarah's red mittens vanishing into the snow. You think of the whispers Katie described—the Hendersons finally admitting the bells weren't coincidence, that three in a row meant something deliberate. That he was still out there. That he always came back.

Of your parents' hallway chest, growing heavier every December.

Tomorrow, another bell will appear.

The bells will come again.

And this time, you'll be here to see it.

For now, you go to bed. Turn to page 41

CHECK INTO THE PINE HOLLOW INN

The Pine Hollow Inn rises out of the storm like a relic, its Victorian trim strung with tired strings of coloured lights. The website called it "rustic charm with modern amenities." To you, it looks like a house that's been trying to smile for too long.

It was here when you were a child, but you don't remember it. You've never been inside. Now here you are.

As you enter, the lobby smells of pine cleaner and old radiator heat. A tree stands in the corner, its ornaments mismatched and sagging. At the front desk, Katie Wilson looks up. Her hair is mostly grey now, but you'd know her anywhere. She was Tommy's sister. Tommy Wilson, the boy who vanished two years before Sarah.

Her eyes widen. "Jenny Matthews," she says, like it tastes bitter.

You force a smile. "Room for one?"

Katie hesitates, then slides the guest book toward you. The pen rattles against the paper as you sign your name.

"You're really back," she murmurs.

The lobby feels too quiet, as though the Inn itself is listening. You wonder what your editor would say if she could see you now: hiding in a second-rate hotel instead of knocking on your parents' door.

You're not ready to face them. Not tonight.

But you're here.

And that means the King of Christmas can't hide forever.

Do you:
Tell Katie why you're back Turn to page 25
Ask Katie about the bells Turn to page 34
Go straight up to your room Turn to page 31
Head to the bar down the street for that drink Turn to page 19

ASK KATIE ABOUT THE BELLS

You start toward the staircase, each step dragging with the weight of everything you didn't say. Then you stop, exhale hard, and force yourself to turn back.

Katie's watching you, arms folded now, like she knew you'd hesitate.

"My parents still get them," you say. The words scrape your throat raw. "Every Christmas Eve. A bell on the doorstep."

For the first time, Katie's expression cracks. Her eyes shimmer, though she blinks hard against it. She nods once, sharp, like a soldier acknowledging a wound.

"Yeah," she says softly. "Mine too. Every year. Even last year when he…"

"Amy," you cut in. Her name lands between you like a strike. Retribution for the way Katie pulled you up about calling them 'the others.' You won't let Amy, or Sarah, or any of them, be faceless victims.

Katie's jaw trembles, but she doesn't look away.

"Amy," she echoes. "She was just eight. My niece used to play with her at the school playground. And still…" She shakes her head, voice rough. "Still, the bell came. Like it was a game he couldn't stop playing."

The lobby falls silent again. The tree in the corner glints weakly in the dim light, ornaments sagging as though the branches can't carry their weight.

Katie grips the desk so hard her knuckles go white. "If you're really here to write this story, Jenny, you better write it right. Because these bells, they don't just mean the past. They mean he's still out there. Taking Amy means he is still out there."

You want to say something—anything—but your throat locks. You see her face flicker in and out of Sarah's, the same mix of hurt and disbelief. Katie stayed. She bore it. And you? You ran.

"I'm not here for headlines," you finally manage. "I'm here because it's time. Because someone has to end this."

Katie lets out a short, bitter laugh. "End this? You think waltzing back into town after twenty years is going to change anything? The cops never stopped him. The town just learned to live with it. And you…" she points at you with a quick, shaking hand "…you want to turn it into a story."

"That's not fair," you say, sharper than you mean. "Every article I've ever written was Sarah. Every case I covered, it was Sarah in my head."

"Maybe," Katie says. "But while you were writing about other people's ghosts, the rest of us were living with ours."

Her eyes drop to the desk, and when she speaks again, her voice is quieter. "You know what it's like to have a bell land on your doorstep every Christmas morning? You know what it does to you? To open that door and wonder if it means he's coming back for you? Or worse, that he already has and you just don't know it yet?"

You picture your mother, stiff-backed at the kitchen table, pretending not to see the bell glinting on the porch. Your father carrying it inside with the Sunday paper, setting it on the pile in the hallway chest like it was nothing more than junk mail. And all the while you, a thousand miles away, pretending the distance made it easier.

Katie's gaze snaps back up, hard again. "Don't you dare screw this up. If you tell this story, Jenny, it has to hurt. It has to make people *listen*. Otherwise, you're just another outsider writing about an urban legend in the mountains. And I'm not giving you that. That's not what he is, and both of us know it."

Do you:

Stand up to Katie Turn to page 36

Say nothing more; just go to your room Turn to page 31

STAND UP TO KATIE

You could take the key, walk away, climb the stairs, and shut yourself in a strange bed until morning. That would be easy. Cowardly.

Instead, you force yourself to look Katie in the eye.

"You think I don't care. You think this is just copy for me. But I'm here because I do care. Because in all these years, the police haven't come anywhere near to solving this."

Katie blinks slowly, her expression caught somewhere between exhaustion and contempt. Then she lets out a low, humourless laugh. "Solve it? Jenny, they gave up years ago. When Amy was taken, they pretended to care — but really, they were pissed the whole thing got dragged back into the light. Eight kids gone, and the closest we ever had to justice was a couple of half-hearted search parties and a sheriff who told us to keep our kids indoors on Christmas Eve."

Her words rattle in the quiet lobby.

You shake your head. "I've read the case files. There was evidence—footprints, notes, bells. They could've…"

"They didn't." Katie's voice slices through yours, sharp and final. "You know what the files don't show? How fast they gave up. How quick they were to write it off as runaways or accidents, anything but what it was. They couldn't stand admitting that someone was taking our kids right under their noses. So they buried it. Pretended it was legend. Easier that way."

"Urban legend," you mutter before you can stop yourself.

Katie's eyes snap to yours, and her face hardens. "Don't call it that. He's real, Jenny. You know it, I know it. He's not some campfire story. He's out there, and he's still taking them."

Her words hang heavy, filling the space between you with something darker than the winter night outside. You swallow hard, and for the first time since you drove back into Pine Hollow, you allow yourself to say the thing you've been circling all along.

"That's why I'm here. Not for headlines, not for The Beacon. I want to find him. I want to stop this once and for all."

Katie stares at you, unblinking. The air feels tight, charged, like the moment before a storm breaks. Then she shakes her head and lets out a bitter laugh.

"End this? You think waltzing back into town after twenty years is going to change anything? The cops never stopped him. The town just learned to live with it. And you..." She points at you with a quick, shaking hand. "...you want to turn it into a story."

"That's not fair," you snap, your voice sharp enough to cut. "Every article I've ever written was Sarah. Every case I covered, it was Sarah in my head. You think it was some kind of escape? You think I was running from her?"

Katie's jaw clenches. For a long, taut moment, the two of you glare at each other across the desk, bound together by grief and fury. Then she exhales, shoulders sagging just enough to show the crack in her armour.

"Maybe," she says finally. "But while you were writing about other people's ghosts, the rest of us were living with ours."

Her eyes drop to the desk. When she speaks again, her voice is quieter, hoarse. "You know what it's like to have a bell land on your doorstep every Christmas morning? You know what it does to you? To open that door and wonder if it means he's coming back for you? Or worse, that he already has and you just don't know it yet?"

The image sears into you. You picture your mother, stiff-backed at the kitchen table, pretending not to see the bell glinting on the porch. Your father carrying it inside with the Sunday paper, setting it on the pile in the hallway chest like it was nothing more than junk mail. And all the while you, a thousand miles away, pretending the distance made it easier.

It didn't. It never did.

Katie's gaze flicks back up, sharp again, as though she regrets showing you the crack in her voice. "Don't screw this up. If you tell this story, Jenny, it has to hurt. It has to make people listen. Otherwise, you're just another outsider writing about freaks in the mountains. And I'm not giving you that. That's not what he is, and both of us know it."

You swallow. "Then help me. I can't do this alone."

Katie studies you for a long time, the muscles in her jaw working, her eyes scanning your face as though she's trying to decide whether you're bluffing. You don't flinch. You let her see the rawness under your words, the part of you that isn't the journalist, isn't the daughter, isn't the survivor. Just the girl who lost her sister and never stopped looking for her.

Finally, Katie exhales through her nose, slow and tired. She leans back, smoothing her sleeves in that old, nervous way you remember from school. "You want help? Fine. But don't expect me to hold your hand. Ask your questions, write your story. Just don't you dare walk away this time."

You nod. "I won't."

Katie doesn't smile. She doesn't soften. She simply turns back to the guest book, tapping her pen against the page. The conversation is over—for now.

You slip the key into your pocket, the brass cold against your palm. Upstairs waits Room 12, and the long night ahead.

Go upstairs to your room Turn to page 31
Ask Katie about the bells Turn to page 39

ASK ABOUT THE BELLS

You start toward the staircase, each step dragging with the weight of everything you didn't say. Then you stop, exhale hard, and force yourself to turn back.

Katie's watching you, arms folded now, like she knew you'd hesitate.

"My parents still get them," you say. The words scrape your throat raw. "Every Christmas Eve. A bell on the doorstep."

For the first time, Katie's expression cracks. Her eyes shimmer, though she blinks hard against it. She nods once, sharp, like a soldier acknowledging a wound.

"Yeah," she says softly. "Mine too. Every year. Even last year, the same night he took Amy. The bells never stopped."

Something clenches in your chest. What kind of monster abducts a child and still makes time to deliver bells to the families of the others?

You try to stay calm as you ask, "You've kept them?"

Katie's fingers drum against the desk, restless.

"Of course I kept them. What else was I supposed to do? Throw them out with the trash? Pretend they weren't sitting there on the porch every Christmas morning like… like a reminder that he's still out there?" She lets out a shaky breath. "I've got a shoebox full of them upstairs. Can't bring myself to open it anymore. Can't bring myself to open it anymore. And tomorrow there'll be another."

You picture your own parents' hallway chest, the weight of silver inside it. The quiet ritual of avoidance they built around it.

Katie sees the flicker in your face and softens, just slightly. "It's not just us. Not just your family. Rachel's left town before that first anniversary, but I know David's parents got them. At least they did until his mom passed away… and you know what happened to his dad." She pauses, the unspoken story hanging heavy between you.

"Claire Henderson's family were the first to mention the bells, so I know they got them. But they don't talk about it anymore. Won't talk about it. I wouldn't even try."

Her fingers tighten on the counter. "Daniel's parents and Emily's too. Both of their families moved away. Can't blame them. But the Crawfords..." Her voice lowers. "Tomorrow will be their first. Christmas Eve. That bell's coming for them next."

You nod slowly, the scope of it pressing down on you like snow on a roof. "What does it mean? What kind of message does a bell give? And why keep coming back? Haven't the police ever staked out the houses? Waited to see who leaves them?"

You'd think after eight children they'd try. But apparently they never have.

Katie gives a humourless smile. "If it is a message, no one has ever figured it out. The cops sure as hell haven't. All they saw were trinkets. But those bells... they're proof, Jenny. Proof he's real."

Her voice drops, steady now. "He's not an urban legend. He's not a story parents tell their kids to make them behave. He's flesh and blood, and he's still walking those woods. And if you've really come back here to find him..." she swallows, meeting your eyes squarely "...then maybe this time someone finally should."

For a heartbeat, neither of you speaks. The air between you is heavy with decades of silence broken at last.

You close your fist around the key. "I will. For all of them. With your help."

Katie exhales, tired, but she doesn't look away.

"Then you'd better get some sleep. Tomorrow, it starts again."

You make your way to room 12 Turn to page 31

YOU GO TO BED

You peel off your coat, but the cold lingers in your bones. The quilt smells faintly of mothballs and stale smoke, but you climb beneath it anyway, too tired to care.

The silence of the room is thick, broken only by the tick of the radiator and the groan of wind at the eaves. You lie on your back, eyes fixed on the cracked ceiling, and wait for sleep to come.

When it does, it isn't merciful.

The dreams are a blur of snow and shadows. Sarah's red mittens darting between the trees. A bell swinging on an invisible string, silent but deafening. The shape of a man in a red coat, his face hidden, watching you with the stillness of something carved from ice.

You try to run, but the snow drags at your legs. The bells multiply—hundreds of them—each one marking the path you didn't take, the years you weren't here. And always, always, Sarah is ahead of you, her small figure receding until she is swallowed by white.

You jolt awake, chest heaving, the room black around you. For a moment you don't know where you are, until the radiator coughs and you remember: Pine Hollow. Room 12.

You press the heel of your hand to your eyes, but the image lingers: mittens, bells, the red blur at the treeline.

Sleep comes again, shallow and fractured, dragging you under in short bursts until grey light leaks through the curtains.

Morning. Christmas Eve.

You wake to the colourless light of winter pressing through the curtains. For a moment, you don't know where you are. Then the quilt's scratch against your skin, the smell of old plaster, and the hollow quiet of the Inn remind you.

Sleep didn't help. What scraps you managed were jagged with images—Sarah's mitten in the snow, a bell you couldn't silence, trees that seemed to lean closer every time you turned. You've woken more exhausted than when you lay down.

And the thoughts start. The *what ifs.*

What if you'd told the truth that night, owned up to the bracelet? What if Sarah had stayed in the house instead of storming out? What if he had chosen you? Would she be the one sitting here now, alive, whole, and you the name carved into cold stone?

The questions tumble, relentless. What if you'd come back years ago, faced this instead of running case after case in every other town but your own? What if you'd been braver, sooner? Could Amy still be alive?

Your hand tightens on the notebook beside you, the names etched there like scars. Each one a fork in the road, each one a path not taken. Life isn't supposed to be a game of choices. There's no flipping back, no re-roll of the dice. Just this: the trail of bells behind you, and the next one waiting ahead.

You roll onto your side and stare at the shadowed corner of the room, throat thick. You've told yourself it was fear that kept you from crossing the street to your parents' house last night. But lying here, with the morning pressing in, you know better.

It isn't fear. It's the weight of thirty years of silence. The way their eyes will ask questions you can't answer. The way those bells, lined up in their hallway, will sound louder than any words.

You press your forehead against your arm and breathe slowly, but the thoughts won't let go. What if you never went at all? What if you packed up the car, drove south until the mountains were a memory? What if you let the bells keep coming, as they always have?

But you already know the answer. Whatever paths you imagine, whatever choices you replay, they all narrow to one road. The one you've been avoiding since the day Sarah vanished.

You have to go home.

The thought sits in your chest, immovable. Not because you want to, not because you're ready, but because there's no other choice left.

You push yourself upright. The room seems smaller now, as though it knows what you're about to do. You gather your things slowly, delaying the inevitable, but every fold of fabric, every click of the zipper only brings you closer.

Across town, the house waits. The house you fled. The house that still breathes with Sarah's absence, every wall holding the echo of her last night.

You imagine the porch, the sagging steps you once ran up two at a time, the windows your mother still dresses with garlands every December. You see the hallway chest in your mind, heavy with silver. You see your father's silence, your mother's face hard with hope she no longer believes in.

You left when you were eighteen and haven't been back since. But now, there's no more stalling. Whatever waits inside, it's time to face it.

Do you:
Go home Turn to page 70
Stop at the bar for a shot of courage Turn to page 47
Try to find Katie before you go Turn to page 61

You don't ease into it; there's no gentler way.

"I'm here because it isn't over," you say. "Amy Crawford. Last Christmas Eve. He's still doing this. He has to be stopped."

Your father's head snaps up. Your mother's fingers tighten around her cup until you fear it'll crack. For a heartbeat, the room feels tilted, the floor not quite under you.

"He's not done," you go on, before fear can make you soften your words. "The bells prove it. He keeps coming back. He's out there—flesh and blood, not a story. I can't ask you to live through another Christmas pretending he turned to smoke."

Your mother flinches at *pretending*, but she nods, once. "Is that what they say in Boston?" she asks, voice thin. "That we pretend?"

"No," you say quickly. "That's what I say about *me*. I pretended the distance made it easier to breathe. I told myself there was nothing left to do. Then Amy was taken and—"

"And you remembered you had a sister," your father says. It isn't cruel; it's bare. It lands like cold air.

"I remembered I had a job to do," you say. "And that I've been avoiding the only story that mattered."

The house seems to lean forward. You lower your voice. "If he took Amy, he's active. There's a pattern to people like this. Gaps. Returns. Sometimes a trigger. I don't know why the years stretch and compress the way they do here, but I know he didn't stop on his own. Which means we can interrupt him. We can put something in his path he isn't expecting."

Your father studies you as if gauging weight and durability. "What? A byline? A camera?"

"Pressure," you say. "Attention he can't control. Questions asked in the right order, in the right places. And yes—if I have to camp on doorsteps tonight, I will. If I have to stand at the tree line where the footprints end, I will. I am not leaving this to next year's bell."

Your mother's composure slips; you see the storm beneath it. "Don't say *tonight*," she whispers. "Don't say it like it's a thing that can happen again."

"It is a thing that can happen again," you say, and the truth tastes terrible. "That's why I'm here."

Your father stands, looks you dead in the eye and shuffles across the room.

Your father has something to give you. Turn to page 65

BACK TO YOUR PARENTS

You tell yourself you'll drive home. Face your parents. Walk into that house and put the folder on the table like a white flag.

But the thought makes your stomach knot. If you couldn't face them last night, what makes you think you can face them now? Not with Amy's name still fresh in the air, not with Sarah's ghost pressing against your back.

You picture your father's face if you walk through that door with nothing but another dismissal from the sheriff. You picture your mother's eyes, hollowed out from years of not knowing. You can't do it. Not yet.

Your hands tighten. There are only two roads left to take.

You could go back to the Pine Hollow Inn, decide on your next move and collect what you need or head up to the old ski resort, where the first abduction took place in 1976.

Back to the Inn Turn to page 77
Up to the ski resort Turn to page 55

GO TO THE BAR

It's 10am, and Pine Hollow isn't Boston. The bar won't open for hours, and even if it did, nothing strong enough exists to make this easier.

This one is on you to face.

Go home Turn to page 70

READ THE FILE

The paper is soft at the edges, worn from decades of handling. Your father has been carrying this longer than you've been carrying your notebooks, and somehow that makes your chest ache.

You sit back down, folder balanced across your knees. The room feels too quiet, as though the house itself is listening for what you'll find.

"I didn't think you'd want to see it," your father mutters, rubbing at his jaw. "But if you're set on digging, better to start with mine."

You open the folder.

The first page is a crude map of Evergreen Lane — houses drawn as boxes, the treeline sketched with a blunt pencil. Notes spider from the edges: *Red sedan parked two nights in a row. Volunteer Santa walked past Henderson house after service.* Your father's handwriting is blocky, determined, the lines pressed deep into the paper.

You've seen this before — not the paper itself, but the angle. Police reports, photocopies in case files, transcribed interviews. But here, in your father's hand, the words carry a different weight. This isn't evidence. It's obsession turned survival.

Your mother places a hand on your shoulder. "He wrote every Christmas Eve," she says softly. "Even if there was nothing. Especially if there was nothing."

You turn another page. Dates march down the margins: 1981, 1982, 1983. The year Tommy vanished. The year after. The year after that. Every December 24th is underlined. Next to them: what cars passed by, who walked their dogs, which porch lights burned late. Some years, the lists are frantic, entire blocks of scrawled names and descriptions. Other years, they're sparse. A single sentence. *Snow heavy. Bells anyway.*

Your throat tightens. "Dad…"

He shrugs, eyes on the floor. "I couldn't stop the bells. But I could write down who was looking away."

You flip forward. Some pages carry details you recognise from police files, but here they're raw, untouched by bureaucratic tone. *Deputy missed the footprint by garage. Said drift. Not drift. Weight in the snow. Heel dug in.*

The words jolt you. You look up. "You wrote it down."

Your father nods once, curt. "I didn't have the heart to tell you then. But I couldn't let it vanish."

You move on. The folder becomes a chorus of voices you half-remember from the town:

Mrs Callahan saw a tall man in a red coat at the market in 1985.

The Wilsons' dog barked all night in 1995.

A janitor at the school asked about locks on classroom doors too many times.

You've heard most of these stories, watered down through rumour and report. But here, they're immediate, written the night they happened. You can feel your father's hand pressing into the paper, trying to force permanence into things that slipped away.

Halfway through, you stop. A page from 2009 — Emily's year. Your father's writing is more frantic here, lines crammed into every inch of the margin.

One line freezes you.

Delivery van. White. No logo. Parked two streets over, engine running. Same plates noted in 1995, scratched out of registry. Told sheriff. Dismissed.

You whisper the words aloud.

Your mother frowns. "I remember that year. You said the truck was nothing."

Your father doesn't meet her eyes. "They told me it was nothing. Said plates get reused, trucks get sold. But I knew I'd seen it before."

Your pulse quickens. In Boston, you dug through archives, flagged inconsistencies. But you never saw this detail. The plate number itself is smudged, nearly illegible, but the repetition—the same van fourteen years apart—sticks like a burr in your mind.

"This wasn't in the files," you say.

"Because I stopped giving them my pages," your father answers. "They treated me as if I were the one seeing ghosts. Better to keep my ghosts in a folder."

You turn to the last section. The handwriting grows shakier in recent years, the ink fading, but the notes remain: *Amy. Note on her pillow. Brother's lie. Footprints to the woods. Bells anyway.*

You shut the folder gently.

The silence in the room is thick. You're not surprised by what's inside — not really. You've read it all before, in one form or another. But seeing it through his eyes, through his refusal to stop watching even when everyone else turned away, steals your breath.

He kept this. Year after year. Just like your mother kept placing the bells in the chest, refusing to hide them in the attic. This was how they carried Sarah.

"This is more than ghosts," you say. "That van…"

"Could be coincidence," your father cuts in.

"Or it could be the first real thread we've had in decades."

Your mother's eyes dart between you both. "If you pull it, what happens?"

"Then we see what unravels," you say.

The folder lies between you on the coffee table, fragile but heavy. For a moment, none of you moves. The house feels charged, like the air before lightning.

At last, your father clears his throat. "So," he says, voice raw. "What now?"

Visit the Crawford family Turn to page 56
Go to Sarah's grave Turn to page 67

GO TO THE POLICE

You sit in the car outside the sheriff's office with the heater wheezing and the folder open across your lap. The notes are your father's hand: clipped lists, scrawled times, fragments of evidence that should have meant something to someone. A crude map. Dates underlined again and again.

You haven't had more than an hour with it, but already you know: it's more thorough than anything you've seen in an official file. More human too. Not evidence, but obsession turned survival.

You tell yourself it might not make a difference. They'll wave you away. They always have. But you can't say you've done everything if you don't at least give them this chance.

And last year. Amy. Isn't that enough? Isn't that fresh enough to matter?

You close the folder and sit for one last breath before forcing yourself into the cold.

The Pine Hollow Sheriff's Department looks smaller than you remembered: a squat brick box with salt stains and a sagging flag. Inside, the air is stale with coffee and radiator heat. A string of lights droops along the reception window.

The deputy behind the glass looks up when you approach. He's young, polite, face too new to remember Sarah.

"Morning. How can I help you?"

"I need to speak with the sheriff. It's about the disappearances." You slide the folder across.

He hesitates, something flickering across his face. Then he nods, businesslike. "I'll let him know. One moment."

He disappears. When the door opens again, it's not him, it's Sheriff Larkin. Broader than you remember, hair greyer, his eyes colder. He doesn't greet you. Just says, "This way," and steers you down the hall, away from ears that might be listening.

The office is cramped, sour with coffee. A child's crayon Christmas card leans on the desk: *Merry Christmas, Daddy*. The sight of it here feels obscene.

He gestures to the chair opposite, then drops heavily into his own. Silence stretches. His gaze rests on the folder like it's something contagious.

"I've seen this before, Jenny." His voice is flat, practiced. "Bill's shoved these same papers across this desk more times than I can count. And now it's you, sitting here with the same file."

Bill. Your father. He and Larkin seem to be on first-name terms, but not in the way friends use names, more like sparring partners who never stop circling, who know every move the other will make.

He hasn't even looked at it properly. Just glanced at the pages like they're some crank's conspiracy board. You've seen *this* before—cops who'd rather close a case than solve it. Who mistake the absence of easy answers for the absence of answers entirely.

"I've worked cases cops like you gave up on," you say, keeping your voice level. "I've found evidence your people missed. This file contains forty years of observations."

"Forty years of a grieving man seeing patterns in random noise," Larkin cuts in.

Random noise. That's what he called it. Your father's meticulous documentation, reduced to static. You stand, gathering the folder. Fine. You've worked around worse cops than this.

"Why are you here? Press, or…"

Larkin's unfinished words burn in the air.

Your throat tightens. He can't even say her name. You can. You have to.

"Or Sarah's sister?"

His jaw twitches, but he doesn't answer.

Your voice rises. "Have you even read what's in here? Do you even care? Do you at least care about Amy?"

His mouth pulls into something between a smirk and a grimace. "Amy was last year, after fifteen years of nothing. This town thought maybe it was over. People let themselves believe it. And then…" He flicks two fingers toward the window. "We went over every inch of ground. Patrols, dogs, the whole circus. Came up empty, same as always. You think you're the first person to drag in a file and tell me it changes things?"

"Will there be a stakeout tonight?" you snap. "You've got another chance. Another family. You could at least try to see where the bells are coming from."

That does it. His hand slams the desk. "The goddamn bells. You think this is television? You think I can post men outside houses every December, waiting for a jingle in the snow? We don't even know if it's the same man. Could be one. Could be two. Could be he's been dead ten years and someone else is keeping it alive for kicks."

"He? You mean *The King of Christmas*," you cut in. The name feels heavy on your tongue, wrong to speak aloud, like a curse loosed into the room.

For the first time, his eyes flick up to yours.

"Call it what you want. Doesn't change a damn thing. This is what you came back for? To play detective with your father's notes?"

"The bells. They mean someone's still out there," you say, leaning forward, your voice wavering. Try as you might to stay in your hard-nosed-reporter persona, this is personal. Of course this is personal.

The sheriff leans back, eyes like stone. "Or they mean nothing at all. You want to gamble this town's peace of mind on shadows? Be my guest. But don't expect me to bankroll your ghosts."

You open your mouth to argue, but he's already pushing himself to his feet. The chair legs screech against the floor. "We're done here."

He comes around the desk, guiding you toward the door with the weight of his body, not quite shoving, but close.

"You should leave it alone, Jenny. That's the kindest thing I can tell you."

Your heart hammers. You clutch the folder tighter. "He'll be back tonight. For the bells. Maybe for another child. And you're what...?" Your hand cuts toward the desk, toward the crayon-scrawled card still propped there. "Going home to your family Christmas? What if he comes for your child next?"

Larkin stops in the doorway, his hand pressed to the frame as though bracing himself. For a beat his jaw works, his throat tight, but no words come out. Then he opens the door, sharp and final.

"We're done," he repeats.

And you're out in the corridor. The folder in your arms is everything, and it's nothing. Years of your father's obsession, and years of doors slammed in his face. Scraps of a puzzle no one here ever wanted to fit together, because fitting it together would mean admitting they'd rather look away.

You press it against you, throat tight, and walk out. The deputy doesn't meet your eyes as you pass.

If you want answers, you'll have to find them yourself.

Stop in at the Pine Hollow Inn. Turn to page 77
Back to your parents Turn to page 46

UP TO THE SKI RESORT

The car groans awake under your hands, headlights spearing through the snow. Headlights in the morning sums this town up too well.

You take the northern road that will lead you just out of town, determination grinding against fear.

The ski resort.

Rachel Van Vleet. Eleven years old. The first girl to be taken. The name that everyone remembers when they talk about Pine Hollow and the eight taken children. They always remember the first, and now they remember the last. You were a baby, then, and Sarah wasn't even born. You still know the story. Her story.

Rachel was an only child, unlike the others. A comer-inner, just like your family ... not born here, never fully belonging. You've searched for patterns, for something that connects the children beyond Christmas Eve and the bells. You've tried to reason why Sarah was chosen and not someone else. Not you.

Your thoughts are lost in a time long past when you reach the edge of town. There, where the road narrows to a single lane between the trees, a snowplough blocks the way, broadside across the asphalt. Its yellow lights pulse in the flurries, harsh and unreal. A sheriff's cruiser idles behind it, the driver's face shadowed. An orange cone sinks into the drift, already half-buried.

You slow, roll down your window, cold air slicing in. There's no way past. The plough fills the road like a barricade.

There's no way for you to reach the ski resort. Not yet.

With a curse, you pull a slow three-point turn. Headlights sweep the trees, skeletal branches clawing at the night, and then you're heading back into Pine Hollow, the mountain still waiting, silent and untouched.

Time to go back to the inn. Turn to page 77

VISIT THE CRAWFORD FAMILY

The Crawfords live two streets over, in the newer part of town where the houses all look like they were built from the same blueprint. Amy's face has been staring out of their front window for the past year. Missing posters, community vigils, candle stubs melted onto the porch railing. You've covered families like theirs for decades, but never in your own town, never this close.

Your grip tightens on the steering wheel. This isn't just another case. This is Sarah. And Sarah's absence is stitched through everything that's happened since.

You park at the curb and sit for too long, staring at the neat siding, the faint Christmas lights drooping across the eaves. There's no excuse left. You force yourself out of the car, up the walk, each step heavier than the last.

You tell yourself this is about the story. It's easier that way. Thinking like a reporter, not like a sister. The Crawfords are the newest case, the freshest wound, the place any journalist would start. But under that excuse, another truth presses harder: Amy's absence feels like Sarah's all over again. If you can face their grief, maybe you can face your parents. And if you can't... you shouldn't even be here.

The door opens before you knock. A man stands there. Amy's father, though his face is more haggard than the photographs that ran in the paper. His eyes go flat the moment they land on you.

"No press," he says, voice raw. "We've had enough of you. Go."

"I'm not..." you start, but he's already shutting the door.

You catch it with your palm, the edge biting into your hand. "Please. I'm not here for a headline."

His eyes flash with anger. "You've all said that. And every one of you printed her picture anyway. You think I don't know what they whisper? Another child gone. The King of Christmas takes another. You feed on it."

Your heart hammers, but you keep your voice steady. "I know what it feels like to have a sister taken. I know what the bells mean."

The door halts mid-swing. His mouth works, but no sound comes.

A woman appears behind him: Amy's mother. Her face is pale, her arms folded tightly across her chest as though she's holding herself together. "What did you say?"

You draw a breath that shakes in your chest. "Sarah Matthews. Nineteen eighty-six. She was my sister."

The silence is thick, broken only by the faint crackle of Christmas lights straining in the cold.

At last, the woman speaks. "Sarah." Her voice trembles. "We heard about her. Everyone in this town did. But you…" She looks at you sharply. "You left."

"I did." The words scrape on their way out. "And I regret it every day. But I'm here now, because I can't run from it anymore. I want to find out what happened to Sarah. To all of them. To Amy."

Amy's father exhales through his teeth, his anger folding into something closer to exhaustion. He leans a shoulder against the doorframe. "You think you're going to solve it? After the police, after the FBI, after all the cameras went away?"

You shake your head. "I don't know if I can. But I have to try. And I can't do that without you."

Amy's mother studies you with eyes rimmed red. "We don't want our daughter turned into a story."

"She already is," you say quietly. "He made her into one the moment he took her. But if I do this right, if I can tell it honestly, maybe it can be more than a cautionary tale people whisper about. Maybe it can be a record that forces him into the light."

The woman's lips press thin. She glances at her husband. "We said no more press."

He runs a hand over his face, weariness settling on his shoulders. "Maybe she's not just press." He looks back at you, searching your expression. "You say you lost Sarah. You say you know. Then tell me this: why now? Why come back after all these years?"

You swallow hard. "Because Amy was taken. Because the bells never stopped. Because this isn't over. If I walk away again, I'm complicit."

His jaw tightens, then relaxes. Slowly, he pulls the door wider. "Five minutes," he says. "That's all."

Inside, the house smells faintly of pine and wax. The tree in the corner is bare of gifts. On the mantel, a school portrait of Amy smiles out. Gap-toothed, her hair in a crooked braid. The sight hits harder than you expect, like a hand closing around your lungs.

Amy's mother gestures stiffly toward the couch. You sit, your notebook heavy in your pocket, though you're not sure you can bring yourself to use it yet.

"She liked skating," her mother says suddenly, voice distant. "We bought her skates last year. She was practicing figure eights on the driveway Christmas morning." She presses her lips together, as if punishing herself for remembering out loud.

"She wasn't bad," a small voice says from the doorway.

You turn. A boy stands there, thin and pale, hair sticking up as though he's been crying for hours. Amy's brother. His hands twist in the hem of his sweatshirt, knuckles white.

"She wasn't bad," he says again, voice breaking. "It should've been me. He should've taken me. I broke the console. She was always covering for me. And then…" His throat closes around the rest. He swipes angrily at his eyes but can't stop the tears.

The floor seems to tilt beneath you. The words strike too close, pulling you backward through decades to your own reflection: I stole the bracelet. I let Sarah take the blame. And then she was gone.

"It wasn't your fault," you whisper, though your throat tightens around the words.

He stares at you, wet-eyed and trembling, and for a moment you see yourself at eleven. Terrified, drowning in a guilt that didn't belong to you.

Amy's mother rises and draws the boy into her arms, rocking him with a desperation that makes your chest ache. Her sobs fill the room, raw and unhidden.

Amy's father sits rigid, jaw working, his hand pressed to the arm of the chair as though it's the only thing keeping him anchored. He looks at you then, not with a challenge at first but with a blunt, weary curiosity.

"So, tell me straight," he says. His voice is small against the room. "You're just here for the story, then? Another piece to make someone sell subscriptions?"

You feel the old defence rise (the practiced line you've used in interviews a hundred times) and for a beat you almost use it. Then the truth comes out of you, harsher and simpler. "I thought I was," you say. "That was part of it. But I… nobody has done anything. The police walked away. State teams came once, took notes, left. The techniques (DNA, cameras, everything everyone promises in press releases) those are for big towns. For big budgets."

"Nobody cares," Amy's father breathes.

The mother snorts, not a laugh but a brittle sound that carries years of waiting. She pulls the boy in close.

"Even Amy," she says. "Even last year. They promised updates, rechecked what we'd already told them. They put a couple of cruisers on the road for a week, and that was it. Then they said the trail was cold. Then they said resources." She looks at her husband. "Resources. As if grief can be budgeted away."

He nods, jaw working. "They have the tools," he says. "They have the language. But no one's willing to sit out a December night when their own kids are upstairs. Not in these parts. Not for us."

Silence folds around those words, brittle as the ice crusting the gutters outside.

Amy's mother strokes her son's hair, eyes fixed somewhere you can't see. Her voice is thin, but it cuts. "So what now?"

You look at them, at the father sunk into his chair like the weight of years might finally pin him there, at the mother clutching the boy who thinks it should have been him. You feel the folder burning against your side, your father's scrawled notes pressed to your hip like contraband.

What now?
Go to the police Turn to page 51
Go to Sarah's grave Turn to page 67

TRY TO FIND KATIE

You head downstairs. Katie isn't at the desk, instead her sister, Siobhan, stands in her place. Same jawline, same tired eyes. She looks at you once with a long, measuring glance that flickers with something you can't quite read. Recognition. Maybe pity. Maybe blame.

Then, without a word, she rises.

The office door closes behind her with a soft but deliberate click, leaving you in the lobby alone.

No words. No help. Just the reminder that you're on your own.

Go home Turn to page 70

DRIVE TO THE OLD SKI RESORT

You close the folder gently. "I'll figure it out."

Your mother nods as if she wants to believe you, though her eyes stay down. Your father presses his hand over yours for a moment — brief, awkward, heavy with everything unsaid. It feels like a benediction and a farewell.

"I'll come back later," you promise, though you don't know if that's true.

You almost wish them a Happy Christmas, but Christmas has never been that way. Not since 1986. Not since Sarah.

Instead, you rise in silence, tuck the folder under your arm, and pull on your coat. At the door, you glance back. They're still at the table, two figures framed in the yellow light of the kitchen window. You know they'll stay there long after you've gone.

Outside, the air stings your lungs. The car groans awake under your hands, headlights spearing through the snow. Headlights in the morning sums this town up too well.

You take the northern road that will lead you just out of town, determination grinding against fear

The ski resort.

Rachel Van Vleet. Eleven years old. The first girl to be taken. The name that everyone remembers when they talk about Pine Hollow and the eight taken children. They always remember the first, and now they remember the last. You were a baby, then, and Sarah wasn't even born. You still know the story. Her story.

Rachel was an only child, unlike the others. A comer-inner, just like your family — not born here, never fully belonging. You've searched for patterns, for something that connects the children beyond Christmas Eve and the bells. You've tried to reason why Sarah was chosen and not someone else. Not you.

You don't want to believe it was because you stole Barbara's bracelet and blamed it on her. That's ridiculous. Isn't it?

Your thoughts are lost in a time long past when you reach the edge of town. There, where the road narrows to a single lane between the trees, a snowplough blocks the way, broadside across the asphalt. Its yellow lights pulse in the flurries, harsh and unreal. A sheriff's cruiser idles behind it, the driver's face shadowed. An orange cone sinks into the drift, already half-buried.

You slow, roll down your window, cold air slicing in. There's no way past. The plough fills the road like a barricade.

You grip the wheel until your knuckles pale. There's no way for you to reach the ski resort. Not yet.

With a curse, you pull a slow three-point turn. Headlights sweep the trees, skeletal branches clawing at the night, and then you're heading back into Pine Hollow, the mountain still waiting, silent and untouched.

Read your father's file Turn to page 48
Visit the Crawford family Turn to page 56
Go to Sarah's grave Turn to page 67

YOU WANT JUSTICE

You set the cup down and meet both of their eyes.

"I'm here because we need justice," you say. "Not just for us. For Rachel. David. Claire. Tommy. Daniel. Emily. Amy. For Sarah. This isn't about telling a sad story. It's about naming what was done and making the person who did it answer for it."

Your father's posture changes almost imperceptibly, a straightening of the spine. Your mother draws in a breath that trembles less than the others. The word has weight in this house; it rings differently from *closure* or *hope*. Justice isn't soft. It's a reckoning.

"Justice," your mother repeats, tasting it

"I can't promise the law will do anything it didn't do before. But there are other ways justice makes itself known. Truth has a shape. It leaves fingerprints even when people think they're wearing gloves. I'm going to find those marks. I'm going to put them in the open." You hold your mother's hand as you speak.

Your father leans forward, elbows on his knees, hands linked. "You'll write it where the world can see."

"Yes," you say. "And I'll take what I find to anyone who will act. It's not just an article. It's a case."

Your mother rises without speaking and walks to the mantel. She lifts a photograph: the four of you in front of the house. She brings it back and lays it on the table. "People said we should put away the pictures," she says. "That it hurt too much. But I thought, if we hide her, doesn't that help him?"

You look at Sarah's face, her laugh caught mid-bloom, hair escaping its clip, the stubborn chin you also inherited. "Justice," you say again, softly, to her. "You deserve it."

"I have something that might help," your father says, pulling himself to his feet.

See what Dad has for you. Turn to page 65

AT THE MATTHEWS HOUSE

Your father opens a narrow drawer in the sideboard and pulls out a paper folder, its edges softened by handling. "This is mine," he says. "Not the cops'. Notes. Times. Faces I don't trust." He offers it like something contraband. "I started it the second year. I didn't want to be the man who only waited for bells."

You take it with both hands. Inside: lists in blocky handwriting. The names of men who worked the slopes when the resort still sputtered along. Teachers. A groundskeeper who never returned from an off-season job. The janitor who started asking too many questions about the classrooms' locks. A delivery driver who switched routes every winter. And dates—so many dates—of odd cars on the street, of charity Santas at the grocery store, of power flickers near the woods.

"This is... a lot," you say, throat tight.

"I was a man with a hammer," he says. "Everything looked like a nail. The police smiled and said they'd *consider* it." The word curdles. "I stopped showing them."

"It matters," you tell him. "Patterns are made precisely of this: ordinary lines that intersect."

Your mother sits again, drawing her hands together.

You gather the folder, the photo in your mind, the map forming across your thoughts.

"We noted everything," your mother says. "Because no one else would." She hesitates. "Jenny... if you do find him—what then?"

You meet her eyes. "This ends. And Sarah..."

Your mother nods once, slowly.

Your father coughs, bringing his hand to his face to cover his emotion.

The three of you sit there with the folder between you like a small, necessary fire. Outside, snow keeps falling, indifferent. Inside, something that isn't indifference stands up in your bones.

Not hope. Not yet. But the engine of justice turning over, stubborn and cold, and catching.

Clearing the tears from his throat, your father asks, "So, where do you start?"

You could...
Read your father's file Turn to page 48
Visit the Crawford family Turn to page 56
Go to Sarah's grave Turn to page 67
Drive up to the old ski resort Turn to page 62

GO TO SARAH'S GRAVE

The morning has dulled to pewter by the time you turn off the road and into the churchyard. Snow drifts in lazy sheets, blurring the edges of the world. The heater fights the cold, but your breath still clouds faintly in the car. You cut the engine, and the silence roars in its place.

For a long moment, you just sit there, hands clenched on the wheel, watching the slope of white beyond the glass. Rows of headstones march up the hill, dark teeth biting through the snow. Somewhere among them is her name.

When you finally open the door, the cold slams into you. It slices your lungs, sharp as glass, and your eyes water instantly. You bury your chin into your scarf, but it doesn't help. Nothing could. The air here is colder than anywhere else in town, colder because of what waits on the hill.

Your boots crunch through the powder as you climb, each step leaving a clean, solitary mark. You keep your gaze low, watching the prints form, because looking ahead feels too much like searching for her.

You find the stone more quickly than you expect. Smaller than it should be, set low in the earth. A rectangle of granite, edges already softened by thirty winters, the name cut sharp enough to last another thirty.

SARAH MATTHEWS
1977—1986

Nine years. A whole life in nine years.

Your breath catches. You lower yourself without thinking, knees sinking into the snow, gloves pressed flat to the frozen face of the stone. The cold stings through fabric.

She isn't here. She never was. No body beneath, no coffin lowered, no ground broken. Just a stone to make the town believe the story was finished. A headstone to anchor grief, because grief with no anchor will drag you under.

Your hand trembles over her name.

What you mourn isn't only the girl stolen in the snow, but the sister you were never allowed to grow up with.

You will never hear the cadence of her teenage voice, that perfect mix of defiance and hope.

Never steal each other's clothes and laugh about who wore them worse.

Never share lipstick shades, or argue about who gets the bathroom first.

Never whisper about crushes, the kind that feel like the end of the world.

Never let her curl up on your sofa after her first heartbreak—or would you have given her your bed and taken the sofa yourself, listening to her cry until she slept?

Never watch her discover a career, light up when she spoke about it, complain when it demanded too much.

Never hear her tell you she was moving to the city, or getting married, or staying single because she loved her life too much to change it.

Never sit across from her at Christmas, year after year, trading stories only sisters tell, all the shorthand of a lifetime of knowing each other.

Nine years. That's all you were given.

Snow gathers on the crown of the stone. You brush it away, as if keeping the letters clear might keep her memory from fading. The scarf at your throat is damp with your breath, your chest aching from the weight pressing in.

All those years you stayed away, convincing yourself distance would soften the loss, and still it gnawed at you. You tried to turn it into something you could outrun: work, headlines, deadlines. But absence doesn't thin. It sharpens. Every year without her has been another cut.

You close your eyes, and for a moment you can almost see her, mittened hands clumsy with the cold, cheeks flushed red, hair escaping her hat in messy curls. She is always nine years old in your memory. Always on the edge of vanishing.

This is why you came back. Not for a headline. Not even for justice, though you keep telling yourself that's the reason. You came back because you can't spend the rest of your life holding on to just six years of her.

You rise slowly, knees stiff, brushing snow from your coat. The headstone looks smaller now, as if it's sinking into the hill, retreating under the weight of winter.

There will never be answers here. Only absence, carved in stone. But it's enough. Enough to remind you why you can't stop, why you can't turn away again.

Your boots crunch as you walk back down the slope. Each print is deliberate, heavy, a promise pressed into the snow: you will not let her vanish a second time.

The only question is where to start.

Police Turn to page 51
Pine Hollow Inn Turn to page 80

THE MATTHEWS HOUSE

The snow is falling harder now, a steady veil across the windshield. You sit behind the wheel, engine idling, breath fogging the cabin glass. Evergreen Lane lies hushed, dressed in the kind of Christmas quiet you used to love as a child. The house waits, crouched beneath its garlands and ribbons, exactly where you left it.

Last night you parked on this same street, headlights off, hands locked around the steering wheel until they cramped. You watched the porch light flicker against the falling snow, but you couldn't move. Thirty years you've been away, and still you couldn't summon the courage to walk up those sagging steps and knock. You told yourself you'd try in the morning. The truth was simpler: you were terrified.

And yet here you are. Morning has come, and the house hasn't vanished.

Your chest tightens. It's not just a house. It's the place that swallowed your sister whole. The day Sarah vanished, the heart of this family cracked open, and you fled through the fracture lines.

You grip the steering wheel until your knuckles burn. The "what ifs" creep in again, as they always do when you let your guard down. What if you had made a different choice that night? What if you hadn't stolen Lucy Johnson's bracelet, hadn't plotted to pin the blame on Sarah? What if you'd gone outside with her instead of sulking upstairs? What if it had been you?

Each question lands like a blow. You've asked them for years, in every city, in every borrowed apartment where the silver bells followed you. None of them ever gave you an answer.

You draw a shaky breath. Whatever choices you've taken, however many roads you've fled down, they all end here. With the choice you least want to face. Going home.

You kill the engine. The sudden silence roars in your ears. Snow taps against the windshield like insistent fingers, urging you forward.

The walk across the street feels impossibly long. The snow clutches at your boots. Each step sinks deeper than the last until you reach the porch. The wood groans beneath your weight, the same sound you remember from childhood. Except now it feels like judgment.

Your hand hovers over the door. You haven't told them you're coming. For all they know, you are still hundreds of miles away, tucked into your Boston apartment with deadlines for company.

They aren't expecting you.

Maybe they stopped expecting long ago.

The door swings open before you can knock.

Your mother stands there. Her hair is silver now, pulled back neatly, but her eyes are the same. Sharp, searching, wet with disbelief. For a long heartbeat, neither of you speaks.

Then she reaches for you.

Her arms are fierce around your shoulders, her cheek pressed against yours. You catch the faint scent of flour and cinnamon, the ghost of a Christmas Eve morning that should have been ordinary.

"Jenny," she breathes, as though saying your name might undo the years. "Jenny."

Your throat closes. You cling to her, every muscle trembling. You didn't deserve this welcome. You expected anger, maybe even blame. But all you feel is her relief, pouring over you like warmth after frostbite.

Behind her, a shape moves in the hallway. Your father.

He stands a few steps back, hands braced on the frame of the living room door. His face is unreadable, carved into lines you don't recognize. The years have weighed on him differently. Heavier, harder. He doesn't speak. Not yet.

Your mother pulls you inside, fussing with your coat, as though she can catch up on thirty years by straightening your collar. "You're frozen. Sit, sit. I'll make coffee."

You let her guide you to the familiar sofa, every inch of the house screaming with memory. The ornaments on the tree glimmer faintly, mismatched as ever. The garlands sag in the window boxes. Time here has moved, but not much. The air feels thick with absence.

Your father lowers himself into his chair. The same chair. He looks at you across the gulf of the coffee table.

"You should have called," he says finally. His voice is low, rough, like gravel.

"I know." Your voice wavers. "I couldn't."

Silence hangs, broken only when your mother returns with mugs of steaming coffee. She sets one in front of you, her hand brushing yours. Her eyes are red but steady. "You're home. That's what matters."

The word 'home' splinters something inside you. Because you're not sure it is anymore.

You wrap your hands around the mug for steadiness. The warmth seeps into your palms, but not deep enough. You glance at your father. His gaze hasn't softened.

The moment stretches until you know you have to speak. The truth presses against your ribs, desperate.

"I didn't just come to visit." Your voice sounds foreign in the small room. "I came because it's time. Because I need to know what happened to Sarah. I need to write it. I need to find him."

Your mother stills. The relief on her face falters, replaced by something smaller. Fear, maybe, or resignation.

"Jenny…" Her hand trembles against her cup. "Some things are better left alone."

The words slice through you. After all these years, she still says it. Leave it alone. Pretend the bells are nothing but decorations, pretend the wound isn't still bleeding.

But you can't. Not anymore.

You lean forward, the words spilling now.

Do you:

Tell them you need **closure** Turn to page 74

Tell them it's **not over** Turn to page 44

Tell them you need **justice** Turn to page 64

YOU NEED CLOSURE

You keep your hands wrapped around the mug, like warmth might steady the tremor in your voice. "I came because I can't live with not knowing anymore. None of us can. We need closure. We need to know what happened to Sarah."

Your mother's eyes fill again. She sets her coffee down with care, as if any sudden movement might tip the room into chaos.

"Closure," she repeats. "People love that word. Pastors, counsellors, neighbours who don't know what to say. They send pies and say, 'I hope you get closure.'" Her mouth trembles. "It's a door they imagine you can shut."

"I know," you say. "It isn't a door. It's a corridor that never ends. But it can't go on like this."

Across from you, your father stares at the rim of his cup. "Closure doesn't bring a child back," he says. "Closure is a word the living use to make time behave."

You lean forward. "It's a word for remembering without choking on it. It's a way to carry her without... without bleeding every time a bell shows up."

His gaze lifts finally to yours. There's something raw there, some old, exposed wire. "What makes you think you can do what the police could not?" he asks. No anger in it, just the weight of decades.

"Because I won't look away this time," you say. "Because I've learned how to follow threads other people miss. Because I know this place, and I know Sarah, and I know what it feels like to fail her. If closure is a fantasy, then at least tell me it's a better one than pretending."

Your mother flinches at that word '*pretending*' and her eyes slide to the hallway. You follow her glance. The chest sits where it always has, at the end of the runner, its lid polished from countless hands. You don't need to open it to feel the years stacked inside.

"Your father wanted to put them in the attic," your mother says softly. "I said no. I... I couldn't box her away."

He doesn't contradict her. The silence between them is practiced, as old as the bells.

You set the cup down and stand. Your legs feel unsteady, but you make yourself walk to the chest. The wood is cool. Your fingers hover over the lid before you lift it.

Silver. A shimmer like frozen light. Bells in small cloth bundles, bells loose, bells with thin lengths of ribbon tied through their loops. You don't touch them. You just look until your eyes blur.

Your mother's voice comes from behind you, small and steady. "Sometimes I'd imagine the sound they'd make if they rang. Not in my head. In this house. As if they were trying to tell us something we weren't hearing."

You swallow. "I used to imagine that, too," you say. "In Boston. I never told you."

She is beside you now, her hand on your shoulder. "We stopped telling each other things," she admits. "It was the only way to get through a day."

Your father joins you, slow, reluctant. He looks down at the bells as if they might look back. "Closure," he says again, but the word has changed shape in his mouth. "If we knew... even something small... where she went, who took her... what those first hours were like..." His voice thins. "What if knowing is worse?"

"It might be," you say. "But not knowing is a poison, and we've drunk it for twenty-nine years."

He exhales through his nose, long and frayed. "And you'll drink the worst of it for us now, is that it?"

"I can carry some of it," you say. "Finally."

Your mother nods. "Then we help you." The decision seems to land on her like snowfall. Silent, complete. "We help you look. We tell you everything again, even the parts we packed away because repeating them made our tongues feel like paper."

She closes the chest carefully, as if not to wake anything. "We never told you this," she says, eyes on the wood. "The night before Sarah disappeared, she asked me if she could sleep with the curtains open. She said she wanted to watch the snow. We said yes. I've thought of that a thousand times. How we were the ones who let the darkness in."

Your father shakes his head. "No." It's firm. "We can't do that to ourselves anymore. The harm belongs to the man who did it."

You return to the sofa. The house feels full of breaths you've all been holding for thirty winters. "Tell me everything," you say. "From your memories, not the reports. The way she laughed that morning. Who came to the door. The phone calls. Anything the files flattened. We build the whole day back, detail by detail. And when we get to the place where the path vanishes, we keep going."

Your father's mouth fights a grimace that isn't quite a smile. "You sound like your editor."

"I sound like your daughter, who can't stand this anymore," you say.

The clock in the hallway ticks on. A sound you avoided using last night in your mind because it carried reproach. But now it's just measure. Your mother sits, fingers interlaced, thumbs rubbing each other like a small prayer. "What do you need first?" she asks.

"Anything," you whisper. "Anything that can help."

They trade a look you can't read. Then, your father rises.

Your dad has something for you. Turn to page 65

BACK TO PINE HOLLOW INN

The drive back through town feels longer than it should. The folder sits on the passenger seat like a second body, the sheriff's rejection still buzzing in your ears. Amy's name, Sarah's name, all of them, swatted away as if they were nothing but irritants. Brick walls. Everywhere you turned.

By the time the Inn comes into view, snow has thickened to a curtain, soft but relentless, muffling the world. The place looks almost warm against the storm, with windows glowing amber, smoke curling into the sky. For a moment you let yourself believe it could feel like safety.

Inside, the lobby smells of lavender polish and wood smoke. The heat is a shock after the cold, but it doesn't ease the weight in your chest.

Katie looks up from behind the desk the moment you enter. Relief flickers through you before you can stop it. This morning it was Siobhan there, stiff and watchful, her eyes following you like you were a problem she was already tired of. But now it's Katie, open-faced, eager, the closest thing you've had to an ally since you came back.

"You're back," she says quickly, as though she's been waiting. Tommy was her brother. You've both lost someone. Her face is a reminder that you're doing this for her as much as for yourself…for Tommy as much as for Sarah.

"So? What's new?"

You drop the folder onto the counter. "What's new is the sheriff won't lift a finger. I laid it out for him. Everything. I even begged him for a stakeout. He just waved me off. Laughed." Your voice hardens. "Fifteen years since the last one, a girl taken just last year, and he acts like it's nothing."

Katie's face flickers. "I knew they wouldn't help," she says quietly.

You press your hand flat on the folder. The word you used still echoes in your mind. Stakeout. The sheriff dismissed it, but maybe he was right about one thing: if anyone's going to sit in the cold waiting for those bells, it won't be him.

It'll have to be you.

The thought lodges sharp in your chest, but you don't speak it. Not yet.

Katie watches you closely. "So, what now?" she asks.

What now, indeed. You could tell her what you're thinking, let her in on it. Or you could keep it to yourself.

Tell Katie. **Turn to page 171**
Keep the plan to yourself. **Turn to page 87**

BACK IN ROOM 12

You climb the stairs to Room 12, each step creaking under your weight.

Inside your room, you close the door and lean against it. The folder goes on the bed. Your father's map spreads across the faded quilt - four houses circled in red, four families still waiting for bells.

You check your phone.

Five hours until midnight. Five hours to rest, to prepare, to decide which house to watch.

You set an alarm for 9:30 PM. That gives you two hours of sleep and time to get into position before the bells come.

The bed is narrow but clean. The pillow smells of detergent and pine. You lie down fully clothed, just for a moment, just to close your eyes.

Sleep takes you faster than you expect, dragging you down into dreams of red mittens and silver bells and Katie's voice saying family is everything over and over like a prayer or a warning.

When the alarm goes off, you're already reaching for your coat.

Where do you go?
The Wilsons' Turn to page 184
The Hendersons' Turn to page 89
The Crawfords' Turn to page 178
Your parents' Turn to page 227

PINE HOLLOW INN

The drive back through town feels longer than it should. The folder sits on the passenger seat like a second body, its weight pulling at you every time you glance at it. Amy's name, Sarah's name, all of them, scrawled across your father's pages like unanswered prayers. Brick walls. That's all you've ever known from this town.

You don't bother with the sheriff. You don't need to. You already know what he'd say: that the bells mean nothing, that the past means nothing, that resources don't stretch far enough for ghosts. You don't need his contempt to remind you: you're on your own.

By the time the Inn comes into view, snow has thickened to a curtain, soft but relentless, muffling the world. The place looks almost warm against the storm, with windows glowing amber, smoke curling into the sky. For a moment you let yourself believe it could feel like safety.

Inside, the lobby smells of lavender polish and wood smoke. The heat is a shock after the cold, but it doesn't ease the weight in your chest.

Katie looks up from behind the desk the moment you enter. Relief flickers through you before you can stop it. This morning it was Siobhan there, stiff and watchful, her eyes following you like you were a problem she was already tired of. But now it's Katie, open-faced, eager, the closest thing you've had to an ally since you came back.

"You're back," she says quickly, as though she's been waiting. Tommy was her brother. You've both lost someone. Her face is a reminder that you're doing this for her as much as for yourself. For Tommy as much as for Sarah.

"So? What's new?"

You drop the folder onto the counter. "What's new is I know better than to waste my time on the police. They'll never lift a finger. Fifteen years since the last one, a girl taken just last year, and my dad says they act like it's nothing. Like it never even happened."

Katie's face flickers. She shakes her head, voice cutting. "They're never going to help."

She's right. They're never going to help. Even tonight, the police won't stake out any of the houses that will receive bells.

You press your hand flat on the folder. The word forms in your mind and sticks there, jagged as glass: stakeout. If anyone's going to sit in the cold waiting for those bells, it won't be them.

It'll have to be you.

The thought lodges sharp in your chest, but you don't speak it. Not yet.

Katie watches you closely. "So, what now?" she asks.

What now, indeed. You could tell her what you're thinking, let her in on it. Or you could keep it to yourself. Or go further and tell your parents directly.

Tell Katie. Turn to page 171
Keep the plan to yourself. Turn to page 87

GO INSIDE YOUR PARENTS' HOUSE

You grab your phone and flashlight, leaving everything else in the car. The walk across the street feels longer than it should, your boots crunching through fresh snow. The porch light casts its yellow glow across the steps: the same steps you climbed this morning, the same door you knocked on.

That was only twelve hours ago, but it feels like days.

You knock. Wait. The door opens almost immediately.

Your mother stands there, still dressed, eyes widening when she sees you. "Jenny?"

"Can I come in?"

She steps back without a word, and you're inside, pulling off your boots in the same entryway where you stood this morning. Your father appears in the living room doorway, concern etched across his face.

"I thought you were staying at the Inn," he says.

"I was." You meet his eyes. "I want to do a stake out. I mean, I am. I am going to. And I realised…" Your voice cracks slightly. "I realised I can't do this alone. Not tonight."

Your mother's hand finds your arm. "You want to watch from here."

It's not a question. She understands immediately.

"The bell will be left here tonight," you say. "One of the four houses. I need to see who places it. But if I stay in the car, I'll freeze. Or fall asleep. Or…"

"Or you'll be alone," your father finishes quietly.

You nod, throat tight. "You're the only people I can trust. Katie and Siobhan… I want to trust them, but…"

You don't finish. You don't need to. Whether it's instinct or something they said, something about them makes you hesitate. And right now, hesitation means you can't rely on them.

Your mother guides you to the sofa, the same sofa where you sat this morning, coffee growing cold as you talked about Sarah. The folder your father gave you is still in your car, but its contents are burned into your memory. The map with the four houses circled in red. The years of observations. The weight of his obsession turned survival.

"Of course you can stay," your mother says. "We'll watch together."

Your father settles into his chair.

"Have you ever tried to watch before?" you ask.

Your father's laugh is bitter, empty. "Every year. Every single Christmas Eve since 1987, we've watched. Taken turns. Sat by the window. Left the porch light on, turned it off, tried every combination we could think of."

"And?" Your voice is barely a whisper.

"And the bell always comes," your mother says quietly. "We've never seen who leaves it. Not once in thirty-nine years. We watch all night, we don't sleep, and then in the morning…" She gestures helplessly. "It's there. On the porch. Like it appeared out of nowhere."

The hair on the back of your neck stands up. "That's impossible."

"We know," your father says. "But it happens anyway."

You think about the other families. The Hendersons, the Wilsons. Have they tried watching too? Have they spent years staring out windows, waiting for something they never see? Will the Crawfords watch for the first time tonight?

"Maybe three of us will make the difference," you say, though you don't quite believe it.

Your mother's hand tightens on yours. "Maybe."

But tonight, that changes. It has to.

You settle in to wait. Turn to page 84

INSIDE YOUR PARENTS' HOUSE

You settle into the waiting.

Your mother turns off the living room lamps, leaving only the kitchen light burning dim. Your father pulls the curtains in the front windows, but leaves a gap just wide enough to see the porch and the street beyond. You position yourself at the kitchen window where your mother suggested: the side angle that gives a clear view of the front steps and the approach from either direction.

The three of you sit in near darkness, tea cooling on the table, watching the empty street. Snow falls steadily, accumulating on the porch railing, the mailbox, your car parked across the street. The neighbourhood is silent. No cars. No movement. Just the hush of Christmas Eve settling over Pine Hollow like a held breath.

You check the street. Nothing.

Check the porch. Nothing.

The minutes crawl.

Your father shifts in his chair, the leather creaking. Your mother hasn't moved from her position by the front window gap. You can see her silhouette, rigid, unblinking.

Thirty-nine years they've done this. Thirty-nine years of watching, waiting, never seeing.

Your eyes burn from staring into the darkness. You blink hard, refocus.

Headlights appear at the end of the street.

All three of you tense.

A vehicle crawls toward the house, moving slowly through the snow. It's a truck. Dark coloured. As it passes under the streetlight, you see the marking on the door.

Sheriff's Department.

The truck pulls to a stop in front of your parents' house. Not across the street where you parked. Right in front, blocking the view of the porch.

"What's he doing here?" your mother whispers.

The driver's door opens. A figure emerges: tall, heavy coat, Sheriff's Department hat. He pauses, looks at the house, then starts up the walk toward the porch.

Your father stands. "I'll see what he wants."

"Dad, wait..." You start to protest, but he's already moving to the door.

The knock comes. Three sharp raps.

Your father opens it, and cold air rushes in along with the sheriff. Sheriff Larkin. Older, late fifties, with deep lines carved around his eyes and a practiced smile that doesn't quite reach them.

"Bill," he says, nodding at your father. "Sorry to bother you so late."

"Sheriff." Your father's voice is neutral, careful. "What can I do for you?"

"Just making rounds." Larkin stamps snow off his boots but doesn't step inside. "After last year, we're doing check-ins on the families. Making sure everyone's all right tonight."

There's a weight to those words. After last year. After Amy Crawford. After fifteen years of silence broke and the nightmare started again.

Your father's jaw tightens. "We're fine."

"Good, good." Larkin's eyes move past him, scanning the room. They land on you standing in the doorway between the kitchen and living room. His expression shifts. Larkin nods slowly, and there's something almost approving in it. Like he's checking a box on a list. "Nice that you've got family with you tonight. That's good. That's real good."

Your mother appears behind your father, hands clasped tight. "We appreciate you checking, Sheriff."

"Just doing our job." He glances back toward his truck, then at the street, then finally at your father again. "You folks planning to stay up much longer?"

The question lands strange. Not threatening exactly, but pointed.

"Not too late," your father says carefully.

"Good, good. Get some rest. Tomorrow's a big day." Larkin tips his hat, that same practiced smile. "Merry Christmas, folks. Stay safe tonight."

The emphasis on those last words makes your skin prickle.

"Merry Christmas," your father echoes hollowly.

The door closes. The sheriff's boots crunch down the steps. You move to the window, watching as he climbs back into his truck, starts the engine. The headlights sweep across the front of the house as he pulls away.

And there, on the path, clearly visible in the glow of the porch light...

A silver bell.

What do you do?

Run after the sheriff. Turn to page 103
Stay with your parents. Turn to page 119

KEEP THE PLAN TO YOURSELF

You open your mouth, the words right there: *I'm going to stake out the houses tonight. Watch for whoever places the bells.*

But something stops you.

Katie's still here. Still in Pine Hollow. Still running this Inn with her sister, still living in the house where Tommy disappeared.

Katie's been here through all of it. Four more disappearances. Four more families shattered. One of them was yours.

And she's still here.

That doesn't happen by accident.

"I'm going to spend Christmas Eve with my parents," you hear yourself say. The lie comes easily, smooth as old habit. "I haven't been home for Christmas in years. It feels like the right thing to do."

Something shifts in Katie's expression. Her shoulders drop slightly, tension you hadn't noticed bleeding out of them. "Oh," she says, and there's genuine warmth in it. "Jenny, that's good. That's really good."

"I should have gone straight there when I arrived instead of coming here first," you continue, building the story as you go. Professional habit - make the lie detailed enough to be believable. "I've been so focused on the investigation that I forgot they're the reason I came back in the first place."

Katie nods, reaching across the counter to touch your hand briefly. The gesture surprises you. "Family is everything," she says, and her voice catches slightly. "Especially at Christmas. Especially when you've lost someone."

She means it. You can see it in her eyes - the memory of Tommy, the weight of all these Christmases without him. This isn't just platitude. This is lived experience. Lived experience that you share.

"They need you there," Katie continues. "More than they need you out here chasing ghosts in the cold. And you need them too, even if you haven't let yourself admit it yet."

The words hit harder than they should. Because she's not wrong. You do need them. You've needed them all the time that you've been away, but you've been too terrified to reach for them.

"I'll head over there after I get changed," you say. "Probably won't be back until Christmas Day."

"Take your time." Katie squeezes your hand once before letting go. "There's no rush. The Inn will be here when you need it. You'll still have to pay for that room though." She laughs, but it seems like a half joke. This is the only inn in the town, and it has only twelve rooms. People don't come here on purpose anymore.

She turns back to her paperwork, and you recognise dismissal when you see it. But it's a kind dismissal. Gentle. She thinks you're doing the right thing.

She doesn't know that in six hours, you'll be watching one of four houses, waiting for whoever places those bells.

She doesn't know that you're not going to let another Christmas Eve pass with nothing but silence and silver bells.

She doesn't know that you've finally stopped running.

You pick up the folder, tuck it under your arm. "Thank you, Katie. For everything."

"Of course." She glances up with a smile that seems genuine, tired but genuine. "Merry Christmas, Jenny."

"Merry Christmas."

Go to your room. Turn to page 79

GO TO THE HENDERSONS'

You head toward Maple Drive. The Hendersons. Claire's family. The oldest victim family still here.

As you turn onto their street, you notice several houses are lit up too. People are home. Not everyone went to church tonight.

The curtains are drawn at the Henderson house, but you can see the flicker of a television through the crack between them as you pass.

You park three houses down, far enough to be unobtrusive but close enough to watch. Your father's map rests on the passenger seat, Henderson house circled in red. You settle in to wait.

The heater hums. Your coffee thermos sits in the cup holder, steam curling from the open top. Outside, the street is empty. Silent.

You watch the house. The upstairs window. The porch. The street in both directions. Your breath fogs the windshield, and you wipe it clear with your glove. Your phone sits in your lap.

Minutes crawl past.

Then movement catches your eye. Not at the Henderson house - further down the street. A figure emerges from between two houses, dark coat, hood up, walking with purpose.

Your pulse quickens. You grab your phone, thumb hovering over the camera. The figure is walking toward you, toward the Henderson house.

Is this it? Are they going to place a bell?

The figure walks past your car. Past the Henderson house without slowing. Doesn't even glance at it. Continues up the street, turns left at the corner, disappears from view.

Just someone out for a walk on Christmas Eve.

You lower your phone. Let out a breath you knew you were holding. False alarm.

You check the time. Still early. The bells could come anytime between now and morning. This could be a long night.

You take a sip of coffee. Wipe the windshield clear again. Stare out at the empty street, the Henderson house dark except for that single downstairs lamp flickering through the curtains.

What are you even doing here? Sitting in a freezing car, watching a house where an elderly couple are probably just watching television, trying to get through another Christmas Eve without their daughter…

Tap tap tap.

You jump so hard your knee slams into the steering wheel. Pain shoots up your leg.

A face at your window. Close. Too close. A man.

Your heart stops.

He's standing right there, bent to peer in at you, face half-shadowed in the dim streetlight. Elderly, weathered, wearing a thick winter coat. You didn't see him approach. Didn't hear footsteps in the snow.

How long has he been standing there? Watching you?

He gestures: roll down the window.

Every instinct screams at you to start the car, to drive away. Your hand moves to the keys still in the ignition. Your phone is in your lap; you could call someone, but who? The police? The same police who've done nothing for forty-nine years?

The man taps again, more insistent. Three sharp raps against the glass.

Your breath comes fast and shallow. The windows are fogging faster now. Your pulse hammers in your ears.

This is Pine Hollow. The town where children vanish.

And there's a stranger at your car window in the darkness of Christmas Eve.

You have seconds to decide.

What do you do?

Roll down the window. Turn to page 94

Drive away. Turn to page 102

REFUSE AND GO BACK

"No." You take a step backward, away from the truck. "I'm not getting in."

Larkin's expression hardens. "Miss Matthews…"

"Someone just left a bell on my parents' porch while you were distracting us. I don't know if you're incompetent or complicit, but either way, I'm not going anywhere with you."

For a moment, you think he might push it. Might insist. Might do something worse.

But then he shrugs, climbs back into the truck. "Suit yourself. But don't say I didn't try to help."

He pulls away, taillights disappearing into the snow.

You stand there for a moment, heart hammering, cold seeping through your coat. Then you turn and walk back to your parents' house.

Go back inside. Turn to page 97

YOU GO ALONE

You shake your head.

"No, Dad. You're staying here too."

His face hardens. "Absolutely not."

"You just told me Mum's too old for this. You're older than she is."

"By two years…"

"You're eighty-two years old. If something happens up there… if the building's unstable, if there's anything dangerous there, if…" Your voice catches. "I can't risk losing you too."

"You're not going alone." His voice is firm, final. "That's not happening."

"Dad…"

"No." He stands, and you see the man he used to be: strong, immovable, protective.

"It's not your choice…"

"It's absolutely my choice." His hands grip the folder so tightly his knuckles go white. "You think I'm going to let you drive up that mountain by yourself? What if something happens? You don't know what condition the lodge is in. It's been abandoned since 1977. What do I tell your mother? 'Sorry, I let our only remaining daughter disappear too'?"

The words hit like a physical blow.

"I've already lost one daughter," he continues, voice breaking. "I will not lose another. If you're going up there, I'm going with you. That's not negotiable."

You stare at him. See the desperation behind the determination. The decades of helplessness finding an outlet. The fear that if he doesn't go, if he doesn't do something, he'll spend whatever time he has left wondering if he could have made a difference.

"I'm going," he says again. "The only question is whether you fight me on it and wake your mother, or whether we leave now, together, and let her sleep."

His jaw is set. His eyes hard. You recognise that look. You inherited it from him. The stubborn determination that won't be moved.

What do you do?
Give in. Let him come. Turn to page 140
Stand firm. Call his bluff. Turn to page 109

ROLL DOWN THE WINDOW

You press the button. The window descends halfway. Cold air rushes in, sharp and biting.

"You're Bill Matthews' daughter," he says. Not a question. His voice is rough, aged.

You can see him better now in the glow of the streetlight. Elderly, seventies maybe, wearing a thick wool coat fastened up close to his chin. Deep lines carve his face. He looks exhausted. And familiar, somehow.

"Who are you?" Your voice comes out steadier than you feel.

"Harold Henderson." He straightens slightly. "This is my house you're watching."

Your stomach drops. Claire's father. The first victim whose family stayed in Pine Hollow.

"Mr Henderson, I'm…"

"I know who you are." He glances back at his house, then at you. "I know what you're doing. And I'm telling you: go home."

"I'm trying to help…"

"You're going to get someone killed." His voice drops. "Maybe yourself. Maybe someone's child. But sitting out here on Christmas Eve, watching houses…" He shakes his head. "You don't understand what you're playing with."

"Then explain it to me." You lean toward the window. "Please. I know about the bells. I know someone is still leaving them. I know…"

"You don't know anything." He looks past you, scanning the dark street. "And if you're smart, you'll keep it that way." His eyes come back to yours. "Drive away. Go back to Boston. Leave this alone."

He knows as much about you as you do about him, it seems.

"I can't do that. My sister…"

"Is gone." The words are brutal in their simplicity. "Just like my Claire. Just like all of them. And us still being here, still getting those bells every year…" His voice cracks. "That's the price we pay for staying alive."

"What does that mean?"

He doesn't answer. Just straightens up, starts to turn away.

"Mr Henderson, please…"

He stops. Looks back. For a moment, you think he might say something. Might give you something to work with.

Instead: "My wife is inside. Watching television. Trying to pretend tonight is just another night. When a bell appears on our porch, she'll find it in the morning like she always does. And we'll put it with the others. And we'll survive another year." He meets your eyes. "That's all any of us can do. Survive."

He walks away. Back toward his house. Up the porch steps. The door opens, closes. The porch light stays on.

You sit in your car, hand still on the window button, cold air still pouring in.

He didn't tell you to call the police. Didn't offer to help. Just told you to leave.

Because he's scared. Or because he's complicit. Or both.

You check your watch. It's gone eleven.

You can't stay here. Not with Mr Henderson knowing you're watching. Not when he could call someone, warn them, compromise whatever happens tonight.

You close the window. Put the car in drive.

Henderson's words echo in your head: *You're going to get someone killed.* Maybe yourself.

He's right. You can't do this alone. Sitting in a car, watching houses, waiting for something to happen - that's not investigation. That's surveillance. And you're not equipped for this.

You need help. You need people you can trust.

You need your parents.

The drive to Evergreen Lane takes five minutes. Your hands are steadier now. The fear is converting to something else. Purpose, maybe. Or just exhaustion with being alone.

Your parents' house appears through the falling snow, porch light still on. Waiting for you. Like it always has been.

You park in the driveway this time. No more hiding. No more watching from a distance.

You have questions. You have suspicions.

But you have parents who stayed. Who endured forty years of bells. Who never stopped looking for answers.

Maybe that's where you should have started.

Go inside. Turn to page 82

GO BACK TO YOUR PARENTS

Your mother meets you at the door, pulling you inside before you can even speak. "What were you thinking, running after him like that?"

"I wanted him to see the bell. To do something." You're shaking, from cold, from adrenaline, from the realisation settling over you like ice.

Your father closes the door, locks it. "And?"

"He didn't care. He called it a prank. Told me to go home and rest." You look between them. "But that's not the worst part."

They wait.

"The timing. He showed up at exactly 11:18. Right when the bells are always left. His truck blocked the view of the porch. He kept us all distracted while someone…" Your voice cracks. "He was part of it. The distraction was deliberate."

Your mother sinks onto the sofa. Your father's face has gone grey.

"Forty years," he whispers. "Forty years we've been watching, and they've been…" He can't finish.

"Thirty-nine," your mother corrects automatically, and the precision of it, the way she's counted every single year, breaks something in your chest.

You sink down beside her. "We need to figure this out. If the sheriff is involved, if this is bigger than one person…" You think about Katie and Siobhan's fear, their warnings. About the way the whole town seems to look away. "We need a plan."

Your father moves to the window, looks out at the empty street. The bell still sits on the porch, silver and mocking.

"What kind of plan?" he asks.

Make a plan with your parents. Turn to page 114

"No." Your voice comes out harder than you intended. "You need to investigate this. Right now. Someone was just here, they couldn't have gone far…"

Larkin's expression shifts. The sympathetic mask slips, just for a moment, and you see something colder underneath. His eyes move past you to your parents' house, where your mother and father are silhouetted in the doorway, watching. Then back to you.

He's sizing you up. Calculating something.

"All right," he says finally. "You want me to investigate, we'll investigate. Get in the truck."

The invitation sounds wrong. Everything about this feels wrong. "What?"

"You want to catch whoever did this, we need to move fast. They're on foot, can't have gotten far in this snow." He gestures to the passenger door. "Come on. Let's go find them."

Your parents are still watching from the doorway. Your mother takes a step onto the porch, concern etched across her face. Your father's hand is on her arm, holding her back.

Larkin waits, one hand on the truck door, patient and still. The engine idles, exhaust curling into the cold air.

Every instinct screams that getting into that truck is a mistake.

But if you refuse, if you back down now, he'll drive away and nothing will change. The bell will sit on the porch. Another year will pass. Another Christmas will come.

"Well?" Larkin prompts. "You coming or not?"

Get in the truck. Turn to page 111
Refuse and go back. Turn to page 91

REFUSE SHERIFF'S TERMS

"No."

The word hangs in the warm air of the truck cab.

Larkin's expression doesn't change, but something shifts in his posture. "No?"

"I'm not leaving. I'm not dropping this. And I'm sure as hell not making promises to you." Your hand tightens on your phone. "Now unlock this door."

He studies you for a long moment. Then he sighs, like you've disappointed him.

"Well," he says quietly. "That's unfortunate."

He puts the truck in drive.

"What are you doing?" Your voice rises. "Let me out. LET ME OUT!"

You pound on the window, on the door, but the truck is already moving, heading away from town, toward the dark woods and the mountain beyond.

"Screaming won't help," Larkin says, almost conversationally. "Nobody out here to hear you."

You try your phone. No signal. The bars have disappeared, like they've been swallowed by the dark.

The truck climbs higher. The road narrows. Snow piles deeper on either side.

You know where he's taking you.

The old ski resort. The place where Rachel Van Vleet disappeared. The place where it all started.

"My parents know I'm with you," you try. "They saw me get in your truck."

"They saw you run after me. They saw you talking to me. Did they see you get in?" He glances at you. "Memory can be funny like that. Especially when people are upset. Stressed. Grieving."

The woods press closer. The headlights catch on snow-laden branches, on the rusted warning signs half-buried in drifts.

OLD SKI RESORT - CLOSED - NO TRESPASSING

"You don't have to do this," you say. Your voice shakes.

"I really do." He sounds genuinely regretful. "You had your chance, Jenny. You could have taken the out I offered. But you just couldn't leave it alone, could you? Just like your father. Just like all the others who thought they could stop this."

"Stop what? What is this? Who's the King of Christmas?"

Larkin laughs, short and bitter. "You still think there's some monster out there? Some boogeyman stealing children? God, you really don't understand."

The lodge appears ahead, a dark mass against darker trees.

He parks at the base, kills the engine. Silence crashes in.

"Here's the truth," he says, turning to face you fully. "This town has secrets. Old secrets. And we keep them buried because that's how we survive. That's how we protect what's ours. Your sister? She was part of that. Amy Crawford? Part of that. And if you keep pushing…" He reaches across, unlocks your door manually. "You'll be part of it too."

The door swings open. Cold air floods in.

"Get out."

"What?"

"Get out. Walk back to town. It's about five miles. Should take you a couple hours in this snow. You'll freeze a little, but you'll make it." His eyes are flat, cold. "And when you do, you get on that plane. You leave Pine Hollow. And you never come back."

You stare at him. "You're just going to let me go?"

"I'm giving you one more chance." His voice hardens. "Don't make me regret it."

You climb out into the snow. The truck door slams behind you.

Larkin leans out the window. "Five miles, Jenny. Straight down the road. Don't wander off into the trees. People get lost in these woods. People disappear."

The truck's engine roars to life. Headlights sweep past you as he turns around, heading back down the mountain.

And then you're alone.

In the dark.

In the snow.

What do you do?

Walk back to town. Turn to page 213

Go into the lodge. Turn to page 356

DRIVE AWAY

Your hand moves. Not to the window button. To the keys.

You twist the ignition. The engine coughs, catches.

The man steps back, startled. His mouth moves, saying something, but you can't hear over the blood roaring in your ears.

You throw the car into drive. In your rearview mirror, you see him standing in the street, watching you go. Just a shape in the darkness. A man you'll never identify.

Your hands shake on the wheel. Your breath comes in gasps.

You don't stop until you're three blocks away, pulled over on a side street, engine idling, heart still hammering.

Was that smart? Or cowardly?

Was he dangerous? Or was he trying to help?

You'll never know.

You check the time. You could still try again, somewhere else.

But you don't. You don't circle back to try the Wilsons or the Crawfords. That moment at the Henderson house - the fear, the uncertainty, the realisation that you have no idea who to trust - has shown you something. You can't do this alone.

Sitting in cars, watching houses, waiting for strangers to appear at your window - that's not investigation. That's paranoia. And it's going to get you killed.

You need help. You need people you can trust. You need your parents.

The drive to Evergreen Lane steadies you. The decision made, the path clear. Your parents' house appears through the falling snow, porch light still on. Waiting for you. Like it always has been.

You have questions. You have suspicions. But you have parents who stayed. Who endured forty years of bells. Who never stopped looking for answers.

Go inside. Turn to page 82

RUN AFTER THE SHERIFF

You yank open the door and bolt into the cold.

"Jenny!" your mother calls, but you're already down the steps, boots slipping on the fresh snow.

"Sheriff!" Your voice cuts through the night. "Sheriff, wait!"

The truck stops. Brake lights flare brighter. The driver's door opens and Larkin steps out, one hand on the door frame, looking back at you with an expression you can't quite read.

You're breathing hard by the time you reach him, cold air burning your lungs. You point back at your parents' house. "There's a bell. On the porch. Someone just left it while you were here."

He follows your gesture, squints at the porch. The bell is clearly visible under the light, small and silver and impossible.

"Well," he says slowly. "How about that?"

The words are wrong. Too casual. Too unsurprised.

"How about that?" you repeat. "Sheriff, someone just left evidence of a crime while you were standing in my parents' doorway. Don't you think that's…"

"Evidence of what crime, exactly?" His tone is patient, almost patronising. "I'm not sure any of us knows what those bells mean."

"You know what it means. You know what those bells mean."

"I know what people *say* they mean." He shifts his weight, glances back down the street. "But saying and proving are two different things. Could be kids. Could be someone playing a prank. Could be anything."

Your hands curl into fists. "After last year? After Amy Crawford? You really think…"

"I think," he interrupts gently, "that you're upset. Which is understandable. It's Christmas Eve, emotions run high, especially for families that have been through what yours has." He looks at you then, really looks at you, and there's something calculating behind the sympathy. "Why don't you go back inside, get some rest. I'll make a note of it in my report."

A note in his report. Forty years of bells, and he'll make a note.

You could push harder. Demand he investigate, refuse to let him leave, force him to acknowledge what just happened.

Or you could go back to your parents. Process this. Figure out what his presence here really meant.

What do you do?

Push the point - Don't let him dismiss this. Turn to page 98
Go back to your parents - Something's wrong. Turn to page 97

NO

You think about Sarah. About the bell on your parents' porch. About eight children vanishing and a town that's chosen silence over justice.

"No."

"Then let's go."

You both climb out. The cold hits immediately, sharp and biting. This high up the mountain, the wind cuts through your coat like it's nothing.

Your father opens the truck bed, pulls out two heavy-duty flashlights. Hands you one. "Stay close," he says. "And if anything feels wrong, the structure feels unstable, floor seems weak, anything - we leave. Understood?"

"Understood."

The two of you approach the main entrance. The front doors hang askew, one barely attached to its hinges. Snow has drifted into the entrance, creating a small slope.

Your father pushes the door. It groans, scrapes against the floor, but opens wider.

You step inside. Turn to page 155

TRUST YOUR FATHER

You force your hand back. Grip the door handle instead. Lock your fingers around it.

Trust him.

He's driven these roads for forty years.

He knows what he's doing.

Your father fights the wheel, trying to bring the truck back under control. The tyres scream. The engine roars. The sheriff's headlights are everywhere, turning the world into nothing but white light and falling snow.

For one impossible second, you think he's going to make it.

The truck straightens. The curve begins to pass. You can see the road continuing ahead, winding up the mountain.

And then the shoulder gives way.

Not dramatically. Not with a crack or a lurch. Just… the edge crumbles under the truck's weight, weakened by snow and decades of erosion, and suddenly there's nothing beneath the passenger-side tyres.

"No," your father breathes.

The truck tilts. Tips. And then you're not on the road anymore.

You're falling.

The sensation is impossible. Weightless. Endless. Your stomach lurches into your throat. Your mother is screaming. The truck is tumbling, rolling, and through the windshield you see stars, then trees, then darkness, then stars again.

This is what it feels like to fly.

This is what it feels like to die.

"I'm sorry," your father says, or maybe you imagine it, because the noise is too loud, metal shrieking and glass breaking and something heavy slamming against something else, over and over and over.

You should have grabbed the wheel.

The thought comes clear and bright in the chaos: you should have grabbed it, you should have done something, you should have, you should have...

The truck hits the bottom.

The impact is total. Absolute. The world becomes nothing but force and sound and pain. Your body slams against the seatbelt, against the door, against surfaces you can't identify. Something breaks inside you. Several somethings. You can feel them breaking, hear them breaking.

And then everything stops.

You're upside down. The truck is on its roof. The headlights are still on somehow, pointing up through shattered glass at the slope above you, at the road so far away it looks like stars.

You can't breathe right. There's something wrong with your chest. Wet sounds when you try to inhale.

"Mum?" you whisper.

She doesn't answer.

"Dad?"

Silence.

You try to turn your head, but you can't move. Can't feel your legs. Can't feel anything below your waist.

Through the broken windshield, you can see snow falling. So peaceful. So quiet.

Far above, on the road, red and blue lights appear. Sheriff Larkin's truck, stopped at the edge. You watch his silhouette emerge, watch him look down at the wreckage.

He stands there for a long moment.

Then he gets back in his truck and drives away.

You close your eyes.

The snow keeps falling.

THE END

You died at the bottom of a ravine off Mountain Road, Christmas Eve, 2025. Your father died on impact. Your mother died within seconds. You survived for almost three minutes, paralysed and unable to call for help.

Sheriff Larkin later filed a report stating he'd found your rental car abandoned at your parents' house. He speculated you'd all left Pine Hollow together, perhaps heading back to Boston. The wreckage wasn't discovered until spring thaw, when hikers spotted metal glinting in the ravine.

By then, it was too late to determine what really happened.

The King of Christmas continued his work.

You keep your tone gentle but firm.

"This is what I do, Dad. I investigate. I go places, I ask questions, I put myself at risk. That's my job. It's not yours."

"She was my daughter…"

"And she was my sister." Your voice cracks despite your best effort. "But I'm the one who can still climb mountains. I'm the one who has nothing to lose. You and Mum have each other. You need to stay together. Stay safe."

Your father opens his mouth to argue, then closes it. His shoulders sag slightly.

"If something happens to you up there…" he whispers.

"Nothing's going to happen to me." You touch his arm. "I'll be back for the Christmas dinner."

You look at him, this old man who's been carrying Sarah's ghost all these years. Who's filled folders with observations and maps and desperate theories. Who's never stopped searching.

"I'm going," you say. "And you're staying. Both of you. That's final."

For a long moment, your father just stares at you. Then, slowly, he nods.

"When?"

"Now. While Mum's still asleep. No point lying for me. She'll know where I am."

Pain flickers across his face, but he doesn't argue.

"Jenny." He catches your wrist. "Please…"

"I'll be careful."

Twenty minutes later, you're in your car. The sun is just beginning to rise, painting the snow pink and gold.

Your father watches from the window as you pull away. You can see him in the rearview mirror, standing there, getting smaller, until you turn the corner and he's gone.

Evergreen Lane. Main Street. The edge of town.

The mountain road rises ahead of you, winding up into the Frost Mountains. The ski resort is maybe thirty minutes away if the road is clear. Maybe longer if it's not.

You drive in silence, watching the trees close in on either side.

You're alone. Completely alone.

For the first time since you arrived in Pine Hollow, that doesn't feel like freedom.

It feels like a mistake.

Then you see them. Headlights in your rearview mirror. Too close. Too fast.

A cruiser. Dark coloured. Moving up behind you quickly.

Your hands tighten on the wheel.

The vehicle gets closer. Closer. Right on your bumper now.

Red and blue lights flash across your dashboard.

Sheriff's Department.

Your stomach drops.

What do you do?

Pull over. Turn to page 145
Keep driving. Turn to page 138

GET IN THE TRUCK

You climb into the passenger seat.

The door closes with a heavy thunk. The interior smells of coffee and leather and something else, something metallic that makes your stomach turn. The radio crackles with static.

Larkin gets behind the wheel, puts the truck in drive. "Where did you see them go?"

"I didn't. I just saw the bell after you..." You stop yourself.

"After I what?" He glances at you as he pulls away from your parents' house. In the rearview mirror, you can see them still standing in the doorway, growing smaller.

"Nothing."

The truck moves slowly down the street, headlights cutting through the falling snow. Larkin scans the yards, the spaces between houses, the tree line at the end of the block.

"Footprints would show in this snow," he says conversationally. "Unless they knew to walk on already-packed surfaces. Driveways. Sidewalks. Someone smart enough to avoid leaving tracks."

You don't respond. Your hand finds your phone in your pocket. Battery at 84%.

"You know," Larkin continues, "your father tried this once. Years back. Sat up all night watching. Thought he could catch whoever was leaving the bells." He shakes his head. "Never works. The bells always come anyway."

"How do you know that?"

"Small town. People talk." He turns left at the intersection, away from the main street, toward the older part of Pine Hollow where the houses thin out and the woods press closer. "Your dad's been obsessed with this for decades. Can't be healthy, carrying that kind of weight."

The road narrows. Fewer streetlights. More shadows.

"Where are we going?"

"Following the logical path. Whoever left that bell had to come from somewhere." He gestures ahead, where the road curves toward the tree line. "Probably parked up here, walked in, walked out. That's how I'd do it."

That's how I'd do it.

Your hand tightens on your phone.

The truck slows as you reach the end of the residential area. Here, the pavement gives way to gravel, and beyond that, the forest. No cars. No tracks. Nothing but snow and trees and darkness.

Larkin puts the truck in park but leaves the engine running. He turns to face you, one arm draped over the steering wheel.

"See anything?" he asks.

"No."

"Me neither." He's quiet for a moment. Then: "You should have stayed in Boston, Jenny."

The words land like ice in your chest.

"What?"

"Your parents. They've made their peace with what happened. Forty years is a long time to carry grief, but they've learned to live with it. And then you show up, stirring everything back up, asking questions nobody wants to answer." His voice is calm, almost gentle. "Some things are better left alone."

"My sister…"

"Your sister is gone." He says it flatly. "She's been gone since 1986. And coming back here, poking around, doing your stakeouts… it doesn't change that. It just makes things harder for everyone."

You reach for the door handle. It doesn't open.

Larkin watches you try it once, twice. "Child locks," he explains. "Safety feature. Can't have people falling out while we're moving."

"We're not moving."

"Not yet."

Your heart hammers against your ribs. The phone in your hand - you could call someone. But who? Your parents are back at the house. Katie and Siobhan? You don't trust them. 911 would just route back to the sheriff's department.

To him.

"Here's what's going to happen," Larkin says, still in that calm, reasonable tone. "You're going to get on a plane tomorrow. Go back to Boston. Write your little article about small-town legends and Christmas mysteries, make it sound spooky for your readers. But you leave out the names. You leave out the families. And most importantly…" He leans closer. "You leave out what you think you know."

"And if I don't?"

His smile doesn't reach his eyes. "Then I can't guarantee your safety. Pine Hollow can be dangerous this time of year. All that snow and ice. People slip. Cars go off roads. Accidents happen."

The heater blows warm air, but you've never felt colder.

"Let me out."

"Sure." But he doesn't move to unlock the doors. "Just as soon as we have an understanding."

What do you do?

Agree to his terms. Turn to page 126
Refuse. Turn to page 99

The three of you sit in the darkened living room, voices low, the bell on the porch like an accusation you can't ignore.

"If the sheriff is part of this," you say, "then we can't go to the police. And if Katie and Siobhan warned me off, if the whole town has been looking away for decades, then we're on our own."

Your father pulls out his folder, spreads the pages across the coffee table. The map. The timeline. The four houses circled in red.

"The families who get bells," you say, studying the map. "Henderson, Wilson, us... and presumably tonight add the Crawfords. These are the families who lost children."

You're thinking out loud, stating the obvious. This is what you do when you're trying to put the pieces together, trying to build the story.

"The victims," your mother confirms quietly.

"But why keep leaving them?" You look at the bell on the porch, visible through the window. "Year after year. What's the point?"

Your father's voice is hollow. "I think it's to remind us. To let us know that he's still out there." He traces the timeline with one finger. "After Sarah, no other child was taken until nine years later. Daniel Peak, in 1995. Then after him, sixteen years passed. Nothing until Emily in 2009. And then nothing until Amy last year. Another fifteen-year gap."

The numbers sit heavy in the air. Nine years. Sixteen years. Fifteen years. The first five children were taken in a ten-year period. You can't help but wonder what changed.

"But all that time," your father continues, "the bells kept coming. To us. To the Wilsons. To the Hendersons. Every single Christmas Eve, without fail. To remind us..." His voice cracks. "To remind everyone. He's always watching. He's always there. He could come back whenever he chooses."

Your mother's hand trembles against her coffee cup. "Forty years of wondering if this will be the year. If he'll take another child. If he'll take someone we know. Someone we love."

The terror of it settles over you. Not just the loss, but the ongoing psychological torture. The annual reminder that the person who destroyed your family is still out there. Still in control. Still choosing when to strike.

And then you ask the question. The one that cuts through everything else. The question every good journalist learns to ask.

"Why?"

Your parents look at you.

"Why would he do this?" You lean forward. "Not just take the children, but why the bells? Why the yearly reminders? Why the gaps between victims? Serial killers usually escalate. They take victims more frequently over time, not less. The gaps get shorter, not longer. But this person can stop for nine years, sixteen years, fifteen years... and then start again. That's not loss of control. That's the opposite."

Your father stares at the timeline. "What does it mean?"

"It means this isn't about compulsion. It's not about some uncontrollable urge." You pull the folder closer, studying the dates, the names, the pattern your father has been trying to decode for forty years. "This is deliberate. Planned. Someone who can wait years between victims, who can maintain this level of control, who keeps leaving these reminders..."

You look up at them both.

"This person thinks they're right. They think what they're doing is justified. The bells aren't just terror, they're a message. 'I'm still here. I'm still watching. And I'll be back when I decide another child deserves it.'"

The silence stretches.

"Deserves it," your mother repeats, her voice barely a whisper.

Your father's face has gone grey. "Naughty children," he says quietly. "That's what the urban legend says. The King of Christmas takes naughty children."

"What if it's not a legend?" you say. "What if this person thinks they are justified?" You think about Sarah, about the bracelet, about your lie. About small towns and gossip and how everyone always knows everyone else's business.

"That's insane," your mother breathes.

"It's been going on nearly fifty years," you say, scanning the notes spread across the coffee table. "This isn't random. Whoever's behind it believes they're doing something righteous, like they've built an entire moral code to justify it." You tap the gaps in the timeline, the stretches of silence. "These pauses... maybe those were the years when no one fit his idea of 'bad enough.' Or maybe something shook his faith in the mission. Something that made him stop, made him question whether he was still the hero of his own story."

Your father's hands still on the papers. "After Sarah... nine years of nothing."

You meet his eyes. Something passes between you in that moment, something unspoken but understood. Sarah's case was different somehow. Something about what happened to her made the King of Christmas pause.

"So, what do we do?" your mother asks. "How do we find someone who's been doing this for so long?" She leans in closer and brings her voice to a whisper, even though it's only the three of you in the room. "Someone who might have the sheriff protecting him?"

The word *might* carries the weight of everything that just happened. The perfectly timed visit. The sheriff interrupting their stake out. The bell appearing while they were all distracted. The countless years of police inaction suddenly feel less like incompetence and more like design.

"Do you really think…" you start to say, as the idea swims in your mind.

Your father's voice is rough. "If the sheriff… if the department has been…" He can't finish. Can't say it out loud. That the people who were supposed to protect them, supposed to find Sarah, might have been protecting her killer instead.

You look at the bell on the porch. At the timeline. At years of bells and terror and silence.

You know where to start. There's only one place an investigator ever starts.

"We go back to the beginning," you say. "To the first victim. Rachel Van Vleet, 1976. We need to understand why it started. What triggered it. Who had access, who had motive…" You stop, the pieces clicking together. "Her family owned the ski resort. They left town right after she disappeared."

"They couldn't stay," your mother says softly. "Not after losing their daughter like that. That's what everyone says."

"That's what everyone says," you repeat. "But maybe there's something there. Something that got overlooked, or something that would make more sense now that we understand the pattern. The resort's been abandoned since 1977. Almost fifty years. If there are any clues left about what happened to Rachel, about why it started…" You trail off, knowing how thin this sounds. An abandoned building, decades of decay and weather. But it's something. "It's where this began. It has to tell us something."

Your father moves to the window, looks out at the dark street. "The ski resort," he says quietly. "After all these years."

The three of you stand in silence for a moment. Outside, snow continues to fall, covering the street, the houses, the bell on your porch.

"When?" your father asks, turning to face you both.

Your mother's voice is barely a whisper. "We could go now. Tonight. Before anyone knows we're suspicious."

"It's nearly midnight," your father says. "Christmas Eve. The roads…"

"Will be empty," you finish. "No one around to see us. But it'll be pitch dark up there. We'd need flashlights, and we wouldn't be able to see much."

"Tomorrow then," your mother says. "Christmas Day. Everyone will be home with their families. The roads will still be quiet, but we'll have daylight."

They both look at you.

You're exhausted. Your body aches, your eyes burn. Every professional instinct says to wait, to rest, to go prepared in daylight when you can actually see what you're searching for.

But the bell sits on the porch. The sheriff knows you're asking questions. And somewhere out there, someone who's been getting away with this without hindrance might be deciding right now what to do about the Matthews family getting too close to the truth.

What do you do?

Go now. Tonight. Before anyone can react. Turn to page 127
Wait until tomorrow. Rested and in daylight. Turn to page 123

STAY WITH YOUR PARENTS

"No," you whisper.

Your father looks at you. "Jenny?"

"Don't chase him. Don't..." You're staring at the bell, at the perfect timing, at the truck that blocked your view. "Something's wrong."

Your mother understands first. Her hand finds yours, grips tight. "You think he..."

"I think he showed up at exactly the right time. I think his truck was positioned exactly right. I think he kept us all distracted for exactly long enough." Your voice is steady despite the way your hands shake. "I think that wasn't a coincidence."

Your father closes the door, locks it with shaking hands. The three of you stand in the entryway, the truth settling over you like snow.

"Forty years," your father says finally. "Forty years I've been trying to catch whoever does this. And the sheriff..." He can't finish.

"Thirty-nine," your mother corrects automatically, and the precision of it, the way she's counted every single year, breaks something in your chest.

You move to the window, watching the sheriff's taillights disappear. "We need to figure this out. If he's involved, if this is bigger than one person..." You think about Katie and Siobhan's fear, their warnings. About the way the whole town seems to look away. "We need a plan."

Your father joins you at the window. Outside, the bell sits on the porch, silver and mocking.

"What kind of plan?" he asks.

Make a plan with your parents. Turn to page 114

GRAB THE WHEEL

Your hand closes on the wheel. You yank it hard to the right, trying to pull the truck back from the edge, back onto the road, back to safety.

"Jenny, no!" your father shouts.

But you're already moving. Already pulling. Already trying to save them.

Your father fights you reflexively. His hands jerk the opposite direction, trying to maintain his line.

For one terrible second, you're both pulling. Both steering. Both in control and neither in control.

The truck lurches violently. The tyres lose all traction.

You're not sliding anymore.

You're spinning.

The world rotates. Headlights sweep across trees, snow, darkness, more trees. Your mother is screaming. Your father is swearing. You're still gripping the wheel, still pulling, and then the truck completes its spin and you're facing backwards down the mountain and the sheriff's headlights are coming straight at you and...

The tree hits the driver's side.

The sound is unimaginable. Metal shrieking, glass exploding, your father's body jerking sideways against his seatbelt. The impact throws you against your door, your head cracking against the window. The airbags deploy with gunshot cracks, white fabric slamming into your face, into your chest, stealing your breath.

And then stillness.

Terrible, ringing stillness.

You're alive. You can feel your heart hammering. Can taste blood in your mouth. The airbag is deflating slowly, plastic smell choking you.

"Dad?" you croak.

He doesn't answer.

You turn your head, though it hurts, though your neck screams in protest.

Your father is slumped in his seat. The driver's side door is caved in, crushed inward by the tree. His head is tilted at an angle that isn't right. Blood runs from his temple, dark and steady.

"Dad?" you say again.

Nothing.

"Bill!" Your mother's voice from the back, thin and broken. "Bill, wake up! Wake up!"

But he's not waking up.

You reach for him with shaking hands. Try to find a pulse. Your fingers are numb, clumsy. You can't tell if you're feeling his heartbeat or your own.

"Mum," you manage. "Mum, we need..."

You need to call for help. You need to get out of the truck. You need to do something.

But when you try to move, your body doesn't respond right. Everything feels distant. Disconnected. There's a strange warmth spreading through your chest, and you look down and see red blooming across your coat.

Oh.

"Jenny?" your mother says. "Jenny, baby, stay with me. Stay with..."

Her voice is fading. Getting smaller. Like she's moving away from you. But she's not moving. You're the one who's leaving.

The last thing you see is snow falling through the shattered windshield, peaceful and silent, covering everything in white.

THE END

You died in a car crash on the mountain road to the Pine Hollow Ski Resort, Christmas Eve, 2025. Your father died on impact when the truck struck the tree. You died two minutes later from internal injuries. Your mother died three minutes after that, trapped in the wreckage.

Sheriff Larkin called it in at 12:14am. Reported finding the wreckage after seeing taillights leave the road. An accident. A tragedy. Lost control on the icy curves.

The King of Christmas continued his work.

WAIT UNTIL CHRISTMAS DAY

"Tomorrow," you say. "Christmas Day. While the town's distracted, while everyone's pretending everything is normal. We go up there, and we look. Really look. Not for answers necessarily, but for... anything. Anything that helps us understand."

Your father nods slowly. Your mother's hand finds his.

"Together," she says.

"Together," you echo.

Outside, the bell sits on the porch, silver and accusatory. But for the first time in thirty-nine years, your family has something they haven't had before.

Not a solution. Not even a solid lead.

But a direction. A place to start.

And sometimes, that's enough.

Your mother stands, collecting the tea mugs. "You should try to get some rest. Both of you. We'll need to leave early, before the town wakes up."

"Thanks," you say. "I guess I'm sleeping in my old room?" Though you know sleep won't come easily.

Your mother's face softens with something complicated: grief, maybe, or hope, or just the weight of having her daughter home after so many years away. "I changed the sheets this afternoon. Just in case."

Your father gathers his folder, handling the pages with careful reverence.

"Dad," you say as he turns toward the hallway. "Thank you. For never giving up. For keeping all of this."

His eyes glisten. He nods once, sharp, and disappears down the hall.

You climb the stairs, each step creaking under your weight. The hallway at the top is exactly as you remember: the same faded wallpaper, the same family photos in their frames. You pause at Sarah's door, but you can't bring yourself to open it. Not tonight.

Your old room waits at the end of the hall.

You push open the door. It's smaller than you remember, the way childhood spaces always are. Your mother has kept it neat: the bed made with fresh sheets, your old desk cleared of clutter. But traces of who you were remain: a poster on the wall, a shelf of books, the window that overlooks the backyard and the tree line beyond.

You sit on the bed, pull off your boots. The mattress dips under your weight, groaning like it resents the intrusion after so many years.

You lie back, stare at the ceiling. The same water stain in the corner, shaped vaguely like a map of some country you still can't name. How many nights did you lie here as a child, staring at that stain, unable to sleep after Sarah vanished?

Your mind won't stop. The pattern. The gaps. The sheriff's perfectly timed visit. Katie and Siobhan's fear. The bell on the porch.

Rachel Van Vleet. Eleven years old. 1976. The first.

Eventually, you fall asleep, thinking that same question: *Why?*

Sleep comes in fits, shallow and restless. You dream of snow and bells and red mittens disappearing into white. You dream of Sarah's face, always nine years old, always on the edge of vanishing.

When you wake, grey light filters through the curtains. Your phone says 6:23am.

Christmas morning.

You sit up, every muscle stiff and protesting, and nearly jump when you see the figure sitting at the edge of your bed.

"Dad." Your heart hammers. "You scared me."

"Sorry." His voice is low, barely above a whisper. He's already dressed in his heavy winter coat, boots on, folder in his hands. "Your mother's still asleep. I wanted to talk to you before…"

He stops. Starts again.

"She's eighty years old, Jenny. The resort is up the mountain, the building's probably falling apart, we don't know what we'll find up there." His hands tighten on the folder. "It could be dangerous. How about the two of us sneak out now, before she wakes. We'll leave a note, of course. We'll be back before Christmas lunch, and she'll be safe and warm here."

You stare at him. "You're eighty-two, Dad."

He gives you the look. The same one he used to give you when you were a teenager and tried to use logic against him. The look that says I know exactly what you're saying, and I'm going anyway.

"I've been waiting since Sarah was taken to do something besides sit and watch," he says quietly. "I'm going. The question is whether we bring your mother too, or whether we protect her from whatever we find."

Whatever we find. Not just danger. Not just an abandoned building. But truth. Answers. Things that might be harder to bear than all the years of not knowing. You can't take Mum. You know you can't.

You look at your father, really look at him. The deep lines around his eyes. The way his hands shake slightly, whether from age or cold or anticipation. The grey in his hair that's closer to white now. He's an old man.

But he's also been a prisoner in this house for thirty-nine years, and this is his first real chance at parole.

What do you do?

Agree. Go with just your father. Turn to page 140
Tell Dad you're going alone. Turn to page 92

AGREE TO SHERIFF'S TERMS

"Fine." The word tastes like ash. "I'll go back to Boston. I'll leave it alone."

Larkin studies you for a long moment, weighing the truth of it. Then he nods and clicks something on his door panel. The locks disengage with a soft thunk.

"Smart girl."

You

yank the door open and stumble out into the snow. The cold hits you like a slap, but you've never been more grateful for it. Solid ground. Open air. Distance from him.

"I'll give you a ride back," he offers.

"I'll walk." You're already moving, back toward the lights of town, toward your parents' house. But not to see them, to get into your car and leave.

You don't look back to see if he's following.

Your phone buzzes. Text from your mother: *Where are you? Are you okay?*

You don't answer. You just walk, boots crunching through the snow, breath fogging in the cold. The streetlights blur through tears you didn't realise were falling.

You made it out. You're alive.

But you gave up. You promised to leave, to abandon Sarah, to let the King of Christmas keep his secrets.

The weight of that promise settles over you like a shroud.

THE END

You survived, but at what cost? By agreeing to the sheriff's terms, you chose safety over truth. Sarah remains lost. The bells will continue. And Pine Hollow's dark secret stays buried.

Sometimes survival means compromise. Sometimes it means betrayal.

GO NOW

You make the decision before you can talk yourself out of it.

"Now," you say. "We go now."

Your mother's face goes pale in the lamplight, but she nods. Your father is already standing, that look of grim determination settling over his features. The same look he's worn for forty years every time Christmas Eve comes around.

"All right," he says. "Let's do this."

The next fifteen minutes feel surreal. Your mother moves through the kitchen with practiced efficiency, filling a thermos with coffee, wrapping sandwiches in foil that no one will eat. She pulls winter coats from the hall closet, your father's heavy parka, her own thick wool coat with the toggle buttons. She hands you a knitted hat.

"It'll be below freezing up there," she says, and her hands are shaking as she adjusts the scarf around your neck. You're fifty years old and she's tucking you in like you're eleven again.

Your father is in the garage. You hear him rummaging, the clatter of tools. He emerges with two heavy-duty flashlights, checking the batteries, clicking them on and off.

"These are good," he says. "Military grade. I got them after..." He doesn't finish. After Sarah. After he started his research. After he spent years preparing for something like this and never actually going.

You have your phone, but the battery is at fading. You should charge it. But that would mean delay, and delay means time to reconsider, and reconsideration means you'll talk yourselves out of this.

"Ready?" your father asks.

You're not ready. None of you are ready. You're about to drive up a mountain in the middle of the night on Christmas Eve with your parents who are in their eighties, to investigate an abandoned building that's been decaying for nearly fifty years, after watching the sheriff prove himself complicit in a decades-long conspiracy.

This is insane.

"Ready," you say.

Your father's truck is in the driveway. Ancient Ford, bought used in the nineties and maintained with the kind of obsessive care men of his generation give to vehicles. He gets in the driver's seat automatically, a habit so ingrained none of you question it.

You slide into the passenger seat. Your mother climbs in the back, the thermos clutched in her lap like a talisman.

The engine turns over on the second try. The heater sputters to life.

Your father backs out of the driveway. The street is empty, silent, blanketed in fresh snow. The bell sits on the porch where the sheriff left it, catching the light. A promise. A threat.

You don't look back.

"Road's bad," your father mutters.

He's right. The snow is coming down harder now, thick flakes that swirl in the headlights. The ploughs haven't been through in hours. The truck's tyres crunch through several inches of fresh powder.

"Maybe we should wait," your mother says quietly from the back. "Until morning. When we can see."

"We're ready now," your father says, unwavering. He's been ready for decades; maybe he was just waiting for you to come home to do this with him.

You leave Pine Hollow behind. The road begins to climb. The trees press in on both sides, dark and dense. The headlights carve a tunnel through the falling snow, but beyond that circle of light, there's nothing but blackness. The mountains loom invisible above you, felt rather than seen.

The silence between the three of you is heavy until your father finally speaks.

"Did you have chance to read my notes?" he asks you.

"Some of them," you say. "You should have been a journalist," you add with a half-laugh. You can't manage a full one, not here, not now.

He doesn't smile; his face is haggard in the dashboard light, eyes fixed on the road.

"I made some notes about the logging camp," he continues. "It was up where the ski resort is now. Frost Timber Company ran it from the thirties through the late sixties. They clear-cut half the mountain. Built roads, a processing facility, workers' housing. The mill in town was supposed to handle the lumber, but the camp did most of the heavy work on-site."

You don't know why he's telling you this, but it's better than the silence. Your mother is silent in the backseat; she must have heard all this before.

"Why did it close?" you ask.

"Economics. Timber prices dropped, easier to import from Canada. The company went bankrupt in sixty-nine." He navigates a curve, the truck fishtailing slightly before the tyres catch. "Van Vleet family bought the land for almost nothing in seventy. Built the ski resort over the old camp. Used some of the existing structures, paved over others."

"Uh-huh," you reply, not quite sure how to answer.

"Logging camps have infrastructure. Kiln vents, equipment pits, drainage shafts, storage cellars. Some of it would have been twenty, thirty feet down. I put the maps in that folder with everything else."

"Maps?" You shuffle into a more upright position, interested now.

"The logging camp and the ski resort. The Van Vleets wanted to make money, not spend it. Turns out they did neither, but…"

Your mother leans forward between the seats. "Bill, you never said... Is the land dangerous?"

"Three separate inspectors flagged the old logging infrastructure as hazardous. But the Van Vleets had connections. They got the violations waived."

"Jesus," you whisper.

"The resort closed in seventy-seven. Six months after Rachel Van Vleet disappeared. The family just... left. Boarded it up and walked away. Didn't sell. Didn't demolish. Just abandoned it." He glances at you. "Forty-eight years of weather damage, structural decay, and underneath it all, those old logging pits still there. Unstable ground. Rotted wood covering open shafts."

"We'll have to be careful," you say.

"We'll have to be very careful." He takes another curve, slower this time. "The snow will cover everything. You won't be able to see where solid ground ends and a covered pit begins. One wrong step and you drop twenty feet onto concrete or rusted metal."

The truck's heater is blasting, but you feel cold.

"Maybe this is a mistake," your mother says quietly.

"It's too late for that," your father replies.

And that's when you see the headlights behind you.

At first, you think it's nothing. Another vehicle heading up the mountain. But they're moving fast. Too fast for these conditions.

"Dad," you say.

"I see them."

The headlights are getting closer. They're not maintaining distance. They're gaining.

Your father presses the accelerator. The truck speeds up, engine straining.

"Bill, don't..." your mother starts.

"I know what I'm doing."

But the headlights keep coming. Closer. Closer. And then they're right behind you, high-mounted and bright, flooding the truck's cabin with harsh white light.

Through the rear window, you can make out the shape of the vehicle.

A Sheriff's Department truck.

"Oh god," your mother whispers.

"Hold on," your father says.

He accelerates harder. The truck surges forward, fishtailing on the snow. The speedometer climbs. Forty-five. Fifty. Too fast. Way too fast for these conditions.

Behind you, the sheriff matches your speed. His headlights are blinding, turning the world into a whiteout of snow and light.

A curve is coming up. You can see the warning sign, that yellow diamond with the arrow bending sharply left.

Your father isn't slowing down.

"Dad," you say. "Dad, the curve…"

"I know."

But he's not slowing down. His hands are locked on the wheel, his jaw set, and you realise with creeping horror that he's not sure he can slow down. The truck is moving too fast, the road is too slick, and if he hits the brakes now you'll spin out.

The sheriff's headlights fill the world. Blinding. Inescapable.

The curve is here. Now.

Your father tries to take it. The wheel cranks left. The truck starts to turn.

But it's too much speed. Too sharp a curve. Too old a man with reflexes that aren't what they used to be.

The back end starts to slide.

"Bill!" your mother screams.

You watch it happen in fractured, crystalline clarity. The truck is sliding. The curve is sharper than it looked. The edge of the road is coming up fast.

Your hand moves toward the wheel. Instinct. Terror. The need to do something.

You could grab it. Wrench control away from your father. Force the truck back onto the road.

Or you could trust him. Let him handle it. He's driven these roads for forty years. He knows what he's doing.

The edge is right there.

Your hand hovers.

The world holds its breath.

What do you do?

Grab the wheel. **Turn to page 120**

Trust your father. **Turn to page 106**

PROTECT YOUR PARENTS

The words come out before you can stop them. Before you can think about what you're doing.

"Okay."

Larkin straightens. Satisfied. "Smart choice."

"I'll go back. I'll call my boss. I'll..." You swallow. Can't quite say it. "I'll stay."

"Good." He steps back from your car. "Turn around. I'll follow you back to Evergreen Lane. Make sure you get there safe."

You execute a careful three-point turn on the narrow road. The sheriff's cruiser pulls in behind you. Lights still flashing. Escorting you back to your prison.

The drive down feels longer than the drive up. Every turn. Every mile. Taking you further from the truth. Further from justice. Further from Sarah.

Your parents' house appears ahead. Warm lights in the windows. Your father probably watching. Waiting for you to come back.

You park. The sheriff pulls up behind you. Waits.

You walk to the door. Your father opens it before you can knock.

"Jenny?" He looks past you at the sheriff's truck. "What happened? Are you..."

"I'm fine." Your voice sounds hollow. "I'm staying, Dad. I'm moving back home."

The confusion on his face breaks your heart.

"Moving back? But your job, your apartment..."

"I'll figure it out." You step inside. The sheriff's truck is still there. Still watching. "Can we talk about this later? I need to make some calls."

You call your editor. Tell him you need extended leave. Family emergency. Your parents need you. You'll be working remotely from Pine Hollow for the foreseeable future.

He's not happy. But he agrees. Three months. Then you need to be back, or they'll have to fill your position.

Three months becomes six.

Six becomes twelve.

Your apartment in Boston goes to someone else. Your things arrive in boxes. You unpack them in your old bedroom. The one that overlooks the mountains.

Your parents are grateful. Confused, but grateful. They don't understand why you gave up your life in Boston. You tell them you needed a change. Needed to be closer to family.

They don't ask too many questions. They're old. They're tired. They're just happy you're home.

You take a job at the Pine Hollow library. Part-time. Quiet. No one bothers you there.

Sheriff Larkin stops by sometimes. Just checking in. Making sure you're settling in okay. Making sure you understand.

You understand perfectly.

Katie Wilson nods to you at the grocery store. Doesn't quite meet your eyes. You're one of them now. Part of the system. Complicit in the silence.

Christmas Eve comes.

You watch from your bedroom window as a figure in dark clothes moves through the neighbourhood. Leaving bells. One at the Henderson house. One at the Wilson house. One at your parents' house: still, always, after all these years.

The figure doesn't see you watching. Or maybe they do. Maybe they know you're there and they know you won't do anything. Can't do anything.

You are a prisoner in Pine Hollow. Not behind bars. Behind threats. Behind the knowledge that one phone call, one article, one attempt to expose the truth, and your parents die.

So you stay quiet.

You shelve books. You make dinner. You help your father with his endless research that goes nowhere. You hold your mother's hand when she cries on Christmas Eve. You watch the bells accumulate in the hallway chest.

Thirty-nine becomes forty. Forty becomes forty-one.

You grow older. Your parents grow older.

The King of Christmas continues his work.

And you do nothing.

Every night, you lie in your childhood bed and stare at the ceiling and think about Sarah. About the story you never wrote. About the justice you never served.

About the person you used to be before you made the choice to protect your parents by sacrificing yourself.

Some prisons have bars. Some have guards. Some have nothing but the knowledge that leaving means someone you love will die.

You are sixty-one years old when your father passes. Stroke. Quick. Peaceful, they say.

You are sixty-eight when your mother follows him. Heart failure. She'd been declining since your father died.

You bury them next to Sarah's empty grave. Two Matthews family members in Pine Hollow soil, one forever missing.

You are sixty-eight years old, and your parents are gone and the threat that kept you silent is gone with them.

But it's been seventeen years. Seventeen years of silence. Of complicity. Of being part of the system instead of fighting it.

And you... you are the woman who stayed silent. Who could have spoken and didn't. Who chose survival over truth.

You think about writing the story. Finally writing it. Exposing everything.

But your hands don't move to the keyboard. Your mouth doesn't form the words.

Seventeen years of silence is a hard habit to break.

The bells keep coming on Christmas Eve. Different houses now. New families. New victims. Even now.

Even now.

And you do nothing.

You do nothing until you die.

THE END

You lived the rest of your life in Pine Hollow, trapped by the sheriff's threats and your own choice to prioritise your parents' safety over truth and justice.

The story was never written. The King of Christmas was never exposed. The system continued.

You died at seventy-three, still living in the house on Evergreen Lane. They found you in your childhood bedroom, looking out at the mountains.

Some people say that's not a bad way to go. Peaceful. At home. They're wrong.

YES

"Wait." Your hand finds the door handle but doesn't open it. "Maybe we should…"

"It's too late for that."

Your father's voice is gentle but firm. He's already out of the truck, already standing in the snow, flashlight in hand. Looking up at the building with an expression you've never seen before, something between fear and determination and desperate hope.

"I've waited too long for this moment," he says. "I'm not turning back now. But if you want to stay in the truck, stay warm, I understand. I can do this alone."

You look at him. Eighty-two years old, standing in the snow on Christmas morning, about to walk into a building that's been abandoned since 1977. About to face whatever truth has been hiding here for half a century.

Alone.

"No," you say, and climb out. "We're doing this together."

He nods, and you see relief in his eyes.

The two of you approach the main entrance. The front doors hang askew, one barely attached to its hinges. Snow has drifted into the entrance, creating a small slope.

Your father pushes the door. It groans, scrapes against the floor, but opens wider.

You step inside. Turn to page 155

KEEP DRIVING

You press harder on the accelerator.

This feels so wrong, but also, so right. You don't trust Larkin. You can't. You're up a mountain, alone in the dark. Snow is falling thick and fast, but you need to get away.

The cruiser is right behind you. Relentless.

He pulls alongside you. You see him gesture: PULL OVER.

You don't.

He swerves toward you.

Your tires hit the shoulder. Gravel spits. You overcorrect, swerve back onto the road.

He does it again. Harder this time.

You're forced right. Off the road completely.

The car is sliding now.

You have to slow to wind between the pines, but Larkin is picking his way through too. Even with your beams on full, it's dark out here.

How did this happen?

You were meant to be gathering information.

Some time ago, you were meant to be writing a story.

Now you're on the run from the sheriff, bumping over the forest floor in a hire car that you'll never get the deposit back on.

Shit, shit, fucking shit.

His red and blues are still flashing, but there's no siren now. The light shines around you, bathing the forest in ice then fire, ice then fire. Over and over as you look for some kind of path to follow.

This doesn't seem like such a good idea anymore.

But then you check your mirror again, and he's stopped.

Did he hit a tree? An animal? You didn't hear anything, you...

And then you realise why, in the worst possible way.

He stopped because he knows this area, and you don't.

He stopped because he knows what is ahead.

Now you know too. The hood tips; the world drops. The road is gone, replaced by air and the black mouth of a ravine. You're falling, weightless, headlights sliding off empty space toward the rock floor below.

Headlights spin; rock rushes up. There's a white-hot crack of impact, and then nothing.

THE END

You died in a ravine off Mountain Road outside Pine Hollow, Christmas Eve, 2025.

The wreckage wasn't discovered until spring thaw, when hikers spotted metal glinting through the melt. By then, it was too late to prove what really happened.

The King of Christmas continued his work.

You take a breath, let it out slowly. Look at your father, at the determination in his eyes, the decades of helplessness finally finding an outlet.

"Okay," you say quietly. "We go together. Just us."

Relief floods his face, followed immediately by resolve. He nods once, sharp. "Get dressed. Quietly. I'll finish the note."

You move as silently as you can, pulling on layers: thermal shirt, heavy sweater, jeans, thick socks. Your winter coat. Gloves. Hat. Every sound feels amplified in the early morning quiet. The creak of a floorboard. The rustle of fabric.

You grab your phone; it's 100% charged. You take your flashlight. Slip them into your pockets.

Downstairs, your father has left a note on the kitchen table, weighted down by the saltshaker:

Gone up to the old resort to look around. Back before lunch. Don't worry. We're being careful.

Love,

Bill and Jenny

Don't worry. As if that's possible.

Your father hands you a thermos of coffee he's already poured, still hot from last night's pot reheated. His folder is tucked securely under his arm. He's thought of everything.

"Ready?" he whispers.

You nod.

The two of you slip out the front door into the grey pre-dawn cold. The street is silent, blanketed in fresh snow. Every house dark. Christmas morning, and Pine Hollow sleeps, or pretends to.

Your father's truck is in the driveway. You climb in, and he starts the engine. It rumbles to life, sounding too loud in the morning quiet. You both hold your breath, watching the house.

No lights come on. No curtains move.

140

He backs out slowly, headlights off until you're at the end of the street. Then he flicks them on and turns toward the mountain road.

Neither of you speaks for the first few minutes. The weight of what you're doing - sneaking away from your mother on Christmas morning to investigate an abandoned building where the first child disappeared - sits heavy between you.

The town slides past, dark and silent. The church. The closed shops. Katie's Inn. All of it sleeping under snow.

The road begins to climb.

"Thank you," your father says finally, voice rough. "For coming back. For believing there's something worth finding."

Your throat tightens. "Of course, Dad."

"Your mother and I... we never blamed you for leaving. For staying away. You had to make a life."

"I should have come back sooner."

"You're here now." He glances at you, and in the dashboard light you can see the emotion in his eyes. "That's what matters. You're here, and we're finally doing something. After all these years."

The truck climbs higher. Trees press closer on both sides, heavy with snow. The road narrows, curves. Your father drives carefully, both hands on the wheel, leaning forward slightly to peer through the windshield.

The morning is still grey, that strange pre-dawn light that's neither dark nor day. Snow continues to fall, light and steady.

"I used to think about doing this," your father says quietly. "Going up there. Looking around. But I never had the courage. And after a while, I convinced myself there wouldn't be anything to find anyway. That I was chasing ghosts."

"You kept documenting, though. All those years."

"Because I couldn't do nothing. Even if nobody looked at it, even if it never helped. I had to do something." His hands tighten on the wheel. "But this. Actually going there. Actually looking. That's different."

"We might not find anything," you say. You need to say it, need to manage expectations. "It's been almost fifty years. The building's probably just... empty. Decayed. Nothing left."

"Maybe." He's quiet for a moment. "But maybe not. And we'll never know if we don't look."

The trees thin slightly, and through them you catch glimpses of the mountain rising ahead, white against grey sky.

And then, as you round a curve, it appears.

The Pine Hollow Ski Resort.

Your father slows the truck to a crawl, both of you staring.

It's larger than you expected. A sprawling structure of wood and stone that once must have been impressive but now stands hollow and abandoned. The main lodge building is three stories, with wings extending from the central structure. The windows are dark, many broken or boarded. The roof sags in places. Snow has drifted against the walls, nearly covering the first-floor windows on the north side.

The parking lot, if you can call it that, is just a flat expanse of snow. No tracks. No signs anyone has been here in years.

Your father pulls in slowly, stops near what might have once been the main entrance. Kills the engine. The silence is profound.

"Well," he says. "Here we are."

You both sit for a moment, staring up at the building. In the grey morning light, it looks less like a resort and more like a corpse, something that died decades ago and has been slowly rotting ever since.

"Last chance to turn back," you say quietly.

Your father looks at you. "Do you want to?"

Yes. Turn to page 137
No. Turn to page 105

EXPLORE THE SERVICE CORRIDOR

"Let's be thorough," you say. "Check the service areas first."

Your father nods, and you both move toward the darker corridor. Your flashlight beams sweep ahead, catching on institutional green walls, peeling paint, exposed pipes along the ceiling.

The corridor is narrow, claustrophobic. Doors line both sides, most closed, a few hanging open. You check the first one: a storage closet. Metal shelving, rusted and empty except for mouse droppings and the brittle remains of cleaning supplies.

The next door: another storage room. Same story. Shelving, decay, nothing useful.

Your father tries a door on the opposite side. It opens to reveal a larger space, maybe a maintenance room once. More shelving, some old tools so rusted they're unidentifiable. The concrete floor is cracked, water damage evident.

"Nothing here," he says.

You continue down the corridor, checking each room methodically. Supply closets. A small bathroom with fixtures long since frozen and cracked. A room that might have been an office, but empty now except for a metal desk frame and some water-stained papers too degraded to read.

At the end of the corridor, a door marked *Service Entrance*. You try it: locked from the inside, or maybe rusted shut. Either way, it doesn't budge.

"Dead end," your father says. "Just storage and staff areas. Nothing personal. Nothing that would tell us about Rachel."

You turn back, retracing your steps through the corridor to the lobby. Your flashlight catches on the Private door again, waiting behind the reception desk.

"That's where we need to look," you say.

Your father nods.

Continue to Private door Turn to page 158

TAKE THE RIGHT DOOR

You move toward the door on the right. Rachel's room. That's why you came here, after all.

Your hand touches the doorknob, and you pause.

"Wait," you say.

Your father looks at you.

"We should be systematic. Document everything properly." You gesture to the left door. "Master bedroom first, then Rachel's room. If we're doing this, we do it right."

Your father nods slowly. Professional. Methodical. The way you've built your career.

"You're right. Left to right."

You take the left door. Turn to page 160

PULL OVER

You ease your foot off the accelerator. Signal. Pull to the side of the mountain road.

The sheriff's cruiser stops behind you, lights still flashing. You watch in the rearview mirror as he climbs out. Slow. Deliberate. Taking his time.

He approaches your driver's side window. You roll it down.

"Happy Christmas to you, Miss Matthews." Sheriff Larkin leans down, one hand resting on your roof. His face is pleasant. Friendly, even. Like he's just making a routine stop. "Heading up the mountain pretty late."

"Just going for a drive," you say. Your voice is steadier than you feel.

"Uh-huh." He glances at the road ahead. At the direction you were heading. Toward the resort. "Funny thing. I've been following you since you left your parents' house."

Your blood runs cold.

"I hoped you were just going back to your room at the Inn." Larkin's smile doesn't reach his eyes. "But here you are. You're a smart woman, Miss Matthews. Too smart for your own good, maybe."

"I don't know what you..."

"The ski resort." He says it flat. Final. "You're going up to the old lodge place. Poking around. Asking questions. Investigating."

You say nothing.

"Here's the thing about this town," Larkin continues. His voice is conversational. Almost kind. "We look out for each other here. We protect our own. You comer-inners never understood that. Your father didn't. All that digging, researching, making noise. We tolerated it because he'd already lost everything. What more could we take?"

He leans closer. You can smell coffee on his breath.

145

"But you, Jenny. You still have something to lose."

"Is that a threat?"

"It's a fact." He straightens slightly. "Your parents are back at that house on Evergreen Lane. Eighty-two and eighty years old. Fragile. Vulnerable. It'd be a shame if something happened to them. A fall on those icy porch steps. A gas leak. A home invasion gone wrong. This town can be dangerous for people who don't fit in."

Your hands clench on the steering wheel.

"So, here's what's going to happen," Larkin says. "You're going to turn this car around. Drive back to your parents' house. And you're going to call your boss at that fancy Boston paper and tell them you're extending your vacation. Indefinitely. Looks like you're moving back to Pine Hollow, Miss Matthews. Welcome home."

The words don't make sense at first. You stare at him.

"Wait." Your voice comes out shocked. "You want me to STAY? I thought... I thought you'd want me gone. Out of town. Back to Boston where I can't cause problems."

Larkin's smile is patient. Like he's explaining something to a slow child.

"You know too much now, Jenny. Can't have you running back to Boston with all those questions. All those theories." He taps the roof of your car. "No, we need to contain you. Keep you where we can see you. Where we can make sure you understand how things work here."

"You're insane."

"I'm practical." His voice hardens. "Your parents are old. They're going to need someone looking after them. Someone nearby. You're going to be that someone. You're going to move into that house on Evergreen Lane. You're going to be a good daughter. A quiet daughter. And every single day, you're going to remember that their safety depends on your cooperation."

The horror of it settles over you. Not exile. Prison. A lifetime sentence in Pine Hollow, watching your parents age, knowing that one wrong move, one attempt to expose the truth, and they die.

"Your parents might just need you," Larkin continues. "They're not getting any younger. Be a shame if you weren't around when something happened."

The threat is clear. Perfectly clear.

Your parents are alone at the house. No protection. No defence against whatever the sheriff might do.

What do you do?

Protect your parents. Do what he says. Turn to page 133
Refuse - Stand your ground. Call his bluff. Turn to page 152

"Window," you breathe. "There has to be…"

You rush to the window in Rachel's room, your father right behind you. Your flashlight beam finds old glass, single-pane, painted shut decades ago. Beyond: darkness and a two-story drop to snow-covered ground.

"We could break it," you whisper. "Climb down…"

"I'm eighty-two," your father says flatly. "I'd break my hip. Or my neck."

The footsteps reach the top of the stairs. The apartment door opens.

"Back stairs," you say desperately, pulling your father toward the main room. "Service entrance, there has to be…"

But you already know there isn't. You came through the front entrance. You saw the layout. One way in, one way out.

"I know you're here."

The voice freezes you both. Rough, aged, male. Coming from the living area.

"I can smell you. The disruption. Someone's been through my things."

You're standing in the middle of Rachel's room, exposed, nowhere to hide now, the window useless behind you.

"The ladder's down. The bins are open." A pause. "Careless."

Footsteps. Coming toward Rachel's room.

Toward you.

Your father grabs your arm, pulls you back toward the corner, but it's too late, you're too exposed, there's no time…

The door swings wider.

Ho Ho Ho Turn to page 176

TAKE THE RIGHT DOOR

You and your father cross the small living area to the door on the right. Neither of you speaks. The weight of what you just found in the loft—the bells, the evidence—presses down like the low ceiling above.

Your hand finds the doorknob. Cold metal. You turn it.

The door swings open.

A child's bedroom.

Your flashlight beam sweeps across walls that still show the ghosts of posters: discoloured rectangles where paper once hung, a few tattered corners still clinging to pushpins. One remains mostly intact: a kitten hanging from a branch, "HANG IN THERE" faded to pale brown letters.

A single bed against one wall. The frame is solid, but the bedding has deteriorated to shreds; what might have been a quilt now just rotted scraps. On the pillow, arranged carefully: stuffed animals. A bear, a rabbit, something that might have been a dog. The fabric is ragged, eaten by time and moths, but they're positioned deliberately. Facing outward.

"Jesus," your father breathes.

This was Rachel's room. And it's been… preserved.

A bookshelf stands against one wall. Your beam picks out spines: faded, colours shifted, but titles still legible. *Anne of Green Gables. A Wrinkle in Time. Charlotte's Web. The Secret Garden.* Books that an eleven-year-old girl loved in 1976.

Your throat closes. *Anne of Green Gables.* Sarah's favourite.

But it's the dresser that stops you both.

While everything else in the room shows decades of decay, the dresser top is different. Dust-free.

A gallery of framed photographs, arranged with deliberate care. Your beam illuminates them one by one:

Rachel as a baby. Rachel maybe five, gap-toothed smile. Rachel in a school photo, dark hair neatly combed. Rachel in a ski parka, grinning in front of this very building.

And in the centre, larger than the others: Rachel at what looks like ten or eleven. Dark eyes bright, hair pulled back, that same stubborn chin you see in every photo. This one has been dusted recently; you can see the cloth marks in the thin layer of dust around the frame.

Surrounding the central portrait, arranged in a perfect circle: seven fresh pine cones.

Not fifty-year-old pine cones. Fresh. Maybe a few weeks old at most. The scales still tight, the scent of pine faint but present when you lean closer.

Your father makes a sound, half sob, half gasp.

"Someone's been maintaining this," you whisper. "For decades. They've been coming here, dusting these photos, leaving fresh pine cones..."

A shrine. This isn't an abandoned child's room. It's a shrine to a dead girl, tended with obsessive care for forty-nine years.

You pull out your phone with trembling hands. This has to be documented. All of it.

Frame the shot: the dresser top, the gallery of photos, the pine cones in their perfect circle.

Tap. Flash.

The light illuminates dust motes swirling in the air, disturbed by your presence. How long since someone else stood here? Days? Hours?

Closer shot: the central portrait of Rachel, the fresh pine cones clearly visible.

Tap. Flash.

Wide angle: the whole room, showing the contrast between the preserved shrine and the decades of decay everywhere else.

Tap. Flash.

Your father hasn't moved. He's staring at Rachel's face in the photographs, his own face twisted with something between grief and horror.

"This is where it started," he says hoarsely. "This is why. Rachel."

You lower the phone, look at the shrine again. At the careful arrangement. The devotion. The impossible maintenance spanning half a century.

"The Van Vleets left in 1977," you say slowly, working it through. "Six months after Rachel disappeared. Everyone knows that. So, who's been coming here? Who's been doing this?"

Someone who needed to keep her memory alive?

Your father's hands are shaking. "And why?"

The bells in the loft. The shrine in Rachel's room. The modern clothes in the master bedroom. It all connects, but you don't understand how yet. Don't understand why.

"We should go," your father says suddenly. "We have the photos. We have evidence. We need to get back to town, to your mother, to..."

A sound cuts him off.

Distant but unmistakable.

A door. Opening. Below. A door that you know has a sign marked 'PRIVATE'.

Footsteps on the stairs.

Someone's coming.

Hide. Turn to page 175
Arm yourself. Turn to page 163
Look for another way out. Turn to page 148

YOU REFUSE

"No."

The word hangs in the cold air between you.

Larkin's expression doesn't change. "Excuse me?"

"No." Your voice is stronger now. "I'm not giving you anything. I'm not going back. And I'm sure as hell not moving to Pine Hollow."

"Miss Matthews…"

"You're threatening my parents. Threatening me. You're complicit in decades of child murders. You think I'm just going to roll over because you flash a badge and make threats?"

Larkin's face hardens. "I think you're going to be smart about this."

"I am being smart." Your hand moves to your door handle. "I'm driving to the state police. Right now. I'm telling them everything. About the bells. About the disappearances. About you."

You try to open the door but Larkin's hand slams it shut. He leans in close, his face inches from yours.

"You're making a mistake."

"Get away from my car."

"I'm trying to help you, Jenny. Trying to give you a chance to do this the easy way."

"There is no easy way." You meet his eyes. "Not when children are dying."

For a long moment, Larkin just stares at you. Then he straightens. Steps back.

"All right," he says quietly. "Hard way it is."

He walks back to his cruiser. Gets in.

You watch in your rearview mirror, heart pounding. Is he leaving? Did you win?

The cruiser's engine revs. Then it surges forward.

Straight into your rear bumper.

The impact jolts you forward against your seatbelt. Your head snaps back against the headrest.

"What the…"

He hits you again. Harder this time. Your car lurches forward, tires slipping on the icy road.

You throw your car into drive, stomp on the accelerator. The car shoots forward, fishtailing slightly before the tires catch.

Behind you, the cruiser follows. Lights flashing. Engine roaring.

He's not stopping you. He's chasing you.

The mountain road twists ahead. You take the first curve too fast, feel the back end start to slide. Correct. Keep going.

Your phone is in your pocket. Still there. Evidence. You just need to get down the mountain. Get to the state police. Get somewhere safe.

The cruiser is right behind you. He hits your bumper again with a calculated tap that sends you into the guardrail. Metal screams. Your side mirror explodes.

"Jesus!" You pull away from the rail, back to the centre of the road.

Another curve. Sharper this time. You brake, turn…

The cruiser clips your rear quarter panel.

Your car spins. The world rotates. You see trees, sky, road, trees, sky…

The guardrail again. This time you hit it straight on. The rail holds for one terrible second, bending, groaning under the impact.

Then it snaps.

Your car tilts. Tips. Goes over the edge.

You're falling. Tumbling. The car rolls, metal shrieking, glass shattering. Your body slams against the door, the roof, the window. Pain everywhere and nowhere and…

The car hits something solid. Stops.

You're upside down. Hanging from your seatbelt. Blood running into your eyes. Can't tell if it's from your head or your face.

Everything hurts.

You try to move. Can't. Your legs won't respond.

Through the shattered windshield, you see boots approaching. Slow. Deliberate.

Sheriff Larkin crouches down, looks into the wreckage.

"Told you," he says. His voice is almost sad. "Should've done it the easy way."

You try to speak. To curse him. To say something. But your mouth won't form words.

"You're a good investigator, Jenny Matthews. But this is Pine Hollow." He reaches through the broken window. You feel his hand in your pocket. Taking your phone. "Nobody leaves Pine Hollow unless we let them."

He stands. You watch his boots walk away.

You hear the cruiser's door open. Close. Engine start.

He drives away.

Leaves you there. Upside down. Bleeding. Dying.

The cold seeps in fast. Or maybe it's the blood loss. Hard to tell. Everything is getting fuzzy. Distant.

You think about Sarah. About how you tried. How you almost made it.

Almost isn't enough.

Your eyes close.

You don't open them again.

THE END

You died on Mountain Road in a car accident on Christmas morning, 2025.

Sheriff Larkin reported finding your vehicle at the bottom of a ravine hours later. He said you'd been driving recklessly, lost control on the ice, went through the guardrail. Tragic accident.

No one questioned it.

The King of Christmas continued his work.

ENTER THE LODGE

The two of you approach the main entrance. The front doors are closed but intact; weathered wood, windows dark. Snow has drifted against the threshold.

Your father tries the handle. It turns.

Unlocked.

You exchange a glance. After fifty years, the front door is simply unlocked. Not boarded. Not chained. Just... waiting.

Your father pushes. The door resists, scraping against the floor with a groan that echoes through the building. He puts his shoulder into it, and it gives, swinging inward slowly, protesting every inch from decades of disuse.

The darkness inside is immediate. You both flick on your flashlights, two beams cutting through the gloom.

The lobby opens before you.

Even in ruin, you can see what this place once was. Two stories high, dark wood beams supporting the ceiling. A massive chandelier hangs in the centre, wrought iron, bulbs long dead, swaying slightly in a draft you can't feel.

The walls are wood-panelled, stained dark, water damage blooming across them in patterns that look almost deliberate. Furniture fills the space, frames of couches and armchairs, upholstery rotted to tatters, mouse nests spilling from the cushions. A stone fireplace dominates the far wall, its hearth filled with black shapes that might have been logs once.

And mounted on the walls on either side of the fireplace, animal heads. A massive elk with antlers spreading wide, at least twelve points. A black bear. A mountain goat. All watching the empty lobby with glass eyes.

"Jesus," your father breathes.

Your beam finds a metal coat rack standing near the entrance, frame still upright despite the decades. A few scraps of fabric hang from the hooks, all that remains of coats left behind.

You move deeper into the space, boots crunching on debris. Your flashlight sweeps across to find a long reception desk, the wood scarred and water-stained but solid. Behind it, a tarnished metal sign hangs crooked on the wall: Pine Hollow Ski Lodge - Established 1970 - Van Vleet Family, Proprietors."

"They just… left it all," you whisper.

"Or they never got the chance to come back," your father says quietly.

You move around the reception desk. Nothing sits on its surface—no papers, no guest book. But the desk itself is intact, drawers still there. An old cash register squats to one side, ancient mechanical thing of metal and keys.

Your father reaches out, hesitates, then presses the largest key.

The drawer springs open with a DING that cracks through the silence.

You both freeze, hearts hammering, the sound echoing up into the rafters.

Inside the drawer: tarnished coins still sorted in their compartments. A few bills so degraded they're barely recognisable, but the denominations are visible. Maybe twenty dollars total.

"Who abandons cash in the register?" you say.

Your father's jaw tightens. "Someone who left in a hurry. Or someone who couldn't bear to come back."

You look at the lobby again, at the furniture, the mounted heads, the coat rack with its sad fabric scraps. The front door was unlocked. Just stiff from decades of weather and neglect, but not secured. Not boarded. Not chained.

This place should have been foreclosed, seized, sold. Even in small towns, someone always wants the land.

Unless people were afraid to touch it.

156

Your flashlight beam catches on something else: a corridor leading deeper into the building on one side. And behind the desk, a door marked with a small brass plaque: Private.

Your father sees it too. "Maybe that leads to the family quarters. Where they lived."

Where Rachel lived.

You exchange a look with your father. His face is pale in the flashlight glow, but his jaw is set with determination.

"We came here for answers," he says quietly. "Let's find them."

Explore the service corridor. Turn to page 143
Go through the Private door. Turn to page 158

GO THROUGH PRIVATE DOOR

You move around the reception desk to the door marked *Private*. Your father reaches for the handle, hesitates.

"Ready?" he asks.

You nod.

He turns the handle. It clicks. Unlocked, like the front door.

The door opens onto a staircase climbing into darkness. Narrow, steep, the kind of utilitarian stairs that weren't meant for guests. Staff access to the family quarters above.

"Up there," your father says quietly. "That's where they lived. Where Rachel lived."

Your throat tightens. This is it. Not the public face of the resort, but the private space. The family home above the failing business.

You start climbing, your father behind you. The stairs creak under your weight, wood protesting each step. The sound echoes in the narrow stairwell, multiplying, making it seem like more than two people ascending.

At the top, another door. Plain, no lock visible.

You reach for the handle. It turns easily. The door swings open.

Your flashlight beam sweeps into the space.

It's warmer here. Noticeably warmer than the lobby below. The apartment is small, maybe four hundred square feet. A living area opens before you, with a tiny kitchen visible off to one side. Two other doors lead off this main room.

The furniture is simple, practical. A couch facing where a small television must have sat. A table with three chairs. Everything is covered in dust, fabric rotted, surfaces warped, but the shapes remain. You can read the life that happened here in the arrangement of objects.

"It's like they just… left," your father whispers.

Your beam catches on something on the wall near the kitchen. A corkboard. You move closer.

Faded papers are pinned to it. A child's drawing in crayon, the colours bleached to ghosts but the lines still visible: a house, a mountain, stick figures holding hands. The writing across the top is barely legible: Me and Mommy and Daddy.

Rachel drew this.

Your father's breath catches. He's seen it too.

"She was eleven," he says, voice rough. "When she disappeared. She drew this when she was younger."

You both stand there, staring at the simple drawing. A child's vision of her family, her home, her world. Before everything ended.

"There are other rooms," you say finally, gesturing to the two doors leading off the main space.

Your father nods. "I'd guess at master bedroom… and Rachel's room."

Your stomach knots. Rachel's room. Preserved or decayed? Empty or frozen in time?

What do you do?

Take the door on the left. Turn to page 160
Take the door on the right. Turn to page 144

TAKE THE LEFT DOOR

You move to the door on the left. Your hand hovers over the handle for a moment before you turn it.

The door swings open.

Your flashlight beam sweeps the space. A bedroom. The master bedroom. A double bed, stripped bare, mattress water-stained and sagging. A dresser with drawers hanging open at odd angles. A closet door ajar, showing empty hangers. Through an open doorway, you glimpse a small bathroom: toilet, sink, shower stall, all coated in grime.

Your father steps in beside you, his beam joining yours. "The parents' room."

You move to the dresser. Your flashlight illuminates the first drawer: empty, wood swollen from decades of moisture. The second holds rotted fabric, maybe sheets or clothing, impossible to tell now.

The third drawer stops you.

Folded clothes. Men's clothes. Jeans, t-shirts, flannel shirts.

But these aren't from the seventies.

Your torch catches on details: modern denim, darker wash, slim cut. A t-shirt with a logo you recognise, a craft brewery that opened in the 2000s. These aren't old. They're faded, worn, but not decades old.

"Dad." Your voice comes out strangled.

He's already beside you, staring at the clothes. His hand reaches out, then pulls back, as if touching them might make them real.

You pull open the fourth drawer with trembling hands. More clothes. Different sizes, different styles. Some look nearly new. One t-shirt still has the tag attached.

"Someone's been here," your father whispers. "Recently."

"Living here? Do you think...?" You lift one of the shirts carefully. The fabric is stiff, but the organisation is deliberate.

Folded. Placed with care. "These aren't just abandoned. They're... maintained."

Your hands are shaking. The enormity of what you're seeing...what it means...threatens to overwhelm you.

And then your training kicks in.

Document. Evidence. You need proof.

You pull out your phone, check the battery: 100%. Thank God you charged it overnight. You frame the shot: the open drawer, the modern clothes clearly visible, the context of the decrepit bedroom around it.

Tap. The flash illuminates the space.

"What are you doing?" your father asks.

"My job." Your voice is steadier now, purpose grounding you. "We need evidence. Photos. Documentation. Otherwise, it's just our word."

You take another photo, closer this time, showing the brewery logo, the tag still attached to one shirt. Then a wide shot of the whole dresser, the room, establishing context.

Your father watches you work, and something in his expression shifts. Relief, maybe. Or recognition. His daughter, the journalist, doing what she does best.

You lower the phone, check the images. Clear. Undeniable.

Your beam sweeps up again, catches on the square hatch in the ceiling above the bed.

"There's a loft," you say. "Storage space. If someone's been living here, using this place..." You look at your father. "There might be more up there. Supplies. Evidence."

"Or we check Rachel's room first," your father says quietly. His voice is strained. That's why you came here, after all. To understand what happened to Rachel. To find the beginning of all this.

You stand there, torn. The loft could have crucial evidence, more modern supplies, maybe documents, something that explains who's been here and why. But Rachel's room is personal, immediate. The heart of the mystery.

And there's something else: a growing unease. You're standing in someone's active living space. Modern clothes in the drawers. Fresh maintenance throughout the apartment. What if whoever lives here comes back while you're exploring?

You've already decided to be methodical and professional.

You check the loft. **Turn to page 167**

"Find something," you hiss. "Anything we can use."

The footsteps are still on the stairs. Steady. Unhurried. You have seconds.

Your father moves to the main room, you follow. Your flashlight sweeps desperately across the space. The furniture is rotted, useless.

The footsteps reach the top of the stairs.

Your beam catches on something in the corner. A coat rack. Metal. The base is heavy, cast iron, the kind that would hurt if you swung it.

You grab it, nearly drop it; heavier than expected, at least twenty pounds. Your father reaches for a broken chair leg, tests its weight.

The apartment door opens.

"I know you're here."

The voice makes your skin crawl. Rough, aged, conversational.

"I can smell you. The disruption. Someone's been through my things."

You and your father position yourselves in the main room, backs to the wall, weapons ready. Not hidden. Not running. Facing him.

"The ladder's down. The bins are open." A pause. "Careless."

Footsteps cross the living area. Slow. Deliberate.

Coming toward you.

A man appears in the doorway to Rachel's room, then turns, sees you standing there in the main room.

Santa Claus.

The thought hits you before logic does: the red suit, the white trim, the elderly face framed by a hood. Your brain screams *Santa* even as your eyes register the details: not a costume but a ski jacket, red with white fur trim around the hood and cuffs. Not a suit but outdoor gear. Not jolly but weathered, deep lines carved into a face that's seen too many winters.

Eighties, like Dad, maybe older. White hair visible beneath the hood.

Not Santa. But close enough to make your skin crawl.

He sees the coat rack in your hands. The chair leg your father grips. And stops.

For a long moment, he just stands there. Staring at the weapons. At you. At your father.

And you see him clearly for the first time. Old. He's *old*.

You knew it intellectually: the King of Christmas has been taking children since 1976. Of course he'd be elderly now. But standing here with a twenty-pound coat rack raised like a club, facing down the monster you've feared your entire life, you'd expected... something else.

Someone younger. Stronger. More threatening.

Not this.

His hands hang at his sides, empty, trembling slightly. The red jacket sags on shoulders that have thinned with age. When he breathes, you can hear it; not laboured, but audible. Present. Real.

The King of Christmas. The nightmare. The legend that's stolen children for half a century.

He's just a man. An old man who looks like he could be someone's grandfather.

Your father sees it too. The coat rack doesn't lower, but his grip shifts. Uncertainty flickering across his face. You can read his thoughts because they mirror yours: *This is what we came to fight? This is the monster?*

"You're armed." The man says it like an observation, not a threat. Not even surprised. His pale blue eyes, watery with age, move between the coat rack and the chair leg. "Interesting."

"Stay back." Your voice doesn't shake as much as you expected. The weight of the weapon helps. "We don't want trouble. We're leaving."

"With weapons." He tilts his head slightly, the movement careful, like his neck hurts. "That doesn't look like leaving. That looks like you're preparing to hurt an old man."

Not a monster. Not a legend. Just an old man in a red jacket, standing in his apartment on Christmas morning, facing two people who broke into his home.

It should make this easier. Should make him less frightening.

It doesn't.

Because monsters you can hate cleanly. But a man? An old man who clearly lives alone, who's maintained a shrine to his dead daughter for forty-nine years, who looks at you with empty, exhausted eyes?

That's more complicated. That's worse.

"Only if you try to stop us," your father says. His voice is stronger than yours, but the chair leg wavers slightly in his hands. Old joints. Old muscles. How long can either of you hold these weapons raised?

"Or what?" The man takes a slow, careful step forward. Not aggressive, just movement. The kind an elderly person makes when their knees ache. "You'll hit me? Kill me in my own home?"

"If we have to." But your voice cracks on the words. Because looking at him—really looking at him—you're not sure you could.

"You won't." He takes another careful step. "You're not killers. I can see it in your eyes. You're scared. Desperate. But you're not capable of..."

"Don't." Your father lifts the chair leg higher, even though the effort shows on his face. "Don't test us."

The man looks between you both. At the weapons still raised. At your father's face, carved with decades of grief. At yours, probably showing fear and determination in equal measure.

"Put down the weapons," he says again. But different this time. Quieter. "Please. I'm not going to hurt you. Just... put them down. We'll talk."

He sighs. Not theatrically. Just… tired. The sound of someone who's carried something heavy for too long.

"I'm too old for this," he says quietly.

And then he moves. Not toward you. Toward the chair by the window: the one with the faded cushion, the one that looks used. He lowers himself into it slowly, one hand gripping the armrest for support, his knees protesting audibly as he sits.

He settles back with a small wince. Adjusts his position. Then looks up at you both, still standing there with your weapons raised.

"My knees," he says simply. "They can't take much standing anymore."

The coat rack is still heavy in your hands. Your arms are starting to shake from holding it raised. Your father's chair leg wavers.

The man in the red jacket sits quietly, hands resting on the armrests. Waiting.

You can't hit a sitting old man. You physically can't make your body do it.

Your father lowers the chair leg first. Not setting it down, just lowering it to his side, still gripped in his hand. Still ready. But no longer threatening.

You follow suit. The coat rack comes down, the weight of it pulling at your tired arms. You keep your fingers wrapped around the pole. Just in case.

The man nods slightly. "Thank you."

The three of you exist in silence for a moment. Him sitting. You and your father standing, armed but no longer aggressive. The morning light filters through the grimy windows, turning the dust motes into small galaxies.

"Now," the man says. "Let's talk about why you're really here."

What do you say?
"We're investigating the disappearances." Turn to page 181
"We lost someone too." Turn to page 192

CHECK LOFT WITH DAD

"The loft," you say. "Let's check it first. If someone's been living here, there might be supplies up there, documents, something that explains all this."

Your father nods, but when you both move to stand beneath the hatch, you look at him, really look at him. Eighty-two years old. The ladder, when it drops, will be steep. The loft opening narrow.

"I'll go up," you say. "You keep watch down here. If you hear anything...anyone coming...warn me."

"Jenny..."

"Dad. You've been up since before dawn. You drove us up here. Let me do this part." You soften your voice. "Please. I need you down here. I need to know someone's watching my back."

He wants to argue. You can see it in his face. But he also knows you're right.

"Five minutes," he says finally. "You're up there for five minutes, then you come down. I don't care what you find."

"Deal."

You climb onto the bed. The mattress sinks under your boots, springs groaning. The frame sags, soft from years of damp. You steady yourself with one hand against the wall.

The hatch has no cord, no handle, just a wooden panel flush with the ceiling. You brace your flashlight under your arm, reach up, and push.

Nothing. Stuck.

You shift your stance, push harder.

The panel jerks. Shifts an inch. Then...

A sharp crack. The hatch swings open.

The ladder drops fast, metal flashing in your beam. You lurch back, boot slipping on the sagging mattress. It slams into the bedframe where your head just was: metal on wood, loud as a gunshot.

You catch yourself against the wall, heart hammering.

"You okay?" Your father's voice is tight.

"Yeah. Yeah, I'm fine." You stare at the ladder, now swaying slightly. "It just… dropped."

"Be careful."

You grab the ladder. The rungs are cold, rust rough beneath your palm. You test the first rung with your weight. It holds. Second rung. Third.

You climb.

Your head clears the opening. The loft is bigger than you expected, the full length of the apartment below. Low ceiling, beams slanting down at the sides. You have to crouch.

"What do you see?" your father calls up.

"Boxes. Lots of boxes." You haul yourself up, boots finding solid plywood. "I'm going to look around."

You sweep your flashlight across the space. Dozens of cardboard boxes, stacked in corners, some splitting with age. And newer ones too, plastic bins with snap lids. Modern. Out of place.

You move carefully, the plywood creaking under your weight. Open the first cardboard box: papers. Old invoices, maintenance logs from 1975, 1976. The paperwork of a dying business.

Another box: moth-eaten curtains. Another: broken ski gear.

Nothing useful yet. Just the remnants of the Van Vleet's failed resort.

But then your beam catches on the plastic bins. Blue, opaque, the kind you'd buy at any hardware store. Too new for this place.

You drag one toward you, pop the latches, lift the lid.

Inside: Christmas.

Garlands, strings of lights, ornaments. Enough to decorate the entire lobby below.

You brush aside the tinsel, and something glints beneath.

Bells.

Dozens of them. Layer on layer, heavy and silent, their silver dulled but unmistakable.

Every one identical to the bells that have haunted your parents' doorstep for thirty-nine years.

"Holy shit." The words burst out of you, too loud, echoing in the confined space. "Holy shit, holy shit…"

"Jenny?" Your father's voice sharp with alarm from below. "What is it? What's wrong?"

You can't answer. Can't breathe. Your hands are shaking so hard you nearly drop the flashlight.

This is it. This is the evidence. Not just one bell, not just a coincidence: dozens of them, hundreds maybe, stored in bins that shouldn't exist in an abandoned building. Proof that someone has been using this place. Proof that the King of Christmas is real, has been real, has been operating out of this lodge for decades.

"Jenny, talk to me…"

"Bells, Dad." Your voice cracks. "The bells. All of them. This is where they come from."

You hear his sharp intake of breath even from down in the bedroom.

Your hands are still shaking but you force them steady. Pull out your phone. Frame the shot: the open bin, the layers of silver bells clearly visible, the modern plastic container in the decrepit loft.

Tap. Flash.

Another angle. Closer, showing individual bells, their tarnish, their uniformity.

Tap. Flash.

Wide shot: the bins, plural, all of them lined up. Evidence of scale. Evidence of planning.

Tap. Flash. Tap. Flash.

Your breath comes in gasps. Decades of terror. Decades of your parents opening their door on Christmas morning to find these on their porch. And here they are. The source. The proof.

"I'm coming down," you call to your father. "We need to see the other room. We need to see everything before…"

Before what? Before someone comes back? Before you lose your nerve? Before the weight of what you've found crushes you completely?

You climb down the ladder carefully, legs weak, hands still trembling. Your father's face is pale in the flashlight glow.

"You found them," he says. It's not a question.

"Yeah." You show him the photos on your phone. Image after image of silver bells, stored like inventory, waiting to be distributed. "This is real, Dad. All of it. The King of Christmas. He's been here. Maybe for decades."

Your father stares at the photos, his jaw working. When he looks up, his eyes are wet.

"Rachel's room," he says hoarsely. "We need to see it. We need to understand why this started. Why Rachel."

You nod. The other door waits across the small living area. The door you haven't opened yet.

The door to Rachel Van Vleet's bedroom.

Go to Rachel's room. Turn to page 149

TELL KATIE

"What now?" Katie asks again, softer this time, as if she already senses the answer and is afraid of hearing it.

You open your mouth before you can stop yourself. "I'm going to do a stakeout tonight."

The words hit the air like a dropped glass. For a heartbeat the lobby is all soft lamplight and polished wood, then it's just silence, sharp and cold as the snow outside.

Katie blinks. Her hands hover above the desk, fingers curled, like she's bracing. She forces a thin smile. "Jenny... that's... brave. But it's too dangerous. You shouldn't."

"If the police won't do it, someone has to," you say. Your palm stays flat on the folder, as if anchoring yourself to the details inside. "Nobody is doing anything. I can't come back here and do nothing too."

Katie shakes her head, still smiling but the light has gone out of it. "It's not that simple."

"What's not?"

"Everything." She leans forward. "Fifteen years, Jenny. Fifteen years without a bell. We thought maybe..." Her voice falters. "We thought maybe he'd stopped. Maybe he was gone. And then Amy last year proved we were wrong. Don't you see? That's what makes it worse. He came back."

She sounds like she's explaining a superstition or a rule.

"That's exactly why someone needs to watch," you say. "He visits every year. Every Christmas Eve, he leaves the bells. It's blowing my freaking mind that no one in forty damn years has just sat outside and waited for him. It's absolutely ridiculous that you all just..."

"Stop." Her voice sharpens, but you've already bitten back your words. "You don't know what you're talking about."

Before you can say anything else, the office door opens. Siobhan steps out, closing it behind her with a soft click. She doesn't bother pretending she didn't hear.

"You can't do this," she says flatly. "You think you're going to catch him? The police have tried for decades. You think you'll do better? You're meant to be writing a story, not getting yourself killed."

Her eyes are hard, but it's more than anger. You catch a flicker of something deeper, something that looks like fear.

"I have to try," you say.

"Try what?" Siobhan steps closer. "Sit in a car until you freeze? Shine a flashlight so he knows exactly where you are? What happens if he sees you?"

"Then I'll see him," you say. "I want to see him. I want to know who it is. I want to stop this. Don't you? Don't any of you?"

Katie's voice is a thread. "Jenny, please."

But Siobhan keeps on. "Do you even understand what you're playing with? Do you know what it felt like? Fifteen years we thought he was finished. We let ourselves believe it. And then he came back. Fifteen years, and then Amy. She was my daughter's best friend. Did you know that? Is that in your folder? No? No. I thought not."

You glance at Katie. Her hands are trembling now. Suddenly their desperation makes a different kind of sense. They're not only worried about you. They're worried about her. Siobhan's daughter.

"What's her name?" you ask in an almost stutter.

"None of your business, out of towner. Why don't you just go back over to your parents', spend some time with them for once, and try to enjoy Christmas. We don't need you coming here stirring things up." Siobhan hisses.

Katie is silent, but if she feels any differently than Siobhan does, she doesn't show any sign of it. If you thought she was going to be your ally, you just realised how wrong you were.

"I'm sorry. I didn't mean to stir anything. I'm not asking anyone to come with me," you say carefully. "I'm not asking for your blessing. I'm telling you what I'm going to do."

"And we're telling you not to," Siobhan snaps.

"Because you're worried about me," you offer, giving them a way to soften.

Siobhan's eyes flash. "Because it's pointless. The police couldn't do it. One woman alone won't do better. This is a small town," she says, too quickly. "He knows how we move."

"What?"

Katie clears her throat, trying to pull things back. "Just…please, Jenny. Don't. Think it through. You've got other avenues. People to talk to. Records. If you push on the story, maybe you force the police to act. Be a journalist. Write the story. Tell everyone about the King of Christmas. Maybe you don't have to throw yourself into the snow at midnight to prove a point."

"It's not a point," you say softly. "It's a person."

"Exactly," Siobhan mutters, but doesn't explain.

You're aware of the clock ticking on the wall. Of the snow thickening against the window. Of a feeling like stepping over a line you can't see.

Katie leans in, lowering her voice. "You don't understand."

"No," you say. "I really don't. But I have to…"

"Stop it." Her hands slam the desk before she can stop herself. "Stop talking like you're invincible."

Katie's eyes flick to Siobhan. Siobhan shakes her head, a minute warning.

"Look, if you want me to leave…" you say, although you know that your only other option is to go back to your parents' house and stay in the room that overlooks the place you last saw Sarah.

Katie lets out a breath you can tell she has been holding.

"No," she says, giving you a smile that looks forced. "We wouldn't send you out there. In the snow."

"On Christmas Eve," Siobhan adds with matching fake kindness. "Please, stay. But please, don't do this."

Tell them you'll drop the idea. **Turn to page 220**
Tell them you'll drop the idea (but you won't). Turn to page 318
Refuse to back down. Turn to page 183

HIDE

"Hide," you hiss. "Now."

Your father doesn't argue. You both move fast, or as fast as an 82-year-old man and his exhausted daughter can move. The footsteps are still on the stairs, steady, unhurried.

The closet. You yank open the door; empty hangers, nothing else. Not enough room for both of you.

"Under the bed," your father whispers.

You drop to your knees, pull up the rotted bedspread. The gap underneath is narrow, maybe a foot of clearance. The springs sag low. You'd have to squeeze, and even then...

"There's no room," you breathe. "Dad, there's nowhere..."

The footsteps reach the top of the stairs. A door opens; the apartment door. He's in the main living area now.

Your father grabs your arm, pulls you toward the corner behind the open door. You press yourself against the wall, your father beside you. If someone opens the door fully, they'll see you immediately. But if they just glance in...

Footsteps cross the living area. Slow. Deliberate.

You hold your breath. Your father's hand finds yours, squeezes. His palm is sweaty, or maybe that's yours.

The footsteps stop. Silence.

Then: "I know you're here."

The voice is rough, aged. Male. Not angry, almost conversational. Like he's commenting on the weather.

"Someone's been through my things."

Your heart hammers so hard you're certain he can hear it.

"The ladder's down. The bins are open." A pause. "Careless."

Footsteps again. Coming closer. Toward Rachel's room.

Toward you.

The door swings wider. Turn to page 176

HO HO HO

A man stands in the doorway.

Santa Claus.

The thought hits you before logic does: the red suit, the white trim, the elderly face framed by a hood. Your brain screams *Santa* even as your eyes register the details: not a costume but a ski jacket, red with white fur trim around the hood and cuffs. Not a suit but outdoor gear. Not jolly but weathered, deep lines carved into a face that's seen too many winters.

Eighties, like Dad, maybe older. White hair visible beneath the hood.

Not Santa. But close enough to make your skin crawl.

He sees you immediately. Looks right at you, pressed against the wall like children playing hide and seek.

"There you are."

Your father steps forward, putting himself between you and the man. "We don't want trouble. We're leaving. Right now."

The man doesn't move from the doorway. Just stands there, blocking the exit, studying you both with eyes that are wrong, somehow. Not angry. Not surprised. Just… empty.

And that's when it fully registers.

He's old.

You knew it logically: the King of Christmas started taking children in 1976, forty-nine years ago. Of course he'd be elderly. But knowing it and *seeing* it are different things.

The King of Christmas. The monster. The legend that's haunted Pine Hollow for half a century.

He's just a man.

His hands, when he reaches up to lower his hood, shake slightly. Arthritis, maybe. Or just age. The red jacket hangs loose on a frame that's thinned over the decades. His breathing is audible in the quiet; not laboured, but present. Real. Human.

You'd expected a monster. Something you could hate cleanly, fight clearly, run from without guilt.

Not this. Not an old man who looks like he could be someone's grandfather. Not someone who moves with the careful stiffness of bad knees and an aching back.

Your father sees it too. You can tell by the way his defensive stance wavers, confusion flickering across his face. Like he's also trying to reconcile the myth with the reality standing three feet away.

"Leaving," the man repeats. His voice is rough, aged, but not threatening. Just tired. "After breaking into my home. After going through my things. After disturbing her room." His gaze shifts to the dresser, to Rachel's shrine. "No. I don't think so."

"Please." Your father's voice is steady despite the trembling in his hands. "We're just trying to find out what happened. We need to know."

"You need to know." The man's mouth twists. "That's why you came here?"

Your mind races. How do you answer? What do you say to a man who's been living in this shrine for forty-nine years, who's blocking your only exit, who looks at you with those empty eyes?

An old man. Just an old man.

It's just a man.

What do you say?

"We're investigating the disappearances." Turn to page 181
"We lost someone too." Turn to page 192

THE CRAWFORDS'

You head toward Oak Street.

The Crawfords. Amy's family. The most recent victim. The wound is fresh; raw in a way the others have had decades to scab over.

The drive through Pine Hollow is quiet. Christmas Eve has emptied the streets. The houses glow with warm light, televisions flickering in living rooms, families settling in for the night. You pass the church, its parking lot full for evening service, voices rising in hymn through the open doors. *Silent night, holy night...*

You turn onto the street.

The Crawford house is modest. Ranch-style, beige siding, a small front porch with a railing wrapped in lights. A plastic snowman stands in the yard, slightly deflated. There's a wreath on the door.

And in the front window, a small artificial tree. Unlit.

You park three houses down, far enough to be unobtrusive but close enough to watch. The folder rests on the passenger seat, your father's map on top, Crawford house circled like a target.

You settle in to wait.

The heater hums. Your coffee thermos sits in the cup holder, steam curling from the open top. You take a sip. It's hot, bitter, and grounding. Outside, the street is empty. Silent.

You're watching the house, planning your vantage points, when the front door opens.

A man steps onto the porch. It must be Mr Crawford. Forties, thinning hair, wearing a flannel shirt and jeans. He's looking directly at your car.

Your stomach drops.

He starts walking toward you. Not hurried, but deliberate. His face is hard.

You consider driving away. But that would look worse. So you roll down your window as he approaches, letting the cold air slice in.

"Can I help you?" His voice is flat, controlled. Barely containing something underneath.

"Mr Crawford, I'm…"

"Don't." The word is sharp. "Don't say anything. You need to leave."

A woman appears in the doorway of the Crawford house. Mrs Crawford, arms wrapped around herself. Behind her, barely visible, a child; she's small, maybe six or seven. Amy's sibling. Another child who will grow up without her sister.

"I'm not here to bother you," you say quietly. "I just want to understand what happened. To all of them. To stop this."

"By staking out my house on Christmas Eve?" His jaw works. "You think I don't see you? You think I don't know what you're doing?"

"I'm trying to help."

"You're trying to write a story." He leans closer, and you can see his eyes are red-rimmed, exhausted. "You're trying to turn my daughter into content. Into something people read with their morning coffee and forget by lunch."

"That's not…"

"It's too fresh." His voice cracks on the last word. "It's too goddamn fresh. We're trying to get through tonight. Trying to keep it together for…" He glances back at the house, at the child in the doorway. "We have another daughter. You understand that? Another little girl who's terrified Santa might be real and might come for her too."

Your throat tightens. "I understand. I'm sorry. I'll go."

"You do that." He straightens. "And if I see you on this street again, I'm calling the sheriff. You're harassing a grieving family. Pretty sure that's against the law."

"I'm sorry," you say again. Because you are. Because you understand grief that raw, that fresh wound. Because you remember your parents the year after Sarah vanished, and how they would have reacted to someone like you.

He walks back to his house without another word. Mrs Crawford ushers the child inside. The door closes. The porch light stays on.

You sit in your car, hands on the wheel, shame burning in your chest.

You can't stake out here. Not with them watching. Not with a child in that house who's already terrified.

You need to choose another location.

Where do you go?

The Hendersons' Turn to page 89
The Wilsons' Turn to page 184
Your parents' Turn to page 227

INVESTIGATING THE DISAPPEARANCES

You fall back on what you know. The investigative approach. Clinical. Controlled. Anything to keep the terror from spilling out.

"We're investigating the disappearances. The missing children. We found the bells. We found Rachel's shrine. We have photos. Evidence. People know we're here."

"Rachel." The man stops. The name lands like a physical blow. His empty expression cracks, just for a moment. Pain flashes across his face before the emptiness returns. "You were in her room."

"We saw everything," you say. "The photos on the dresser. The fresh pine cones. Someone has been maintaining it. For decades. You?"

You're testing your hypothesis like a good journalist, even now.

"Don't." The word is sharp. "Don't talk about her room. Don't talk about what you saw. You had no right…"

"We have every right." Your father's voice hardens. "This is a crime scene. Has been for forty-nine years. Eight children disappeared from Pine Hollow, and you…" He stops. Stares at the man. Really stares. "You've been living here. All this time? You know what happened to them."

The man's jaw works. His hands are clenched into fists.

"You don't understand what you've walked into," the man says finally. "What this place is. What I've had to do."

"Then explain it." Your father's voice is steady. "Make us understand. Why the bells? Why the children? Why…" His voice catches. "Why my daughter?"

The man's eyes snap to your father.

"Your daughter?"

"Sarah Matthews. Disappeared Christmas Eve, 1986. She was nine years old." Your father's voice breaks. "We've gotten a bell on our doorstep every Christmas Eve since."

Something shifts in the man's face. Not guilt. Not exactly. But…
recognition? Pain?

"Matthews," he repeats. "You're Bill Matthews."

Your father nods slowly, and asks "And you are…?"

The man stares at him. Then at you. Then back at your father.
And laughs.

It's not a pleasant sound. Short, bitter, almost disbelieving.

"You haven't figured it out yet?" He looks between you both.
"The local investigator and his big-shot city journalist daughter? I
don't know whether to be offended or disappointed in you."

Your blood runs cold. Because of the way he says it - like he
KNOWS you, like he's been waiting for this moment.

"You're the King of Christmas," you say.

The man tilts his head slightly. Acknowledging. But his eyes stay
on your father.

"Who am I, Bill?"

Your father stares at him. You can see him processing - the red
jacket, the shrine to Rachel, the apartment at the abandoned ski
resort, forty-nine years of hiding.

"Van Vleet?" your father breathes.

The man's mouth curves. Not quite a smile. "Robert Van Vleet.
Yes."

"Fuck." The word slips out before you can stop it.

Because suddenly it all makes sense. Rachel Van Vleet, the first
victim, 1976. The ski resort closing six months after her death. The
family leaving town but never selling the property. The shrine
maintained for forty-nine years by someone who loved her.

Not a monster hiding in an abandoned building.

A father who never left his daughter's side.

The King Speaks. Turn to page 202

REFUSE TO BACK DOWN

You shake your head, the words coming harder, sharper. "No. I'm not changing my mind. I'm doing the stakeout tonight, and nothing you say will stop me."

Katie flinches as if you've raised your voice at her. Siobhan's mouth tightens into a grim line. For a moment neither of them speaks, and the silence feels like ice forming over deep water.

"Jenny," Katie whispers. "Please. Don't…"

"I have to," you cut in. "I didn't come back here just to shuffle papers and write a sad feature about bells and rumours. If no one else will face him, I will. I'd rather freeze to death on the edge of those woods than spend another year pretending this isn't happening."

Siobhan steps closer, her face hard with fury and something darker. "You think you're brave? You're reckless. You'll get yourself killed, and you'll drag the rest of us back into the nightmare with you."

"Maybe," you say. "But if I do nothing, another kid could end up like Sarah. Like Tommy. Like Amy. That's worse than reckless."

The three of you stand locked in a stalemate: Katie trembling, Siobhan glaring, you burning with defiance. At last, Siobhan shakes her head in disgust and stalks back into the office, slamming the door behind her.

Katie lingers, her eyes glassy with fear. "I can't stop you," she says finally. "But don't expect anyone here to save you if he…"

You hold her gaze. "I don't need saving."

With the folder under your arm and your pulse hammering, you climb the stairs toward Room 12. Every step feels like a countdown. You've drawn your line in the sand, and the whole Inn seems to creak under the weight of it.

Go back to room 12 Turn to page 278

You head toward Birch Street.

The Wilsons. Katie's house. Tommy's house, even though he was gone before you even moved to this town.

The Wilson house is a two-story colonial, one of the older properties in town, but well maintained. Lights glow in the downstairs windows. Christmas lights hang from the eaves, blinking red and green in steady rhythm. Someone's home. Someone's waiting.

You park beneath a birch tree, white bark ghostly in the streetlight. Unlike most roads in Pine Hollow, Birch Street actually has birch trees. It was the original. The others just borrowed the naming pattern.

You remember riding your bike here as a kid, running your hand along the papery bark, pretending these trees held some secret about Tommy Wilson's disappearance. They didn't, of course. Trees don't talk.

But tonight, maybe the house will.

You settle in to wait.

Outside, the street is empty. Silent. A few cars parked along the curb, snow-covered. No movement.

You watch the house. The lit windows. The Christmas lights blinking their cheerful pattern, oblivious to the darkness underneath.

Minutes crawl past.

Your phone sits in your lap, 67% battery, screen dark. You resist the urge to check it, to scroll through old emails, to do anything that might make you visible. You're here to observe, not to be observed.

Minutes crawl past.

The upstairs light goes out. Then the downstairs dims. Someone's going to bed.

You check your watch. 11:03pm.

The street remains empty. No cars. No pedestrians. Just the soft hiss of snow beginning to fall again, dusting the windshield in patterns that blur your view.

You wipe the glass with your glove, lean forward, squinting.

Time moves like frozen honey. 11:14. 11:22. Your coffee grows cold. The windows fog with your breath. You wipe them clear again and again.

11:27pm.

A figure appears at the far end of the street, moving along the sidewalk. Not trying to hide, but not lingering either. Just someone out for a walk on Christmas Eve.

Except no one goes for walks on Christmas Eve at 11:30 at night.

The figure turns onto the Wilson's walkway. Climbs the porch steps. Bends down, placing something on the doormat.

Your heart hammers. This is it. This is what you came for.

Your phone is in your hand. Camera already open. One click and you'll have proof. Evidence. Something concrete to show the police, to put in your article, to prove this is real.

But the figure is already straightening, preparing to leave. In seconds they'll be gone.

Your other hand is on the door handle. You could stop this. Right now. Catch them in the act, force them to explain, make them talk.

The figure turns.

You have to choose.

What do you do?

Take photographs. Turn to page 207

Get out and apprehend them. Turn to page 186

APPREHEND THEM

You're out of the car.

You're running.

Your boots hit snow, pavement, snow again. The figure straightens, starts to turn.

You crash into them.

Both of you go down hard on the porch, the impact knocking the air from your lungs. You're grappling, holding on, your voice raw: "I've got him! Katie! KATIE!"

"Get off me!" The voice is male, panicked, thrashing. "Get OFF!"

"KATIE!" You're shouting now, half-pinning the man, adrenaline making you strong. "Call the police! I've got him!"

The porch light blazes on. The door flies open.

Katie stands there in her pyjamas and robe, face white with shock.

"Jenny? What are you…"

"Call 911!" You've got the man's arm twisted behind his back now, journalist instincts replaced by pure fury. "He just placed a bell! I saw him!"

Katie doesn't move. She's staring at the man, then at you, then at the silver bell glinting on the doormat between you.

"Katie, CALL THE SHERIFF!"

For three long seconds, Katie just stands there, frozen. Then something shifts in her face.

"Inside." Her voice cuts through the cold, and she's moving towards you and the man you are struggling to hold onto. "Quick. Let's get him in."

She moves fast, stepping onto the porch, grabbing the man's other arm. "Jenny, help me."

You nod and tighten your grip. It's easier with Katie holding on to him too. He's not going anywhere. Two middle aged women with decades of grief are plenty enough to overcome a single person.

Together, you half-drag, half-push the man through the door. He's not fighting anymore, just stumbling, breathing hard.

Katie slams the door. Throws the deadbolt.

You get your first look at the man in the dim light.

He's in his fifties, not much older than you, balding, wearing a Canvas Lumber jacket. Ordinary. Completely ordinary.

He could barely have been school age when the first child went missing.

It doesn't make sense.

This can't be the King of Christmas.

Katie guides you into the kitchen, and pulls out a chair with one arm while still holding onto him with the other.

"No trouble now," she says. "I've got a child asleep upstairs."

A child? You shoot her a look as she guides the man to the seat.

"Lily," Katie says. "Siobhan's daughter. I'm babysitting while she…"

The man grunts as you pull his arm behind him.

"I'll get some rope," Katie says.

"Good," you and the man say at exactly the same time.

Good?

You study his face for a moment, trying to put the pieces together, but nothing fits.

Nothing fits until Katie steps behind you and throws a loop over rope over your body.

"What the fuck?"

It's all you can think of to say, as you stretch your arms, try to turn around, try to break free.

The man is back on his feet, spinning you into the chair, helping Katie with the rope. The two of them bind you, rough hessian pressing your winter coat against your skinny arms.

What the fuck.

You'd like to say more, but you hear a ripping sound behind you and Katie slaps a piece of duct tape over your mouth.

"Lily really *is* upstairs, and I'm not having you say or do anything that puts her in danger," she says, almost apologetically.

"You need me to stay, or are you going to deal with her?" the man says.

You still don't know who he is. You don't recognise him. You don't even know if he recognises you. The only thing you know for certain right now is that this is *not* the King of Christmas.

Katie looks at him for a long moment.

"Siobhan will be back soon. I can do this."

He wavers.

"I said I can DO this." Katie gives an emphatic tug on the rope that's already too tight around your chest.

The man nods and heads for the door.

The house falls silent except for the ticking of the kitchen clock and your harsh breathing through your nose.

Katie sinks into a chair across from you. For a long moment, she just stares at the table. When she finally looks up, her eyes are wet.

"You should never have come back," she says.

You try to speak, but the tape muffles everything into angry sounds.

"I know." Katie's voice breaks. "I know how it hurts. But Jenny…" She wipes her eyes with the back of her hand. "You don't understand how this works. You've been gone too long. You don't know what it's like to live here."

She stands, moves to the counter. Picks up a glass. Sets it down again without filling it. Her hands are shaking.

"We protect our children." Her voice drops to a whisper. "Lily is eight years old. She's upstairs right now, asleep, dreaming about Christmas morning. And if I let you expose this, if I let you break the system…" She closes her eyes. "He'll take her. Just like he took Tommy. Just like he took Sarah."

You're shaking your head, thrashing against the ropes.

"I know you don't understand," Katie says. She comes closer, crouches in front of you so you're eye to eye. She reaches out, touches your face gently. "But you understand too much."

Your eyes widen. Your chest is tight. You can't breathe properly through the tape.

Then she's back on her feet, behind you. Metal clanks in a drawer. Her footsteps come back across the room.

"I'll tell your parents you had to go back to the city," she says. "They're used to you not being around."

Those are the last words you hear before blood fills your throat. You feel that before you realise that there's a knife in Katie's hand. The warmth, the taste, the air not getting to where it should anymore.

The blood, spreading down your chest, soaking into your coat. Your ears fill with the sound of your own heartbeat, too loud, then too faint, then…

Nothing.

THE END

You died in Katie Wilson's kitchen on Christmas Eve, 2025.

Your parents received a text from your phone around 2 AM: "Emergency at the paper. Have to get back to Boston. Sorry I couldn't stay for Christmas. Love you both." *They believed it.*

The King of Christmas continued his work.

THE MASTER BEDROOM

The master bedroom is sparse. This was where the Van Vleets slept. A double bed, stripped bare, mattress water-stained and sagging. A dresser with drawers hanging open at odd angles. Through an open doorway, you glimpse a bathroom coated in decades of grime.

You're still shaking from Rachel's room. The shrine. The fresh pine cones. The dust-free photos. Someone's been maintaining that space.

You move to the dresser, hands unsteady. Your torch illuminates the first drawer: empty, wood swollen. The second holds rotted fabric.

The third drawer stops you.

Folded clothes. Men's clothes. Jeans, t-shirts, flannel shirts.

But these aren't from the seventies.

Modern denim. Darker wash, slim cut. A t-shirt with a logo you recognise - a craft brewery that opened in the 2000s. Worn but not old. Faded but not decades-faded.

You pull open the fourth drawer with trembling hands. More clothes. Different sizes. One t-shirt still has the tag attached.

The pine cones in Rachel's room. Fresh. Weeks old. And now this: modern clothes, organised, folded carefully.

Someone's been here. Recently. Not just visiting, living here. Using this space.

And the clothes. They're not stolen, not scavenged. They're placed. Arranged. Like someone's been leaving them.

Why hasn't anyone mentioned it? You've been asking questions all over Pine Hollow. No one said people use the old ski lodge. No one warned you.

Maybe they don't know.

Or maybe they do know. Maybe they've always known. Maybe the silence isn't ignorance, it's something else.

Your breath comes faster. Your hands won't stop shaking.

Someone lives here. Someone who maintains Rachel's shrine, who keeps her photos dust-free, who arranges pine cones with care.

You don't understand. But you understand enough to know you're not safe.

The hatch above the bed catches your eye. Storage. Loft space.

You need to leave. Every instinct says get out, get to your car, get back to town. Call your parents, tell them what you found, let someone else figure out what it means.

But the loft. If someone's been living here for years, using this as a base, there might be evidence up there. Something that explains the maintenance, the supplies, the *why* of all this.

Something you could show authorities outside Pine Hollow. Proof.

Pull open the hatch. Turn to page 251

WE LOST SOMEONE TOO

You can't do this. Can't stand here with your investigator mask on, pretending this is just another story, just another interview.

Not in this room. Not with your father beside you, grief written in every line of his face.

"We lost someone too." Your voice cracks on the words. "My sister. Sarah."

The man goes very still. His eyes move to your father, then back to you.

"Sarah Matthews," your father says quietly. "She disappeared Christmas Eve, 1986. She was nine years old."

Something flickers across the man's face. Recognition. And something else. Something that might be pain.

"We've gotten a bell every Christmas Eve since. And every year we've spent not knowing what happened to her. If she suffered. If she called for us. If she…"

You can't finish. Can't say *if she died alone.*

The way you said *we've gotten a bell* only reminds you how it was your parents who stayed, who suffered this every year. It was you who left. You who built a life in Boston while they opened their door every Christmas Eve to find another silver bell on the porch. The bells might as well have been Fed-Exed to your apartment too, but at least you had the luxury of distance. At least you could pretend to move on.

Your father doesn't correct you. Doesn't point out that you weren't there for most of those bells. He just sits beside you, and that somehow makes it worse.

The man's jaw works. He looks toward the doorway, toward Rachel's room.

"You've been maintaining this place," you say, following his gaze. "Rachel's room. The shrine. You knew her."

His eyes snap back to you. For the first time, you see real emotion. Pain, sharp and immediate.

"Don't," he says quietly. "Don't say her name."

"Rachel," your father says, and the man flinches like he's been struck. "Rachel Van Vleet. She lived here. She disappeared Christmas Eve, 1976. She was the first. She…"

"I know when she died." Each word is clipped, precise. "I was there."

The admission hangs in the air.

You were there.

"You're him," you breathe. "You *are* the one who's been taking the children."

He doesn't deny it. Just sits there, watching you both, as if you're gathered for a cosy chat, not this. Not whatever this is.

Your father stares at him. You can see him processing. The red jacket. The shrine to Rachel. The apartment at the abandoned ski resort. The years of hiding.

"*Van Vleet?*" your father says slowly. "Are you Robert Van Vleet?"

The man's expression shifts. Something like relief. Or maybe resignation.

"Yes," he says finally. "I'm Robert Van Vleet."

Your father goes pale. "But… you're Rachel's father. Rachel was the first victim. The King of Christmas took Rachel in 1976. That's how this all started."

Van Vleet's expression goes carefully blank.

"If you're the King of Christmas," you say slowly, trying to make the pieces fit, "then who took Rachel? Or did someone else… is there someone else? Did you take over after…"

"No." The word is sharp. Final.

"Then I don't understand." Your father's voice rises slightly. "Rachel disappeared Christmas Eve, 1976. Seven more children have disappeared since then. The King of Christmas has been taking children for forty-nine years. But if Rachel was the first victim, if YOU'RE her father, then…"

"Rachel…." Van Vleet's voice is hard. Controlled. "That's not what happened. I would never have hurt her. Never."

The words hang in the air.

"What does that mean?" you ask.

Van Vleet looks toward Rachel's room. At the carefully arranged shrine. At the drawings on the wall visible through the doorway.

"It means," he says finally, "that you don't understand what happened. What any of this really is." He turns back to you both. "The story everyone tells, the legend of the King of Christmas taking naughty children, it's not the whole truth."

"Then tell us the truth," your father demands.

The King speaks. Turn to page 202

PHONE SOMEONE

You grip your phone, hands slick with sweat. The battery icon glows red: 5%.

No signal bars. You shift, tilt it toward the ceiling, desperate for a flicker. One dot appears. Then vanishes. Then again.

Maybe enough. Maybe.

The whistling continues below, soft and unhurried, curling up the ladder like smoke.

He sees you when you're sleeping.

You can't let him see you, not at all.

You freeze, thumb hovering over the screen.

Who do you call?

Katie at the Inn. **Turn to page 259**
Your parents. **Turn to page 296**
911 **Turn to page 200**

HEAD UP TO THE SKI RESORT

The road narrows as you climb into the Frost Mountains, the town falling away in the rearview like a set piece struck from a stage. Pines crowd the shoulder, their branches hunched with snow, their shadows striping the tarmac in black ribs that appear and vanish in your headlights. The air turns sharper the higher you go. The heater's on full, but the cold here is different: older, cleaner, angled like glass. Your tyres hiss over patches of black ice and catch again, and each bend feels like a decision you can't take back.

You pass nothing for miles. No cabins tucked in the trees, no glow from windows, no orange tongues of snowplough lights. Just the dark spine of the mountain and the long white breath of the road, unwinding ahead of you.

When the sign rises out of the beam—PINE HOLLOW SKI LODGE—it startles you enough to flinch. The letters are bleached to bone, the arrow pointing into a stand of spruce that looks identical to every other stand of spruce for the last ten miles. You take the turn anyway, the gravel track punching up through the snow like a scar. The car shudders across ruts the weather has opened and closed for decades. The forest parts with a sigh of branches, and the track spills you into a flat, white expanse that was once a parking lot.

You kill the engine, and the silence empties the car like a vacuum. The tick of cooling metal sounds brazen out here. You sit for a moment with your hands on the wheel, thumbs pressed to the plastic, feeling the rhythms of your pulse through your skin. Then you open the door and the cold reaches in first, clean and absolute, and takes you.

Back at the Pine Hollow Inn you made the call: no theatre, no waiting in cars, no stakeout. You're here to follow the story, and this is where it started. The first page. The first abduction.

The lot is a crater of ice and cracked tarmac glazed over by years of freeze and thaw. A drift has swallowed half a row of parking bumpers so only their rounded spines show. Lift chairs lie half-buried where they must have been dumped when the cables were stripped, their seats upended, their bars blotched with rust the colour of dried blood. The ticket booth leans, an off-kilter cube, its windows caved and boot-scuffed, a graffiti heart scorched to a smudge.

The lodge sits at the far end, a low, sprawling thing squatting into the slope like a creature that chose not to move and simply let the snow build up around it. Boards crosshatched over the windows don't quite meet; in the inches of gap, the darkness inside looks physical, like a slow flood. The roofline sags. A metal gutter has torn away and speared itself into a drift where icicles accrete around it in thick glass columns.

You pull your coat tighter and start across the lot. The snow comes up over your boots, past the cuff once and then again, and the cold seeps at your socks. The only sound is the careful crush of your own steps. If there's wind, it's somewhere else. If there are birds, they've decided you are not worth announcing.

As a child, the resort wasn't a place so much as a rumour. Your mother had called it "up there," the way people point at heaven.

Up there, where people with money used to come in winter. That stopped long before you moved to town.

Your bike could never have made this climb, and you were never allowed to try. The lodge existed for you the way castles exist for children who glimpse them from a motorway: not real enough to touch, but real enough to want. You used to imagine its carpet and the ridge of the counter where they once handed out hot chocolates with cream folded into peaks. You imagined an indoor pool, blue as a bruise. You imagined other children coming to town on their holidays.

And somewhere in there, once upon a time, lived Rachel Van Vleet.

When you were a child, all you knew was that she was the first taken. You knew she was an out-of-towner, like your family, because the Van Vleets belonged to the lodge the way you never quite belonged to Pine Hollow. Their mailbox wasn't on Maple or Birch; their name lived up there. And yours, despite years of school photos and bake sales, never quite fit in either. Always *The Matthews who moved in '83*, the *comer-inners*. Forty years on, it hasn't washed off your parents. Still, they stay.

The Van Vleets weren't part of anything, not really. Sometimes, as a child, you felt the same: close enough to see the rooms where other people's lives happened, never quite invited to sit down. Maybe that's why the small rebellions started. Pocketing Barbara's bracelet and blaming it on her. Taking what didn't belong and pretending it did. A mean, glittering act that felt like proof you could make something yours, if only for a minute. You told yourself it was nothing. Kids are cruel, and then they grow. But the memory still nicks when you touch it, a tiny cut that never heals clean.

Now you're an adult, you know more. You've read the case files and the press clippings. You've obsessed over this town and its disappearances as fiercely as your father, maybe more. You've uncovered the details you ignored as a child, but none of the ones that still burn: Who is the King of Christmas, and why did he take Sarah?

Up here, the distance feels familiar. The mountain made a boundary for the Van Vleets. The town made one for you. And somewhere between them, a girl disappeared.

You picture Rachel on the lobby carpet where the window light pooled, bootlaces undone, the air tasting of iron and chlorinated towels. In season there were other families, a bustle that looked like community if you squinted. But before Rachel vanished, the bustle had thinned. Pine Hollow fell off the maps that mattered; each year the brochure photos aged a little more while newer places threw brighter light.

On Christmas morning, 1976, Rachel Van Vleet's parents woke to find her gone.

You stop halfway across the lot with that sentence in your head, as if speaking it aloud would demand a bow. Then you move again, because it feels wrong to stand exposed with that room lodged in your lungs.

The lodge swells as you approach. Boards cross the windows at the height of your face; you can see where someone pried them once and where someone else hammered them back. Nails failed first. Screws came later. The door sits centred under a shallow porch, its wood gone grey and furred with a fine bloom where cold has raised the grain.

You step back and look beyond the eaves, up the mountain. The runs score the slope in long, healed-over cuts, trees ending, dropping, beginning again. If you squint, you can trace a single lift line where the towers still climb, crossbeams stripped, pulleys dead.

If you go inside the lodge, there will be rooms like mouths. There will be papers gone soft with damp that still hold language. There will be a wall that remembers where a shelf was and a lighter rectangle where a picture hung. There will, maybe, be nothing that matters to anyone except you. If you climb, there will be wind on the slope. There will be the discipline of your breathing. There will be the angle of the mountain and the exact, unarguable fact of distance. Up there, the world won't be made of rooms where people say no. It will be made of cold and gravity and the evidence of your own feet.

Find a way into the lodge. Turn to page 208
Walk the hill to the ski runs while it's still light. Turn to page 288

CALL 911

You dial 911, hands shaking so hard you nearly drop the phone.

One ring.

"911, what is your emergency?"

"I'm at the old ski lodge," you whisper, fighting to keep your voice steady. "On Frost Mountain. Someone broke in. He's in the building. I need help."

"Which lodge, ma'am?"

"Pine Hollow. The old Van Vleet place." Your voice cracks. "Please, he's climbing up here right now, there are… there are bells, so many bells, and I found…"

You want to tell them everything. Make them understand. But the words tangle with sobs, and you need to be QUIET.

"Ma'am, I'm connecting you to the Sheriff's Department."

"No, please, just send…"

Click. Hold music. Three seconds that feel like hours.

Click.

"This is Sheriff Larkin."

"Sheriff!" Relief floods through you for one desperate second. "This is Jenny Matthews. From Evergreen…" You haven't lived there for years. It doesn't matter. "I'm at the ski lodge. Someone's here. You need to send help NOW…"

"Jenny." He says your name like a period at the end of a sentence. "Where exactly are you."

Not a question. He knows. He's always known.

"The loft." Your voice breaks completely. "Above the apartment. He's climbing the ladder. Please…"

Silence stretches.

"Sheriff?"

"I can't help you, Jenny."

The words are quiet. Final.

"What?" You're sobbing now, can't help it. "You have to... you're the police..."

"You shouldn't have gone up there." He sounds tired. Resigned. "You should've stayed away."

"Please... I found bells, I found..."

"There's nothing I can do." A pause. "I'm sorry."

Click.

He hung up.

You stare at the phone. 2%.

The whistling drifts up through the hatch. The ladder creaks.

No one is coming. No one will help.

You're completely alone.

What do you do?

Hide among the boxes. Turn to page 395

Van Vleet is quiet for a long moment. You can see him weighing something. Deciding how much to reveal. Then he begins to talk.

"Rachel died here," he says finally. "Christmas Eve, 1976. But she wasn't taken by some monster in the night. She…" He stops. Swallows hard. "It was an accident."

"An accident," your father repeats. His investigator brain is working now, you can see it. "But… you left. After Rachel died. You and your wife. Everyone says you closed the resort and left Pine Hollow six months later."

Van Vleet says nothing.

"No." Your father's voice changes. "No, you didn't leave. You…" He looks around the apartment. At the maintained furniture. At Rachel's shrine. At the evidence of decades of habitation. "You've been here. The whole time. You shut the place down and you… you stayed."

"The town said you left," you add. Your mind is racing. "Everyone believes you left. But you didn't. You've been living here. Hiding here. For forty-nine years."

Van Vleet's jaw tightens but he doesn't deny it.

"Jesus Christ," your father breathes. "The whole town lied. They all knew you were here. They've been lying for nearly fifty years about…"

He stops. Stares at Van Vleet.

"Your wife," he says slowly. "Marcie. Where is your wife?"

The temperature in the room seems to drop.

Van Vleet's expression goes flat. Empty. "Gone."

"Gone where?" you press.

"Just gone." His voice is hard. Final. The same tone he used about Rachel. A door slamming shut.

But there's something in his eyes. Something that makes your skin crawl.

Your father sees it too. "Mr Van Vleet. Where is your wife?"

"That's not your concern."

"You've been here alone for forty-nine years," you say quietly. "Maintaining Rachel's room. Living in this apartment. But Marcie... she didn't stay with you, did she?"

Van Vleet's hands clench. "I said that's not your concern."

The way he won't answer. The way he's gone rigid. The way the grief on his face has transformed into something harder, colder.

"What did you do?" You can't stop the question coming out.

Van Vleet's eyes flash. "What I had to do. What anyone would do when their world falls apart and the person who should have been there, who should have understood..." He stops. Takes a breath. "Marcie wanted to leave. After Rachel. She wanted to sell this place, move away, forget. As if we could forget." His voice is bitter now. "As if our daughter was something we could just leave behind like broken furniture."

"So, you..." Your father can't finish the sentence.

"So, I made sure she stayed." Van Vleet's voice is flat. Matter-of-fact. "Where she belongs. With Rachel. With me. All of us together, the way we're supposed to be."

The words settle over you like ice.

He killed her. His wife. Because she wanted to leave.

"You've been alone here," you whisper. "For forty-nine years. Just you and..."

"And Rachel." Van Vleet looks toward her room again. "I'm never alone. She's always here. I keep everything the way she liked it. The drawings. The pine cones. Everything."

Your father's voice is hollow. "And the other children? Sarah and Tommy and all the others? Why them?"

Van Vleet turns back to you both. When he speaks, his voice is different. Harder.

"Because Rachel's death meant something. It had to mean something." His hands are shaking now. "I thought that if I told the

203

truth about what happened, no one would care. They would blame me, blame her. Oh, Bill Matthews of Evergreen Lane, you know exactly what it's like in this backward little shithole. You know what people like them think about people like us."

Your father sits forward, visibly bristling at the words. This man is comparing himself to your father. This man who destroyed his life.

"A child has an accident on a site that people already think is dangerous and… what? It's forgotten within a week. Or worse, it's all they think about when they see you. A child that's abducted though? Well…"

"You wanted people to feel sorry for you?" Your father's voice is low. Dangerous.

Van Vleet's eyes flash. "I WANTED PEOPLE TO CARE." His composure cracks, voice rising. "MY DAUGHTER WAS DEAD AND I WANTED PEOPLE TO CARE."

The words echo in the small apartment.

"And they still didn't." You almost feel something like sympathy, but you push it down. He doesn't deserve it.

"No," Van Vleet says, trying to control his voice now. "I told them she was taken. That someone had come in the night, on Christmas Eve, and we had woken to an empty bed. But no one cared. The police said they'd done what they could, but that was nothing. The people in town. Bill, you know, don't you? You know how they treated me, because you're a comer-inner too. You're the same as me."

Your father explodes.

"THE SAME?" He's on his feet, the chair scraping violently backward. "You think we're THE SAME?"

Van Vleet flinches back in his seat.

"My daughter was MURDERED." Your father's voice is shaking, his hands clenched into fists. "She was taken from our garden. She was nine years old. She was INNOCENT. And you…"

He points at Van Vleet, his whole body trembling. "YOU killed her. You murdered my child to maintain your COVER STORY."

"Dad..." you start, but he's not done.

"Your daughter died in an accident." The words are daggers. "An accident that happened because YOU didn't secure your property. Because YOU cut corners. Because YOU were negligent. And instead of facing that, instead of taking responsibility, you created a MONSTER. You BECAME that monster. You murdered SEVEN CHILDREN so people would feel sorry for you instead of blaming you."

Van Vleet's face has gone pale.

"We are NOT the same." Your father's voice drops to something more dangerous than shouting. "I spent thirty-nine years searching for my daughter. Begging for help. Getting doors slammed in my face. While you..." He gestures around the apartment. "You spent your time hiding in your dead daughter's bedroom, murdering children, and pretending you were the victim."

The silence that follows is absolute.

Your father is breathing hard, still standing, still furious. Van Vleet sits frozen in his chair, staring up at him.

"Don't you EVER," your father says quietly, "compare yourself to me again."

"David Drake. Claire Henderson. Tommy Wilson. Sarah Matthews. Daniel Peak. Emily Taylor. Amy Crawford." You list the names like a mantra. "You murdered seven children so people would care that your daughter died in an accident you could have prevented."

Then it hits you. Hard.

"Why did no one stop you?"

Turn to page 463

TAKE A PHOTO TO ZOOM IN LATER

You pull out your phone, fingers clumsy inside your gloves. The screen lights up, brightness shocking against the muted grey of the afternoon. You frame the weathered post, the faded letters barely visible even through the camera lens. The phone struggles to focus in the flat light, the letters swimming in and out of clarity.

Click.

The mechanical shutter sound feels absurdly cheerful up here, a small piece of the modern world intruding on all this white silence.

A notification flashes at the top of the screen: **Battery 15%**

The cold is draining it faster than you expected. You should have charged it fully at the Inn, should have brought a portable battery. Too late now. You shove the phone back into your pocket, the metal already ice-cold against your palm.

You can zoom in later, when you're somewhere warm, somewhere with better light and steady hands. For now, you have the image captured. That's what matters. That's what a journalist does: document first, analyse later.

The post stands silent behind you as you turn back to the slope. Whatever it says, you'll know soon enough.

You keep climbing. Turn to page 360

TAKE PHOTOS

You raise your phone.

The camera clicks once. Twice. Three times. The figure frozen in each frame - bent over the doormat, bell glinting in their hand, face partially visible in the porch light.

You zoom in. Click again. The bell. The figure's coat. Their shoes leaving prints in the snow.

Evidence. Finally, evidence.

The figure straightens, glances around one more time, then walks away. Down the porch steps, back along the sidewalk, disappearing into the darkness between streetlights.

You wait, heart hammering, until they're completely gone.

Your hands are shaking as you review the photos. They're good. Clear enough. The bell is visible. The figure is identifiable, at least to someone who knows them. You have proof that someone placed a bell on the Wilson porch at 11:28pm on Christmas Eve.

But what do you do with it?

What do you do?

Go to Katie's door and show her the photos. Turn to page 216

Drive straight to the police station with the evidence. Turn to page 233

FIND A WAY INTO THE LODGE

You circle the lodge. The stillness presses close. Somewhere in the trees, a single clack—ice letting go and striking ice. The sound travels out and doesn't return. You wait longer than it earns, as if it might mean something twice.

The sky is a low, blank ceiling. You picture the road back: the hairpins, the patch where the car fishtailed and your stomach pretended it didn't. Then you picture the routes if you stay: the side where the rentals came back, the slope toward the treeline, the service door with your scarf over your nose and a torch gripped in your teeth. You can't take them all. You can't leave without choosing the first shape of the story you'll tell about this place.

You step to the service door and press your palm flat to the metal. The cold is clean, almost medicinal. You imagine Rachel's mother coming through in a nightgown and boots before dawn because some sound woke her, and going back to find an empty bed in Rachel's room.

You turn away, sharp, because your head is full of things that did not happen to you, and then turn back to the door and test the handle.

Cold metal, rough with rust. The screws holding it are orange with corrosion, barely gripping the wood. Loose. Decades of weather have worked at the mechanism.

Pull gently. Turn to page 212
Pull hard. Turn to page 210

EXPLORE THE KITCHEN

You move to the kitchen. The sink holds dishes. Ceramic plates gone brown with grime but still recognisable as dishes. Why? Who leaves dishes in the sink when they have six months to pack up?

The small refrigerator door hangs open, interior gutted. Someone cleaned it out thoroughly. But other things remain: the dishes, the furniture, Rachel's drawing on the corkboard. It's selective. Deliberate.

Your fingers trail along the counter, disturbing dust that swirls in the grey light. Six months between Rachel's disappearance and their departure. That's not fleeing in panic. That's time to grieve, to decide, to pack what matters and leave what doesn't.

But what kind of parents leave their daughter's drawing pinned to the wall? Leave the furniture arranged exactly as it was? The couch still facing the television. The chairs still tucked under the table. The corkboard untouched.

Most people would pack it all up. Box the memories. Take them somewhere new, or store them, or give them away. Anything but leave it here like a preserved moment.

Unless they couldn't bear to disturb it.

Or unless they planned to come back.

You're rationalising. You know you are. But standing in this space, imagining Rachel running through it, you can't help but feel for the Van Vleets. They were out of towners, like you. They were a family who lost everything.

Two doors lead off the main room.
Take the left Turn to page 228
Take the right Turn to page 290

PULL HARD

You pull hard. The handle comes away in your hand with a sharp snap—rusted screws giving up all at once. The door swings open from the momentum.

You stand there holding the useless handle, feeling foolish and exposed. Christ. Professional journalist, breaking evidence.

The handle's corroded where the screws were, metal flaking like rust-coloured snow. You set it on the porch railing—can't exactly reattach it now. Already compromised. No point stopping now.

The doorway yawns open, darkness thick despite your phone's flashlight. The door hangs crooked now, won't close properly even if you tried. Wind catches it, making it creak and shift.

You could still leave. But you're here, the door's broken, and somewhere inside is the truth about Rachel Van Vleet—the first name in a list that includes your sister.

You step through. Behind you, the door swings in the wind, banging softly against the frame. Announcing your presence to no one.

You enter the lodge. Turn to page 223

TRY TO CLIMB OUT NOW

You don't waste time. Adrenaline is a drug and you're high on it, the pain distant and manageable. You have to move NOW, before your body realises how broken it is, before the shock wears off and leaves you helpless.

You push yourself up, every muscle protesting. Your right hand finds the wall; rough concrete, decades of grime and ice. You pull, trying to stand, trying to get your feet under you.

Your left leg buckles the moment you put weight on it.

The pain isn't distant anymore. It's immediate, electric, a white-hot spike that shoots from ankle to hip. You collapse, gasping, and the impact of hitting the ground again sends fresh agony through your ribs.

For a moment you can't see, can't think, can't do anything but ride the wave of pain until it crests and begins—barely—to recede.

You're on your side now, curled around your ruined leg, breath coming in short, sharp gasps. The adrenaline is still there, but it's not enough. Not nearly enough.

You force yourself to look around. Turn to page 403

PULL GENTLY

You pull gently, feeling the mechanism resist. The handle turns with a grinding protest, metal on metal, the sound loud in the mountain silence. The door groans but gives, swinging inward on hinges that haven't moved in years. The hinges shriek—a long, rusty complaint that echoes and dies.

You freeze, listening. No response. No footsteps. No voices. Just your own breathing and the whisper of wind through pine branches.

The doorway opens onto darkness. Your phone's flashlight cuts a narrow beam into shadow, catching on dust motes that swirl in the disturbance. The air that comes from inside is different: stale but not as cold as it should be, like the building is holding onto something.

You could still turn back. Document the exterior, come back with better equipment, with someone else. But you're here now. The door's open.

You step through, pulling the door closed behind you until it settles against the frame with a soft click.

You enter the lodge. Turn to page 223

WALK BACK TO TOWN

You watch the taillights disappear down the mountain road, swallowed by trees and snow. Five miles. You've walked farther than that. You're in decent shape. You have your phone, even without signal. You have your flashlight.

You can do this.

The road is a pale ribbon through the darkness, barely visible under fresh snow. You start walking, boots crunching. Your breath clouds white in the beam of your flashlight.

The cold bites immediately. The kind of cold that finds every gap in your clothing, every exposed inch of skin. Your ears burn. Your fingers ache even inside your gloves.

You walk faster. Generate heat. Keep moving.

The trees press close on both sides, heavy with snow. Somewhere in the distance, you hear something crack. A branch breaking under ice. Or something else.

You keep walking.

Your phone is dead weight in your pocket. No signal this far up. Even if you had one, who would you call? Your parents? Katie? They'd never make it up here in time.

Keep walking.

The road curves. You follow it, flashlight beam swinging through the darkness. How far have you gone? A mile? Less? It's hard to judge distance in the dark, in the cold, when every step looks like the last.

Your teeth are chattering now. The shivering has started, that deep-body tremor that means you're losing heat faster than you can generate it.

Should have gone into the lodge. Should have found shelter, started a fire, waited until morning.

No. The lodge is where children disappear. The lodge is where it all started.

The road. Stick to the road.

Another curve. The trees thin slightly and you catch a glimpse of the valley below, the distant lights of Pine Hollow barely visible through the snow. So far away. Too far.

Your legs are heavy. Each step takes effort. The cold is inside you now, settling into your bones.

And then you hear it.

An engine.

You stop, turn. Headlights appear around the curve behind you, bright and blinding.

Relief floods through you. Larkin came back. Changed his mind. Or someone else, some late-night driver heading down the mountain.

You wave your flashlight, stepping to the side of the road. "Hey! HEY!"

The truck accelerates.

The realization hits a second before the bumper does.

He never intended to let you walk away.

The impact throws you into the air. You have a moment of weightlessness, almost peaceful, before you hit the ground. Snow cushions nothing. The world is white and red and then nothing at all.

The truck's brake lights glow red through the falling snow. It sits there for a moment, engine idling.

Then it backs up.

The tire catches your arm first. You feel the bone snap, distant and strange, like it's happening to someone else. You try to scream but your lungs won't fill.

Sheriff Larkin climbs out. His boots crunch in the snow beside your head.

"Told you not to wander into the woods," he says quietly. "But you never were good at listening."

He drags your body off the road. It doesn't take long. You don't weigh much, and the snow is deep here, piled against the trees.

By morning, you'll be buried. Just another person who got lost in the Frost Mountains. Just another name added to Pine Hollow's long list of winter tragedies.

The truck drives away, taillights fading into the dark.

The snow keeps falling.

THE END

You died from blunt force trauma when Sheriff Larkin ran you down on the mountain road. He then dragged your body into the woods where it will never be found.

Your mistake was believing he would actually let you walk away. When a man who serves the King of Christmas offers you mercy, it's not mercy. It's a trap. The moment you refused to leave Pine Hollow, your fate was sealed. Larkin's "generous offer" to walk back to town was never an act of compassion. It was simply choosing where and how to dispose of you.

You trusted a wolf who smiled and showed you the door.

The King of Christmas continued his work.

TAKE THE PHOTOS TO KATIE

You're out of the car before you can second-guess yourself.

The photos feel like fire in your cell phone as you cross the street. Proof. Real, undeniable proof. Katie needs to see this. Katie needs to know that someone is placing bells, that you caught them, that this changes everything.

You climb the porch steps, careful not to disturb the bell still sitting on the doormat. You'll need that too. Evidence.

You take a photograph of it, lying there like a bomb.

Then you knock on Katie's door. Quiet but firm.

For a long moment, nothing. Then footsteps. The porch light blazes on. The door opens a crack.

Katie stands there in her pyjamas and robe, face creased with sleep. "Jenny?" She blinks. "What are you doing here? It's almost midnight."

"I need to show you something." You hand her your phone. "I was watching your house. Someone came. Someone placed the bell."

Katie looks down at the silver trinket in the snow.

"The bell," she repeats. "You saw?"

"Yes!" You can't contain your excitement, but Katie has a stone-faced stillness that you read as shock.

"You were watching my house."

"Yes! I got photos."

She scrolls through them.

"Look," you say, jabbing your finger at an image on the screen. "This person - do you know them? We need to call the police right now, we need to…"

"Jenny." Katie's voice is quiet. Careful. "Come inside."

"We don't have time to…"

"Inside. Now." Her eyes flick past you, scanning the dark street. "Before someone sees you standing on my porch at midnight with your phone out."

She's right. It could be dangerous. He could come back.

You follow her in.

The living room is warm, dim. A Christmas tree in the corner, lights unplugged. Katie closes the door, throws the bolt. Turns to face you.

"Let me see everything," she says.

She swipes through the pictures. You got a lot. You did well.

"See? This person came at 11:27. Placed the bell. Left. I got clear shots of their face, their…"

"Dennis Harper," Katie says quietly. "He works at the grocery store."

You stare at her. "You know him?"

"Of course. Everyone knows everyone in Pine Hollow." She looks up at you. "Can I ask you something?"

"What?"

"Why didn't you stop him? You were right there. You could have confronted him, caught him. Why just take pictures?"

The question catches you off guard. "I… I thought documentation was more important. Evidence that would hold up…"

"You wanted proof before you acted." Katie nods slowly. "That's very professional of you. Very *journalist*." She's still holding your phone. "Can I get you something? Coffee? Tea? You must be freezing after sitting in that car."

"Katie, we need to call the police. Show them these photos. They can pick up Dennis Harper tonight, question him…"

"Of course." Katie moves toward the kitchen. "But first, sit down. Warm up. You're shaking."

You are shaking. Adrenaline and cold and the weight of what you've discovered. You sink onto the couch.

Katie disappears into the kitchen. You hear water running. The clink of mugs.

She still has your phone.

She returns a few minutes later with two steaming mugs. Herbal tea, by the smell. She hands you one, sits in the chair across from you. Your phone rests on the arm of her chair.

"Drink," she says gently. "You look like you need it."

You take a sip. It's hot, slightly bitter, soothing. You take another.

"You've never seen before?" you ask. "All these years and you've never…?"

Katie shakes her head slowly.

"How lucky that you came back," she says, but her voice is flat.

Something's not right.

"All… these…"

Your voice sounds wrong.

Your mouth feels wrong.

Your wrong feels head.

No. That's not…

"What…?"

Your eyes ask the question that your drugged brain can't build.

"I'm sorry," Katie says with an expression that looks just the opposite. "My niece is upstairs asleep. I can't let you put her in danger."

"Whaaa…? I…"

You don't understand, that's what you want to say, but even with the poison working its way through your system there are shreds of understanding seeping through.

Whatever is going on in Pine Hollow, Katie is part of it.

And if the sister of someone who was taken is part of this…

Maybe everyone is.

"I'm sorry," Katie says again, as the room starts to darken around you.

She stands, picking up your phone, and holds it up to your face to reopen the lockscreen.

"I'll tell your parents you had to go home," she says. "Don't worry. They don't need to know they lost you too."

No.

It's too late. There's nothing more to say. No more decisions to make.

Your eyes close, and the darkness takes you.

THE END

You died in Katie Wilson's living room on Christmas Eve, 2025, poisoned by a woman trying to protect her niece. But from what?

Your parents received a text from your phone: "Emergency at the paper. Have to get back to Boston. Sorry I couldn't stay for Christmas." They believed it.

The King of Christmas continued his work.

DROP THE IDEA

Your throat feels tight, but you force the words out.

"Fine. You're right. I won't do it."

Relief flickers across Katie's face. Siobhan's expression stays hard, but her shoulders ease just slightly.

"I'm sorry," you add, quieter than you mean to. "I shouldn't have said anything."

Katie nods quickly, seizing on your surrender. "Get some rest, Jenny. That's all anyone can do."

You gather the folder against your chest and head for the stairs. Each step creaks beneath your boots, louder than the words you swallowed. By the time you reach the hallway, you feel hollow, as if you've been scolded like a child and sent to bed.

Inside Room 12, the air smells faintly of radiator heat and old dust. You close the door, set the folder on the bed, and press your palms to your face. The idea of sitting out in the dark, waiting for something you might not even see, seems absurd now. You're not a cop. You're not invincible. You're a reporter, and reporters work with stories, not stakeouts.

You sink onto the bed, forcing your breath steady. Fine. No stakeout. Not tonight. There are other ways forward: interviews, records, the long, careful work of piecing truth together. Dangerous or not, you'll do your job the way you always have.

The storm thickens outside the window, snow hissing against the glass. You open the folder, thumbing through your father's notes, and let the weight of other possibilities settle in.

You spread the pages across the bed. You've read thousands of case files. Police reports, witness statements, forensic analyses. Your father's handwriting is spidery and desperate, but the information is information. You know how to extract signal from noise. You've done this your entire career: taken raw evidence and shaped it into narrative. This is just another file. Just another case.

Except it's not.

You push the thought away and focus on the pages. Some are maps: hand-drawn sketches of Evergreen Lane, the tree line, the routes between houses. Others are timelines, lists of names, fragments of overheard conversations your father captured in his blocky handwriting. There's even a crude map of the old logging camp, overlaid with a sketch of where the ski resort stood. How much changes in a small town, you think. How much stays the same.

Your eyes jump from date to date, looking for the pattern. 1980, 1981, 1983, 1986. You're trained to spot inconsistencies, to find the gaps that matter. Some pages are dense with your father's observations: cars, strangers, odd behaviours. You flip past them. Context is useful, but you need the skeleton first. The structure.

1980: Claire Henderson.

Your father's blocky handwriting hovers on the page: *No one mentions bells until Hendersons receive their THIRD.* Underlined twice. Another note in the margin: *Won't talk now.* The page smells faintly of old coffee and winter air trapped in paper. You can almost hear the hush that must have followed that first admission; a town realising coincidence with a timetable isn't coincidence at all.

1978: David Drake.

A thinner line of ink. *Mother deceased.* Then a harder, darker stroke: *Father unreachable.* The words feel like frost. Not dramatic, just killing-cold. Your father has circled the date, then scratched at the circle until the paper thinned. Whatever he learned here, it wasn't from official files.

1976: Rachel Van Vleet.

Below your father has drawn blunt arrow to a sketched map of the **ski resort**. Another margin note: *Out-of-towners. Where did they go?*

Then, one last sentence, cramped: *Do they still get bells, wherever they are?*

You sit back, palms flat on the quilt. The story isn't linear here; it radiates from the mountains, the crumbling lifts, the shuttered lodge, the empty runs blowing with spindrift. If there is a beginning to this story, it isn't just a bell on a porch. It is a door opening in that resort, and a family losing their daughter then leaving town within six months.

It's a mother recognising that the bells started coming the year after her own daughter was taken, and never stopped even though four decades passed.

You close your eyes and hear Katie's warning again: *the Hendersons won't talk about the bells.* Maybe they can't. But they were the first to name them, and first truths tend to leave echoes.

The resort offers a different kind of truth: the kind that doesn't have to speak.

You gather the pages, feeling the shape of a choice settle in your hands.

Will you

Pay a visit to the Hendersons? Turn to page 244
Drive up to the ski resort? Turn to page 196

YOU ENTER THE LODGE

The darkness is immediate, absolute, until your phone's flashlight cuts a narrow beam into it. A hallway extends ahead, walls close enough to touch on both sides. The floor is concrete, cracked and uneven, with patches of ice where water seeped through and froze. Your breath clouds white in the beam.

It's warmer inside than out, but only just. The building holds cold differently; here it's trapped, stale, the kind that seeps into your bones slowly.

The smell hits you: mildew, old wood, something chemical and sharp underneath. Rodent droppings. The specific decay of a place where organic and synthetic materials break down together in the dark.

You're in a service corridor. Staff entrance. The walls are painted institutional green, paint peeling in long strips. Pipes run along the ceiling, wrapped in deteriorating insulation that hangs in grey tatters. Doors line both sides. You poke into storage closets, maintenance rooms, the infrastructure guests never saw.

One door hangs open. Your light catches metal shelving inside, cleaning supplies in plastic bottles gone brittle with age, mops with wooden handles warped from decades of temperature swings.

This is the back of house. The hidden machinery that kept the resort running. You're seeing it from the wrong side, the employee perspective, and it feels like trespassing in a way the front entrance wouldn't have.

At the end of the hallway, maybe thirty feet ahead, the darkness shifts to something lighter. Grey instead of black. Natural light filtering in from somewhere.

You move toward it, your footsteps too loud on concrete, each step echoing and multiplying until it sounds like someone's following you.

You stop. Listen. Nothing. Just your own breathing and the building settling around you, wood contracting in the cold with soft groans that could almost be voices if you let yourself imagine.

Don't imagine. Document. Move.

The hallway ends at a doorway. No door, just the frame, opening onto a larger space. The light comes from there—windows, probably, high ones, letting in the last of the afternoon.

You step through.

The first thing you see is the back of a long wooden counter. Front desk. You're standing where the staff stood, looking out at the lobby from the wrong side, and the perspective is all wrong. Like walking onto a stage from the wings and seeing the audience seating from behind the curtain.

The lobby opens up before you: two stories, ceiling high above, supported by dark wood beams. A chandelier hangs in the centre, massive thing of wrought iron and dead bulbs, swaying slightly in a draft you can't feel. The walls are wood-panelled, stained dark, water damage blooming across them in patterns that look almost deliberate.

Furniture fills the space: frames of couches and armchairs, upholstery long since rotted to tatters. Mouse nests spill from the cushions. The coffee tables are intact, solid wood, but their surfaces are warped from decades of moisture. The stone fireplace dominates the far wall, but you guess there hasn't been any heat from it for a long time. Your breath fogs in front of you and you wish for a moment for logs.

Underneath the decay, the structure holds. And the layout remains a map of what this place was.

A rusted coat rack stands near what must be the main entrance, frame still upright, hooks intact. Scraps of fabric hang from two of the hooks, all that remains of coats left behind.

A metal sign hangs crooked on the wall behind the front desk: "Pine Hollow Ski Lodge - Established 1970 - Van Vleet Family, Proprietors." The letters are tarnished but legible.

You move around the counter, examining the front desk. The wood is scarred and water-stained but solid. Nothing sits on its surface. No papers, no guest book, nothing that would have survived five decades of exposure. But the desk itself is intact, drawers still sliding open on rusted runners.

The cash register squats to one side, ancient mechanical thing of metal and keys. Unlike everything else, it looks almost preserved. You press the largest button. The drawer springs open with a DING that cracks through the silence.

You freeze, heart hammering, the sound echoing up into the rafters.

Inside the drawer: tarnished coins still sorted in their compartments. A few bills so degraded they're barely recognisable as currency, but the denominations are visible: ones, fives. Maybe twenty dollars total. More than forty-nine years ago, anyway.

Who abandons cash in the register?

And why is this place still standing? Failed resort, missing child, owners who fled; the property should've been foreclosed, seized, sold decades ago. Even in small towns, someone always wants the land. Unless people were afraid to touch it.

This isn't abandonment. This is avoidance.

And the police search? Where's the evidence? No tape, no seals, no signs they systematically processed this scene. Maybe time erased it. Or maybe they never searched as thoroughly as they should have.

The thought sits wrong, but you push it away. You're here for answers, not to second-guess decade-old police work.

You pull out your phone. You need photos: the lobby, the cash register, the coat rack with its fabric scraps. Every detail matters.

This is your story, your evidence. The resort frozen in time, the Van Vleets' abandoned business, the place where it all started.

The screen lights up. 6%.

What?

You stare at the number, not understanding. It was at 54% when you left the Inn. You're sure of it. You remember checking it before you got in the car, seeing the battery indicator comfortably in the green.

That was… what, an hour ago? Less?

Cold. The cold drains batteries. You knew that, should've anticipated it, but not THIS fast. Not from 54% to 6% in under an hour.

Your chest tightens.

6% in an abandoned building, miles from town, no one knowing you're here, temperature dropping as the sun sets. If the battery dies completely, you have no light. No way to call for help. No navigation back down the mountain if the weather turns.

You could take photos now. Document everything while you still have the chance. Take photos that could matter, that could mean something if you can connect them to Rachel's disappearance, to Sarah's, to all of them.

But every photo drains the battery faster. Every flash, every moment the screen stays lit. The camera is the single biggest power draw.

Or you could save it. Minimal use, just for light when absolutely necessary. Keep enough battery to call someone if you need extraction. If something goes wrong.

Take photos. Turn to page 237
Save your battery. Turn to page 269

STAKEOUT AT YOUR PARENTS

On Evergreen Lane, you sit in the cold car, engine ticking as it cools, and stare at the house across the street. Through the front window, you can see the living room lamp casting its warm glow. Someone's awake. Of course they are. Your mother never sleeps on Christmas Eve. Not since Sarah.

Thirty-nine years without her. Merry Christmas.

You came here because this felt like the right tactical choice; your parents' house is one of the four that will receive a bell tonight. You could watch from the car, see who places it, maybe even follow them. Stay separate. Stay in control.

But the cold is already seeping through your coat, and you know yourself well enough to admit the truth: you'll fall asleep out here. Or freeze. Or lose your nerve entirely and drive back to the Inn with nothing to show for it but frostbite and shame.

And there's something else, something that's been gnawing at you since you drove back into Pine Hollow. Since you were old enough to leave, you've been running from this house, from these people, from the guilt that lives in every corner of your childhood bedroom. Maybe it's time to stop running. Maybe it's time to let them in.

You kill the engine. The sudden silence is profound.

Go inside. Turn to page 242

THE MASTER BEDROOM

The master bedroom is sparse. This was where the Van Vleets slept. A double bed, stripped bare, mattress water-stained and sagging. A dresser with drawers hanging open at odd angles. A closet door ajar, showing empty hangers. Through an open doorway, you glimpse a small bathroom - toilet, sink, shower stall, all coated in grime.

You move to the dresser first. Your torch illuminates the first drawer - empty, wood swollen from decades of moisture. The second holds rotted fabric, maybe sheets or clothing, impossible to tell now.

The third drawer stops you.

Folded clothes. Men's clothes. Jeans, t-shirts, flannel shirts.

But these aren't from the seventies.

Your torch catches on details: modern denim, darker wash, slim cut. A t-shirt with a logo you recognise - a craft brewery that opened in the 2000s. These aren't old. They're faded, worn, but not decades-old.

Someone's been here. Recently. Using this space.

You pull open the fourth drawer. More clothes. Different sizes, different styles. Some look nearly new. One t-shirt still has the tag attached.

Your mind races. Squatters? Homeless people using the abandoned building as shelter? That would explain the warmth, the maintenance, why the apartment hasn't completely disintegrated.

But the arrangement bothers you. The clothes are folded. Organised. Not thrown in, not rummaged through. Placed carefully, like someone's been leaving them. For someone else to find.

A donation system, maybe? Local churches sometimes leave supplies in abandoned buildings for transients. You've heard of that in cities. Could happen in small towns too. The explanation doesn't quite fit, but you don't have a better one.

But why hasn't anyone mentioned it? You've been asking questions all over Pine Hollow. No one said: "Oh yeah, people use the old ski lodge as a shelter." No one warned you that squatters might be up here.

Maybe they don't know. It's isolated, miles from town. Or maybe it's so commonplace no one thought to mention it.

Or maybe…

You push the thought away. The explanation is uncomfortable enough without adding conspiracy theories.

Above the bed, you notice a square hatch in the ceiling. Storage space. Attic or loft. There might be something up there still.

Pull open the hatch. Turn to page 230
Go back and explore the other room. Turn to page 420

PULL OPEN THE HATCH

You climb onto the bed. The mattress sinks under your boots, springs groaning. The frame sags, soft from years of damp. You steady yourself with one hand on the wall.

The hatch has no cord, no handle. Just a wooden panel flush with the ceiling. You raise your torch, press the end against it, and push. Nothing. You shift your stance, feel the mattress compress beneath you, and push harder.

The panel jerks. Shifts an inch. Then...

A sharp crack. The hatch swings open.

The ladder drops fast, metal flashing in your beam. You lurch back, boot slipping on the sagging mattress. It slams into the bedframe where your head just was. Metal on wood, loud as a gunshot.

You catch yourself against the wall, pulse hammering. The ladder sways, still intact. Above, darkness yawns: one way up, one way down. You push that thought away.

Just a quick look. Five minutes.

You grab the ladder. The rungs are cold, rust rough beneath your palm. First rung. Second. It holds. You climb.

Your head clears the opening. The loft is bigger than you expected. The full length of the apartment below. Low ceiling, beams slanting down at the sides. You crouch, torch sweeping the space.

Boxes. Dozens of them. Cardboard splitting, stacked in corners. Others, plastic bins, sit newer, out of place. The air is thick with dust; you taste it when you breathe.

You haul yourself up, boots on plywood. Solid. Someone built this to bear weight.

You open a box: papers. Old invoices, maintenance logs from 1975, 1976. The paperwork of a business already dying. Another holds moth-eaten curtains. Another, broken ski gear.

Nothing useful. Just the remnants of a life packed away.

Still, if the Van Vleets really left after Rachel vanished, why leave all this? Files, linens, supplies. You'd expect emptiness. Bare walls, not rooms caught mid-breath, as if someone stepped out one winter and never came back.

The thought sticks as you move deeper into the loft. Your torch catches on something that doesn't belong here: a row of opaque blue bins, snap-lid, modern. The kind you'd buy anywhere. Too new for this place.

You drag one toward you, pop the latches, lift the lid.

Inside: Christmas.

Garlands, strings of lights, ornaments dulled by time. Enough to deck the entire lobby of the lodge.

You brush aside a tangle of tinsel, a cracked glass bauble, a velvet ribbon turned grey with dust. They're old (the originals, from the resort's first winters) but they couldn't have been left here like this. Not packed so neatly, not in boxes that didn't exist fifty years ago.

You shift the top layer aside, and something glints beneath. Bells. Dozens of them. Layer on layer, heavy and silent, their silver dulled but unmistakable.

Every one identical to the bells that haunt your parents' doorstep.

And then the connection hits you. The folded clothes in the dresser downstairs, modern denim, shirts with fresh creases. The same careful hands that placed those drawers have been here, too. The clothes, the decorations, the bells. Not remnants. Preparations.

Someone's been keeping this place.

A sound breaks the stillness.

A door slams below. Hard, sudden, close enough to shake dust from the rafters. You jerk upright, heart in your throat. Silence follows for a beat... and then, faint but unmistakable, comes whistling.

A tune you know too well.

The notes drift up through the cracks in the floorboards, light and careless, echoing through the hollow rooms. A Christmas song, in an empty lodge.

Santa Claus is coming to town.

You kill the torch. Darkness presses close, thick as cloth.

The whistling goes on, unhurried, tuneless between verses.

He's here.

Your thoughts splinter into choices:

Hide. **Turn to page 395**
Get out of the loft. Now. **Turn to page 362**
Phone someone. **Turn to page 195**

TAKE THE PHOTOS TO POLICE

You start the car.

The police station. That's where this evidence needs to go. Sheriff Larkin might not have taken your father's research seriously, but this is different. This is photographic proof of someone placing a bell on Christmas Eve.

The drive through Pine Hollow is short. The station is on Main Street, a squat brick building with two cruisers parked outside. Lights on inside. Someone's working the night shift.

You park, grab your phone, check the photos one more time. Clear. Damning. Perfect.

The front door is unlocked. A blast of warm air hits you as you step inside.

The lobby is small, fluorescent-lit. A desk behind protective glass. A deputy you don't recognise looks up from his computer.

"Help you?"

"I need to see Sheriff Larkin. It's urgent."

The deputy glances at the clock on the wall. 11:48pm. "Sheriff's not here. You can talk to me, or come back in the morning."

"This can't wait until morning." You pull out your phone. "I have evidence of a crime in progress. Someone placing a bell at a victim's house. Tonight. I have photos."

The deputy's expression changes. Something flickers in his eyes. Not surprise. Recognition.

"Photos," he repeats slowly.

"Yes. Clear images. I can identify the person. I watched them place a bell on the Wilson porch less than thirty minutes ago."

The deputy stands. "Let me make a call. Have a seat."

He disappears through a door marked AUTHORISED PERSONNEL ONLY.

You wait. The plastic chairs are uncomfortable. The clock ticks. You review the photos again, making sure they're all there, all clear. Five minutes pass. Ten.

The door opens. Sheriff Larkin steps through.

"Miss Matthews." His voice is carefully neutral. "Deputy Carson says you have some photos to show me."

"Yes." You stand, relief flooding through you. "I was conducting a stakeout at the Wilson house. I witnessed someone placing a bell. I got photographic evidence."

"I see." Larkin gestures toward the door. "Why don't you come back to my office. We can look at them properly."

You follow him through. The hallway is narrow, lined with filing cabinets and wanted posters. His office is at the end - small, cluttered, smelling of coffee and old paper.

He closes the door behind you. Gestures to a chair.

You sit. Pull out your phone. Start swiping through the photos.

"This is at 11:27pm," you explain. "The Wilson house on Birch Street. You can see the figure approaching. Here they're placing the bell. Here's a close-up of their face. Do you recognise them?"

Larkin studies the screen. His jaw tightens.

"Dennis Harper," he says quietly.

"You know him?"

"Everyone knows everyone." He looks up at you. "Can I see your phone?"

You hand it over. He swipes through the photos slowly, methodically. Then he closes the photo app. Opens your messages. Your call log.

"What are you doing?" you ask.

"Checking if you sent these to anyone." He looks at you over the screen. "Did you? Email them to yourself? Upload them to cloud storage?"

Something cold settles in your stomach. "Why does that matter?"

"Because," Larkin says, setting the phone on his desk, "I need to know how big of a problem we have."

"Problem?" You stand. "Those photos are evidence of…"

"Of Dennis Harper doing exactly what he was told to do." Larkin's voice is flat. "Along with three other people placing bells at three other houses tonight."

The room tilts. "What?"

You look at the door, because something tells you that you should be trying to get through it now.

You need to get out of here.

Nothing good is about to happen.

"Don't think about it," Larkin says. Not a threat. Just a fact. "Carson's outside. You won't make it past the lobby."

"You're supposed to protect people."

"I am protecting people." He stands, points at the crayoned Christmas card on his desk. "I have a son. He's seven years old." His voice cracks. "He's *seven*. Do you understand?"

You don't understand, but at the same time you do.

"This is insane…"

"This is survival." Larkin moves around the desk. "And you just made it very complicated. If Dennis Harper saw you, he'll report it. And when the King of Christmas learns someone was watching, learns the system was compromised…" He closes his eyes. "Another child will be taken. To remind us…"

"Then stop him!" Your voice breaks. "Help me stop him!"

"That's not how this is going to go down," he says, reaching for something on his belt.

Not his phone.

His gun.

"I have a son," he says quietly. "I have to protect him. That's all any of us are doing. Protecting what's left."

The last thing you see is his hand, steady, raising the weapon.

The last thing you hear is his voice, sad and resigned: "I'm sorry."

Then the gunshot.

Then nothing.

THE END

You died in Sheriff Larkin's office on Christmas Eve, 2025.
The King of Christmas continued his work.

TAKE PHOTOS

Behind the desk, a door marked with a small brass plaque: "Private."

You try the handle. It turns. Unlocked.

The door opens onto a staircase climbing into darkness. Narrow, steep, the kind of utilitarian stairs that weren't meant for guests. These lead up to staff quarters, probably. To where the owners lived while running the business.

To where the Van Vleets lived.

To where Rachel grew up.

Your throat tightens.

This is it. Not the public face of the resort, but the private space. The family home above the failing business. Where Rachel had a bedroom, where she played, where she woke up Christmas morning before she vanished.

If there are answers, they're up there.

The stairs creak under your weight, wood protesting each step. The sound echoes in the narrow stairwell, multiplying, making it seem like more than one person is climbing. You pause, listening, but there's nothing. Just your own footsteps reflected back at you.

The stairs end at a door. Plain, no lock. You turn the handle and step through.

Your torch beam sweeps the space—a single open room, living area, maybe four hundred square feet. There's a kitchen off to one side, and two other doors leading off this main room. No frills, all function.

You pull out your phone. 5%. That's what you have. But you need these photos. This is evidence—the Van Vleets' apartment, preserved, the family home where Rachel lived.

You raise the phone, frame the shot: the living area, the couch, the table, all of it in one wide angle. Tap. Flash illuminates dust motes swirling. The image saves.

4%.

The apartment is warmer here. Not warm, but noticeably less cold than the lobby below.

The furniture is simple, practical: a couch facing a small television, a table with three chairs. Everything covered in dust, fabric rotted, surfaces warped—but the shapes remain. You can read the life that happened here in the arrangement of objects.

You take another photo: the temperature won't show, but the context will. The furniture arrangement, the preserved layout.

Tap. Flash.

4%. Still.

Your torch finds a corkboard on the wall near the open kitchen door. Faded papers pinned to it. You step closer. A child's drawing in crayon, the colours bleached to ghosts but the lines still visible: a house, a mountain, stick figures holding hands. The writing across the top is barely legible, faded to pale brown: *"Me and Mommy and Daddy."*

Rachel drew this.

Your throat tightens.

You frame it carefully, make sure the writing is visible.

Tap. Flash.

3%.

Your heart rate picks up. Three percent. Maybe ten photos left, maybe less. You need to be strategic. Document what matters most. Take a few more photos and leave before dark falls.

The Van Vleets came here with dreams. Young couple, buying a struggling ski resort, believing optimism and hard work would be enough. Rachel sitting on that couch watching cartoons. Robert making coffee while his wife reviewed reservations. Ordinary life, mountain isolation, building something.

Then Christmas Eve 1976. Rachel was gone. Within six months, the Van Vleets vanished too, destroyed by grief.

That's the story.

But standing here with your phone dying and your torch beam catching on details that don't fit: the apartment too preserved, the dust not thick enough, the smell of fresh pine underneath decay. You know the story is wrong.

Document first. Analyse later.

Two doors lead off the main room. You need to see both, photograph both, before your phone dies completely.

From here you can
Explore the kitchen. Turn to page 241
Open the door to the left. Turn to page 247
Open the door to the right. Turn to page 257

SAVE YOUR BATTERY

You could call your parents. Tell them where you are. But that 12% might be all you have. Up at the lodge earlier, when your phone died, you had no way to take photographs, no way to contact anyone. You learned that lesson already.

Better to keep it in reserve. Just in case.

You slip the phone back into your pocket.

Through the windshield, you watch the dark lodge and wait for the sheriff to return.

You'll see your parents soon enough. After this. When you have real answers to share.

You'll tell them everything then.

The service door opens. Turn to page 282

EXPLORE THE KITCHEN

You move to the kitchen. The sink holds dishes—ceramic plates gone brown with grime but still recognisable as dishes. Why? Who leaves dishes in the sink when fleeing?

The small refrigerator door hangs open, interior gutted. Someone cleaned it out. Someone took the time, in their grief and panic, to empty the refrigerator before leaving. That doesn't match the narrative of parents so destroyed they walked away from everything.

Your fingers trail along the counter, disturbing dust that swirls in the grey light. How much time did they have between Rachel's disappearance and their departure? Enough to clean out perishables. Enough to decide what to take and what to leave. Enough to make it look like they left in a hurry without actually leaving in a hurry.

Or maybe grief does strange things to people. Makes them perform small tasks like washing dishes or emptying refrigerators, because the enormity of loss is too much to face directly.

You're rationalising. You know you are. But standing in this space, imagining Rachel running through it, you can't help but feel for the Van Vleets. They were out of towners, like you. They were a family who lost everything.

There's nothing here you want to waste your phone's battery on. The dishes, the cleaned-out fridge: they're details, context, but not evidence of what you need to prove. Save the battery. You have maybe eight or nine photos left before the phone dies completely.

Two doors lead off the main room.

Take the left door. Turn to page 247
Take the right door. Turn to page 257

GO INSIDE FOR THE STAKEOUT

You grab your phone and flashlight, leaving everything else in the car. The walk across the street feels longer than it should, your boots crunching through fresh snow.

That was only twelve hours ago, but it feels like days.

You knock. Wait. The door opens almost immediately.

Your mother stands there, still dressed, eyes widening when she sees you. "Jenny?"

"Can I come in?"

She steps back without a word, and you're inside, pulling off your boots in the same entryway where you stood this morning. Your father appears in the living room doorway, concern etched across his face.

"I thought you were staying at the Inn," he says.

"I was." You meet his eyes. "I want to do a stake out. I mean, I am. I am going to. And I realised…" Your voice cracks slightly. "I realised I can't do this alone. Not tonight."

Your mother's hand finds your arm. "You want to watch from here."

It's not a question. She understands immediately.

"The bell will be left here tonight," you say. "One of the four houses. I need to see who places it. But if I stay in the car, I'll freeze. Or fall asleep. Or…"

"Or you'll be alone," your father finishes quietly.

You nod, throat tight. "You're the only people I can trust. Katie and Siobhan… I want to trust them, but…"

You don't finish. You don't need to. Whether it's instinct or something they said, something about them makes you hesitate. And right now, hesitation means you can't rely on them.

Your family has always been different, here. Your parents have lived here for over four decades and they are still comer-inners. And you? What are you now?

Your mother guides you to the sofa, the same sofa where you sat this morning, coffee growing cold as you talked about Sarah. The folder your father gave you is still in your car, but its contents are burned into your memory. The map with the four houses circled in red. The years of observations. The weight of his obsession turned survival.

"Of course you can stay," your mother says. "We'll watch together."

Your father settles into his chair.

"Have you ever tried to watch before?" you ask.

Your father's laugh is bitter, empty. "Every year. Every single Christmas Eve since 1986, we've watched. Taken turns. Sat by the window. Left the porch light on, turned it off, tried every combination we could think of."

"And?" Your voice is barely a whisper.

"And the bell always comes," your mother says quietly. "We've never seen who leaves it. Not once in thirty-nine years. We watch all night, we don't sleep, and then in the morning…" She gestures helplessly. "It's there. On the porch. Like it appeared out of nowhere."

The hair on the back of your neck stands up. "That's impossible."

"We know," your father says. "But it happens anyway."

You think about the other families. The Hendersons, the Wilsons. Have they tried watching too? Have they spent years staring out windows, waiting for something they never see? Will the Crawfords watch for the first time tonight?

"Maybe three of us will make the difference," you say, though you don't quite believe it.

Your mother's hand tightens on yours. "Maybe."

But tonight, that changes. It has to.

Continue to stakeout at your parents'. Turn to page 293

THE HENDERSONS

The Hendersons' house looks smaller than you remember. A squat Victorian with its curtains drawn, the garlands on the porch out of kilter with the sorrow you know exists within.

You hesitate at the gate, the folder pressed to your chest, and the old ache stirs. After Sarah vanished, you used to walk past the other houses: Tommy Wilson's, Claire Henderson's, David Drake's. The four town families. Your father called them the *ones who stayed*.

The ski resort was always out of bounds, and there was no one there to pay your respects to anyway, if that's what you thought you were doing.

To be honest, you never really knew.

For you, those three houses here in Pine Hollow became landmarks. No one else went missing until after you left, no more houses added to your route after Sarah. For nine years, the town breathed again.

You were already at college when the silence broke. One of the first years you didn't come home for Christmas. You were with friends instead, half-drunk on spiced wine in a cramped apartment strung with fairy lights, when your mother called. She talked about the cards, the presents, the roast goose, her voice striving for cheer. Then, almost as an afterthought, she said Daniel Peak had been taken.

Her words tilted the room. You remember the laughter of your friends in the background, the clink of glasses, and how far away it all suddenly felt. You pressed the receiver harder to your ear, waiting for her to tell you it was a mistake, a rumour. But all she said was, "*Another boy, same as before.*"

You didn't come home that year, not even after the call. And by the next Christmas, Pine Hollow was no longer just the place you left. It was a place that kept swallowing children while you pretended distance could keep you safe.

And now, three decades later, you're standing on the Hendersons' porch with snow in your hair and the same hollow in your chest.

You knock.

The door opens a crack. A woman peers out. You recognise her, but she's thirty years older now, lined deep, her sweater pulled high at the throat. She doesn't ask your name. She doesn't need to. Her eyes flicker with recognition, then sharpen into something harder.

"We don't talk," she says. Her voice is hoarse, clipped.

You clear your throat. "I'm not here for headlines. I just... Claire was..."

Her hand tightens on the doorframe. "Don't say her name."

The words freeze you.

"You hear me?" she snaps, louder now. "Don't you dare come onto my porch, dragging up ghosts you left behind. You ran off to your big-city paper, didn't you? Left the rest of us here to carry it. And now you come back, stirring it all up like it's a story for you to print?"

You swallow hard. "I just want to understand..."

"You want to understand?" Her voice cracks with fury, but there's fear underneath. "You think you're the first? The police came. Reporters came. They all left, just like you will. Nothing changes. Nothing ever changes."

Through the gap you glimpse the hallway: dark wood, a coat rack bristling with scarves, traces of something like a normal life. But this is *not* normal.

"Please," you whisper. "If you know something..."

Her eyes pin you through the narrow gap with a look that isn't just dismissal, but warning.

The door snaps shut with a violent crack.

The lock slides, heavy and final.

You stand on the porch while the snow swirls around you, pulse hammering, staring at the grain of the wood as if it might soften.

You step back onto the path, your boots sinking deep. The memory of your younger self lingers – eleven years old, twelve, a teenager – circling these same houses year after year, searching their windows for answers. Nothing then. Nothing now.

And still, standing here at forty, you feel the same as you did at eleven: small, shut out, watching doors close while the town pretends not to hear you. The years haven't changed that. You only grew older; the silence stayed exactly the same.

You stand on the porch and resist the urge to knock again. In Boston, you'd have three other sources by now. You'd have triangulated the story, found someone willing to talk. But here, every door closes before you can get your foot in. Every face shuts down at Sarah's name.

Small towns. Everyone protecting everyone else. Or maybe everyone protecting themselves.

You can't work like this; one source at a time, each one a dead end. You need momentum. You need the break that cracks everything open.

You turn your back on the Hendersons' house, the weight of Claire's mother's stare still burning into your spine. Snow drifts across the porch and into your hair, fine as ash. You brush it away and glance down the street. The houses look the same as they did when you were eleven: shutters tight, curtains drawn, each one hiding something.

Enough doors slammed. Enough silence.

If no one in Pine Hollow will speak, then you'll have to look elsewhere. Back to where Rachel Van Vleet disappeared, where the Van Vleet family left and never came back, where your father's notes trace the very first threads of the story. If Pine Hollow won't give you answers, maybe the mountain will.

Head up to the ski resort. **Turn to page 196**

TAKE THE LEFT DOOR

The master bedroom is sparse. This was where the Van Vleets slept.

You raise your phone immediately. Document first, analyse later. Frame the shot: the bed, the dresser, the stark abandonment.

Tap. Flash.

2%.

Through an open doorway, a bathroom; you take one quick shot. Context.

Tap. Flash.

1%.

One percent left. Maybe one photo, maybe two if you're lucky. Make them count.

You move to the dresser, torch under your arm. Pull open the first drawer: empty. Second drawer: rotted fabric. Third drawer...

You stop.

Folded clothes. Men's clothes. Jeans, t-shirts, flannel shirts.

But these aren't from the seventies.

Your torch catches on details: modern denim, darker wash, slim cut. A t-shirt with a logo you recognise - a craft brewery that opened in the 2000s. These aren't old. They're faded, worn, but not decades old.

Someone's been here. Recently. Using this space.

You pull open the fourth drawer. More clothes. Different sizes, different styles. Some look nearly new. One t-shirt still has the tag attached.

Your mind races. Squatters? Homeless people using the abandoned building as shelter? That would explain the warmth, the maintenance, why the apartment hasn't completely disintegrated.

But the arrangement bothers you. The clothes are folded. Organised. Not thrown in, not rummaged through. Placed carefully, like someone's been leaving them. For someone else to find.

A donation system, maybe? Local churches sometimes leave supplies in abandoned buildings for transients. You've heard of that in cities. Could happen in small towns too. The explanation doesn't quite fit, but you don't have a better one.

But why hasn't anyone mentioned it? You've been asking questions all over Pine Hollow. The sheriff, Katie… No one said: "Oh yeah, people use the old ski lodge as a shelter." No one warned you that squatters might be up here.

Maybe they don't know. It's isolated, miles from town. Or maybe it's so commonplace no one thought to mention it.

Or maybe…

You push the thought away. The explanation is uncomfortable enough without adding conspiracy theories.

You raise your phone with shaking hands. Frame the drawer, the modern clothes clearly visible, the tag still attached to one shirt.

Tap. Flash.

The screen goes black.

You tap again. Nothing. You hold the power button. Nothing. Dead.

But you got the shot. The modern clothes are documented. Proof someone's been here recently. That's something. That's evidence.

Except now you have no phone. No way to take more photos.

Above the bed, you notice a square hatch in the ceiling. Storage space. Attic or loft. There might be something up there still.

Pull open the hatch. Turn to page 352
Go back and explore the other room. Turn to page 345

FIGHT HIM

You lunge at him.

Your fist aims for his face. He moves, faster than you expected, and your knuckles connect with empty air.

You try again. Clawing. Kicking.

He catches your wrist. Twists. Pain shoots up your arm.

And then he laughs.

"HO HO HO!"

The sound echoes through the reception area. Deep. Jolly. Completely wrong.

"Try harder, little girl." He's still laughing, that twisted Santa laugh. "HO HO HO!"

You're not a little girl. You're fifty years old. You want to make it to fifty-one. You want to get out of here, go home, tell someone, anyone what you've found.

It doesn't seem to matter what you want.

He spins you around.

You're facing the fireplace now, the mounted animal heads on either side.

A massive elk. Antlers spreading wide, twelve points at least.

"Let me show you something," he says, voice still carrying that horrible cheer.

He shoves you toward the wall.

You try to stop yourself but you're off balance, stumbling...

The antlers rush toward you.

You feel them puncture. One through your shoulder. One through your side. One...

The pain is blinding.

You're suspended. Mounted. Like the elk whose antlers hold you.

"There we go," he says, stepping back to admire his work. Still that smile in his voice. "Now you're part of the collection."

You try to speak. Blood fills your mouth.

"HO HO HO!" he laughs again. "Merry Christmas, Miss Matthews."

The room tilts. Darkens.

Your last thought: *This can't be how it ends.*

But it is.

THE END

You died in the Van Vleet Ski Lodge on Christmas Eve, 2025, impaled on a mounted elk's antlers. Your body was never found. The King of Christmas added you to his collection.

Your parents waited for a call that never came.

Two Matthews daughters lost to Pine Hollow. Both vanished on Christmas Eve. Both never found.

The King of Christmas continued his work.

GO INTO THE LOFT

You climb onto the bed. The mattress sinks under your boots, springs groaning. The frame sags, soft from years of damp. You steady yourself with one hand on the wall.

The hatch has no cord, no handle. Just a wooden panel flush with the ceiling. You raise your torch, press the end against it, and push. Nothing. You shift your stance, feel the mattress compress beneath you, and push harder.

The panel jerks. Shifts an inch. Then...

A sharp crack. The hatch swings open.

The ladder drops fast, metal flashing in your beam. You lurch back, boot slipping on the sagging mattress. It slams into the bedframe where your head just was. Metal on wood, loud as a gunshot.

You catch yourself against the wall, pulse hammering. The ladder sways, still intact. Above, darkness yawns: one way up, one way down. You push that thought away.

Just a quick look. Five minutes.

You grab the ladder. The rungs are cold, rust rough beneath your palm. First rung. Second. It holds. You climb.

Your head clears the opening. The loft is bigger than you expected. The full length of the apartment below. Low ceiling, beams slanting down at the sides. You crouch, torch sweeping the space.

Boxes. Dozens of them. Cardboard splitting, stacked in corners. Others (plastic bins) sit newer, out of place. The air is thick with dust; you taste it when you breathe.

You haul yourself up, boots on plywood. Solid. Someone built this to bear weight.

You open a box: papers. Old invoices, maintenance logs from 1975, 1976. The paperwork of a business already dying. Another holds moth-eaten curtains. Another, broken ski gear.

Nothing useful. Just the remnants of a life packed away.

Still, if the Van Vleets really left after Rachel vanished, why leave all this? Files, linens, supplies. You'd expect emptiness. Bare walls, not rooms caught mid-breath, as if someone stepped out one winter and never came back.

The thought sticks as you move deeper into the loft. Your torch catches on something that doesn't belong here: a row of opaque blue bins, snap-lid, modern. The kind you'd buy anywhere. Too new for this place.

You drag one toward you, pop the latches, lift the lid.

Inside: Christmas.

Garlands, strings of lights, ornaments dulled by time. Enough to deck the entire lobby of the lodge.

You brush aside a tangle of tinsel, a cracked glass bauble, a velvet ribbon turned grey with dust. They're old (the originals, from the resort's first winters) but they couldn't have been left here like this. Not packed so neatly, not in boxes that didn't exist fifty years ago.

You shift the top layer aside, and something glints beneath. Bells. Dozens of them. Layer on layer, heavy and silent, their silver dulled but unmistakable.

Every one identical to the bells that haunt your parents' doorstep.

And then it hits you. The folded clothes in the dresser downstairs, the shirts still smelling faintly of detergent, the shrine of pine cones and faded photographs laid out with impossible care. Every piece arranged by the same hands.

This place isn't abandoned. It's tended. Loved, even.

The clothes, the decorations, the bells. None of them leftovers from another life.

They're offerings. Devotion disguised as order.

Someone hasn't just been keeping this place.

They've been keeping it alive.

A sound breaks the stillness.

A door slams below. Hard, sudden, close enough to shake dust from the rafters. You jerk upright, heart in your throat. Silence follows for a beat… and then, faint but unmistakable, comes whistling.

A tune you know too well.

The notes drift up through the cracks in the floorboards, light and careless, echoing through the hollow rooms. A Christmas song, in an empty lodge.

Santa Claus is coming to town.

You kill the torch. Darkness presses close, thick as cloth.

The whistling goes on, unhurried, tuneless between verses.

He's here.

Your thoughts splinter into choices.

Hide. Turn to page 395

Get out of the loft. Now. Turn to page 362

Phone someone. Turn to page 195

THE HENDERSONS STAKE OUT

You head toward Maple Drive.

The Hendersons. Claire's family. The oldest victim family still here, forty-five years of bells, forty-five years of silence.

The drive through Pine Hollow is quiet. Christmas Eve has emptied the streets. You pass the church. The parking lot is full, windows glowing warm with candlelight. Voices rise in hymn: Silent night, holy night…

But as you turn onto Maple Drive, you notice that several houses are lit up too. People are home. Not everyone went to church tonight.

The curtains are drawn at the Henderson house, but you can see the flicker of a television through the crack between them as you pass.

You park three houses down, far enough to be unobtrusive. Your father's map rests on the passenger seat, the Henderson house circled in red.

You settle in to wait. The heater hums. Your thermos of coffee sits in the cup holder.

Outside, the street is empty. Silent.

You watch the house. The upstairs window. The porch. The street in both directions. Your breath fogs the windshield, and you wipe it clear with your glove.

Minutes crawl past.

Movement catches your eye. Not at the Henderson house, further down the street. A figure emerges from between two houses, dark coat, hood up, walking with purpose.

You grab your phone, zoom in as much as the camera allows. The figure is walking toward you, toward the Henderson house.

Your pulse quickens. Is this it? Are they going to place a bell? It's still early. What time does it happen? From what you know, it's random. It could be anytime. This could be a long night, or this could be it, right now.

All you know is that there are four bells to be placed at four houses. This is a small town, it's not as though Santa on his sleigh has to circumnavigate the world, dropping off his shitty little bells.

The figure walks past your car, keeps walking. Past the Henderson house without slowing. Doesn't even glance at it. Continues up the street,

You watch as the figure turns left at the corner, disappears from view.

Just someone walking through the snow on Christmas Eve. It's not too late yet for it to be abnormal. In the City the night would just be getting going. Here, it's surprisingly peaceful considering the town's history, especially on this night.

You lower your phone. Let your eyes unfocus. Your breath fogs the windshield, and you wipe it clear with your glove, stare out at the empty street, the Henderson house dark except for that single downstairs lamp.

What are you even doing here? Sitting in a freezing car, watching a house where an elderly couple…

Tap tap tap.

You jump so hard your knee slams into the steering wheel. Pain shoots up your leg.

A face at your window. Close. Too close.

A man.

Your heart stops.

He's standing right there, bent to peer in at you, face half-shadowed in the dim streetlight. You didn't see him approach. Didn't hear footsteps in the snow.

How long has he been standing there? Watching you?

He gestures: roll down the window.

Every instinct screams at you to start the car, to drive away. Your hands move to the keys still in the ignition. Your phone is in your lap; you could call someone, but who?

The man is elderly, you can see that much now. But that doesn't mean safe. Ted Bundy looked trustworthy too.

The man taps again, more insistent. Three sharp raps against the glass.

Your breath comes fast and shallow. The windows are fogging. Your pulse hammers in your ears.

This is Pine Hollow. The town where children vanish. Where everyone stays silent. Where you're investigating a killer who's operated for forty-nine years.

And there's a stranger at your car window.

You have seconds to decide.

What do you do?
Roll down the window. Turn to page 381
Drive away. Turn to page 446

TAKE THE RIGHT DOOR

The bedroom is small. A child's room.

You raise your phone immediately. This must have been Rachel's room. You need it documented.

Your torch beam sweeps across walls showing ghosts of posters. One remains: a kitten, "HANG IN THERE" faded to pale brown. You frame the shot.

2%.

A single bed, bedding deteriorated to shreds. On the pillow: stuffed animals arranged deliberately. Bear, rabbit, dog. Ragged but positioned with care.

You photograph them.

1%.

One percent left. One shot, maybe two. Choose carefully.

A bookshelf against the wall. Your torch picks out spines: *Anne of Green Gables*, *A Wrinkle in Time*, *Charlotte's Web*.

Anne of Green Gables. Sarah's favourite.

Your throat tightens, but you don't have time for emotion. Document first.

The dresser across from the bed, that's what matters. While everything else shows fifty years of decay, the dresser top is different.

Dust-free.

A gallery of framed photos arranged with deliberate care. School photos of Rachel at different ages. Family snapshots. The central photo: Rachel at eleven, dark hair, bright eyes.

And surrounding it, arranged in a perfect circle: seven pine cones.

You lean closer. The pine cones aren't scattered, they're placed. Each perfectly formed. Your torch catches their surfaces: dry but not brittle, brown but not grey.

Fresh. Weeks old, maybe a month.

Someone's been here. Recently. Maintaining this.

This is the shot. This is the evidence.

You raise your phone, frame it carefully: the central photo of Rachel, the circle of seven pine cones, all of it clear and documented.

Tap. Flash.

The screen goes black.

You tap again. Nothing. Power button—nothing. Dead.

But you got it. The shrine, the fresh pine cones, proof of maintenance. That's something. That's evidence.

Except now you have no phone. No way to take more photos. No way to call for help.

Something catches your eye behind Rachel's photo. You tilt the large frame forward with your free hand.

Another picture, smaller, half-hidden. Rachel's mother. Formal portrait. A single white stone sits on this frame.

Seven offerings for Rachel. One for her mother. Why separate? Why hidden?

You reach for your phone reflexively—then stop. Dead. You see this crucial detail but can't document it.

Your hand trembles. The torch beam wavers.

Someone has been coming here for decades. Letting everything else rot while maintaining this shrine. Fresh pine cones. Dust-free photos. Obsessive care.

You have the photo. The shrine with the pine cones. But there's more here. More you need to understand.

The master bedroom. You haven't seen it yet. If this is Rachel's preserved room, what's in the parents' bedroom? What else has been maintained?

You need to see it. Even without the phone, you need to know.

Go to the master bedroom. Turn to page 262

You scroll to the Pine Hollow Inn number, thumb slipping on the screen.

You press call.

"Pine Hollow Inn, Katie speaking."

"Katie…" Your voice comes out as a harsh whisper. "Katie, it's Jenny. I'm at the Van Vleets'. The old lodge. You have to listen to me."

"You're WHERE?"

"There's a fucking shrine in Rachel's room." The words hiss out, frantic. "Fresh pine cones. Photos dusted. Someone's been maintaining it for decades. And the clothes. Katie, there are modern clothes in the bedroom. Someone lives here. Someone's BEEN here."

Below you, a sound. The apartment door.

Opening.

Your breath catches. You press the phone harder to your ear, crouching lower in the loft.

"And the loft," you whisper, barely audible. "I'm in the loft. There are boxes everywhere. Bells, Katie. Hundreds of silver bells. This is where they come from. This is…"

"You're there NOW?" Her voice goes sharp. "Tonight?"

Footsteps below. Heavy. Crossing the main room.

"Katie, someone just came in." Your voice breaks. "Someone's downstairs. I need help. I need… please, you have to send someone, you have to…"

"Jesus Christ, Jenny." Not concern. Fury. Terror. "What have you DONE?"

"I need help!" You're begging now, whispering so hard your throat aches. "Please, Katie, call the police, call someone, he's…"

"He goes up there on Christmas Eve." She cuts you off. "Every single year. If you're in that building tonight…"

The footsteps stop below. Right beneath you.

"Katie…"

"You just killed a child." Her voice shakes. "Do you understand me? He'll know someone was there. He'll take another one tonight. Because of YOU."

"I don't…what do you…"

You needed her to understand. You needed someone who lost Tommy to understand what you found. The shrine. The clothes. You need someone to help you to make sense of it.

But Katie already knows. The way she said it. He goes up there. She's always known.

"Katie, please." You're crying now, tears hot on your cheeks. "I found everything. Sarah…this is about Sarah too. The bracelet. I need to tell someone. I need…"

Another voice cuts through, female, higher pitched, frantic: "Is she still there? Katie, is she STILL THERE?"

Siobhan.

Katie's response is sharp, directed away from the phone: "I'm handling it!"

"My daughter…" Siobhan's voice cracks with panic. "If he thinks we told her anything, if he thinks we helped… Katie, what if he comes for her? What if tonight…"

"I KNOW." Katie's voice breaks. Then, back into the phone, desperate: "Jenny, I can't help you. Do you understand? I can't. Put the phone down. Don't move. Don't…"

Click.

Dead line.

You stare at the phone. 4%.

Siobhan's daughter. The terror in her voice. What if he comes for her? What if tonight…

The town doesn't just know. The town is hostage.

And you just walked into his base. On Christmas Eve. The night he comes for the bells.

No help. No help is coming. They can't help you without endangering their own children.

You're alone.

The whistling starts below. Soft. A Christmas song twisted into nightmare.

He sees you when you're sleeping. He knows when you're awake.

The footsteps resume. Coming toward the bedroom. Toward the hatch you left open.

Toward you.

A beam of light appears below. Torch sweeping across the bedroom, catching on the dresser, the bed, the ladder.

The whistling stops.

"Well." The voice is rough, aged, but strong. "Someone's been visiting."

Your heart hammers so hard you're certain he can hear it.

The ladder creaks. Weight on the bottom rung.

He's climbing.

What do you do?
Try to fight. Turn to page 416
Hide among the boxes. Turn to page 395

TAKE THE LEFT DOOR

The master bedroom is sparse. This must have been where the Van Vleets slept. A double bed, stripped bare. A dresser with drawers hanging open.

You move to the dresser, torch in hand. No phone to document this. Just your eyes, your memory.

First drawer: empty. Second: rotted fabric.

The third drawer stops you.

Folded clothes. Men's clothes. But not from the seventies.

Modern denim. A t-shirt with a brewery logo from the 2000s. Contemporary. Recent.

You pull open the fourth drawer. More clothes. Different sizes. One still has the tag attached.

Your hand moves to your pocket—the phone—then stops. Dead. You're looking at crucial evidence and you can't photograph it.

Someone's been here. Living here. The shrine in Rachel's room, the fresh pine cones, and now modern clothes, supplies, organised like offerings.

You photographed the shrine. You have proof of the maintenance, the ritual. But not this. Not the modern clothes, not the proof someone's living here NOW.

The shrine shows obsession. These clothes show habitation.

Together, they'd tell the complete story. Separately...

Above the bed, a square hatch in the ceiling. Storage. Loft.

You have photos of the shrine. That's something. But without proof of current habitation, how much can you prove? The pine cones are recent, yes, but these clothes, this evidence of ongoing supply...

You're standing in someone's active living space with no phone, no way to call for help, and the light is fading outside.

The loft might have more evidence.

Or you could leave. Now. Photos of a shrine with fresh pine cones. That's proof of maintenance, of someone returning regularly. Maybe it's enough.

What do you do?
Pull open the hatch. Turn to page 438
Leave now with the photos you have. Turn to page 340

GO TO KATIE AT THE INN

The Pine Hollow Inn glows warm against the snowfall, its windows amber squares in the white void. You kill the engine and sit for a moment, hands shaking on the wheel. Not from cold, but from the adrenaline still flooding your system.

You found something. You actually found something.

The lodge. The evidence someone's been there.

Your phone sits in the cup holder, screen glowing faintly. Fifteen percent. Not much, but enough to show the photos. Enough to prove you're not crazy. Enough to show Katie what you found.

Katie. Katie lost Tommy. Katie will understand. Katie will believe you.

The wind tries to shove you back as you push through the Inn's front door. Inside, warmth hits like a wall, along with the smell of cinnamon, maybe, or nutmeg. No doubt the mulled wine warming for tonight. The Christmas scent should feel comforting but instead it makes your stomach clench.

Katie looks up from behind the desk. Her face shifts through surprise, concern, and something else you can't quite read before settling on worry.

"Jenny? You're covered in snow. Are you all right?"

"I went to the lodge." The words tumble out too fast, too loud. "Katie, I went up to the old ski resort and I found... you need to hear this. Is there somewhere we can talk?"

Katie's eyes widen. She glances toward the office door, then back to you. "The lodge? Jenny, that place is..." She stops herself. "Come on. Let's get you warm. Siobhan!"

The office door opens and Siobhan emerges, wiping her hands on a towel. Her gaze lands on you and something hardens in her expression, but it's gone so fast you might have imagined it.

"She's been up to the ski lodge," Katie says quietly.

Siobhan's hands still on the towel. "Has she."

"I found evidence," you say, too hyped to register the flatness in Siobhan's tone. "Someone's been there. Recently. I need to show you. I need to tell someone who'll actually listen."

Katie and Siobhan exchange a look. Quick, weighted, speaking a language you're not fluent in. Then Katie's face softens into something like sympathy.

"Of course," she says. "Come on back. Siobhan, put the kettle on?"

Siobhan nods once and disappears again. Katie leads you around the desk, through a narrow hallway to a small sitting room you didn't know existed. Floral wallpaper, worn sofa, a gas fire already burning in the grate. The kind of space that's private, hidden from guests.

"Sit," Katie says, gesturing to the sofa. "You look frozen. When did you leave the lodge?"

"Maybe an hour ago? I don't know. I drove straight here." You sink onto the cushions, suddenly aware of how exhausted you are. How much your legs ache from climbing. How your hands are still trembling.

Katie sits across from you in a wingback chair. "Start from the beginning. What made you go up there?"

"Sarah." The name comes out raw. "It started with Rachel Van Vleet. The first child taken. I kept thinking… if I could understand what happened to her, maybe I could understand what happened to Sarah. So I went to the lodge. I had to see where Rachel lived."

Siobhan enters carrying a tray. Three mugs of tea, steam curling. She sets it on the low table between you and settles into the other wingback chair, hands wrapped around her own mug. Her eyes never leave your face.

"And?" she prompts.

You reach for the tea, grateful for something to do with your hands. The warmth seeps into your palms. "The place is supposed to be abandoned. Forty-nine years, right? The Van Vleets left after

Rachel disappeared. Everyone says the building's been rotting up there ever since."

"But it's not?" Katie says quietly.

"No." You meet her eyes. "Someone's been maintaining it. I got inside. The apartment where they lived. Rachel's room is like a shrine. Her photos on the dresser, dusted, clean. Fresh pine cones arranged around them. Katie, those pine cones were weeks old, not decades."

Katie's mug pauses halfway to her lips. "Fresh?"

"And that's not all. The master bedroom had clothes in the dresser. Modern clothes. Jeans with tags from brands that didn't exist in the seventies. A t-shirt from a brewery that opened in the 2000s." You lean forward, words spilling faster now. "The apartment is warm. Not freezing like it should be. Someone's been living there. Using it. And I think…"

Your throat closes on the words. Katie and Siobhan wait, faces unreadable.

"I think it's him," you finish. "The King of Christmas. I think he's been hiding in that lodge for decades."

Silence fills the small room. The gas fire hisses softly. Outside, wind throws snow against the window in soft fistfuls.

Katie sets her mug down carefully. "My god."

"You believe me?" The question comes out smaller than you intended, almost childlike. You hate how much you need her answer.

"Jenny." Katie's voice is gentle, her eyes bright. "Of course I believe you. Tommy…" She stops, swallows. "I've been waiting forty years for someone to find something. Anything. And you did it. You actually did it."

The relief that floods through you is so intense it's almost painful. You blink back tears. "I came straight here because I thought… I thought maybe you'd understand."

"I do understand." Katie glances at Siobhan. "We both do."

Siobhan nods slowly. "You have proof? Photos?"

You turn the screen toward them. You wish you could have taken more photos, but what you have is enough for now. The story is clear: this isn't an abandoned building. Someone is using this space.

"Who else knows you went up there?" Siobhan's voice is measured, careful.

"No one. Just you two. I wanted to tell someone I could trust first. Someone who'd believe me instead of trying to shut me down." You lean back against the cushions, exhaustion catching up with the adrenaline crash. "I need to figure out what to do next. The evidence is there, but I need... I need someone to come with me. To see it. To verify I'm not crazy."

Katie and Siobhan look at each other again. That same weighted glance, like they're having an entire conversation without words.

Then Katie speaks. "We should go back up there. Tonight. All three of us. Document everything properly before..." She hesitates. "Before he comes back. If he's really living there, he might notice someone's been inside. We need to get real evidence before that happens."

"No." Siobhan's voice cuts sharp. "That's too dangerous. We don't know what he's capable of. We don't know if he's there now."

"But the evidence..."

"Can be reported to the police. Properly. With official channels." Siobhan turns to you. "Jenny, you found something huge. But if we go up there and something happens... if he's there, if he catches us..." She shakes her head. "We should take this to the authorities. Let them investigate. That's what they're for."

Katie leans forward. "The police have done nothing for forty years. You think they'll suddenly care now because Jenny saw some pine cones? We need more. We need photos, physical evidence, something they can't dismiss. If we all go up there together, with cameras, flashlights, witnesses..."

"Or we could all end up dead," Siobhan interrupts. "Use your head, Katie. This man has been taking children for decades. Killing them. You want to walk into his home? At night? In a storm?"

They're both looking at you now. Waiting.

"What do you think, Jenny?" Katie asks. "You're the one who found it. You're the one who knows what's up there. What should we do?"

The choice sits heavy in your chest. Both options sound reasonable. Both women watching you with concern in their eyes. Katie eager, Siobhan protective. Both of them finally, finally believing you.

Siobhan's right that the lodge could be dangerous. If he's there, if he comes back while you're inside… but the police haven't helped in decades. What makes you think they'll start now?

Katie's right that you need more evidence. Real proof. Photos that survive. Physical items. Something undeniable. But is it worth the risk?

You look between them. Katie leaning forward, hopeful; Siobhan tense, worried. Two women who've lived in this nightmare longer than you have. Two women who lost Tommy, who've watched other children vanish, who've carried silver bells on their own doorsteps.

"I think…" you begin.

What do you do?

Go to the lodge with Katie and Siobhan. Turn to page 319
Go to the police with Katie and Siobhan. Turn to page 427

SAVE YOUR BATTERY

Behind the desk, a door marked with a small brass plaque: "Private."

You try the handle. It turns. Unlocked.

The door opens onto a staircase climbing into darkness. Narrow, steep, the kind of utilitarian stairs that weren't meant for guests. These lead up to staff quarters, probably. To where the owners lived while running the business.

To where the Van Vleets lived.

To where Rachel grew up.

Your throat tightens.

This is it. Not the public face of the resort, but the private space. The family home above the failing business. Where Rachel had a bedroom, where she played, where she woke up Christmas morning before she vanished.

If there are answers, they're up there.

The stairs creak under your weight, wood protesting each step. The sound echoes in the narrow stairwell, multiplying, making it seem like more than one person is climbing. You pause, listening, but there's nothing. Just your own footsteps reflected back at you.

The stairs end at a door. Plain, no lock. You turn the handle and step through.

Your torch beam sweeps the space. A single open room, living area, maybe four hundred square feet. There's a kitchen off to one side, and two other doors leading off this main room. No frills, all function.

The apartment is warmer here. Not warm, but noticeably less cold than the lobby below. The smaller space holds heat better, or maybe the insulation is intact. You can almost imagine what it was like when people lived here.

The furniture is simple, practical: a couch facing a small television, a table with three chairs. Everything covered in dust, fabric rotted, surfaces warped, but the shapes remain. You can read the life that happened here in the arrangement of objects.

Your torch finds a corkboard on the wall near the open kitchen door. Faded papers pinned to it. You step closer. A child's drawing in crayon, the colours bleached to ghosts but the lines still visible: a house, a mountain, stick figures holding hands. The writing across the top is barely legible, faded to pale brown: "Me and Mommy and Daddy."

Rachel drew this.

Your throat tightens.

The Van Vleets came here with a plan. Young couple, entrepreneurial, buying a struggling ski resort and believing they could turn it around. They'd seen the decline in the industry, sure, but they had optimism, energy, a willingness to work eighteen-hour days. And they had Rachel.

You picture them in this space: Robert making coffee while his wife reviewed reservations at the table. Rachel sitting cross-legged on the couch, watching Saturday morning cartoons. Ordinary moments in an ordinary life, high in the mountains, believing they were building something.

The resort failed anyway. The metal poster in the lobby below showed what they were selling: family-friendly slopes, affordable rates, personal service. But Pine Hollow wasn't on the main routes. Bigger resorts had better snow, better amenities, better marketing. Year by year, the reservations thinned. The bills mounted. The optimism curdled into desperation.

And then, Christmas Eve 1976, Rachel disappeared.

You imagine waking up Christmas morning in this apartment, expecting your daughter's excited footsteps, hearing only silence. Running through the lodge, calling her name, checking every room, every closet, every corner. The panic rising as the hours passed. The police arriving. The search parties. The questions that never got answered.

Within six months, the Van Vleets were gone. Left everything behind and vanished, destroyed by grief.

That's the story, anyway.

But standing here, you feel the wrongness under the narrative.

The apartment is too preserved. Not perfectly (the upholstery is shredded, the wood is warped, time has done its work). But the structure of the life remains visible in a way that feels deliberate.

The corkboard with Rachel's drawing hasn't fallen. The dust on the kitchen counter is thick but not decades-thick. The air smells of mildew and decay, yes, but underneath something else. Pine. Fresh pine, like the forest outside brought indoors.

From here you can
Explore the kitchen. Turn to page 209
Open the door to the left. Turn to page 228
Open the door to the right Turn to page 290

STAY IN THE CAR

You keep your hand on the door handle but don't pull.

Stay in the car. Stay safe.

You lift your phone instead, snap more photos through the windshield. The figure is straightening now, turning to leave.

You zoom in as much as you can. Click. Click. Click.

But even as you're taking them, you know they're not great. Too much glare from the streetlight. Too much distance. The hood obscures everything.

The figure walks back down the porch steps. Down the sidewalk. Past your car. You sink lower in your seat, heart hammering. He continues down the street.

They don't even glance at your car.

You watch them go. Walking with that same purposeful stride. Not hurrying. Not sneaking. Just... walking.

Like they do this every year.

They reach the corner and turn. Out of sight.

You sit in the cold car, hands shaking, phone clutched tight.

You look at the photos. Dark shape. Blurry. Hood obscuring face. But it's SOMETHING. Proof that someone placed a bell. Proof this is real.

Not enough to identify them. But something.

You look back at your parents' house. The bell sits on the porch, barely visible in the darkness.

Your parents are inside. Twenty feet away. You could cross the street right now. Show them what you saw. Tell them everything.

Or you could follow that figure. They're on foot. You have a car. You could track them at a distance, see where they go. Maybe they'll lead you to something, or someone, useful.

What do you do?

Go across to your parents' house. Turn to page
Follow the person that left the bell. Turn to page 308

272

"Wait," you say. "Please. Just...talk to me."

He stops. Waits.

"I need to understand. Why? Why all of this?"

Silence. You think he won't answer.

Then: "Because Rachel didn't deserve to die."

Your breath catches. Rachel. Rachel Van Vleet. The first.

"She was a good child," he continues, voice distant. "She was perfect. But this town..." His jaw tightens. "This town never gave us a chance. And when she died... no one cared."

"So you..."

"So I made sure they'd remember." His eyes refocus on you. Sharp. Cold. "I made sure every family in Pine Hollow would know what it feels like to lose a child on Christmas Eve."

"That's insane..."

"Is it?" He takes a step closer. "Or is it justice?"

You back against the wall.

"I don't need to tell you anymore," he says. "No one is going to hear from you again."

"Wait...what *happened* to Rachel? How did she..."

"Die?" He's moving toward you now. "Does it matter? She's gone. They're all gone. And soon you will be too."

You try to dodge. He's faster.

"If this is about Rachel... I could... I'm a journalist. I could tell people... I could make people care..."

But it's too late. His hand closes around your throat.

"I'm sorry," he says quietly. "But you asked the wrong questions."

You claw at his hands. Can't breathe. Can't...

Rachel. Sarah. All the missing children.

You'll never know the truth.

And no one will know what happened here, to you.

THE END

You died in the old ski lodge on Christmas Eve, 2025. Strangled after learning that Rachel Van Vleet's death started everything. Your body was never found.

The King of Christmas continued his work.

PULL OVER

Your heart jumps. You stop the car.

The cruiser door opens. Sheriff Larkin steps out, waves you down.

Relief floods through you. The *SHERIFF*. Finally, someone who can help.

You roll down your window as he approaches.

"Sheriff! Thank God. I saw them! Someone just placed a bell at my parents' house. I followed them, they went that way…" You point. "We can catch them if we…"

"Miss Matthews." His voice is calm. Too calm. "I need you to turn off your engine and step out of the vehicle."

"What? No, we need to follow them, they're getting away…"

"Now, please."

Something in his tone makes your stomach drop.

"Sheriff, I just told you…"

"I heard you." He opens your car door. "Get out. Get in my cruiser. We'll pursue together. You can show me exactly what you saw. We can't have citizens chasing down potentially dangerous individuals."

That makes sense. Of course. He's a police officer. He has a radio, backup, authority. Your little sedan won't help in a pursuit.

You hesitate only a moment, then nod. Turn off your engine. Grab your phone. Step out into the cold.

You walk to the cruiser. He opens the back door.

"The back seat?"

"Standard procedure when we're pursuing a suspect. Keeps civilians secure."

The interior smells like coffee and vinyl. There's a metal cage separating the front seat from the back. No door handles on the inside.

You hesitate.

"Miss Matthews," the sheriff says. "We're losing time."

You get in.

The door closes behind you with a heavy, final click.

Sheriff Larkin walks around to the driver's side. Gets in. Starts the engine.

"Which way did they go?" you ask.

He doesn't answer. Just puts the cruiser in gear and starts driving.

Not the direction you pointed. The opposite direction.

"Sheriff, they went LEFT, not…"

"I know where they went," he says quietly.

Your stomach drops.

"Sheriff Larkin, where are we…"

"Somewhere we can talk." His eyes find yours in the rearview mirror. "Somewhere private."

You try the door handle. Nothing. It's locked from the outside. No way to open it from in here.

"Let me out."

"I'm afraid I can't do that."

"SHERIFF…"

"You should have left when you had the chance, Miss Matthews." His voice is almost… sad. "When Katie warned you. You had so many chances to leave."

Katie. The sheriff. Who else?

They're all part of it.

You pull out your phone. No signal.

There should be one here.

"Where are you taking me?"

He doesn't answer.

You watch through the window as familiar streets pass by. Then unfamiliar ones. Then the town limits sign.

Pine Hollow disappears behind you.

The road starts to climb. Trees close in on both sides, dark and dense. No streetlights. No houses. Just forest and snow and the cruiser's headlights cutting through the darkness.

"Sheriff Larkin, please…"

"I'm sorry." And he sounds like he means it. "I really am. But you couldn't leave it alone."

You're in the back of a police cruiser, locked in, no way out, no way to call for help, being driven into the mountains in the middle of the night by a sheriff who just admitted he's part of the conspiracy.

· You have no idea where you're going.

But you know it's nowhere good.

You're all out of choices. Turn to page 311

BACK IN ROOM 12

You close the door to Room 12 and lean against it, breathing hard. Your hands are shaking; not from cold, but from anger. From the look on Siobhan's face when she slammed the office door. From Katie's fear. From the weight of knowing that in a few hours, you're going to be sitting in the dark, watching for a killer.

The room is exactly as you left it this morning. Bed unmade, your duffel bag open on the chair. You set your father's folder down on the desk and finally exhale. This is more than a story. It always has been.

The window overlooks the street, and through it you can see Pine Hollow settling into Christmas Eve. Lights twinkle on the storefronts. A few people hurry past, bundled against the cold, carrying last-minute gifts.

Normal. It all looks so normal.

You check your phone. 6:48 PM. 34% battery. That won't be enough. You plug it into the charger and watch it climb to 35%, then 36%. Tonight you need to be prepared. Fully charged phone. Flashlight. Warm clothes. Coffee. You'll do this right.

Five hours until midnight. Five hours to prepare, to think, to second-guess yourself into staying here where it's safe.

Except you're not going to do that.

But first, the folder.

You cross to the desk and pull out the chair. The folder is thick, worn at the edges from years of handling. It's just a plain manila folder, the kind you'd use for tax returns or medical records. Except inside is something far more painful than paperwork.

You open it.

The first page is a timeline. Dates marching down the left margin in chronological order:

December 24, 1976 - Rachel Van Vleet

278

December 24, 1978 - David Drake
December 24, 1980 - Claire Henderson
December 24, 1981 - Tommy Wilson
December 24, 1986 - Sarah Matthews

Your throat tightens. Seeing her name there, in your father's handwriting, makes it real in a way it hasn't been for years. You've written about missing children. You've researched cold cases. But this, this is YOUR sister, YOUR family, YOUR father's forty-year hunt.

You know these names. You've always known them. As a child, you used to ride your bike past their houses: David's old place on Birch Street (before his family sold it), Claire's on Maple Drive, Tommy's where Katie still lives. You'd pedal slowly past, staring at the windows, trying to understand what it meant that children could just vanish. Trying to make sense of something that had no sense to make.

You were never allowed to ride up to the ski lodge where Rachel had lived. The mountain roads were too dangerous, your parents said. But really, you think now, they just didn't want you getting too close to where it all started.

The list continues with the names of other children that were never part of your obsession when you were only a child yourself.

December 24, 1995 – Daniel Peak
December 24, 2009 – Emily Taylor
December 24, 2024 – Amy Crawford

The new names are each written by different pens, in the same spidery handwriting. Later additions to the list.

You can't help but wonder if he left the rest of the page blank because he thought there might be more.

The next page is more annotations. Notes about the bells:

First known bell appeared Christmas morning 1979. Drake residence. No one mentions bells until Hendersons receive their THIRD.

He's underlined the final word twice as if he can't quite believe it.

Bells appear every year.

No fingerprints, no DNA, no trace evidence (per police reports)

Bells are identical—silver, approx 2", same manufacturer mark on loop. Purchased where? No local stores carry this exact style.

Why haven't the police looked into this? You've seen countless episodes of Forensic Files where killers are caught because they bought their duct tape at a specific Home Depot, or their rope from a particular hardware store. These bells come from SOMEWHERE. Someone is buying them, or bought them in bulk years ago. That's a trail. That's evidence.

But nobody followed it.

Who places them? When? How do they appear without anyone seeing?

That last question is underlined three times.

Your hands tighten on the folder. Either the police are incompetent, or they don't want to find answers. You're not sure which is worse.

You flip to the next page. A map of Pine Hollow: hand-drawn, photocopied, annotated in your father's blocky handwriting. Red circles mark the houses. Evergreen Lane. Birch Street. Maple Drive. Each circle has a name beside it.

You pull the map closer and study it. The red circles. The victim families. Your father has marked which houses still have the original families living there, which have been sold, which are empty.

Van Vleet – The lodge (left 1977)

Drake - Birch Street (sold 1982)

Henderson - Maple Drive (current)

Wilson - Birch Street (current)

Matthews - Evergreen Lane (current)

Peak - Cedar Lane (family moved 2003)

Taylor – Willow Street (family moved 2012)

Crawford - Oak Street (current)

Four families still in their original houses. Four houses where bells will appear tonight.

It's 7:45pm. You could get ready, get a couple of hours rest and head out.

Which one should you watch?

Decision time.

Make your choice and get ready. Turn to page 298

THE SERVICE DOOR OPENS

The service door opens. The sheriff emerges, flashlight beam sweeping the lot before settling on the cruiser. He walks back, opens your door.

"All right. Building's clear, no one inside. Jenny, can you come show me exactly where you found these things?"

"Sure."

Stepping out and stretching your legs feels better than it should. The mountain air is fresh compared to the cramped back of the cruiser. Whoever designed those things meant for suspects to be uncomfortable.

The sheriff leads, flashlight beam cutting through the dark. You follow him toward the lodge, boots crunching through fresh snow.

"Through here," the sheriff says, pushing through the broken door.

The corridor swallows you.

Into the lobby. Up the stairs. Your footsteps echo in the silence.

At the apartment landing, the sheriff stops. Pulls out his radio.

"We're here," he says into it.

A crackle of response. You can't make out the words.

Your voice is a squeak as you ask, "Who are you talking to?"

The sheriff doesn't answer. Just opens the apartment door.

A figure sits in the middle of the shoddy, faded sofa. Red parka. White fur trim.

It's Santa Claus.

But it's not.

You know it's not.

It's a twisted, warped version of everything Santa Claus is not.

He spreads his arms wide across the back, relaxed. Like he's holding court.

"Do you know who I am?" he asks.

You can't speak. Can't breathe.

"I'm the King of Christmas," he says, almost gently. "I've been maintaining order in this town for almost fifty years. Keeping the balance. Making sure naughty children face consequences." His eyes fix on you. "And you, Miss Matthews, have been very naughty."

The sheriff's hand stays firm on your shoulder.

"Breaking into my home. Taking pictures. Coming here to destroy what I've built." The King of Christmas tilts his head. "What did you think would happen?"

"I thought... I thought someone would help..."

"Someone did help." He nods toward the sheriff. "He helped deliver you to me. Just like he's supposed to. Just like everyone in this town does when someone breaks the rules."

Your legs almost give out. The sheriff's grip keeps you upright.

"Emma," the sheriff says quietly. "My daughter. She's seven. She's on the list." His voice is hollow. "I do what I have to do to keep her safe."

The King of Christmas smiles. "Exactly. Everyone makes their sacrifices. Everyone follows the rules. That's how we maintain order."

He pats his knee. "Come here, Jenny. Come sit with me."

"No..."

The sheriff pushes you forward. Across the living room. Past Rachel's corkboard. Past the Christmas decorations rotting in place.

To the sofa.

To him.

"Sit," the King of Christmas says again.

The sheriff forces you down. You land on his lap with a jolt. His arm comes around your waist, holding you in place.

"There we are," he says softly. "Just like when you were small. Sitting on Santa's lap."

You're shaking so hard your teeth chatter.

"What do you want for Christmas, Jenny?" His voice is right by your ear now. Almost tender. "What's your deepest wish?"

You can't answer. Can't think.

"Is it to see your sister again? To know what happened to Sarah?" He shifts slightly, his other hand moving. "She was naughty, you know. Just like you're naughty now."

Something cold touches your throat.

A blade.

"Please," you whisper. "Please don't..."

"Shhh." His arm tightens around your waist. "It'll be quick. That's a kindness I give to those who come alone. No one to watch. No one to carry the image."

The sheriff turns away, facing the window. He doesn't want to see.

"You should have stayed away," the King of Christmas murmurs. "You should have let the past stay buried."

The blade presses harder against your throat.

Your last thought isn't of him.

It's of your parents, waiting at home. Your mother baking, your father with his reading glasses, both of them hoping you'd come back to them.

You never will.

The blade moves.

There's pressure. Then warmth. Then...

The world tilts. Sound becomes distant. The lights blur and fade.

The last thing you feel is his arm still around your waist, holding you like a child who's fallen asleep.

Then darkness.

Complete and final.

THE END

You trusted the law. You went alone.

The sheriff delivered you exactly where the King of Christmas wanted you.

You died on a monster's lap while he hummed Christmas carols.

In Pine Hollow, authority belongs to the King of Christmas. And you walked right into his arms.

DRIVE TO YOUR PARENTS' HOUSE

Every instinct screams: **No.** Something about this is wrong. The way she came out so quickly. The way she's been watching through the curtains. The way she and Siobhan warned you off earlier but now Katie's here, alone, seemingly wanting to talk.

Your hand moves to the keys, not the window button.

You twist the ignition. The engine coughs, catches.

Katie steps back, startled. Her mouth moves—saying something—but you can't hear over the blood roaring in your ears.

You throw the car into drive.

In your rearview mirror, you see her standing in the street, watching you go. Just a shape in the darkness.

Your hands shake on the wheel. Your breath comes in gasps.

Was that smart? Or cowardly?

Was she dangerous? Or was she trying to help?

You'll never know.

You don't stop until you reach Evergreen Lane.

You pull up across the street and kill the engine.

Through the front window, you can see the living room lamp is on. Someone's awake.

Of course they are. It's Christmas Eve. Your mother never sleeps on Christmas Eve. Not since Sarah.

Thirty-nine years without her. Happy shitty anniversary.

You sit in the cold car, engine ticking as it cools, and stare at the house.

You came here because it felt safe. Because Katie's reaction spooked you and you needed somewhere familiar. You came here because where else would you go?

But now that you're here, you have to decide: what next?

You could go inside. Knock on the door. Tell your parents everything, about Katie, about the stakeout, about what you're trying to do. They'd let you watch from inside. You'd be warm. Safe. Not alone.

Or you could stay here. In the car. Watch from across the street. Your parents' house is one of the four that will receive a bell tonight. You could see who places it without involving them, without worrying them, without putting that weight on their shoulders.

They've carried enough of that over the decades.

You look back at the lit window. Your mother moving past, a shadow behind the curtain.

What do you do?
Stay in the car and watch. Turn to page 370
Go inside. Turn to page 242

WALK THE HILL TO THE SKI RUNS

Up the mountain, the runs wait. They don't promise. They don't refuse. They soldier up the slope in slow pale lanes and vanish into a fold you can't see past. For a moment you're certain there's a set of tracks up there, a regularity cut into the white that could be the imprint of someone who knew where they were going. You squint until your eyes water. It's nothing. Or it's everything and the snow has softened it, and either way your doubt and your need take exactly the same shape.

You turn from the lodge and start walking.

The hill rises gentle at first, a slope you barely register through the snow. Your boots find purchase on buried ground, each step a small negotiation between weight and ice. The air tastes clean, metallic, the kind of cold that seems to sharpen the inside of your lungs. Above, the sky holds a pale, exhausted light: late afternoon, not yet dusk. You tell yourself there's time. There's always time when you're moving forward.

Behind you, the lodge shrinks into the white. Ahead, the runs open like pages, blank and waiting. This is better than knocking on doors that won't open, better than sitting in rooms where people look through you like you're already a ghost. Up here, the world is simple: climb or don't, breathe or don't, keep moving or stop.

The first lift tower appears like a skeleton half-eaten by the mountain. The metal frame tilts slightly, its crossbeam sagging where the cable once ran. Snow has drifted against the base, sculpting it into something organic, a bone the earth is slowly claiming. You pass close enough to brush it with your glove, and rust comes away on the fabric like dried blood.

You keep climbing.

The trees thin as you gain elevation, their trunks dark against the white. The runs widen, the open space dizzying after the close press of the forest. Your thighs begin to burn with effort, your breath coming harder. The cold finds its way past your scarf, needling at your throat.

At the second tower, you pause. Something juts from the snow nearby: a post, weathered grey, driven deep into the ground. There are others, you realise, spaced at intervals, marking some kind of boundary. You approach the nearest one. Paint clings to the wood in patches, black letters faded to ghosts. You can make out shapes, angular marks that might be letters, but the words are illegible, erased by decades of weather.

Trail markers, probably. Closed runs. Every ski resort has them. Just to be sure, though, do you

Take a photo to zoom in on the sign later. Turn to page 206
Try to get a better look now. Turn to page 355

TAKE THE RIGHT DOOR

The bedroom is small. A child's room.

Your torch beam sweeps across walls that still show the ghosts of posters. Discoloured rectangles where paper once hung, a few tattered corners still clinging to pushpins. One remains mostly intact: a kitten hanging from a branch, "HANG IN THERE" faded to pale brown letters. The image is bleached nearly white, but you can still make out the shape.

A single bed against one wall. The frame is solid, but the bedding has deteriorated to shreds. What might have been a quilt now just rotted scraps, stuffing from the pillow spilling out like snow.

On the pillow, arranged carefully: stuffed animals. A bear, a rabbit, something that might have been a dog. The fabric is ragged, eaten by time and moths, fur worn to bare patches. But they're positioned deliberately, facing outward, as if someone still tucks them in.

This was Rachel's room.

And they never cleared it.

Your throat closes.

A bookshelf stands against one wall. Your torch picks out spines: faded, colours shifted, but titles still legible. *Anne of Green Gables*, *A Wrinkle in Time*, *Charlotte's Web*, *The Secret Garden*. Books that an eleven-year-old girl loved in 1976.

Anne of Green Gables. Sarah's favourite.

Your hand reaches for it before you can stop yourself. The cover is faded to a uniform tan, original image barely visible. The binding cracks when you open it, pages brittle yellow. No inscription, no name. Just a book that a child loved once.

You put it back carefully, exactly where it was.

The dresser across from the bed is where all the maintenance has been focused. While everything else in the room shows decades of decay, the dresser top is different.

Dust-free.

A gallery of framed photos, arranged with deliberate care. The glass protects them. You can see the images clearly despite the fading. Colours have shifted strange, blues gone entirely, leaving everything tinted yellow-red like aged film. But the faces remain.

School photos showing Rachel at different ages: missing front teeth, gap-toothed grin, more serious as she got older. A family snapshot, the three of them in front of the lodge, mountains behind. A Polaroid of Rachel on skis, face lit with joy. Another of her holding a stuffed rabbit. You glance back at the bed, at the deteriorated rabbit positioned on the pillow. The same one.

The central photo, largest: Rachel at eleven. Dark hair, bright eyes, smile showing permanent teeth coming in. Taken sometime in 1976, months or weeks before she disappeared.

And surrounding it, arranged in a perfect circle: seven pine cones.

You lean closer. The pine cones aren't decorative scatter. They're deliberately placed. Each one perfectly formed, scales intact. Your torch catches their surfaces: dry but not brittle, brown but not grey with age.

Recent. Weeks old, maybe a month.

Fresh.

Someone's been here. Recently.

Not forty-nine years ago. Recently.

Cleaning this specific surface.

Arranging these specific cones.

Something catches your eye behind Rachel's central photo. A frame edge barely visible. You reach out, fingers trembling, and tilt the large photo forward carefully.

Another picture leans against the wall, smaller, half-hidden.

Rachel's mother. Formal portrait, professional. She wears a blouse with a collar, hair styled. No smile, just a direct gaze at the camera.

A single white stone sits on top of this frame. River stone, worn smooth by water, white as bone.

Why separate? Why hidden? Why does Rachel get seven offerings while her mother gets one?

Your torch beam wavers. Your hand is shaking.

The room around you shows fifty years of decay. The posters gone to dust, the bedding rotted, the stuffed animals falling apart. Everything has aged, deteriorated, returned to the mountain.

Except this dresser top. Except these photos. Except these pine cones.

Someone has been coming here. For decades. Letting everything else fall apart while maintaining this one small shrine. Dusting the frames. Placing fresh pine cones. Keeping Rachel's face visible.

Your parents kept Sarah's room for three years before packing it away. Three years of walking past that closed door, of your mother unable to disturb it, of pretending preservation meant something.

This room has been a shrine for forty-nine years.

The Van Vleets left. Everyone knows that. Six months after Rachel disappeared, they packed up and drove away, destroyed by grief.

So, who's been maintaining this?

Your breath comes faster. You need to understand.

You could keep exploring. Or you could leave. Right now. Get to your car, back to town, tell someone what you've found.

Every instinct screams that something is wrong. This isn't an abandoned building. Someone is using this space.

But you're a journalist. You investigate. You find truth even when it's uncomfortable.

Go back and try the other door. Turn to page 190

STAKEOUT AT YOUR PARENTS

You settle into the waiting.

Your mother turns off the living room lamps, leaving only the kitchen light burning dim. Your father pulls the curtains in the front windows, but leaves a gap just wide enough to see the porch and the street beyond. You position yourself at the kitchen window where your mother suggested: the side angle that gives a clear view of the front steps and the approach from either direction.

The three of you sit in near darkness, tea cooling on the table, watching the empty street. Snow falls steadily, accumulating on the porch railing, the mailbox, your car parked across the street. The neighbourhood is silent. No cars. No movement. Just the hush of Christmas Eve settling over Pine Hollow like a held breath.

You check the street. Nothing.

Check the porch. Nothing.

The minutes crawl.

Your father shifts in his chair, the leather creaking. Your mother hasn't moved from her position by the front window gap. You can see her silhouette, rigid, unblinking.

Thirty-nine years they've done this. Thirty-nine years of watching, waiting, never seeing.

Your eyes burn from staring into the darkness. You blink hard, refocus.

Headlights appear at the end of the street.

All three of you tense.

A vehicle crawls toward the house, moving slowly through the snow. It's a truck. Dark coloured. As it passes under the streetlight, you see the marking on the door.

Sheriff's Department.

The truck pulls to a stop in front of your parents' house. Not across the street where you parked. Right in front, blocking the view of the porch.

"What's he doing here?" your mother whispers.

The driver's door opens. A figure emerges: tall, heavy coat, Sheriff's Department hat. He pauses, looks at the house, then starts up the walk toward the porch.

Your father stands. "I'll see what he wants."

"Dad, wait..." You start to protest, but he's already moving to the door.

The knock comes. Three sharp raps.

Your father opens it, and cold air rushes in along with the sheriff. Sheriff Larkin. Older, late fifties, with deep lines carved around his eyes and a practiced smile that doesn't quite reach them.

"Bill," he says, nodding at your father. "Sorry to bother you so late."

"Sheriff." Your father's voice is neutral, careful. "What can I do for you?"

"Just making rounds." Larkin stamps snow off his boots but doesn't step inside. "After last year, we're doing check-ins on the families. Making sure everyone's all right tonight."

There's a weight to those words. After last year. After Amy Crawford. After fifteen years of silence broke and the nightmare started again.

Your father's jaw tightens. "We're fine."

"Good, good." Larkin's eyes move past him, scanning the room. They land on you standing in the doorway between the kitchen and living room. His expression shifts. Larkin nods slowly, and there's something almost approving in it. Like he's checking a box on a list. "Nice that you've got family with you tonight. That's good. That's real good."

Your mother appears behind your father, hands clasped tight. "We appreciate you checking, Sheriff."

"Just doing our job." He glances back toward his truck, then at the street, then finally at your father again. "You folks planning to stay up much longer?"

The question lands strange. Not threatening exactly, but pointed. "Not too late," your father says carefully.

"Good, good. Get some rest. Tomorrow's a big day." Larkin tips his hat, that same practiced smile. "Merry Christmas, folks. Stay safe tonight."

The emphasis on those last words makes your skin prickle.

"Merry Christmas," your father echoes hollowly.

The door closes. The sheriff's boots crunch down the steps. You move to the window, watching as he climbs back into his truck, starts the engine. The headlights sweep across the front of the house as he pulls away.

And there, on the path, clearly visible in the glow of the porch light…

A silver bell.

What do you do?

Run after the sheriff. Turn to page 103
Stay with your parents. Turn to page 119

CALL PARENTS

You scroll to Mom and Dad, thumb shaking so hard you nearly drop the phone.

It rings once. Twice.

"Jenny?" Your mother's voice, immediate alarm. "What's wrong?"

"Mom…" You're whispering, but it comes out choked, broken. "I'm at the ski lodge. The old one. Up the mountain."

"WHERE?" Your father's voice in the background, sharp.

"There are bells," you whisper frantically, trying to control the sobs that want to tear out of you. "So many bells. And… and…"

You want to tell them everything but your throat closes around the words, tears streaming down your face, and you need to be QUIET, he's down there, he'll hear…

"Jenny, what…"

"Someone just came in," you manage, barely audible. "He's climbing up here. I'm trapped."

"Get out!" Your father's voice, louder now, like he grabbed the phone. "Jenny, get OUT of that building!"

"I can't!" The sob finally breaks free, and you clamp your hand over your mouth to muffle it. "I'm in the loft. He's on the ladder. There's no other way down."

"Oh God." Your mother's voice cracks. "Bill, we need to…"

"We're coming!" Your father shouts. "Jenny, hold on, we're getting in the car right now…"

"There's no time!" You can hear the ladder creaking below. The whistling. Soft and terrible. "Please, call someone, send…"

"Who?" Your mother's voice is desperate, breaking. "The sheriff won't… Jenny, WHO can we call?"

The question hangs there. You both know the answer.

No one.

"I found the bells," you whisper, needing them to know even if you can't explain.

Your voice cracks completely. You can't say more. Can't breathe.

"Baby, please." Your mother is crying now too. "Just hide. Just stay quiet. We're coming, we're…"

The footsteps reach the bedroom below. Right beneath you.

"I have to go." You're sobbing. "I love you. I have to…"

"JENNY!" Your mother screams your name. "Don't hang up! Stay on the…"

But he's climbing. You can hear the ladder taking his weight.

You end the call. The last sound is your mother screaming.

3% battery.

There's nowhere to run.

No one to help you.

Hide among the boxes. Turn to page 395

YOU MAKE YOUR CHOICE

The map stares back at you, the red circle around the house like a target. You check your watch again. 7:52 PM. You have time. Not much, but enough to prepare properly.

You stand and cross to the bed, begin laying out your supplies like a soldier preparing for deployment. Phone, now at 89%. You leave it charging. Flashlight. Extra batteries. Your notebook and pen. The folder. The timeline. The map. Your father's notes about the bells.

Gloves. Hat. Scarf. The warmest socks you packed.

You pull out your thermal underwear and change, layering yourself against the cold. Jeans over the thermals. Your thickest sweater. Your heavy winter coat.

You look at yourself in the small mirror above the dresser. You look tired. Old. Determined.

8:30pm.

You should rest. You should lie down, close your eyes, conserve energy for the long night ahead. That's what a smart investigator would do.

You lie on the bed fully clothed except for your boots and coat. The ceiling has a water stain in the corner, shaped vaguely like a map of some country you can't name. You stare at it and try to quiet your mind.

It doesn't work.

Your thoughts spiral. Sarah in her red mittens. Your father's spidery handwriting. Katie's fear. Siobhan's anger. The sheriff's dismissal. Eight children. Eight families. Forty-nine years.

You think about the choice you just made. Was it the right one? What if nothing happens there? What if you're in the wrong place and miss everything?

8:48pm.

You close your eyes. Try to breathe slowly. In for four counts. Hold for four. Out for four.

It doesn't help.

You think about what you're about to do. Stake out a house. Watch for whoever places the bells. Confront them if necessary. Follow them if you can. Get evidence. Get answers.

And then what?

You don't let yourself think about the "then what." One step at a time.

9:15pm.

You give up on sleep. Sit up, pull on your boots, lace them tight. Check your phone: 97%. Good enough. You unplug it, slip it in your pocket. Gather the pages from your father's folder. Tuck them inside your coat.

The thermos. You'll need to fill it downstairs.

9:30pm.

You're as ready as you'll ever be.

You pull on your coat, your gloves, your hat. Check yourself one more time in the mirror. You look like someone heading out into a blizzard. Which, in a way, you are.

You open the door carefully, quietly. The hallway is dim, lit only by the faint glow from the stairwell. You listen.

You slip out, close the door with barely a click, and move down the hallway on silent feet.

The stairs creak. You take them slowly, keeping to the edges where the wood is more solid.

At the bottom, you pause. The lobby is empty. The Christmas tree in the corner blinks its tired lights. The front desk is unattended. You move quickly to the small kitchenette and fill your thermos from the still-warm coffee pot, the sound too loud in the silence. No one comes.

You slip out the front door into the crystalline cold of Christmas Eve.

10:02pm.

Your car is where you left it, already wearing a fresh coat of snow. You brush off the windshield with your gloved hand, get inside, start the engine. It coughs, protests, catches.

The heater kicks on slowly. You sit for a moment, hands on the wheel, breath fogging.

This is it.

You put the car in drive.

Where are you heading?

Henderson. Turn to page 254

Wilson. Turn to page 309

Crawford. Turn to page 336

Your parents. Turn to page 335

YOU RUN FROM LARKIN

No. Something in your drugged brain screams: NO.

He locked you up. He brought you here. He's lying.

You turn. Try to run back the way you came.

"Miss Matthews, STOP…"

You stumble into the trees at the side of the road. Branches slap your face. You can barely see.

Behind you: car door slamming. Footsteps.

"You can't run like this! You'll freeze to death out here!"

Maybe. But better than what he'll do.

You push deeper into the forest. Away from the road. Away from him.

Your foot catches. You fall. Get up. Fall again.

Everything is spinning. Which way is down? Which way is town?

You don't know.

"JENNY!"

His voice is close. Too close.

You crawl. Hands and knees. Forward. Any direction.

Your hand finds air.

You pitch forward into nothing.

Falling.

Hitting slope. Rolling. Can't stop. Branches tearing at you. Rocks slamming into you.

You hit the bottom hard.

Everything stops.

You lie there. Can't move. Can't breathe right.

Above you: flashlight beam. Searching.

"Miss Matthews? JENNY?"

You try to be still. Silent.

The beam sweeps over you. Moves on. Comes back.

Finds you.

"Goddammit." Larkin's voice. Frustrated. Sad.

He starts climbing down toward you.

You try to move. Your body won't respond.

Too injured. Too drugged. Too cold.

He reaches you. Crouches down. Shines the light on you.

You see his face. Resigned.

"I'm sorry," he says. "I really am."

He reaches for something on his belt.

Not his radio.

His gun.

"It didn't have to be this way," he says quietly.

The last thing you see is his face. Sad. Tired.

Then the gunshot echoes through the forest.

And nothing.

THE END

You died in the forest outside Pine Hollow on Christmas Eve, 2025. Shot by Sheriff Larkin after attempting to escape.

Your body was never found. The official report stated you left Pine Hollow and never returned.

Your parents waited for a call that never came.

Two Matthews daughters lost to Pine Hollow. Both vanished on Christmas Eve. Both never found.

The King of Christmas continued his work.

SEARCH FOR EVIDENCE

If Rachel fell here, there might be something. Bones, maybe. Clothing. Anything that proves what happened, that turns this legend into truth.

Your right hand sweeps across the concrete, feeling in the dim light. Debris, chunks of old concrete, rust flaking off the rebar—nothing. But you keep searching because if you're going to die here, at least you could die knowing. At least you could have that.

You drag yourself a few inches to the left, ignoring the way your broken leg screams in protest. Your fingers probe the corners, the edges, anywhere something might have settled over fifty years.

Nothing. Just cold concrete and accumulated debris. Dirt and ice and the detritus of decades.

Maybe Rachel isn't here. Maybe she fell somewhere else, or maybe there was no fall at all. Or maybe her bones are buried deeper, under layers you can't reach with one working arm and a body that's already failing.

You slump back, exhausted from the effort. The searching bought you nothing. No proof. No certainty. Just the same questions you came here with, and now you're dying with them unanswered.

The journalist in you wanted evidence, wanted the story. But the mountain doesn't care about stories. It just takes.

Turn to page 307

"Finally," your father says quietly. "Finally someone's taking this seriously."

You don't answer. The words stick in your throat.

There's so much you should say. Thirty years of apologies and explanations and the kind of honesty that should happen between a father and daughter who've been circling each other's grief.

But the silence feels safer. Easier. Old habits.

Your father glances at you, seems to read your face, and nods slightly. Like he understands. Like he always has.

He reaches over and takes your hand anyway.

You squeeze back.

No words needed. Just this: his hand in yours, your shoulder against his, breath fogging the windows, waiting together in the dark.

This is enough, you think. *Whatever happens next, at least we had this.*

The service door opens. Turn to page 339

CALL YOUR PARENTS

Your mother answers on the second ring. "Jenny?"

"Mom. Hi. I just… I wanted to let you know I'm okay. I'm at the old ski lodge with Sheriff Larkin. We're investigating something I found."

"The sheriff?" Relief floods her voice. "Oh, thank God. I was worried when you didn't come back."

"I know. I'm sorry. But I think we might be onto something. The sheriff's checking it out now."

"Be careful up there. That building's dangerous."

"I will. I am." You glance at the lodge, dark against the snow. "Mom, when I'm done here… can I come over? Can we spend Christmas Eve together? All of us?"

Her voice breaks. "Of course. Of course, sweetheart. We'd love that. Your father will be so happy. We'll wait up for you."

"I'll be there soon. I promise."

"We love you, Jenny."

"I love you too."

You end the call. The phone drops to 11%.

Through the windshield, you watch the dark lodge and wait for the sheriff to return.

You told them you'd see them soon.

You meant it.

The service door opens Turn to page 282

FOCUS ON ESCAPING

You ignore the historical implications, ignore the possibility that you're in Rachel's grave. That's not important right now. Getting out is important. You have to get OUT.

You scan the walls, looking for holds, for anything that might help you climb. There: a piece of rebar jutting out about four feet up. If you can reach it, pull yourself up, maybe find another handhold...

You push yourself up with your right arm, trying to get your feet under you. Your left leg buckles immediately, pain so bright it whites out your vision. You collapse, gasping, but force yourself to try again.

This time you keep the weight off the left leg, hop on the right, reach for the rebar with your good hand.

Your fingers brush the metal. So close. You stretch, shoulder screaming in protest, ribs grinding with each movement. You've almost got it...

Your right leg gives out.

You hit the ground hard, the impact driving the air from your lungs. For a moment you can't breathe, can't think, can't do anything but lie there while the pain crescendos and your body trembles with the effort of trying and failing.

The wall is slick with ice anyway. Even if you reached the rebar, you'd never be able to pull yourself up. Your body won't cooperate. The cold has stolen your strength, and the injuries have stolen everything else.

You're not getting out.

The thought arrives with terrible clarity.

You're not getting out.

Go to page 307

HYPOTHERMIA. SORRY.

You try to move again, to sit up, but your body refuses. The left leg is definitely broken, the pain now sharpening into something specific and terrible. Your head throbs with each heartbeat, and there's something wet and warm trickling down your temple that you know is blood.

You need to get out. You need to climb.

Your right hand finds the wall. The concrete is slick with ice, rough with age. You try to pull yourself up, but your fingers slip, won't grip, and the pain from your ribs drives you back down with a gasp that might be a scream.

Again. You have to try again.

But your body won't obey. The commands travel from brain to muscle and arrive garbled, delayed, wrong. Your left arm lies useless at your side. Your left leg is agony. And the cold. The cold is everywhere now, a presence that fills the pit like rising water.

You slump back, staring up at the circle of sky. It's darker now. Evening coming. How long have you been down here? Minutes? An hour? Time feels negotiable, a thing that bends and stretches.

The shivering has stopped. You notice it with a kind of distant curiosity. You should be shivering—you're so cold—but your body has given up that fight. Instead, there's a strange warmth creeping through you, starting at your core and spreading outward like something sweet and heavy.

You know what this is. Some part of you, some rational corner of your journalist's brain, recognises paradoxical undressing, the final stage before the end. Your body thinks it's overheating. Your body is lying to you, trying to make death comfortable.

What do you do?

Fight it - stay awake, stay alert, keep trying. Turn to page 412

Accept it - you're dying, let it be peaceful. Turn to page 418

FOLLOW THE PERSON

You start your car and pull away from the curb.

The figure is a block ahead now, still walking. Not hurrying. Just a steady pace, like someone heading home after a late shift.

You keep your distance. Engine low.

They turn left at the end of Evergreen Lane. You follow, hanging back.

The street is empty. Dark. No one else out at this hour.

The figure continues walking. You creep forward, keeping them in sight.

Then, ahead of you, red and blue lights flash.

A police cruiser pulls across the intersection, blocking your path.

Do you
Pull over, Turn to page 275
Keep going Turn to page 387

THE WILSONS'

You head toward Birch Street.

The Wilsons. Katie's house. Tommy's house, though Tommy has been gone for forty-four years.

The Wilson house is a two-story colonial, one of the older properties in town, but well maintained. Lights glow in the windows: downstairs living room, upstairs bedroom. Christmas lights hang from the eaves, blinking red and green in steady rhythm.

Someone's home.

You park beneath a birch tree, white bark ghostly in the streetlight. Unlike most roads in Pine Hollow, Birch Street actually HAS birch trees. It was the original. The others just borrowed the naming pattern.

You remember riding your bike here as a kid, running your hand along the papery bark, pretending these trees held some secret about Tommy Wilson's disappearance. They didn't, of course. Trees don't talk.

But houses might.

Outside, the street is quiet. A few cars parked along the curb, snow-covered. No movement.

You watch the house. The lit windows. The Christmas lights blinking their cheerful pattern, out of sync with the dread settling in your stomach.

Minutes pass.

Maybe you shouldn't have told them you were coming. The thought niggles at you as you shift in your seat, trying to get comfortable. Having them check on you every few minutes through the curtains is already getting old, and you've barely been here ten minutes. It feels oppressive. Like being monitored instead of doing the monitoring.

But then again, at least someone knows where you are. If anything goes wrong, if you see something, if HE shows up…Katie and Siobhan are right there. They'll have your back. The thought is oddly comforting.

The curtain in the front window moves. Just slightly. Someone's looking out.

Your pulse quickens. There it is again. They see you. They know you're here.

The curtain falls back. The window is dark again, backlit by lamplight from deeper in the house.

You wait.

The curtain moves again. Longer this time. You can't tell if it's Katie or Siobhan. Perhaps it's both of them taking turns to check up on you.

You resist the urge to duck down, to hide. You're here to observe. But it's unsettling. You came to watch their house, but they're watching YOU.

At least they're keeping an eye on you, right? At least you're not completely alone out here.

The curtain drops.

You exhale slowly, breath fogging.

Then the front door opens.

A figure steps onto the porch. Katie. You recognise her immediately. She's wearing a heavy coat, arms wrapped around herself against the cold. She looks toward your car, directly at you.

Katie walks down the porch steps, crosses the yard, approaches your car through the snow. Her face is set, determined.

She reaches your window. Taps on the glass.

Your hand hovers over the button.

What do you do?
Roll down the window. Turn to page 487
Drive away to your parents' house. Turn to page 286

YOU'RE OUT OF CHOICES

The cruiser slows. Turns off the main road onto something unpaved. Gravel crunches under the tires.

Through the window, you see a building emerging from the trees. Large. Dark.

The old ski lodge.

You know as soon as it comes into view, even though you've never been here before. Too far out of town for you to have visited as a kid. Too creepy for you to have bothered with as a teenager.

The windows are boarded. It looks like a shadow, even in the darkness. Like something trying to disappear.

"Why are we here?" you ask.

Sheriff Larkin doesn't answer. Just parks the cruiser and kills the engine.

He gets out. You hear his boots crunch in the snow. Coming around to your side.

Your door opens.

"Come on," he says.

"What?" You stare at him. "Why are we HERE?"

He reaches in, takes your arm.

"Sheriff, what are you...I don't understand, the person who placed the bell went the OTHER way..."

He pulls you out of the cruiser. You stumble in the snow. He steadies you, starts walking you toward the lodge.

"We need to go BACK," you say, trying to pull away. "We're wasting time. They're getting away. If we go back to my parents' street, we can..."

"Miss Matthews."

"Why did you bring me HERE?" Your voice is rising, frustrated now. "This is the old ski lodge. There's nothing here. It's been abandoned for decades..."

"Has it?"

You stop. Look at him. "What?"

But he's not looking at you. He's guiding you forward, up the steps to the entrance.

"Sheriff Larkin, I don't…I saw someone place a bell. Tonight. At my parents' house. We could have caught them. You were supposed to HELP me…"

"I know what you saw."

"Then why…"

You're not making sense of this. Any of this. Why drive out here? Why this building? What does the abandoned lodge have to do with…

The door opens before you reach it.

Light spills out. Warm. Golden.

A figure stands silhouetted in the doorway.

Tall. Red suit. White beard.

Your brain stutters. Stops.

That's not…

That can't be…

"Miss Matthews," the figure says. Voice deep, almost gentle. "I've been expecting you."

And suddenly, horribly, you understand.

The figure steps back, gestures inside.

"Come in," he says. Not a request.

Larkin pushes you forward gently. You stumble across the threshold.

The door closes behind you with a heavy click.

You're in a reception area; wood panelling, a stone fireplace, mounted animal heads on the walls. It looks frozen in time, like the lodge closed yesterday instead of forty-eight years ago. Dust-free. Maintained.

The man in the red suit stands between you and the only exit. He's tall, broad-shouldered, the white beard perfectly matching his persona. But his eyes are cold. Businesslike. And the suit? This close up you can see it's not a Santa suit at all; it's a ski suit.

Behind you, you hear Larkin starting up his cruiser.

Leaving you here.

"Wait…" You turn toward the door but the man in red moves, blocking your path without seeming to hurry.

"Miss Matthews," he says. "Sit down."

There's a chair near the fireplace. Old leather. Worn.

"I'm not…"

"Sit. Down."

His voice doesn't rise. Doesn't need to.

You don't sit.

"You're the *King of Christmas*," you say. Your voice shakes but you force the words out.

"That's what they call me."

And then you say the first thing that comes into your mind.

"What did you do to my sister?"

"The same thing I'm about to do to you."

It's no kind of answer, but you're afraid it's the truth.

The words land like blows. Simple. Direct. Final.

"Please…"

"You came back to Pine Hollow asking questions. Digging. Threatening everything I've built here." He tilts his head slightly. "Did you think there wouldn't be consequences?"

"I just wanted to know what happened…"

He takes a step toward you. "Was it worth it?"

You back up. Your shoulders hit the wall.

He's between you and the door. The only other exits you can see are a doorway behind the reception, and a corridor further back. Dark. Unknown.

Your heart is hammering. Your breath comes in gasps.

You have seconds to decide.

What do you do?

Try to fight him. Turn to page 249
Try to run. Turn to page 329
Try to reason with him. Turn to page 273

GO TO THE SHERIFF

You pull back onto the road and head straight for the sheriff's station. No detours. No stopping at your parents' house or the Inn. You need someone official. Someone with resources, authority, the ability to actually investigate.

The photos on your phone are evidence. Real, documented proof that someone's been using the Van Vleet lodge. The sheriff dismissed you before, but that was when you had nothing concrete. Now you have something he can't ignore.

The station sits on the corner of Main Street, lights on in the front office despite the late hour. You park and hurry inside, out of the cold. Sheriff Larkin looks up from his desk. His expression shifts when he sees you. Something you can't quite read.

"Miss Matthews."

"I found something." You pull out your phone, hands shaking slightly. "I went to the old ski lodge. Someone's been using it. Living there, maybe. I have photos."

You show him the screen. The modern clothes. Rachel's shrine with fresh pine cones.

The sheriff looks at the photos for a long moment. Then he stands. "Where exactly did you take these?"

"The Van Vleet ski lodge. In the apartment upstairs. Someone's been maintaining it. Fresh offerings, recent clothes. The Van Vleets supposedly left in 1977, but…"

"But someone's been there." He comes around the desk, closer than necessary. "Recently."

"Yes. And I think it might be connected to the disappearances. To the King of Christmas."

The sheriff is quiet for a moment, studying your face. Then he picks up his keys.

"All right. Let's go take a look."

You blink. "What?"

"You found evidence of someone using an abandoned building. That's worth investigating." He pulls on his coat. "Come on. Show me what you found."

Relief floods through you. "Thank you. Thank you, I…"

"Don't thank me yet." His smile doesn't quite reach his eyes. "Let's see what we're dealing with first."

You follow him out to the patrol car. He opens the back door (oddly courteous) and you climb in. The door closes with a solid chunk. No handle on the inside.

Your stomach flips, but he's already getting into the driver's seat, starting the engine.

"Sheriff…"

"Relax. Procedure. Can't have civilians opening doors during transport." He pulls out of the lot. "Now. Tell me everything you saw up there."

You talk as he drives, explaining about the apartment, the shrine, the clothes. He nods along, asking occasional questions, seeming genuinely interested.

The road starts to climb. You recognise it. The route back up the mountain.

"I should warn you," you say, "the place is in bad shape. Dangerous. We should probably call for backup…"

"We'll assess first." His hands are steady on the wheel. "No point calling in the whole department for what might be nothing."

"It's not nothing. The evidence…"

"Evidence of someone using a building. Could be squatters. Transients. Happens all the time up here." He glances at you in the rearview mirror. "You're thinking it's connected to the disappearances because you want it to be connected. Understandable. Your sister, all those years… you want answers."

"This isn't about what I want…"

"Isn't it?" His voice is gentle. "You've been carrying Sarah for thirty years. Looking for her in every story you write. Every case you cover. Now you come back here and find... what? An old apartment with some clothes in it? And suddenly you're sure you've found the King of Christmas."

Your throat tightens. "You're doing it again. Dismissing me."

"I'm being realistic." The car climbs higher, trees pressing close on both sides. "But I'm also investigating. That's what you wanted, right? For me to take you seriously?"

He is taking you seriously. He's driving you back up there. That's more than he did before. But something feels wrong.

The lodge appears ahead, dark against the snow. Larkin pulls into the lot, parks near the service entrance.

He kills the engine. The sudden silence is profound.

"Wait here," he says. "I'll take a look around first. If I need you to show me something specific, I'll come get you."

He gets out. The door closes. Through the windshield, you watch him walk toward the building, flashlight beam cutting through the falling snow.

He disappears inside.

Minutes pass. Five. Ten.

You try the door handle. Nothing. The locks are secure.

Your phone glows from your pocket: 12%.

You could call your parents. Tell them where you are. That you're with the sheriff, investigating. That you'll come see them when you're done. That you'll spend Christmas Eve together, finally.

Or you could save the battery. You've learned that lesson already today. Up at the lodge when your phone died and you had no light, no way to call for help. Better to keep that 12% in reserve. Just in case.

What do you do?

Call your parents. Turn to page 305
Save your battery. Turn to page 240

LIE TO KATIE AND SIOBHAN

You draw in a breath, steadying yourself. "All right," you say, softer now. "You're right. I won't do it."

The words taste like ash, but Katie exhales with visible relief. Even Siobhan's glare cools a notch, though suspicion still burns in her eyes.

"Good," Katie murmurs, almost to herself. "That's good." She shuffles the papers on the desk as though the conversation has been filed away too.

You manage a thin smile. "I'll focus on the story. On the records. No more crazy ideas, I promise."

They want to believe you, and for a moment, it looks like they do. Katie even offers a weary smile, as if she's convinced you've come to your senses. Siobhan studies you longer, her gaze sharp, but finally she turns away.

You clutch the folder tighter and excuse yourself, heading for the stairs. Each step creaks underfoot, echoing too loudly in the hush of the Inn.

You go back to your room. Turn to page 451

GO TO THE LODGE

"You're right, Katie. We need real evidence. Something they can't ignore or dismiss. If we go together, document everything properly…" You set your mug down with more confidence than you feel. "That's how we stop him."

Relief floods Katie's face. "Thank God. I was hoping you'd say that."

Siobhan nods slowly, already standing. "If we're doing this, we do it smart. We go now, before the storm gets worse. Before he comes back, if he's not already there."

"Three of us," Katie says, squeezing your hand. "Safety in numbers."

The certainty in her voice steadies you. She's right. You're not alone this time. Not stumbling through a dark building with a dying phone and no one knowing where you are. This time you have allies. Witnesses. People who understand what's at stake.

"I should drive," Siobhan says. "You're shaking. And my car handles better in this weather."

You are shaking. Adrenaline and exhaustion and the weight of finally, finally being believed. "Okay. Thank you."

"Give me two minutes." Siobhan disappears into the office. You hear drawers opening, items being gathered.

Katie stays beside you, her hand still in yours. "We're really doing this," she says quietly.

"We are."

"After forty years. Someone's finally going to see."

The grief in her voice mirrors your own. Tommy. Sarah. All those years of silence and bells and unanswered questions. Tonight, that changes.

Siobhan returns with a canvas bag. "Flashlights. Fully charged. My phone's at ninety percent. Katie, yours?"

Katie checks. "Eighty-five."

"Good. We document everything. Photos, video if we can. Multiple angles." Siobhan's voice is crisp, organised. "Jenny, you lead. Show us exactly what you saw. We verify, we photograph, we leave. In and out in thirty minutes maximum."

The plan sounds solid. Professional. You nod.

The three of you head out to Siobhan's SUV. A sturdy thing built for mountain roads. Katie climbs in back with you while Siobhan takes the wheel. The engine starts with a reassuring rumble.

"Ready?" Siobhan asks, eyes finding yours in the rearview mirror.

"Ready."

The drive up the mountain feels different this time. The dark doesn't seem as oppressive. The snow falling against the windshield is almost peaceful. Katie sits close beside you, her shoulder warm against yours.

"Thank you for trusting us," she says quietly. "I know this can't be easy. Coming back here, digging all this up. But you're doing the right thing."

"I just want to find the truth. For Sarah. For Tommy. For all of them."

"We will." Katie's hand finds yours again in the dark. Her grip is firm, grounding. "Together."

Siobhan navigates the winding road with steady confidence. Her eyes flick to the rearview mirror periodically, catching yours, then Katie's. Some silent communication passing between the sisters that you can't quite read. Probably just nerves. You're all nervous.

"Tell us again what we're looking for," Siobhan says. "Walk us through it so we know what to document."

You describe the apartment. The warmth, the preserved rooms, the evidence of recent habitation. The photos on your phone show some of it, but the full picture needs to be seen in person.

"Modern clothes," Katie repeats. "Contemporary supplies. Fresh maintenance. That's huge, Jenny. That's actual proof someone's been using the space."

"Exactly. The police can't dismiss this. Not when three of us have seen it."

"No," Siobhan agrees. "They can't."

The lodge materialises out of the storm. Dark bulk against darker sky. Your car is still in the lot, already half-buried under fresh snow. Siobhan parks beside it and kills the engine.

Silence crashes in.

"Stay together," Siobhan says. She reaches into the canvas bag, distributing flashlights. "No one wanders off. We go in as a group, we leave as a group."

Katie's hand squeezes yours one more time. "We've got this."

You lead them to the service door. It hangs slightly open where you left it, a dark mouth in the building's side. Your flashlight beam cuts through the opening, illuminating the concrete corridor beyond.

"Through here," you whisper, though you're not sure why you're whispering.

The three of you move down the hallway. Katie walks close behind you, her breathing audible in the enclosed space. Siobhan brings up the rear, flashlight sweeping the walls and doorways.

"God, it is warmer," Katie murmurs. "You're right. It shouldn't be this warm."

Through the corridor, into the lobby. Your lights catch on the furniture, the chandelier swaying slightly in a draft you can't feel. The rusted cash register with its drawer hanging open.

"This way." You lead them toward the stairs.

The stairwell is narrower with three people, your footsteps echoing off concrete. Katie's hand finds your elbow in the dark, steadying herself or steadying you. You're not sure which.

At the top, the apartment door stands open. You step through.

The living room is exactly as you left it. The corkboard with Rachel's drawing. Wait. No. The drawing is gone. Just the tacks remain, pushed into the cork board, empty.

"What is it?" Katie asks, crowding in behind you.

"There was a drawing here. Rachel's drawing. It's gone."

Siobhan moves past you both, flashlight sweeping the space. "Maybe you misremembered…"

"No. It was here. Right here." Your heart hammers. "Someone took it."

The three of you stand in the small living room, lights crisscrossing in the dark. Other things feel different too. The dust on the table has been disturbed. A cushion on the couch sits at a different angle.

"Maybe we should go," you say quietly.

"We just got here." Katie's voice is calm. Steady. "Show us what you found. We came all this way."

She's right. You're being paranoid. The drawing could have fallen. The dust could have been disturbed by your own movements earlier. You take a breath.

"This way."

You lead them to the master bedroom first. The dresser with its hanging drawers. "Here. Look."

Katie and Siobhan crowd around. You pull open the third drawer, the one with the folded clothes. Modern denim. Contemporary t-shirts.

"My god," Katie breathes. She pulls out her phone, starts photographing. "This is incredible. How did no one find this before?"

"No one was looking." Siobhan is examining the clothes, checking tags. "Or if they found it, they didn't want to see it."

You show them the bathroom next, then Rachel's bedroom. The door is closed now. You're certain you left it open. But Katie's already reaching for the handle.

The bedroom is exactly as you saw it. The dresser with its gallery of photographs. The stuffed animals on the bed. The books on the shelf. And surrounding Rachel's central portrait, seven pine cones in a perfect circle.

"Jesus," Siobhan whispers.

Katie steps inside, drawn to the dresser like something's pulling her. Her flashlight illuminates the photographs, the careful arrangement, the fresh pine cones.

"Katie's right," you say. "This is Rachel. Rachel Van Vleet. Someone's been maintaining her room for forty-nine years."

"Who would do that?" Katie's voice is strange. Distant.

"That's what we need to find out."

You're all standing in Rachel's room now, flashlights illuminating different corners. The stuffed animals. The books. The shrine.

That's when you hear it.

Footsteps. From somewhere in the apartment. Not the building settling. Not the wind.

Heavy. Deliberate. Getting closer.

You spin toward the doorway. Your flashlight beam catches movement in the living room. A figure stepping from the shadowed hallway you never explored.

Tall. Broad. Wearing red.

Your brain struggles to process what you're seeing. It can't be. It's not possible.

But he's there. Santa Claus. The King of Christmas. Real. Here. Not a legend or a story but a man in a red suit, hood up, face shadowed.

And he's between you and the only exit.

Katie's hand slips from your elbow. Not panicked. Just releases you. Calmly. Deliberately.

"Katie?" Your voice comes out small.

She doesn't answer. She's looking at Siobhan.

Siobhan nods once. Some silent agreement passing between them.

The figure steps into fuller light. You can see his face now. Weathered, bearded, somewhere between sixty and eighty. His eyes are pale and flat.

"She came here tonight," Siobhan continues. "Found your rooms. Took photographs. Was planning to expose everything." A pause. "We thought you'd want her back."

The words don't make sense. Can't make sense. Your brain refuses to process them.

"We?" you whisper.

No one looks at you.

The man studies you like you're something he'd lost and rediscovered. "The guilty one," he says softly. "The sister who lived."

"Yes," Siobhan says.

Silence stretches. You look at Katie, desperate for her to say something, to explain, to tell you this isn't what it looks like.

But Katie won't meet your eyes. She's staring at the floor, hands clenched at her sides.

"Your daughter is safe tonight, Siobhan," the man says finally.

Relief floods Siobhan's face. Genuine, visceral. "Thank you."

"Wait…" Your voice cracks. "Katie, what is this? What are you…"

"I'm sorry," Katie whispers. Still not looking at you. "Lily. I have to protect Lily."

"We all do what we have to," Siobhan says. She's moving toward the door now, giving the man space to enter fully. "Come on, Katie. We should go."

"No." You back away, bumping into Rachel's dresser. Photographs rattle. "No, you can't… Katie, please…"

Katie finally looks at you. Her eyes are wet but her face is resigned. "I'm sorry, Jenny. I really am. But I can't let him take my niece. I can't lose her like I lost Tommy."

"So you'll let him take me instead?"

"Yes." The word is barely audible.

Siobhan takes Katie's arm, pulling her toward the door. Katie doesn't resist. She walks like someone in a dream, or a nightmare, letting her sister guide her.

"Wait!" You lunge forward but the man blocks your path. Up close he's bigger than he seemed, solid and immovable.

"Don't," he says quietly.

You watch helplessly as Katie and Siobhan reach the doorway. Siobhan doesn't look back. Katie does. Just once, her face streaked with tears.

"I'm sorry," she mouths.

Then they're gone. Footsteps receding down the stairs. The service door opening and closing. An engine starting in the parking lot.

Silence.

You're alone in Rachel's room with the King of Christmas.

He reaches up slowly, deliberately, and pushes back his hood. The face beneath is weathered, lined deep with age and weather. His beard is mostly white, his hair thin. He looks like someone's grandfather. Like he should be handing out candy canes, not...

"You're shaking," he observes.

You are. Your whole body is trembling, teeth chattering despite the warmth of the apartment.

"Please," you whisper. "I won't tell anyone. I'll leave town. I'll never come back..."

"Yes, you will." His voice is almost gentle. "You'll tell everyone. It's what you do. You're a journalist. Your whole career has been about exposing things that should stay buried."

"I won't. I promise. I'll..."

"Stop." He moves closer. You back away until you hit the wall under the window. Nowhere left to go. "Do you know how long I've been waiting?"

"For what?"

"For you." His pale eyes never leave your face. "Thirty-nine years. Took you long enough to come home."

Your throat closes. "I don't understand."

"Don't you?" He tilts his head, studying you like you're a puzzle he's trying to solve. "Sarah was innocent. Genuinely innocent. She kept saying 'I didn't do it, I don't know what you mean, please.' Over and over. She didn't understand why she was being punished."

The room tilts. "You… you're the one who…"

"The bracelet," he continues as if you haven't spoken. "She didn't steal it. She didn't lie about it. She was genuinely confused about why I'd taken her. Because she was actually innocent." His voice drops. "Which meant someone else was guilty."

"No…"

"You." The word is soft but final. "You stole the bracelet. You blamed your sister. You let her carry the guilt for something you did. And then I took her. An innocent child, punished for your sin."

You can't breathe. Can't think. The truth you've carried for thirty-nine years, laid bare by a monster in a red suit.

"That's what broke the pattern," he says. "Why I stopped taking children for nine years after her. Because she proved my whole system was flawed. I was punishing the innocent based on lies told by the guilty. Sarah died because of you, Jenny Matthews. And you've been alive all this time, walking free, pretending you weren't responsible."

"I was eleven," you choke out. "I was a child. I didn't know…"

"Neither was she." His hand moves to his coat. "But she paid anyway."

You see the knife then. Not large or ornate. Just a simple blade, worn smooth with use.

"Please." Tears stream down your face. "Please, I'm sorry. I'm so sorry about Sarah. About everything. Please…"

"I know you are." He sounds almost sympathetic. "But thirty-nine years late, wouldn't you say?"

He moves fast. You try to dodge but there's nowhere to go, your back already against the wall. His hand catches your shoulder, pins you in place.

"Wait!" The word tears from your throat. "Rachel. This is Rachel's room. You're… you're her *father*? Mr Van Vleet."

He freezes. Something flickers across his face. Pain, maybe, or recognition of a name he hasn't heard in decades.

"I was," he says quietly. "Before she was taken from me."

"But then you started taking other children. Making them guilty to prove she was innocent. Punishing them for being alive when Rachel died." Your voice cracks. "How many? How many children have you killed to justify one accident?"

"SHUT UP!"

The knife rises.

You try to wrench free but he's too strong, the wall at your back giving you nowhere to go. The blade catches the light from the fallen flashlights, silver and sharp.

"This is your fault," he says, and his voice is cold now, all sympathy gone. "You made Katie bring you here. You made Siobhan choose. You forced this. All of it. Just like you forced Sarah's death thirty-nine years ago."

"No…"

The blade moves.

There's pressure. Then warmth spreading across your side. Then pain. Bright and sharp and all-consuming.

You're aware of falling. Of the floor coming up to meet you. Of Rachel's stuffed rabbit staring at you with its black button eyes, its worn fur matted with age.

The man crouches beside you. His face fills your vision.

"Tell Sarah hello for me," he says quietly.

You try to speak but only blood comes out. Your vision is darkening at the edges, sound growing distant and muffled.

Your last thought, as the room fades to grey then black, is of that moment. Christmas Eve 1986. Sarah running into the backyard in her red mittens. You watching from the window, bracelet hidden in your pocket, already rehearsing the lies you'd tell.

If you'd just told the truth. If you'd just admitted what you'd done.

Sarah would have lived.

And you wouldn't be dying in a dead girl's room, surrounded by the artifacts of a childhood that never got to finish.

The darkness takes you.

Outside, the storm keeps falling. Katie and Siobhan drive home through the white, windshield wipers beating steady rhythm. They'll go inside. Make hot chocolate. Tuck Lily into bed. Read her a story.

Sleep soundly, knowing their daughter is safe.

By morning, fresh snow will have covered the tracks leading to and from the lodge. The building will stand silent, keeping its secrets for another forty-nine years.

Inside Rachel's room, two sisters' stories finally end in the same place.

THE END

You died in Rachel Van Vleet's preserved bedroom, betrayed by the women you trusted, killed by the man whose daughter's accidental death started everything. Katie and Siobhan sacrificed you to protect Siobhan's daughter Lily—following the rules that keep their children safe in a town held hostage by the King of Christmas.

Sometimes the people who understand your pain are the very ones who'll use it to destroy you.

TRY TO RUN

You bolt. Not the main door, he's blocking that. You panic and run for the doorway behind the reception desk. You vault over the counter, stumble, catch yourself.

A hallway. Dark. You run.

Behind you: "There's nowhere to go."

His voice is calm. Not chasing. Doesn't need to.

You find stairs. Go up. Maybe there's a window, a balcony, something...

The second floor is different. Residential. You're in someone's home. Someone's living room. The wallpaper is faded, a floral style that looks like it's been unchanged since the 1970s. That's when this place was abandoned. Six months after Rachel Van Vleet was taken, her parents left. You've read the reports, but more than that, you know from your childhood. This was where the King of Christmas began: with the abduction of Rachel.

She lived here, she...

You don't have time for any more thoughts. There are three other ways out of this room, and you can see a small kitchen through one of them. You push forward, taking the door to the right. There has to be a way through, a way out...

But what you find is not an exit.

What you find is a child's bedroom.

Pink wallpaper. A small bed with a time-faded quilt, except up close you see it's not faded, it's rotted. Shredded to scraps, stuffing spilling out like snow.

On the pillow: stuffed animals. A bear, a rabbit, something that might have been a dog. Fabric ragged, eaten by time and moths, fur worn to bare patches. But positioned deliberately. Carefully. Like someone still tucks them in.

Rachel's room.

They never cleared it.

Your eyes sweep frantically, looking for windows, for doors, for ANY way out.

A bookshelf.

A dresser.

Framed photos arranged with deliberate care. You don't have time to look at them, but in the centre there's a large portrait of a girl with dark hair. Even through the fade, you can see her smile.

And surrounding that centrepiece, arranged in a perfect circle: seven pine cones.

Fresh. Recent.

It looks like a shrine.

Behind you: footsteps on the stairs. Steady. Unhurried.

You spin. Another door. You lunge for it, yank it open.

It's a bathroom. Tiny. Sink, toilet, shower. One small window above the toilet.

Boarded.

You climb onto the toilet, claw at the boards. They don't budge; nailed from outside, solid.

"No no no…"

Footsteps in the bedroom now.

You jump down, back into Rachel's room.

You're trapped.

The man in the red ski suit stands in the doorway. Blocking it. The only exit.

"This was her room," he says quietly. Looking around. "I keep it exactly as it was. Well." He glances at the rotted bedding, the deteriorated toys. "As close as I can."

"You're insane…"

"And here you are on Christmas Eve, chasing your own ghost."

He steps into the room.

"Rachel was the first. Then the Van Vleets left," you say desperately, backing toward the boarded window. "They abandoned this place. Why are you…"

"Did we?" His voice is cold. "Or did I just let everyone believe that?"

We.

You look at him, a quick calculation running in your mind. His face is lined with age. He could be in his seventies, eighties perhaps. He *could* be Mr Van Vleet, Rachel's father.

Your back hits the wall.

"You're…"

"This is my lodge," he says, looking around the room at the rotted toys, the faded wallpaper, the shrine on the dresser. "My daughter's room."

"But your wife?"

"Long gone." His jaw tightens. "She wanted to confess. Wanted to tell them what really happened. I couldn't let that happen."

The implication settles over you like snow.

"What really happened?"

You should be thinking about a way out, but suddenly all you can do is ask questions.

"Rachel was perfect," he continues quietly. "She didn't deserve what happened. But this town…" His hands clench. "They didn't care. And when she was gone, they just moved on. Like she never mattered."

He's almost on you now. Part of you wants to ask what happened and part of you wants to tear down the boards on the windows and throw yourself out.

"I made sure they'd never forget," he says as he lunges.

You grab for something, anything. Your hand closes around a book from the shelf. It's soft, rotten, mildewed. You throw it at him anyway.

It bounces off his chest. Falls to the floor.

He looks down at the book. Then at you.

"That was hers," he says.

His hand closes around your throat.

You claw at his grip. Can't breathe. Can't…

Your vision tunnels. The photos on the dresser blur. Rachel's face, smiling. The seven pine cones arranged in their perfect circle.

A father's shrine.

Maintained for forty-nine years.

Alone.

Now you're dying in it.

And you'll never know why.

THE END

You died in Rachel Van Vleet's bedroom on Christmas Eve, 2025. Your body was left there, with the photos daughter Robert Van Vleet never stopped mourning.

The King of Christmas continued his work.

The sheriff heads for the door. Your father follows immediately, and you tuck in alongside him, holding his hand.

Outside, the cold hits like a wall. The sheriff's opens the back door and waves for you to enter.

"Procedure," he says, almost apologetic. "Can't have civilians up front during an investigation."

Your father climbs in and shuffles across to let you take the other seat. Something in the way he moves reminds you of how old he is.

The door closes with a heavy chunk.

No handles on the inside.

The sheriff gets in front, starts the engine. The heater kicks on, filling the car with warm air that smells faintly of coffee and leather.

"So," he says, adjusting the rearview mirror. "Tell me everything you saw up there. Every detail."

You talk as he drives, explaining about the apartment, the shrine, the clothes. Your father adds details, questions about the Van Vleets, about who might have had access, about how long someone could have been using the place.

The sheriff nods along, asking occasional questions, seeming genuinely interested.

The road starts to climb. You recognise it: the route back up the mountain.

Through the window, Pine Hollow's lights fade behind you. The trees press closer, their branches heavy with snow. The road narrows to a single lane, winding higher.

Your father's shoulder is warm against yours. His hands rest in his lap, fingers laced together. He's been waiting decades for this moment. For someone official to finally listen. To finally act.

"When we get there," the sheriff says, "I'll need you both to stay in the car while I assess the situation. Standard procedure. Can't have civilians contaminating a potential crime scene."

"Of course," your father says. "Whatever you need."

The lodge appears ahead, a dark shape against darker trees. The sheriff pulls into the lot, parks near the service entrance.

He kills the engine. The sudden silence is profound.

"Wait here," he says. "I'll take a look around first. If I need you to show me something specific, I'll come get you."

He gets out. The door closes. Through the windshield, you watch him walk toward the building, flashlight beam cutting through the falling snow.

He disappears inside.

While you wait:
Talk to your father. Turn to page 344
Stay silent. Turn to page 304

YOUR PARENTS' HOUSE

You throw the car into drive and don't stop until you reach Evergreen Lane.

You pull up across the street and kill the engine.

Through the front window, you can see the living room lamp is on. Someone's awake. Of course they are. It's Christmas Eve. Your mother never sleeps on Christmas Eve. Not since Sarah.

Thirty-nine years without her. Merry shitty Christmas.

You sit in the cold car, engine ticking as it cools, and stare at the house.

You came here because if you're going to stake out, why not do it where your own family are going to get their bell? You want to know who took Sarah, and who is still leaving these twisted keepsakes every single year since. You need answers. The story you came here to write has taken backseat.

But now that you're here, you have to decide: what next?

You could go inside. Knock on the door. Tell your parents everything: about the stakeout, about Katie and Siobhan trying to talk you out of it, about what you're trying to do. They'd let you watch from inside. You'd be warm. Safe. Not alone.

Or you could stay here. In the car. Watch from across the street. Your parents' house is one of the four that will receive a bell tonight. You could see who places it without involving them, without worrying them, without putting that weight on their shoulders.

They've carried enough of that over the decades.

You look back at the lit window. Your mother moving past, a shadow behind the curtain.

What do you do?
Stay in the car and watch. Turn to page 370
Go inside. Turn to page 242

THE CRAWFORDS STAKEOUT

You head toward Oak Street.

The Crawfords. Amy's family. The most recent victim. The wound is fresh, raw in a way the others have had decades to scab over.

The drive through Pine Hollow is quiet. Christmas Eve has emptied the streets. The houses glow with warm light, televisions flickering in living rooms, families settling in for the night. You pass the church—its parking lot full for evening service, voices rising in hymn through the open doors. *Silent night, holy night...*

You turn onto the street.

The Crawford house is modest. Ranch-style, beige siding, a small front porch with a railing wrapped in lights. A plastic snowman stands in the yard, slightly deflated. There's a wreath on the door.

And in the front window, a small artificial tree. Unlit.

You park three houses down, far enough to be unobtrusive but close enough to watch. The folder rests on the passenger seat, your father's map on top, Crawford house circled like a target.

10:32pm.

You settle in to wait.

The heater hums. Your coffee thermos sits in the cup holder, steam curling from the open top. You take a sip. It's hot, bitter, and grounding. Outside, the street is empty. Silent.

You're watching the house, planning your vantage points, when the front door opens.

A man steps onto the porch. Mr Crawford. Forties, thinning hair, wearing a flannel shirt and jeans. He's looking directly at your car.

Your stomach drops.

He starts walking toward you. Not hurried, but deliberate. His face is hard.

You consider driving away. But that would look worse. So you roll down your window as he approaches, letting the cold air slice in.

"Can I help you?" His voice is flat, controlled. Barely containing something underneath.

"Mr Crawford, I'm..."

"Don't." The word is sharp. "Don't say anything. You need to leave."

A woman appears in the doorway of the Crawford house. Mrs Crawford, arms wrapped around herself. Behind her, barely visible, a child; she's small, maybe six or seven. Amy's sibling. Another child who will grow up without her sister.

"I'm not here to bother you," you say quietly. "I just want to understand what happened. To all of them. To stop this."

"By staking out my house on Christmas Eve?" His jaw works. "You think I don't see you? You think I don't know what you're doing?"

"I'm trying to help."

"You're trying to write a story." He leans closer, and you can see his eyes are red-rimmed, exhausted. "You're trying to turn my daughter into content. Into something people read with their morning coffee and forget by lunch."

"That's not..."

"It's too fresh." His voice cracks on the last word. "It's too goddamn fresh. We're trying to get through tonight. Trying to keep it together for..." He glances back at the house, at the child in the doorway. "We have another daughter. You understand that? Another little girl who's terrified Santa might be real and might come for her too."

Your throat tightens. "I understand. I'm sorry. I'll go."

"You do that." He straightens. "And if I see you on this street again, I'm calling the sheriff. You're harassing a grieving family. Pretty sure that's against the law."

"I'm sorry," you say again. Because you are. Because you understand grief that raw, that fresh wound. Because you remember your parents the year after Sarah vanished, and how they would have reacted to someone like you.

He walks back to his house without another word. Mrs Crawford ushers the child inside. The door closes. The porch light stays on.

You sit in your car, hands on the wheel, shame burning in your chest.

You can't stake out here. Not with them watching. Not with a child in that house who's already terrified.

You check your watch. 10:47pm.

You need to choose another location.

Where do you go?

The Hendersons. Turn to page 254
The Wilsons. Turn to page 309
Your parents. Turn to page 335

THE SERVICE DOOR OPENS

The sheriff emerges, flashlight beam sweeping the lot before settling on the cruiser. He walks back, opens your door.

"All right. Building's clear, no one inside. Jenny, can you come show me exactly where you found these things? Bill, you wait here. Keep the heater running, stay warm. This shouldn't take long."

Your father shifts beside you. "I should come too…"

"Appreciate it, but the fewer people tramping around, the better. Evidence preservation." The sheriff's voice is patient, reasonable. "Jenny can show me what she found, I'll document it, then we'll figure out next steps. Ten minutes, tops."

It makes sense. It's logical. But something in your gut twists.

What do you do?

Go with the sheriff alone. Turn to page 423
Insist on staying with your father. Turn to page 441

LEAVE NOW

You have the photos you managed to take before your phone died. And you've seen enough: the modern clothes, Rachel's shrine, the fresh pine cones. Someone has been here. Recently. They might come back, and you don't want to be here when they do. You're a journalist not a private detective. You're a sister, not a superhero.

You can almost hear your editor reminding you to know your limits. Those limits were always emotional, not physical. But right now? Right now they're both.

The apartment presses in around you, too warm, too preserved, too wrong. Every minute you stay increases the risk.

They could come back.

They could be coming back right now.

You need to leave. Get to town. Tell someone what you've found. Come back with help, with authorities, with backup.

This is the smart choice.

You move carefully through the living room, past the corkboard with Rachel's faded drawing, past the couch where a family once sat together. Your torch beam sweeps the shadows one last time.

The apartment door stands open to the stairwell. The same stairs you climbed. Now they're your way out.

You descend quickly, boots careful on the creaking wood. The lobby below is silent, grey light filtering through boarded windows. No movement. No sound.

Almost there.

The service corridor stretches ahead, concrete floor gleaming with ice patches. Your breath clouds in the beam of your torch. Each step echoes, multiplies, sounds like someone following.

You don't look back.

The door. The metal handle, cold against your palm. You push through.

Outside, the mountain air hits you like a wall. Clean, sharp, alive. Snow falls in slow spirals, settling on your shoulders, your hair. The parking lot spreads white and empty before you.

Your car waits where you left it, already wearing a fresh coat of powder.

You run.

The snow clutches at your boots, but you push through it, closing the distance. Twenty feet. Ten. Your hand finds the door handle, wrenches it open. You fall into the driver's seat, slam the door, punch the lock.

Safe. You're safe.

Your hands shake as you jam the key into the ignition. The engine turns over, reluctant in the cold, then catches. Heat begins to trickle from the vents, and you sit there for a moment, breathing hard, staring at the lodge in your rearview mirror.

Dark windows. Silent walls. A building that should be abandoned but isn't.

You reach for your phone, plug it into the car charger. The screen stays black for a long moment, then flickers: Charging... 1%

It'll take time. But you're moving, you're leaving, and that's what matters.

You shift into gear and pull out of the lot.

Heat floods the vents now, almost too warm after the cold of the lodge. Outside, the snow has eased, just a few lazy flakes drifting through your headlights. The road winds down through darkness, the trees pressing close on both sides.

You check the rearview mirror. Again. And again.

Half-expecting to see headlights behind you. A figure in red emerging from the tree line. A man in a coat with white fur trim, watching you flee.

But there's nothing. Just darkness and falling snow.

Your hands tighten on the wheel. You're being paranoid. There was no one at the lodge. No sign anyone was there. You were alone.

Except…

Your breath catches.

What DID you find?

Your hands shake too hard to drive safely. You pull over on a wide shoulder, engine idling, and grip the wheel until your knuckles go white.

The Van Vleets.

It crashes over you all at once: the shrine to Rachel, maintained for forty-nine years. The apartment preserved like a museum. Fresh pine cones arranged just days ago around her photographs.

Maybe they didn't leave town.

Maybe they never left.

Robert Van Vleet. Maybe his wife too. Living up there all this time, hiding in the mountains, maintaining their daughter's shrine.

But why?

Why?

Did you miss something that would have given you more answers? Should you have searched further? Looked harder?

At least you're thinking now.

The King of Christmas took Rachel on Christmas Eve 1976.

The Van Vleets left six months later.

Why?

They left the lodge, didn't sell. No one has run it or repurposed it.

Why?

The King of Christmas took Rachel.

Why?

These are questions you still have to answer.

There was no evidence connecting what you found to the disappearances.

The pieces swirl in your head, refusing to fit together.

If it's not the Van Vleets, it's someone who's obsessed with Rachel Van Vleet.

You don't know who, you don't know why.

Your phone glows from the charging cradle: 8%.

You have photos. You have questions.

What you need is someone who knows this town's history. The Van Vleets' story.

Someone who knows more than you do.

Where do you go?

Take the evidence to

Katie. Turn to page 264
Your parents. Turn to page 366
The sheriff Turn to page 315

TALK TO YOUR FATHER

"Finally," your father says quietly. "Finally someone's taking this seriously."

You turn to him. In the dim light from the dashboard, his profile could be from any year: 1986, 1995, tonight. Time collapses.

"Dad," you say. "I'm sorry. For staying away so long. For not coming back."

"Don't." His voice is rough. "You did what you needed to do. Got out. Made a life."

"But I left you here. With the bells. With all of it."

He looks at you then, and his eyes are wet. "You survived. That's what mattered. Your mother and I... we never blamed you for leaving."

"I blamed myself."

"I know." He reaches over, takes your hand. His palm is warm, calloused. "But you're here now. That counts for something."

"What if this doesn't work? What if we're wrong about..."

"Then we'll figure it out together." His grip tightens. "Like we should have done thirty years ago. Like we'll do from now on. No more distance. No more missed years."

No more missed years.

You lean your head against his shoulder, and he rests his cheek against your hair the way he used to when you were small.

"I love you, Dad."

"I love you too, Jenny. So much."

The service door opens. Turn to page 339

TAKE THE RIGHT DOOR

The second bedroom is smaller. A child's room.

Your torch beam sweeps across walls that still show ghosts of posters. Discoloured rectangles where paper once hung, tattered corners clinging to pushpins. One remains mostly intact: a kitten hanging from a branch, "HANG IN THERE" faded to pale brown.

A single bed. The bedding has deteriorated to shreds. Rotted scraps, stuffing spilling from the pillow like snow. On the pillow, arranged deliberately: stuffed animals. A bear, a rabbit, something that might have been a dog. Fabric ragged, eaten by time, but positioned with care. Still tucked in.

This is Rachel's room.

Your throat closes.

A bookshelf against one wall. Your torch picks out spines: *Anne of Green Gables, A Wrinkle in Time, Charlotte's Web*. Books an eleven-year-old girl loved in 1976.

Anne of Green Gables. Sarah's favourite.

You reach for your phone before you remember. Dead. You got photos of the modern clothes in the master bedroom and then nothing. But you need this. You need Rachel's room documented.

You pull out the phone anyway, press the power button. Hold it. Nothing. The screen stays black.

You try again, thumb jabbing at the button. Wake up. Please.

Dead.

You slip it back into your pocket, useless weight.

The dresser across from the bed draws your eye. While everything else shows fifty years of decay (posters gone, bedding rotted, stuffed animals falling apart), the dresser top is different.

Dust-free.

Your torch illuminates a gallery of framed photos arranged with deliberate care. The glass protects them. Colours have shifted strange, blues gone, everything tinted yellow-red like aged film. But the faces remain.

School photos of Rachel at different ages. A family snapshot in front of the lodge. A Polaroid of her on skis. Another holding a stuffed rabbit. You glance at the bed, at the deteriorated rabbit on the pillow. The same one.

The central photo: Rachel at eleven. Dark hair, bright eyes, smile showing permanent teeth coming in.

And surrounding it, arranged in a perfect circle: seven pine cones.

You lean closer. The pine cones aren't scattered. They're placed. Each one perfectly formed, scales intact. Your torch catches their surfaces: dry but not brittle, brown but not grey.

Fresh. Weeks old, maybe a month.

Someone's been here. Recently. Not forty-nine years ago. Recently. Cleaning this surface. Arranging these offerings.

Something catches your eye behind Rachel's photo. You tilt the large frame forward carefully.

Another picture, smaller, half-hidden. Rachel's mother. Formal portrait. No smile, just a direct gaze.

A single white stone sits on this frame. River stone, smooth, white as bone.

Seven offerings for Rachel. One for her mother. Why separate? Why hidden?

Your hand moves toward your pocket again. The phone, you need to photograph this. You stop. Dead. It's dead. This shrine, these pine cones, this evidence of maintenance; you see it, but you can't prove it.

You have photos from the master bedroom. Proof someone's been using this space. But you don't have this: the shrine, the ritual, the obsessive maintenance of Rachel's memory.

The apartment is warmer than it should be. The clothes are contemporary. The pine cones are fresh.

Your breath comes faster. You're not just investigating an old disappearance. You're standing in someone's active space. Someone who lives here, maintains a shrine here, accepts supplies here.

And you have no phone. No way to call for help if you need it.

The hatch in the master bedroom; the loft. If someone's been living here for years, that's where they'd keep supplies, records, the things that matter. Physical evidence you could take with you.

Or you could leave. Right now. You have photos of the modern clothes. That's something. That's proof of recent habitation. Get to your car, drive to town, show someone. Your parents. Someone who'll believe you.

But without the shrine photo, without the pine cones, without whatever is in the loft, how much of the story can you tell? How much will they believe?

Every instinct screams that something is wrong. That you're not alone here. That staying longer is dangerous.

But you're a journalist. You find truth. You build cases. You need to see more. You need the full story. Don't you?

What do you do?
Go back and enter the loft. Turn to page 352
Leave now with the photo you have. Turn to page 340

"Wait." You hold up your hands. "We can talk about this. We can—"

CRACK.

Your mother drops. Just drops. Like a puppet with cut strings.

"Mom!" Your father lunges toward her.

CRACK.

He falls across her body.

You can't move. Can't breathe. Can't process what just happened.

Larkin lowers the gun slightly. Looks at you.

"That was your parents," he says. Calm. Conversational. "They died because you came back. Because you couldn't leave well enough alone."

Your legs give out. You're on your knees. Can't look away from them. From the blood. From the...

"Sarah died because of you too." Larkin's voice continues. Patient. Like he has all the time in the world. "You blamed her for the bracelet. You lied. And he took her. Forty years of guilt, Jenny. Forty years of knowing it was your fault."

"Please..." Your voice is barely there.

"And now your parents. Also your fault." He shakes his head. "You've always made the wrong choices. Always got people hurt. Everyone you touch."

He raises the gun again. Points it at your head.

"You should have stayed in Boston."

CRACK.

THE END
You died on your knees in your childhood living room on Christmas Eve, 2025. Your parents died seconds before you,

executed without warning while you tried to negotiate with their killer.

The official report called it a home invasion. A drifter, they said. Wrong place, wrong time. Sheriff Larkin responded but arrived too late. He was commended for his investigation. No suspect was ever found.

Pine Hollow mourned the tragedy. The bells kept coming to other houses. Other families. Other victims.

The King of Christmas continued his work.

KEEP DRIVING

You press harder on the accelerator.

I can lose him. I can lose him.

You turn off Main Street onto a side road. Then another. Trying to put distance between you, trying to find somewhere to hide.

The streets blur together as you head out of town. You don't know your way around out here. It's beyond the realms of the area you were allowed to take your bike out to as a child. It's nowhere you wanted to come when you were a teenager. It's trees, more trees, nowhere to hide.

The cruiser is right behind you. Relentless.

He pulls alongside you. You see him gesture: PULL OVER.

You don't.

He swerves toward you.

Your tires hit the shoulder. Gravel spits. You overcorrect, swerve back onto the road.

He does it again. Harder this time.

You're forced right. Off the road completely.

The car is sliding now.

You have to slow to wind between the pines, but Larkin is picking his way through too. Even with your beams on full, it's dark out here.

How did this happen?

You were meant to be gathering information.

Some time ago, you were meant to be writing a story.

Now you're on the run from the sheriff, bumping over the forest floor in a hire car that you'll never get the deposit back on.

Shit, shit, fucking shit.

His red and blues are still flashing, but there's no siren now. The light shines around you, bathing the forest in ice then fire, ice then fire. Over and over as you look for some kind of path to follow.

This doesn't seem like such a good idea anymore.

But then you reach the edge of the treeline and burst out into a wide open clearing.

This could be your chance.

The clearing stretches ahead of you: wide, flat, covered in snow. You could gun it across. Put real distance between you and Larkin. Make it to the tree line on the other side and lose him in the forest.

Or you could stick to the edge. Follow the tree line around the perimeter. Slower, but safer; solid ground, cover if you need it, a way back into the forest if things go wrong.

Behind you, Larkin's cruiser breaks through the tree line. His headlights pin you in place.

You have seconds to decide.

What do you do?
Drive straight across the clearing. Turn to page 389
Stick to the forest edge. Turn to page 447

ENTER THE LOFT

In the master bedroom, you climb onto the bed. The mattress sinks under your boots, springs groaning. The frame sags, soft from years of damp. You steady yourself with one hand on the wall.

The hatch has no cord, no handle, just a wooden panel flush with the ceiling. You raise your torch, press the end against it, and push. Nothing. You shift your stance, feel the mattress compress beneath you, and push harder.

The panel jerks. Shifts an inch. Then…

A sharp crack. The hatch swings open.

The ladder drops fast, metal flashing in your beam. You lurch back, boot slipping on the sagging mattress. It slams into the bedframe where your head just was: metal on wood, loud as a gunshot.

You catch yourself against the wall, pulse hammering. The ladder sways, still intact. Above, darkness yawns: one way up, one way down. You push that thought away.

Just a quick look. Five minutes.

You grab the ladder. The rungs are cold, rust rough beneath your palm. First rung. Second. It holds. You climb.

Your head clears the opening. The loft is bigger than you expected, the full length of the apartment below. Low ceiling, beams slanting down at the sides. You crouch, torch sweeping the space.

Boxes. Dozens of them. Cardboard splitting, stacked in corners. Others, plastic bins, sit newer, out of place. The air is thick with dust; you taste it when you breathe.

You haul yourself up, boots on plywood. Solid. Someone built this to bear weight.

You open a box: papers. Old invoices, maintenance logs from 1975, 1976. The paperwork of a business already dying. Another holds moth-eaten curtains. Another, broken ski gear.

Nothing useful. Just the remnants of a life packed away.

Still, if the Van Vleets really left after Rachel vanished, why leave all this? Files, linens, supplies. You'd expect emptiness—bare walls, not rooms caught mid-breath, as if someone stepped out one winter and never came back.

The thought sticks as you move deeper into the loft. Your torch catches on something that doesn't belong here: a row of opaque blue bins, snap-lid, modern. The kind you'd buy anywhere. Too new for this place.

You drag one toward you, pop the latches, lift the lid.

Inside: Christmas.

Garlands, strings of lights, ornaments dulled by time. Enough to deck the entire lobby of the lodge.

You brush aside a tangle of tinsel, a cracked glass bauble, a velvet ribbon turned grey with dust. They're old, perhaps the originals, from the resort's first winters, but they couldn't have been left here like this. Not packed so neatly, not in boxes that didn't exist fifty years ago.

You shift the top layer aside, and something glints beneath. Bells. Dozens of them. Layer on layer, heavy and silent, their silver dulled but unmistakable.

Every one identical to the bells that haunt your parents' doorstep.

And then it hits you. The folded clothes in the dresser downstairs, the shirts still smelling faintly of detergent, the shrine of pine cones and faded photographs laid out with impossible care. Every piece arranged by the same hands.

This place isn't abandoned. It's tended. Loved, even.

The clothes, the decorations, the bells. None of them are leftovers from another life.

They're offerings. Devotion disguised as order.

Someone hasn't just been keeping this place.

They've been keeping it alive.

A sound breaks the stillness.

A door slams below. Hard. Sudden. Close enough to shake dust from the rafters. You jerk upright, heart in your throat. Silence follows for a beat... and then, faint but unmistakable, comes whistling.

A tune you know too well.

The notes drift up through the cracks in the floorboards, light and careless, echoing through the hollow rooms. A Christmas song, in an empty lodge.

Santa Claus is coming to town.

You kill the torch. Darkness presses close, thick as cloth.

The whistling goes on unhurried, tuneless between verses.

He's here.

Your thoughts splinter into two choices:

Hide. Turn to page 395

Get out of the loft. Now. Turn to page 362

TRY TO GET A BETTER LOOK NOW

You step closer to the post, your boots breaking through the crust with a soft crunch. Lean in, squinting against the glare of snow. The paint has faded to almost nothing, the letters mere shadows of themselves, ghosts pressed into weathered wood.

You pull off one glove, thinking your bare fingers might brush away snow more effectively, might reveal something your covered hand missed. The cold bites immediately, sharp little teeth at your fingertips. You trace the shapes: angular marks that could be D-A-N... something. Below it, N-O... something else.

You shift your weight, trying a different angle. Crouch lower. The letters seem to shift in and out of meaning, like one of those optical illusions that resolves into sense only if you look at it exactly right. But you can't find the right angle. The decades have worn the message smooth.

Your fingers are starting to hurt, a deep ache settling into the joints. You pull the glove back on, flex your hand. It responds slowly, as if the tendons have stiffened.

How long have you been crouched here? A minute? Three? Time feels strange, stretched thin like the light.

You straighten, a little light-headed from the change in position. Your knees protest, stiff from the cold and the static crouch. Whatever words this post once carried, they are lost now. Erased by fifty years of weather, of snow and wind and the mountain's patient indifference.

Just an old trail marker. Just another piece of abandoned infrastructure slowly returning to the mountain.

You turn back to the slope ahead, shaking feeling back into your fingers. Nothing that matters now. Nothing that changes what you came here to do.

You keep climbing. Turn to page 360

GO INTO THE LODGE

You start walking. Down the road, toward town, like he told you to. Your boots crunch in the snow. You don't look back.

Behind you, the truck's engine idles. Waiting. Watching.

You keep walking. Twenty yards. Thirty. The cold is already biting through your coat. Five miles of this. You'll freeze.

The truck moves. Slowly. Following you at a crawl.

He's making sure you actually leave.

You keep your pace steady. Don't look back. Don't give him any reason to doubt you.

Fifty yards. The truck is still there, headlights casting your shadow long and dark across the snow.

Then the engine revs. The headlights swing past you as he turns around. The sound fades as he drives back down the mountain, away from the lodge, back toward town.

You stop. Listen. The engine gets quieter. Quieter.

Gone.

You stand there in the darkness, breathing hard. Your face is already numb. Your fingers ache inside your gloves. Five miles. In this. You won't make it.

And you don't trust that he's actually gone. Don't trust that he won't be waiting somewhere down that road. Waiting to see if you really leave Pine Hollow.

You turn back toward the lodge. Its dark shape looms against the trees. At least it's shelter. At least you can get out of this wind, warm up, figure out what to do next.

You're not investigating. Not yet. You just need to survive the night.

The main entrance is close now. The doors hang crooked, one barely attached. You push through.

Inside, the darkness is absolute until you pull out your phone; 17% battery. The flashlight cuts a narrow beam into the space.

The lobby opens before you. Massive. Two stories high, dark wood beams supporting the ceiling. A chandelier hangs in the centre, wrought iron and dead bulbs, swaying slightly. The walls are wood-panelled, water damage blooming across them in dark patterns. Furniture sits in skeletal arrangements throughout the space; frames of couches and armchairs, upholstery rotted away to nothing.

But it's warmer. Not warm, but out of the wind. Out of the snow.

You move deeper, catching your breath. Your lungs burn from the cold air. You need to warm up. Need to think. The stone fireplace dominates the far wall, too dangerous to try lighting a fire, even if you could find dry wood. But maybe there's a smaller room. Something more enclosed.

That's when you see him.

Sitting in one of the armchairs facing the fireplace. Perfectly still. A figure in red.

Your flashlight beam finds him and your breath stops.

An old man. So old he seems barely human. Thin, bent, wearing a red coat with white fur trim, faded to the colour of rust. Long white beard, yellowed and matted. He's sitting with his hands folded in his lap like he's been waiting.

Like he's been sitting there for forty-nine years.

He looks exactly like Santa Claus would look if he'd died and kept sitting there anyway.

You don't move. Don't breathe.

He turns his head. Slowly. His eyes catch your light and reflect it back. Sharp. Alert. Watching.

"Hello, Jenny."

Your phone almost slips from your hand. He knows your name.

"I—I'm just trying to get warm. I'll leave. I'm leaving right now."

You back toward the door.

He stands. Not fast, but inevitable. Like he has all the time in the world. Like you have nowhere to go.

"You've been very naughty." His voice is gentle. Conversational. Wrong. "Lying to the sheriff. Sneaking back here. Trespassing where you don't belong."

"I'm sorry. I'm leaving."

"No." The word is soft. Final. "You're not."

He takes a step toward you.

You turn and run.

Your boots slip on debris. You catch yourself against a wall. Keep moving. Towards the door. Towards the exit. Towards…

He's there. Between you and the door. You don't know how. He's too old, too slow. But he's there.

Your flashlight catches his face. That terrible Santa Claus smile.

"The naughty children always run," he says quietly. "They always try to leave. But this is where they belong. In the mountain. In the cold. In the dark."

You back away. Toward the lobby's centre. Looking for another exit. A window. Anything.

He follows. Not rushing. Just walking. Steady.

Your foot catches on something. You go down hard, phone flying from your hand. The light spins across the floor, coming to rest against the base of the fireplace.

You scramble backward on your hands. He's above you now. Standing over you.

He reaches into his coat. Pulls out something small. Silver.

A bell.

It rings as he holds it up. One clear note that echoes through the empty lodge.

"This one has your name on it."

You try to crawl away but your back hits furniture. A wall. Something. Nowhere left to go.

He kneels down. His face is close now. You can smell him. Pine needles and old blood and something sweet and rotting.

"Don't be afraid," he whispers. "Sarah wasn't afraid at the end. She was very brave. Just like you're going to be."

His hands close around your throat.

You claw at them. Try to scream. But his grip is iron. Decades of strength preserved in those ancient hands.

The lobby tilts. Your vision narrows. Grey creeping in from the edges.

Your phone's flashlight, still on the floor, illuminates the scene in harsh white light. An old man in a red coat. A woman dying on the floor of an abandoned lodge. A bell lying in the dust between them.

Like a photograph. Like evidence no one will ever see.

The grey becomes black.

The last thing you hear is his voice. Singing, so quietly.

It's *Santa Claus is Coming to Town*.

Then nothing.

Complete and final.

THE END

You died from strangulation in the lobby of the Pine Hollow Ski Lodge. You went inside seeking shelter from the cold, but the King of Christmas was already there. He'd been waiting in that chair, perhaps for hours, perhaps for years. You never learned his real name. You never understood why. You just became another child on his list.

Your mistake was going into the lodge at all. The moment you stepped through those doors, you were already his. Survival and investigation both led to the same place: the floor of that lobby, a silver bell beside your body, your name added to a list forty-nine years old.

The King of Christmas always knows when you've been naughty.

YOU KEEP CLIMBING

The wind picks up as you push higher, no longer absent but present, a living thing that finds the gaps in your coat and presses cold fingers to your ribs. You zip up to your chin, pull your scarf higher, but the cold is insistent, patient. It has time.

Another lift tower. Another set of weathered posts. Between them, half-buried in a drift, you see a foundation, concrete edges jutting from the snow, the ghost of some structure long gone. You crouch beside it, brushing snow away with your glove. The concrete is old, stained dark, cracked by freeze and thaw. Not ski lodge construction. Something older.

The logging camp. This is where it was, before the resort. Before Rachel.

Your heart kicks. The resort was built on the bones of something else, something industrial and dangerous. Heavy equipment, cutting operations, all the infrastructure of a lumber mill that would have sprawled across this slope. And when the Van Vleets opened the ski lodge, they built over it, around it, incorporated what they could and left the rest to rot under snow.

You straighten, looking around with new eyes. How many hazards are still here? How many pits and shafts and unstable structures, hidden now, waiting?

The thought should send you back down the mountain. Instead, it pulls you forward.

If there were hazards here when Rachel lived at the lodge, if there were places a child could fall...

You push the thought away. Rachel disappeared from the lodge itself, from her bedroom. Everyone knows that. But the idea sits in your chest like a stone, cold and heavy.

The wind gusts harder, kicking up loose snow in stinging veils that blur your vision. The light is failing, the pale sky turning grey at its edges. You check your watch; the numbers swim, take a moment to resolve.

But there's something ahead. Not a shape, exactly. More like a wrongness in the landscape, a place where the snow sits different, where the ground seems to dip and recover.

You move toward it.

Your boots break through crust with each step, the snow deeper here, loose and treacherous. The wind screams past, a high keening that sounds almost like voices, almost like warning. You're breathing hard, each inhale a knife of cold, each exhale a cloud that whips away before it fully forms.

The cold has teeth now. It bites at your cheeks, numbs the tip of your nose. Your fingers ache inside your gloves, and you flex them, trying to keep blood moving, but the motion feels distant, like it's happening to someone else's hands.

You're not shivering anymore. That's good, isn't it? It means you're adjusting, your body finding equilibrium with the temperature.

It doesn't mean that. Some part of you knows it doesn't mean that. But that part is getting quieter.

Ahead, through the thickening snow, you catch a flash of colour. Something rust-red against the white, half-buried in a drift.

You move toward it, not thinking now, just following. Your thoughts feel sticky, slow, like they're moving through something thicker than air.

Three more steps and the ground gives way.

There's a moment—less than a heartbeat—when you're suspended, when the world is white sky and white ground and you're floating between them. Then gravity remembers you.

You fall.

Quick! Do you:

Try to grab the sides to slow your fall. Turn to page 365

Tuck your head and brace for impact Turn to page 385

GET OUT OF THE LOFT NOW

You move before you can think.

The ladder groans as you drop down. The mattress swallows you for a beat; you scramble up and sprint for the single door. The bedroom opens straight into the living room and the exit is only yards away.

Almost.

From the stairwell comes the sound of boots on wood. Heavy. Deliberate. He's already coming up.

You freeze. For one terrible heartbeat you imagine the loft above, the twelve blue bins closed and silent, the bells locked away where no clatter can betray you. The silence of them feels obscene now, like evidence being hidden in the rafters.

A man in red fills the doorway, torchlight cutting through the dark. His padded ski suit gleams wetly, streaked with snowmelt and grime. The not-quite-white fur at his cuffs is stiff with ice. His hood shadows most of his face, but you catch glimpses: a beard crusted with frost, a cracked mouth, eyes like cold glass.

Almost Santa Claus.

Almost the opposite.

Instincts flare. Is there anywhere to go? There are two bedrooms, one kitchen. No other exit. You measure distance in heartbeats. None of it is enough.

He steps inside. Slow. Deliberate. The door clicks shut behind him.

You raise your torch like a weapon. "Stay back."

He doesn't.

You swing first. The beam arcs wide, catches his shoulder, glances off the padded fabric. He staggers, just a fraction, and the smile that spreads beneath his beard is small and terrible.

He moves faster than you expect. A hand snatches your wrist, twisting hard until the torch falls from your grip and rolls away, spinning light across the walls. He shoves you back against the sofa, the impact knocking the air from your lungs.

You kick out, catch his thigh. He grunts. You shove at him, claw for the torch, anything, but he's too close. Too strong.

Your arm flails, looking for a weapon and closes on a lamp, still plugged in at the wall. You wrench it free, cord snapping taut, and swing. The shade tears loose, the bulb bursting in a flash of white. Jabbing blindly, he catches your arm, wrenches it down, and your hope clatters to the floor.

You scream. He doesn't flinch.

The torchlight flickers between you, white and strobing, and in each flash you see his face more clearly: the hollowed cheeks, the dark-ringed eyes, the calm certainty.

He leans close, breath frosting the air between you. "You shouldn't have come here."

You slam your knee up, once, hard. He grunts, but his hand doesn't loosen. The other swings.

Pain bursts white across your skull. You drop, hit the floor, the room tilting and spinning. You crawl, reaching for the torch, but the beam slides away from you, rolling to rest beneath the sofa.

Footsteps follow; measured, and patient.

He crouches beside you, breathing steady. You can't move. The world has narrowed to the sound of your pulse and the quiet creak of the floor beneath his weight.

His gloved hand touches your hair, smoothing it back with awful gentleness. You try to pull away, but your body won't answer.

"Say it," he murmurs.

You blink, fighting for focus. "W–what?"

He tilts his head, eyes pale and endless. "Say my name."

The words catch on your tongue, trembling, broken.

"King of Christmas."

He nods once. Almost tender. "Good girl."

The last thing you see is the shape of him, haloed in red and white, standing over you as everything drains away.

Somewhere close, the whistle starts again.

Santa Claus is coming to town.

THE END

You died in the apartment above Pine Hollow Ski Lodge on Christmas Eve, 2025. Van Vleet struck you repeatedly with a blunt object, fracturing your skull. You lost consciousness within seconds and died from head trauma minutes later.

Your body was never found. The official story was that you left Pine Hollow early Christmas morning, heading back to Boston. Your parents received a text from your phone apologizing for leaving so abruptly. They believed it.

The King of Christmas continued his work.

TRY TO GRAB THE SIDES

Your hands fly out, instinct overriding thought. Your right hand catches the edge, rough concrete biting into your palm, and for a heartbeat the fall slows.

But physics has rules. Your upper body jerks to a halt while your legs keep moving. The momentum twists you, rotates you, the world spinning, sky and stone trading places. You try to correct, to right yourself, but there's no time, no room, and the shaft is too narrow. Your shoulder slams against one wall, your hip against the other, and then the orientation is all wrong.

You're falling headfirst now.

The impact is a sound more than a feeling—something breaks that shouldn't break, something fundamental and irreversible. There's no pain. Not exactly. Just a sense of everything stopping at once: thought, breath, the frantic beating of your heart.

The circle of grey sky above tilts impossibly, fades to black.

THE END

You died instantly from the fall. The attempt to save yourself created the rotation that killed you. The truth about Rachel, about what happened in this place, dies unlearned. The mountain claims you before you can even understand why.

Sometimes the instinct to save yourself is exactly what kills you.

GO TO YOUR PARENTS

You pull back onto the road, hands steadier now, and drive straight to Evergreen Lane.

Your parents' house glows warm in the darkness, Christmas lights blinking along the eaves, wreaths on the door. The same decorations they've hung every year since you were a child. Before Sarah. After Sarah. Always the same.

You sit in the car for a moment, engine idling, staring at those lights.

Thirty years you stayed away. Thirty years of phone calls that never said enough, visits that felt like performances, the distance you kept because being here hurt too much.

Not tonight.

Tonight you need them.

You kill the engine and walk up the sagging porch steps. Your hand hovers over the door, then you knock. Once. Twice.

The door opens. Your mother stands there, dish towel in her hands, and for a heartbeat she just stares. Then her face crumples.

"Jenny."

She pulls you inside, into the warm smell of something baking, into the hallway where the chest sits against the wall—the chest full of bells. Your father appears from the living room, reading glasses pushed up on his forehead, and stops dead.

"What's wrong?"

"I need to show you something." Your hands shake as you pull out your phone. 8% battery. The screen glows between you. "I went to the old ski lodge. The Van Vleet place."

Your father's expression shifts. "Jenny…"

"Someone's been there. Living there, or using it. I found evidence. Look."

You show them the photos. Your mother's hand goes to her mouth. Your father leans closer, eyes narrowing.

"What? When did you go? Did you see anyone up there?"

"No. I just got back. I didn't want to wait around. But someone's been there. Someone obsessed with Rachel Van Vleet. And I think…" You swallow hard. "It *must* be connected to the King of Christmas."

Your mother makes a small sound. Your father straightens, jaw tight.

"You shouldn't have gone alone," he says. "That was dangerous."

"I know. But I found something. Evidence. We need to…."

"We need to go to the police." Your father is already reaching for his coat. "Now. Before whoever's up there realises someone was snooping around. You have evidence now. Photos. He can't dismiss this." Your father's voice is firm, the tone you remember from childhood when he'd made a decision and nothing would change his mind. "This is how we do this. Properly. Through the right channels."

Your mother touches your arm. "Be careful. Both of you." Her voice wavers. "Please."

"We will." Your father kisses her forehead. "We'll be back soon."

You want to argue. The law haven't helped in forty-nine years. But your father is already putting on his coat, already heading for the door, and your mother is looking at you with something you haven't seen in decades.

Hope.

"Come on," your father says. "We'll drive together. Show him everything. Make him listen."

Follow your dad to the truck. Turn to page 376

TRY TO GET FREE

You can't just lie here. You have to try something.

You roll onto your side, then your stomach, trying to get your hands where you can see them. The rope is tight, professional knots. Whoever tied you knew what they were doing.

But rope can be loosened. Rope can be cut.

You inch toward the nearest shelf, dragging yourself across the concrete floor. Your shoulder screams where you fell on it. Your wrists burn.

How did you end up here?

The question surfaces through the fog of pain and fear. How did it come to this? Bound. Captive. In some storage room.

You knew Pine Hollow was dangerous. You knew coming back was risky. But you thought the danger was abstract. Historical. A cold case you could investigate from a safe distance, armed with your press credentials and your righteous determination to finally get justice for Sarah.

Even after last year. Even after Amy. You thought this was a story.

The shelf is low. You reach back with your bound hands, feeling along the metal edge.

Rust. Rough metal. Maybe sharp enough.

You start working the rope against it. Back and forth. Small movements.

Sheriff Larkin brought you here. That's the part your mind keeps circling back to. The one person who should have been helping you, protecting you, investigating alongside you. But why?

It's awkward. Your hands are numb. You can't get good leverage.

But you keep trying.

And you know as you work, it was never just a story. This was always your destiny. To come back here. To find out what happened to your sister.

Because none of the other missing children you have written about have been her. And she is the only person who has ever mattered.

The rope frays. Just slightly. You can feel it.

Keep going. Keep...

The rope frays more. You can feel it starting to separate. Just a little more. Just a few more...

The door opens. Turn to page 409

STAY IN THE CAR

You stay put. You came here because it felt safe, but you don't need to drag your parents into this. They've lived with Sarah's absence for thirty-nine years. They don't need to know their daughter is sitting outside in the cold, waiting to see who terrorises them on Christmas Eve.

Better they sleep. Better they don't know.

You settle deeper into the seat, turn off the car completely to avoid drawing attention. The cold seeps in immediately. You pull your coat tighter, tuck your gloved hands under your arms.

The heater's off. The engine's silent. Just you and the night and the house across the street.

Your parents' house.

The last place you saw Sarah alive.

You stare at the porch steps. They are weathered, but the same.

You're not sure what else has changed in all these years.

The living room lamp is still on. You can see shadows moving behind the curtains. Your mother, probably. Cleaning. Organising. Anything to keep her hands busy on Christmas Eve.

Your father is probably in his study. Or sitting in the living room, writing new notes to add to the folder that now sits here on your dashboard.

They're so close. Right there. You could cross the street, knock on the door, fall into your mother's arms.

But you don't.

Minutes pass. The cold deepens. Your breath fogs the windshield and you wipe it clear with your glove.

The street is quiet. Empty. A few houses have Christmas lights still on. Most are dark, families asleep or preparing for bed.

You watch. Wait.

Your mind drifts despite yourself.

Sarah running into the snow. The way she looked back once, mittens bright against the white. The way she smiled, not scared, not worried, just curious. Following footprints like it was a game.

You should have gone with her.

You shake your head, force the thought away. You've spent thirty-nine years with that thought. It doesn't help. It never helps.

Focus on now. On the house. On whoever's coming.

The living room lamp goes off.

You sit up straighter.

Your parents are going to bed. Or at least your mother is. The upstairs bedroom light flicks on a moment later. You can see the glow through the curtains.

They're going to sleep. Like they do every Christmas Eve. Not knowing that in a few hours, there will be another bell on their porch.

The thirty-ninth bell.

You settle in for a long wait.

Time crawls. The cold is relentless. Your toes are numb. Your fingers ache even inside your gloves. You run the engine for five minutes to warm up, then turn it off again. Can't risk being too obvious.

The upstairs light goes off.

Your parents are in bed now. Trying to sleep. Probably failing, like they have every Christmas Eve for thirty-nine years.

You check your phone. Then you see movement.

Down the street. A figure walking. Dark coat, hood up, moving with purpose.

Your pulse quickens.

You grab your phone, pull up the camera, ready to document everything.

The figure is getting closer. Walking on the sidewalk, heading directly toward your parents' house.

This is it. This is what you've been waiting for.

The figure crosses the street, reaches your parents' front walk, climbs the porch steps.

You're snapping photos through the windshield, but the angle is terrible. Too much glare. Too much distance.

You need to get closer.

The figure bends down, places something on the porch.

The bell.

You're snapping photos through the windshield, but the angle is terrible. The glass reflects streetlight. The distance makes everything blurry. You can barely make out the figure's shape, let alone their face.

The figure straightens, starts to turn away.

This is it. Your only chance.

You could stay here. Stay safe. The photos might be useless but at least you'd have something.

Or you could get out. Get closer. Get a shot clear enough to identify them.

Or you could confront them. Right now. Demand answers. End this.

What do you do?
Stay in the car. Turn to page 272
Get out for better photos Turn to page 414
Confront them Turn to page 374

CONSERVE YOUR ENERGY

You're badly hurt. Thrashing around, panicking; that will only make things worse. Better to rest, to think, to let the adrenaline fade so you can assess clearly. You've covered enough trauma stories to know: people who stay calm survive. People who panic die.

You lean back against the wall, slow your breathing. In through your nose, out through your mouth. The cold settles around you, but that's fine. You just need a moment to gather yourself. To think.

The concrete against your back is solid, almost reassuring. You close your eyes, just for a second. Just to clear your head.

When you open them, the sky has darkened. How long was that? A minute? Five? The light is different now, deeper, the grey turning purple at the edges.

You try to move.

Your body doesn't respond.

Go to page 307

CONFRONT THEM

Your hand is on the door handle before you can think it through.

You push the door open, not quietly this time. You're done hiding.

"HEY!"

Your voice cracks the silence like a gunshot.

The figure on the porch freezes. Turns toward you.

You're already out of the car, door slamming behind you, boots crunching in snow as you cross the street.

"I SEE YOU!" you shout. "I know what you're doing!"

The figure doesn't run.

They should run. Anyone caught placing a bell should panic, flee, disappear into the night.

But they just stand there. Watching you approach.

That should tell you something.

It doesn't.

"Who are you?" You're halfway across your parents' yard now, phone in hand, not even pretending to hide it. "What did you do to my sister? What did you do to Sarah?"

The figure takes a step back. But not away. Just... repositioning.

You're ten feet from the porch steps now. Five.

"ANSWER ME..."

A hand clamps over your mouth from behind.

You didn't hear them. Didn't see them. Too focused on the figure in front of you.

Another hand grabs your arm, wrenching it back.

You try to scream but the hand is too tight, fingers digging into your jaw.

Something dark drops over your head: fabric, thick, blinding.

Hood. A hood.

You thrash, try to twist away, but there's someone else now, grabbing your other arm. Two people behind you. Maybe more.

And the figure on the porch. They're not running. They're just standing there. Watching.

Your phone falls from your hand, hits the snow with a soft thump.

You try to kick, to fight, but they're lifting you, dragging you backward, away from the porch, away from your parents' house.

You hear a car door open. Close by. Engine running.

You didn't even notice it there.

No. No no no…

They shove you forward. You hit seats, leather, the smell of cigarettes and pine air freshener.

Hands push you down, hold you down.

The car door slams.

You're trying to scream through the hand still clamped over your mouth, but the sound is muffled, useless.

The car is moving.

You hear voices, low, urgent, but you can't make out words through the hood, through the panic, through the blood roaring in your ears.

You try to sit up. Hands push you back down.

"Stop fighting." A man's voice.

You don't stop. You can't stop.

Something sharp pricks your arm and the world starts to blur even through the darkness of the hood.

Your limbs go heavy. Your thoughts scatter.

You're trying to stay conscious, trying to remember which direction the car is turning, trying to anything…

But the darkness is swallowing you.

The last thought you have before everything goes black:

Your parents are right there. Right across the street. Sleeping twenty feet away and they don't know.

Wake up. Turn to page 400

FOLLOW YOUR DAD TO THE TRUCK

You follow your father out to the truck, and hop up into the front seat beside him. How long has it been, the two of you riding like this? The answer is too long. You could say that's your own fault, but that would be unkind. The memories in this town drove you out, and now, maybe if this lead funnels towards resolution, perhaps there will be no more missed years between you.

Your father's hands are steady on the wheel, but you see the tension in his shoulders. He's been waiting for this since 1986. For a lead. For evidence. For a chance to act instead of grieve.

"I should have come back sooner," you say quietly.

"You're here now." His voice is rough. "That's what matters."

The sheriff's station is only ten minutes away, but the drive feels longer. The truck's heater wheezes, filling the cab with warm air. Christmas lights blur past the windows.

"Dad... what if he doesn't listen? What if he dismisses this too?"

"Then we go over his head. State police. FBI." Your father's jaw sets. "Someone will listen. Someone has to."

You want to believe him. Want to believe that proper channels work, that authority serves justice, that doing things right leads to right outcomes.

But thirty years of silence suggest otherwise.

As you pull up, you can see the lights on in the front office of the station. Your father parks and you both get out, walking up the salted steps together.

Sheriff Larkin sits behind the front desk, paperwork spread in front of him. He looks up when you enter, and something flickers across his face.

"Bill. Jenny."

"We need to talk to you," your father says. "Jenny found something. At the old ski lodge."

The sheriff's expression doesn't change. "That so?"

"Evidence," your father continues. "Someone's been using the Van Vleet place. We have photos."

You pull out your phone, show him the screen. The sheriff looks at the photos for a long moment, then back at you.

"Where'd you say you took these?"

"The Van Vleet ski lodge. The apartment upstairs. Someone's been maintaining it. Fresh pine cones, modern clothes. I couldn't take photos of everything, but there's more. And... it's been used recently."

"Recently." The sheriff leans back in his chair. "And you were trespassing on private property to get these photos?"

Your father steps forward. "That's not the point..."

"Actually, Bill, that's exactly the point." The sheriff's voice is calm, almost gentle. "Breaking and entering. Trespassing. Taking photos inside a private residence." He looks at you. "That's a crime, Miss Matthews."

"It's been shut down since before we ever moved here. It's hardly someone's private residence. But someone is living up there," you say, frustration rising. "Or using it. Don't you want to know who?"

"What I want," the sheriff says slowly, "is for people to understand how things work in this town." His eyes move between you and your father. "You moved here in what, Bill? '83? Forty-two years, and you still don't get it."

"Get what?" Your father's voice hardens.

"That some things are Pine Hollow business. Family business. Not outsider business." The word outsider lands like a slap. "You came here, bought a house, put your kids in our schools, worked at our mill. But that doesn't make you one of us. That doesn't give you the right to go poking around in matters that don't concern you."

"My daughter is gone," your father says, each word clipped. "That concerns me."

"There's no chance." The sheriff stands. "There's just an old man who can't let go, and now he's got his other daughter breaking into abandoned buildings and making wild accusations."

"They're not wild," you say. "The shrine, the clothes, someone's been there…"

The sheriff is quiet for a long moment. His eyes drift to the small Christmas tree in the corner of the office, lights blinking in steady rhythm. Red, green, gold. He sighs, and something in his expression softens.

"All right." He stands, reaching for his coat. "All right. It's Christmas. Let's… let's go up there and you can show me what you found. We'll take it from there. Okay?"

Your father blinks. "You're going to look?"

"I'm going to look." The sheriff pulls on his coat, grabs his keys. "Can't promise anything, but if someone's been using that building illegally, that's worth checking out at least."

Relief floods through you. "Thank you. Thank you, I…"

"Don't thank me yet." But his voice is gentler now. "Let's see what we're dealing with first. Come on."

Follow the sheriff to his cruiser. Turn to page 333

YOU GO INTO THE FOREST

You turn toward the trees.

Immediately you're blind. Total darkness. And your eyes aren't working right anyway.

You put your hands out. Feel for trees. Move between them.

Your foot catches. You fall. Snow in your face. Get up. Keep moving.

Which direction? Downhill. You think this is downhill.

Everything is spinning. You stop. Lean against a tree. Wait for it to pass.

It doesn't pass.

Keep moving anyway.

Behind you: voices. Distant. Or nearby? You can't tell.

You push forward. Hands outstretched. One foot. Then the other.

Your boot finds nothing.

You're falling.

Down. Tumbling. Can't stop. Can't...

You hit something. Hard. Pain explodes in your shoulder, your ribs, your...

Everything.

You lie there. Can't move. Can't breathe right.

Something's broken. Ribs? Shoulder? Everything hurts.

Above you: flashlight beam. Searching.

"Down there! I see her!"

Multiple voices now. They're coming.

You try to move. Your body barely responds.

Crawl. You can crawl.

You drag yourself along the ravine floor. Snow and rocks. Darkness.

Where are you going? Away. Just away.

Your arms give out. You collapse.

So cold. So tired.

The voices are getting closer.

But they sound… farther away too?

Everything is confused. Spinning.

You close your eyes. Just for a second.

When you open them it's darker. Quieter.

Did they leave? Did they not find you?

Or are you just… fading?

You can't feel your hands anymore. Your feet. Your face.

Everything is numb.

You think of your parents. Twenty feet away across the street. That's how close you were when this started.

Now you're… where? Miles away. In the forest. Broken. Freezing.

You think of Sarah. Red mittens in the snow.

Now you'll be just like her. Gone. Lost. Never found.

Your eyes close.

The cold doesn't feel so bad anymore.

Almost warm, actually.

That's wrong. You know that's wrong.

But you can't remember why.

The thinking stops.

THE END

You died of hypothermia and injuries in a ravine outside Pine Hollow on Christmas Eve, 2025.

Your body was found three days later by hunters. The official story was that you fled the sheriff's attempted rescue and got lost in the forest. An accident. A tragedy.

The King of Christmas continued his work.

ROLL DOWN THE WINDOW

You press the button. The window descends halfway. Cold air rushes in, sharp and biting.

"You're Bill Matthews' daughter," he says. Not a question. His voice is rough, aged.

You can see him better now in the glow of the streetlight. Elderly, seventies maybe, wearing a thick wool coat, fastened up close to his chin. Deep lines carve his face. He looks exhausted. And familiar, somehow.

"Who are you?" Your voice comes out steadier than you feel.

"Harold Henderson." He glances up and down the street, nervous. "You appear to be watching my house."

Claire's father. Relief floods through you, followed by caution.

"Yes," you say, your voice unsteady. "I'm here to…" You're about to say *write a story about the King of Christmas*, but that line hasn't gone down too well so far. You change tack halfway through. "I heard about Amy Crawford last year…"

"And you came to write a story about it?"

There's no escaping the truth, it seems.

Henderson looks up and down the street. It's just the two of you. He bends closer to the window and asks, "Can I get in? So we can talk?"

He gestures to the passenger door, and you look over like you don't know what it is.

It makes sense though. The snowfall is constant. It must be near freezing out there. He must be, what, seventy, eighty years old now? He lost Claire in 1980 and she was how old? The answer is in the folder on the dashboard between you, but you can't look now.

It's cold. He's an old man. Maybe he has something to say that will help you.

You unlock the door.

Henderson pulls it open and climbs in awkwardly, folding himself into the seat with a grunt. When he closes the door, the car suddenly feels smaller, the air thicker.

He doesn't look at you. He stares straight ahead, over the top of that folder, through the windshield at the snow falling in the streetlight's glow.

"I understand what you think you're doing," he says quietly. "Coming back. Asking questions. Watching."

You wait.

"But you need to stop."

"Why?"

He finally turns to look at you. His face is haggard, deeply lined. "Because it won't change anything. And it might make things worse."

"Worse for who?"

He doesn't answer immediately. His hands rest in his lap, fingers interlaced. "You came to see if someone would leave a bell here tonight. Didn't you?"

Your breath catches. No point denying it. "Yes. I don't understand why no one…"

"No," he says. His voice is flat, worn smooth by repetition. "You don't understand. That's why you shouldn't be here."

The words hang in the small space between you.

You stare at him until he looks at you, a psychological trick you've honed over your many years of interviewing. When his eyes meet yours, you jerk slightly, involuntarily. There's a deep sadness beneath his gaze, you're sure of it. You've seen that look before.

"Why?" you ask. "Why shouldn't someone come and do something? The police don't seem interested. Even with Amy…"

"Don't," he cuts in. He closes his eyes as though he can sense you reading him and shakes his head. "We thought it was over. Can't you see that? Fifteen years of peace in this town. Fifteen years. People started to feel safe."

"You thought he had stopped," you say, your mind taking notes because pulling out your phone and recording this would be wrong.

"Of course we did." He looks at you with something like pity. "You really don't understand, do you? You think this is about catching someone. About solving it. But it's not. It's about survival."

"I don't…"

"Why do you think your parents stayed?" he asks suddenly. "After Sarah. Why didn't they leave?"

The question catches you off guard. "Because… because they couldn't. This is where she was. They couldn't leave her."

He nods slowly. "That's part of it. That's what we all tell ourselves. We stay because we loved them. Because leaving would be abandoning them." He pauses. "But that's not the whole truth."

"Then what is?"

"We stay because we have to." His voice drops lower. "Because if we leave, there are consequences."

Your stomach tightens. "What kind of consequences?"

He doesn't answer directly. Instead, he says: "My wife and I, we've lived here our whole lives. Born here. Raised our family here. We have two sons. The oldest, he left as soon as he could. Never looked back. Smart kid." There's pride in his voice, but also something like envy. "Never married. Never had children. He's free."

He pauses.

"The younger one… we had him two years after Claire. We needed… we thought…" He doesn't finish. Can't finish. Instead, he half-whispers, *We have grandchildren.*"

There's something heavy in how he says it. Not warm. Not nostalgic. Something darker.

"They play in the backyard where Claire used to play. They don't know about her. They don't know about any of it. They just know we're Grandma and Grandpa who make cookies and tell stories."

He looks at you directly now, and his eyes are wet.

"I'd like to keep it that way."

The meaning settles over you slowly, like snow.

"You're saying... if you left..."

"I'm not saying anything," he says quickly. Too quickly. "I'm just telling you why we stay. Why we don't ask questions. Why we don't make waves."

You stare at him. "You're protecting them."

"We're trying to." His voice cracks. "That's all any of us are doing. Trying to protect what's left. My son... he should never have..."

He looks at you one more time and whatever he was about to say melts into a long silence. Outside, the snow falls steadily, muffling the world.

Finally, you ask: "What? What shouldn't he have done? Why are you telling me all this?"

Mr Henderson opens the car door. Cold air rushes in.

He pauses before getting out.

"Because you're Bill's daughter. And your father's a good man who's suffered enough. I don't want to see him suffer more if something happens to you."

"Nothing's going to happen to me."

He looks at you with that same pitying expression. "That's what we all thought. About our children. Please, leave. Nothing good will come of this."

He climbs out of the car, closes the door, and walks back toward his house without looking back.

You sit in the frozen silence, hands gripping the wheel, mind racing.

What do you do?

Go to the Wilsons' residence Turn to page 309

Go to your parents' home. Turn to page 335

BRACE FOR IMPACT

You pull your arms in, tuck your chin tight to your chest, try to make yourself small even as you fall. It's not a decision, not really, just the body's desperate attempt to protect what matters most.

The impact slams you sideways into concrete.

The world whites out. Not metaphorically. Actually whites out, vision bleaching to nothing as your body hits the bottom of the shaft. Then you're on your back somehow, staring up at a ragged circle of grey sky that seems impossibly distant.

For a long moment you can't breathe. Your lungs have forgotten how. They sit in your chest, empty and still, waiting for permission to work again. When the air finally comes, it arrives as a gasp that turns immediately to a sob of pain.

Everything hurts. Not sharp, not yet—just a massive, overwhelming sense that your body has been fundamentally rearranged, that bones and organs have shifted in ways they were never meant to shift.

You try to move. Your left leg screams in protest, pain so bright it turns your vision grey at the edges. Something's wrong there. Very wrong. You don't look. Looking won't help.

Your phone. You need your phone.

The thought arrives with crystalline clarity. You pat your pocket with your right hand; the left one isn't responding properly, fingers numb or broken or both. Your pocket is empty. The phone must have fallen out during the drop.

You turn your head, each degree of movement sending fresh waves of nausea through your skull. There. A few feet away. The phone lies face-down on the concrete, its case cracked, a spider web of fractures spreading across the back.

You reach for it. The distance is impossible. Your shoulder screams. Your ribs scream. Everything screams. But you stretch, fingers scrabbling against rough concrete, until you touch the edge of the case.

Got it.

You pull it toward you, turn it over. The screen is shattered, a starburst of cracks radiating from a central impact point. You press the power button anyway, desperate, knowing it's futile.

Nothing. Black screen. Dead.

The phone slips from your fingers, clatters against concrete. The sound echoes in the small space, then dies.

What do you do?
Try to climb out now. Turn to page 211
Assess your injuries carefully first. Turn to page 392
Call for help. Turn to page 391

KEEP GOING

You make a split-second decision.

Your foot presses the accelerator instead of the brake.

You swerve around the cruiser, barely missing it. Sheriff Larkin jumps back, shouting something you can't hear.

You wave frantically out your window—*Following someone! Bell-placer! Come on!*—and floor it around the corner.

The figure should be right there. Just ahead.

But the street is empty.

Gone. How are they GONE?

You speed up, checking side streets, driveways, anywhere they could have ducked into.

Nothing.

Behind you, the cruiser's siren wails to life. Red and blue lights fill your rearview mirror.

Shit.

You're fleeing from the police. While chasing a ghost.

You turn right, then left, scanning desperately for the figure. But they've vanished. Melted into the darkness like they were never there.

The siren gets louder. Closer.

You can't outrun a police cruiser. And you've lost the person you were following anyway.

Your heart is hammering. Your hands shake on the wheel.

What were you thinking? You just fled from the sheriff. You're going to be arrested. Or worse.

You round another corner and realise you're driving in circles. You don't even know where you are anymore.

The figure is gone.

The sheriff is hunting you.

And you're alone in the dark with no plan.

The cruiser is right behind you now. Lights blinding in your mirror.

"PULL OVER." The loudspeaker. Sheriff Larkin's voice, amplified and commanding.

There's no way you're stopping now.
Keep driving. Turn to Page 350

DRIVE STRAIGHT ACROSS

You floor it. The car leaps forward, tires finding purchase in the snow. You're flying now, straight across the clearing, the tree line on the far side getting closer…

The car is sliding.

Not fishtailing. Not losing traction in snow.

Sliding. Smoothly. Too smoothly.

Your stomach drops.

This isn't a clearing.

Behind you, Larkin's cruiser has stopped at the edge. Not following. He's not following.

This is a lake.

The sound reaches you.

Crack.

Soft. Almost gentle. Like someone stepping on a twig.

Then another. *Crack.*

Your breath catches.

The car tilts. Front end dipping, just slightly.

"No," you whisper. "No no no…"

CRACK.

Louder this time. Closer.

Water appears at the base of your door. Seeping in. Black. Freezing.

The windshield is pointing down now. The hood is lower than it should be.

You grab for your seatbelt, yank it off. Reach for the door handle.

The car lurches. Tilts further.

You try to push the door open but the pressure is too great, the door too heavy.

The car is sinking.

You're sinking.

The water is at your waist. Your chest. Freezing. Stealing your breath.

You try to climb out the window, but your legs won't move right, the cold is already numbing everything, and the car is tilting more, the windshield pointing straight down now into black water...

You manage one breath before the water covers your face.

It's so cold it feels like fire.

fire ice fire ice

You don't know which way is up. The water is black. The cold is overwhelming.

Your lungs are burning. Your limbs won't work.

Somewhere above you—impossibly far away—you think you see lights. Red and blue. Flashing.

red blue red blue

Sheriff Larkin's cruiser. Still on shore. Still watching.

Still not coming.

Your lungs are screaming. You try to hold your breath but your body betrays you, gasps, and water floods in...

The lights fade.

The cold fades.

Everything fades.

Your last thought, as the darkness takes you:

Sarah.

And then nothing.

THE END

You drowned in Pine Lake on Christmas Eve, 2025.

Your car was never found. Your body was never recovered.

Sheriff Larkin filed a report stating you fled a traffic stop and disappeared into the night. He speculated you might have left Pine Hollow, unable to cope with the memories. Search parties looked for three days before giving up.

CALL FOR HELP

"Help!"

Your voice cracks against the concrete walls, echoes, dies. The sound is smaller than it should be, swallowed by the shaft and the wind and the vast indifference of the mountain.

"HELP!"

Louder this time, ripping your throat. But the wind above swallows it. You're miles from anyone, deep in the mountain, and the storm is getting worse. You know this. You've known it since you started climbing. But you keep trying because what else can you do?

"PLEASE! SOMEONE! HELP!"

The words turn ragged, desperate. Your voice gives out on the last syllable, cracking into something that's half-scream, half-sob.

The silence that answers is absolute.

No one is coming. No one knows you're here. And even if they did, even if someone heard you somehow, they'd never reach you in time.

You're alone.

You force yourself to look around. **Turn to page 403**

ASSESS YOUR INJURIES FIRST

You force yourself to be methodical. The journalist in you, the part that documents and catalogues and makes sense of chaos, takes over.

Left leg: broken. You can tell without looking: the angle is wrong, and there's a grinding sensation deep in the bone when you breathe too hard. Compound fracture, probably. Tibia or fibula or both.

Left arm: something wrong with the shoulder. Dislocated, maybe, or the collarbone snapped. Your fingers won't respond properly. You can wiggle them, but there's no strength, no coordination.

Ribs: at least two cracked on the left side, possibly broken. Each breath is a negotiation with pain.

Head: concussion, definitely. There's something wet and warm trickling down your temple, matting your hair. Blood. You can feel it but you don't touch it. Knowing how bad it is won't help.

You catalogue each injury like you're writing it in your notebook. Like this is a story you're covering, not your own body failing.

The list is long. The list is bad.

But you're alive. For now.

You force yourself to look around. Turn to page 403

KATIE RETURNS

Katie returns from tucking Lily in. She sits on the couch, but she's perched on the edge, not relaxed. Her hands keep moving. Adjusting her mug, picking at her sweater, reaching toward the coffee table where a strand of fairy lights lies coiled.

"You lied to me," Katie says quietly.

Your stomach drops. "What?"

"At the Inn. You said you wouldn't do the stakeout. You looked me in the eye and you lied."

There's no point denying it. "Katie, I…"

"Do you know what you've done?" Her voice is shaking. "Coming here anyway. After I warned you. After I thought I'd convinced you." She picks up the fairy lights, winds them around her hand absently. "Siobhan is out there right now. If she comes back and finds you here, if she thinks I helped you…"

"I'm sorry," you say, standing. "I shouldn't have come. I'll go…"

"It's too late." Katie stands too. The lights dangle from her hand, red and green and white, cheerful colours that suddenly feel wrong.

"Katie…"

"I can't let you leave." Her voice breaks. "You'll tell. You'll write your story. And then Lily… Lily will be next. Do you understand? She'll be next."

"No one has to know I was here…"

"They'll know." Katie is crying now, tears streaming down her face. "They always know. That's how it works. That's how it's always worked."

She moves toward you, lights still in her hands.

"Katie, please…"

"I'm sorry." She's sobbing. "I'm so sorry. But I don't have a choice."

The lights are suddenly around your neck.

You grab for them, fingers scrabbling, but Katie is behind you, pulling tight. The plastic-coated wire bites into your throat.

You can't breathe.

You thrash, knock into the Christmas tree. Ornaments fall, shattering on the floor. The tree tilts but doesn't fall.

Katie is still crying. "I'm sorry, I'm sorry, I'm sorry…"

You try to call out but no sound comes. Just a choked gasp.

Upstairs, you hear movement. Lily.

"It's okay, honey!" Katie calls out, voice strained. "Just go back to bed! Everything's fine!"

Everything is not fine.

Your vision is starting to blur. Your lungs are screaming.

You claw at the lights, at Katie's hands, at anything.

"Please don't fight," Katie whispers. "Please. I don't want you to suffer."

But you do fight. Until you can't anymore.

Until the lights fade. Both the Christmas lights and everything else.

Until there's nothing.

THE END

You died on Katie Wilson's living room floor on Christmas Eve, 2025. Strangled with Christmas lights while Lily slept upstairs.

Katie called Siobhan. Together, they cleaned up the broken ornaments, disposed of your body, and moved your car. By morning, the snow had covered everything.

Your parents never learned what happened to you. The official story was that you left Pine Hollow suddenly, unable to face the memories.

The King of Christmas continued his work

HIDE

You kill your torch. Darkness swallows you whole.

You don't breathe. You don't move.

You scramble backward, away from the hatch, hands fumbling for the stacks of boxes in the pitch black. Your fingers find cardboard, plastic bins, the cold metal of stored bells that shift with a whisper of sound. You press yourself into the corner where the roof slopes lowest, pulling boxes in front of you. Not cover. Not really. Just something between you and the light.

The whistling drifts up through the hatch, soft and unbroken. The notes slide through the darkness, deliberate and patient.

A beam of light appears below. His torch, sweeping the bedroom. It catches on the dresser, the bed, then crawls upward toward the open hatch.

The ladder.

You left it down.

Cold panic grips you. He doesn't need to guess someone's here. The open hatch, the extended ladder. Proof enough.

The beam halts just beneath the opening. Silence stretches, broken only by the whistling.

Then a voice, rough-edged but calm:

"Someone up there?"

Your hand flies to your mouth, stifling the sob that wants to escape. Don't move. Don't make a sound.

He waits.

"I know you're here." Not angry. Almost conversational. "Saw your car down below. City plates."

The ladder creaks. Metal on wood.

He's climbing.

Terror floods through you, turning your limbs to ice. Your torch is clutched in your shaking hand. Off, useless. Even if you turned it on, what would you see? One way up. One way down. And he's on it.

The first rung groans. Then another. Slow. Measured. He's not rushing.

You press yourself deeper into your corner, body trembling so hard you're certain the boxes around you will rattle and give you away. Your breath comes in tiny, stuttering gasps.

His head clears the opening. The beam of his torch lances into the loft, cutting through shadow like a blade.

"Why are you here?" His voice is calm, patient. The torch beam sweeps methodically across the space. "In my home. Going through my things."

You bite down on your hand to keep from whimpering. The beam plays across boxes, dust motes, moving closer.

The beam catches your boot print in the dust.

He stops moving. The light holds there.

"Someone went through the bins." A pause. "The bells. You found the bells."

Your heart hammers so hard it hurts.

"Those aren't for you." His voice shifts, something darker entering it. "You know what happens when people don't follow the rules."

The beam swings toward your corner. Closer.

"You DO know, don't you?"

You don't. You don't know what he means. What rules? What happens? But your throat is closed with terror. You can't answer even if you wanted to.

The light catches the edge of the box in front of you.

"Everyone in Pine Hollow knows." His voice is conversational again, almost friendly. "They follow the rules. They do what they're told. They stay safe."

The beam swings directly onto your hiding place.

"You didn't."

"There."

You explode from your corner, pure terror driving you. Not toward him (you can't, he's blocking the only exit) but away, scrambling deeper into the loft like a trapped animal. Your shoulder slams into boxes. They topple, cascading down with a crash of cardboard and the bright, terrible chiming of bells scattering across plywood.

"No!" The word tears out of you. "No, please…"

His hand closes around your ankle.

You scream. A raw, animal sound. You kick, frantic, boot connecting with something solid. He doesn't let go. His grip is iron.

"Please! Please, I'll leave, I won't tell anyone, please…"

He drags you backward across the floor. You claw at the wood, at the boxes, at anything. Your fingernails splinter. Bells roll beneath you, digging into your ribs, your back.

"Wait! Wait!" You're sobbing now. "I'm looking for my sister! Sarah! Sarah Matthews! I just need to know what happened!"

He stops pulling. For one desperate second you think maybe this will save you, maybe saying her name means something.

"Sarah Matthews." He says it quietly. Thoughtfully. "Nine years old. Christmas Eve, 1986."

"Yes! Yes, please, I just need to know…"

"The bracelet." His voice is soft. "She kept saying 'I didn't do it.' Over and over. 'I don't know what you mean. Please.'"

"She didn't do it!" The words rip out of you. "She was innocent! I was the one who stole it! I blamed her!"

"I know." His hand moves to your throat. Not squeezing yet. Just resting there. You can feel the rough fabric of his glove against your skin. "She died innocent. Confused. Not understanding why."

"No…" You try to wrench away, hands scrabbling at his arm. "Please, I'm sorry, I'll leave, I won't…"

"You're the guilty one." His fingers press lightly against your windpipe. "The one who should have been taken. She died for your sin."

"I didn't mean… I was eleven… please…"

"And she was nine." His grip tightens, just slightly. "Thirty years you've lived. Thirty years she's been gone. Do you know what the rules are, Jenny Matthews?"

You shake your head frantically, tears streaming. You don't know. You don't understand.

"Everyone else does." His voice is almost gentle now. "Everyone in Pine Hollow. They know what happens when you break the rules. When you come where you shouldn't. When you touch what isn't yours."

"Please!" You claw at his hand, trying to pry his fingers loose. They don't move. "Please! I'm sorry! I'm so sorry!"

His other hand grabs your wrist, pulling it away from his throat, pinning it against the floor. You try to use your free hand but it's useless. He's too strong, you're too weak.

"Children pay the price." His voice is matter-of-fact. Final. "That's the rule. That's how it works. The innocent suffer for the guilty."

"No… please… I don't understand…"

"You will."

His grip closes fully.

Your hands push weakly at his arm. Your legs kick at nothing. The bells beneath you chime softly, their sound growing fainter and fainter.

"Tell Sarah hello for me."

Then nothing.

THE END

You died trapped and terrified in the loft, having discovered evidence but not the identity of the killer. You learned that Sarah died innocent—that your childhood lie led directly to her death. You learned there are "rules" that Pine Hollow knows and follows, but you died before understanding what they are.

Who is the King of Christmas? What are the rules? Why does the town stay silent?

The truth remains hidden behind that red hood.

Perhaps if you'd made different choices earlier...

WAKE UP

You wake to cold.

Not the cold of winter air. The cold of stone. Concrete. Something hard beneath you.

Your head throbs. Your mouth tastes like copper and chemicals.

You try to move and can't.

Your hands are behind your back. Tied. Rope, tight, cutting into your wrists.

Where…

You force your eyes open. Everything is blurry at first, shapes without definition.

Slowly, the room focuses.

Small. Dark. Stone walls. Shelves lined with… things. Cans? Boxes? Dusty. Forgotten. A storage room.

One small window near the ceiling, boarded over. No light gets through.

The only illumination comes from under the door, a thin line of yellow light.

And voices.

Outside the door. Talking. Normal conversation. Someone laughs. The sound is jarring, wrong.

You try to remember. What happened? Where are you?

The stakeout. Your parents' house. You saw…

Someone placing a bell.

You got out of the car to…

Then nothing. A gap. Black.

You're trying to piece it together when the door opens.

Light floods in, blinding after the darkness. You squint against it.

A figure in the doorway. Backlit. You can't see their face.

They step inside. A flashlight clicks on, beam sweeping the room, finding you.

The light settles on your face. You flinch.

"Here you are," a man's voice says.

The figure moves closer. The flashlight lowers slightly.

Sheriff Larkin.

Relief floods through you so fast it makes you dizzy.

"Thank God," you gasp. "Sheriff, someone…I don't even remember what happened. I went to do the stakeout. I saw someone leave a bell at my parents' house. I got out of the car and then…"

You try to gesture but your hands won't move. The rope. Right.

"Here, let me show you the photos I took…" You look down at yourself, at your empty hands. "Fuck, where's my phone?"

Larkin doesn't answer.

"Sheriff? Can you untie me? Where am I? What happened?"

He crouches down in front of you. The flashlight beam no longer in your eyes, you can see his face now.

He looks tired. Sad.

But he doesn't reach for the ropes.

"Sheriff Larkin, please, you have to…"

"I'm sorry, Miss Matthews." His voice is quiet. "I really am. But you should have left when you had the chance."

Your stomach drops.

"What? What are you…"

He stands. Turns toward the door.

"Wait…WAIT!" You try to stand but your ankles are tied too. You fall sideways, shoulder hitting the concrete floor. Pain shoots through you. "You're a sheriff! You're supposed to…"

"You were warned," he says quietly. "But you wouldn't listen."

"So… what…? You're… protecting this fucker?"

"We're protecting Pine Hollow." His voice is firm now. Final. "And you're a threat to that."

"I'm a JOURNALIST. I came to investigate what the hell is going on here in Shitsville."

"You're a problem." He steps through the doorway. "And problems get solved."

"LARKIN, you're the SHERIFF. You can't…"

You trail off.

Because he can.

He's already kidnapped you. He's already locked you in a storage room somewhere. He's already chosen the town over the law.

Whatever you thought sheriffs "can't" do doesn't apply here.

Not in Pine Hollow.

Not in Shitsville.

The door closes.

The lock clicks.

You're alone in the dark again. The thin line of light under the door. The voices outside continuing their conversation.

Someone laughs.

Your heart hammers. Your breath comes in gasps.

You're tied up. Somewhere. You don't know where.

And no one knows you're here.

You lie there on the cold floor, wrists burning from the rope, shoulder aching from the fall.

Minutes pass. Or maybe hours. You can't tell in the darkness.

You need to do something. But what?

What do you do?

Try to get free. **Turn to page 368**

Feel around for an exit   **Turn to page 486**

Wait and rush him when he comes back **Turn to page 408**

FORCE YOURSELF TO LOOK AROUND

You force yourself to look around properly now, to see where you've fallen.

Concrete walls rise on all sides, maybe twelve feet high. Fifteen. It's hard to judge distances with your head ringing like this. The walls are old, stained dark with moisture and age, cracked from decades of freeze and thaw. Metal protrudes in places, rusted rebar or piping, corroded to lace by time and weather.

The opening above is ragged, irregular. The snow gave way under your weight, and now you can see the edges where the crust collapsed inward. Snow falls through the gap in lazy spirals, settling on your face, your chest, cold little kisses that might be tender if they weren't another way to die.

This isn't natural. The walls, the shape, the construction— someone built this. Someone dug this shaft or vent or whatever it is, lined it with concrete, used it for something industrial and then abandoned it when the work was done.

The logging camp.

The thought arrives clear and cold. This is what's left of the Frost Timber operation, the infrastructure they built to strip the mountain of trees. Kilns and vents and access shafts, all the machinery of an industry that died fifty years ago and left its bones to rot under snow.

When the Van Vleets opened the ski resort, they built over this. Used what they could, incorporated what made sense, and left the rest. Left the hazards unsealed because sealing them cost money, and money was already tight.

And Rachel lived here. Rachel played here.

Your breath catches, and it's not from the pain.

A child could have fallen into this. Easy as breathing, easy as taking three steps in the wrong direction on a winter afternoon. The snow would have hidden the opening just like it hid it today. One moment running, playing, being eleven years old. The next moment, nothing. Just air and the drop and the impact.

Just like you.

Everyone said the King of Christmas took Rachel. Everyone believed in the monster because it was easier than believing in this: negligence, oversight, a hole in the ground that should have been sealed and wasn't.

What if there was no abduction? What if Rachel just fell?

The thought sits in your chest, heavy as the cold. You don't know. Can't know. Fifty years of snow and ice have erased any evidence. Even if you're lying in the exact spot where Rachel died, even if her bones are somewhere in this pit, buried deeper in debris you can't see, you'll never know for certain.

The truth could be here, and it dies with you.

What do you do?

Focus on escaping. Turn to page 306
Search for evidence. Turn to page 303
Conserve your energy. Turn to page 373

RUN

You don't give them time to think.

"GO!"

You shove your mother toward the kitchen. Your father moves with you, understanding instantly.

Behind you: "Don't…."

You're through the kitchen doorway. The back door is right there. Five feet. Three.

Your father reaches it first. Twists the knob.

CRACK.

The shot is deafening.

Your father jerks. Doesn't fall. Keeps moving. Wrenches the door open.

"Run, run, RUN!"

You push your mother through. Cold air. Snow. Darkness.

Your father is behind you, one hand pressed to his side. Dark wetness spreading.

"Dad…"

"GO!"

You're in the backyard. Your mother is ahead, running for the fence. You grab your father's arm, try to help him.

Another shot. The fence post beside your mother explodes.

She stops. Freezes.

"That's far enough." Larkin's voice from the back door. Calm. Not even breathing hard.

You turn. He's standing there, gun raised, silhouetted by the kitchen light.

"Back inside," he says. "All of you. Now."

Your father is sagging against you. The wound in his side is bad. You can feel the wetness soaking through his shirt.

"He needs a hospital," you say. Your voice shakes.

"Then you better move fast." Larkin gestures with the gun. "Inside. Or the next shot goes in his head."

Your mother is crying silently. She walks back toward the house. Defeated.

You help your father. Each step is agony for him.

Back through the door. Into the kitchen. Your father collapses into a chair.

Larkin follows you in. Closes the door. Locks it.

"Sit," he says. "All of you."

You and your mother sit. Your father is already sitting, hand pressed to the bleeding wound.

Larkin leans against the counter. Gun still in hand but lowered slightly. Not enough to matter.

"That was stupid," he says. "Bill needs medical attention now. And whose fault is that?"

"Yours," you spit. "You shot him."

"I shot him because you ran." Larkin's voice is patient. Like explaining something to a child. "Actions have consequences, Jenny. You should have learned that forty years ago."

The words hit like ice.

"What?" Your voice is barely there.

"Sarah." He says it simply. "You blamed her for the bracelet. You lied. And he took her because of you." Larkin shakes his head. "You've always made the wrong choices. Always got people hurt. Your sister. Your parents. Everyone you touch."

Your mother makes a sound. Half sob, half gasp.

Your father's breathing is getting laboured. Shallow.

"Please," you whisper. "Let them go. Take me. Just let them go."

"Too late for that." Larkin straightens. "You came back. You stirred everything up. You made this necessary."

He raises the gun again.

Your father tries to stand. Can't. Slumps back in the chair.

Your mother grabs your hand. Squeezes.

"I'm sorry," you say. To her. To your father. To Sarah, wherever she is.

"Me too," Larkin says.

And pulls the trigger.

THE END

You died in your childhood kitchen on Christmas Eve, 2025. Your mother died seconds after. Your father bled out in his chair while Larkin watched.

The official report called it a home invasion. A drifter, they said. Wrong place, wrong time. Sheriff Larkin responded but arrived too late. He was commended for his investigation. No suspect was ever found.

The King of Christmas continued his work.

WAIT AND RUSH HIM

You force yourself to breathe slowly. Calmly.

Don't panic. Don't waste energy.

Someone will come back. Larkin, or someone else. And when they do, you'll have one chance.

You work on the ankle rope first. It's easier to reach than your wrists. You bend your knees, bring your feet as close to your hands as you can. Feel for the knots.

Your fingers are numb but you keep trying.

The rope is tight but not impossibly so. Whoever tied it was focused on your wrists: those are the real restraints. The ankles are secondary.

You pick at the knot. Minutes pass. Your shoulders ache from the position.

Finally: give. The rope loosens.

You work it off your ankles, kick it away into the darkness.

Your legs are free.

Now you position yourself carefully. On your side, facing the door. Legs drawn up, ready to kick out.

Your hands are still behind you, useless. But your legs are strong. And free.

You wait.

The voices outside continue. Laughing. Talking. Like this is just another night.

You wait.

Your muscles cramp. You adjust position slightly. Wait more.

Time stretches. Your head throbs. The drugs make everything feel slow and thick.

But you stay ready.

Finally: footsteps approaching the door.

The lock clicks. You tense.

The door opens. Turn to page 409

THE DOOR OPENS

Light floods in. A figure steps through.

Not large. Not the man you're expecting. Someone smaller.

You don't hesitate.

You launch yourself forward, kicking out hard, aiming for their knees...

Your feet connect. They stumble backward with a shout.

You're already moving, rolling, scrambling past them into the hallway on hands and knees.

"HEY..."

You're on your feet. Hands still bound behind you but your legs are FREE. You can RUN.

You run.

Down the hallway toward light. Behind you: shouts. Footsteps.

A staircase. Going up.

You take the stairs fast, using the wall for balance since your hands are tied.

Top of the stairs. A hallway. Doors. Dim lights.

You pick a direction. Run.

Behind you: "She's loose! She's LOOSE!"

A door ahead. You throw yourself against it, turn the handle with your bound hands behind you.

It opens.

Cold air hits you.

Outside.

Snow. Darkness. Trees.

You're out.

You don't know where you are but you're OUT.

Behind you: "She's outside! OUTSIDE!"

You run into the snow. It's deep but you can move, you can RUN properly now.

You need to get your hands free.

You see a tree. Sharp branch jutting out. You back up to it, start sawing the rope against the rough bark desperately.

The voices are getting closer. Lights bobbing through the trees.

Come on come on come on...

The rope frays. Snaps.

Your hands are FREE.

You stop, gasping, trying to orient yourself.

The world tilts. You grab the tree to steady yourself.

Still drugged. Whatever they gave you, it's still in your system. Your vision swims. Doubles. You blink hard, trying to focus.

It's DARK. Not just night, pitch black. And your eyes aren't working right. Everything blurs at the edges.

You turn to look back at the building.

It takes a moment for it to resolve. Stone. Timber. Two stories.

The ski lodge.

Where the first abduction happened.

You're not in town. You're outside Pine Hollow. Up in the mountains.

How far? You try to remember. Three miles? Five? Your drugged brain can't hold the numbers.

Behind you, voices: "She's outside! FIND HER!"

You turn back toward the darkness.

Your legs feel wrong. Heavy. Not quite responding right.

Move. You have to MOVE.

Below you—you think it's below—distant lights. Tiny. Wavering. Or is that your vision?

Town. Pine Hollow. Parents.

That's where you need to go.

You start moving downhill.

Immediately your foot catches on something. A root? A rock? You pitch forward. Hit the snow hard. Your hands break the fall but barely.

Get up. Get UP.

You push to your feet. The world spins. You wait for it to steady. It doesn't.

Fuck it. Move anyway.

You walk. Stumble. Walk. The snow is deep. Each step takes so much effort. Your legs are so heavy.

Are they heavy from the snow or from the drugs?

Both.

The cold bites but distantly. Your face is numb. Your hands are numb. Everything is numb.

Is that hypothermia or the injection?

You don't know.

You keep moving.

Behind you: flashlight beams. Voices.

They're coming.

Focus. You need to FOCUS.

The road. You can see, or you think you can see, a break in the trees ahead. Clearer. The road.

Or the forest. Dense. Dark. To your right.

Which way?

Your brain is sluggish. Trying to work it out.

Road = fast but exposed.

Forest = cover but confusing.

The flashlights are getting closer.

Choose. CHOOSE.

What do you do?

Take the road. Turn to page 437

Into the forest. Turn to page 379

FIGHT IT

No. You won't go gentle into this. You won't let the mountain take you without a fight.

You force your eyes open when they want to close. Bite down hard on your tongue, using the sharp burst of pain to cut through the seductive warmth. The taste of blood fills your mouth, copper and salt. and for a moment it works. For a moment you're alert, present, furious.

You think of Sarah. Of the story you haven't told. Of the truth dying here with you in this pit while the world goes on believing in monsters instead of negligence. You think of your parents opening their door tomorrow morning to find another bell, never knowing you're here, never knowing what you learned.

You try to move your arms. Try to move your legs. Anything. But your body has made its decision without consulting you. The warmth is relentless, patient, and you're so tired of fighting.

The effort drains out of you like water through cupped hands. You can feel it going, can feel yourself surrendering even as some part of you screams to hold on, to stay, to not let go.

But the dark is coming anyway.

It takes you raging, fighting inside your head even as your body grows still. Your last thought isn't peaceful or resigned—it's furious. Furious at the mountain, at the cold, at fifty years of unanswered questions, at dying here alone with the truth locked inside your freezing mind.

The mountain doesn't care about your fury. It takes you anyway.

Above, snow falls into the shaft, silent and patient. It settles on your face, your chest, your outstretched hand. The flakes are small and perfect, each one unique, each one melting against your skin until they're not melting anymore because your skin has no more warmth to give.

The sky darkens to black. The wind keeps blowing. The mountain stands, indifferent.

By morning, fresh snow will have filled the opening, smoothing it over, making it look like nothing was ever there. Just another drift on an abandoned slope. Just another secret the Frost Mountains keep.

THE END

You died in an old logging shaft, forty-nine years after it should have been sealed. You discovered that the old logging camp left dangerous, unsealed hazards—places where a child could fall and disappear.

Maybe that's what happened to Rachel Van Vleet in 1976. Maybe the King of Christmas legend was built on an accident, not an abduction.

But how does that explain why seven more children went missing?

The question dies with you.

This time.

GET OUT FOR BETTER PHOTOS

Your hand is on the door handle before you can think it through.

You push the door open as quietly as you can, slip out into the cold. Your phone is raised, camera focused on the figure who's now straightening up, turning to leave.

You step onto the sidewalk, moving closer, trying to get a clear shot...

A hand clamps over your mouth from behind.

Another hand grabs your arm, wrenching it back.

You try to scream but the hand is too tight, fingers digging into your jaw.

Something dark drops over your head: fabric, thick, blinding.

Hood. A hood.

You thrash, try to twist away, but there's someone else now, grabbing your other arm. Two people. Maybe more.

Your phone clatters to the pavement.

You try to kick, to fight, but they're lifting you, dragging you backward.

You hear a car door open. Close by. Engine running.

No. No no no...

They shove you forward. You hit seats, leather, the smell of cigarettes and pine air freshener.

Hands push you down, hold you down.

The car door slams.

You're trying to scream through the hand still clamped over your mouth, but the sound is muffled, useless.

The car is moving.

You hear voices, low, urgent, but you can't make out words through the hood, through the panic, through the blood roaring in your ears.

You try to sit up. Hands push you back down.

"Stop fighting." A man's voice.

You don't stop. You can't stop.

Something sharp pricks your arm and the world starts to blur even through the darkness of the hood.

Your limbs go heavy. Your thoughts scatter.

You're trying to stay conscious, trying to remember which direction the car is turning, trying to anything...

But the darkness is swallowing you.

The last thought you have before everything goes black:

Your parents are right there. Right across the street. Sleeping twenty feet away and they don't know.

Wake up. Turn to page 400

HIT HIM

Your pulse surges. You tighten your grip on the torch, feel the cold metal bite your palm. He takes one more step forward. Close enough now that you can hear the hiss of his breath through the hood.

You rise, swinging hard.

The torch connects with something solid. His arm, maybe his shoulder. It thuds against his flesh.

He grunts, more surprised than hurt, and the torch in his hand jerks upward. White light floods the loft. You flinch, blinded.

By the time your eyes adjust, he's moving. Fast for someone his size. A red blur, a hand grabbing for your wrist.

You wrench free, swing again, wild. The beam fractures across the walls, slicing over boxes, bells, your own terrified reflection in a strip of broken tinsel.

Then, his voice, quiet and almost amused: "Shouldn't have done that."

He lunges.

You stumble back, hit a stack of boxes. They topple, spilling garlands and bells that clatter across the floor in a shrill cascade.

He's on you before you can recover. A gloved hand catches your arm, jerks you forward. The smell of him (cold air, metal, something faintly chemical) fills your lungs. You twist, drive your elbow back, connect with his ribs. He grunts, but it only spurs him.

You lash out again with the torch, this time higher, aiming for his face. He blocks it with one arm, the other sweeping across in a blur of red.

Pain detonates behind your eyes. A single, heavy blow.

The torch flies from your hand, clattering into the dark. The beam spins wild, flashing bells, boxes, the ceiling, and dies.

You go down hard, head striking the plywood. Bells roll past your cheek, chiming faintly as the sound in your skull expands to a high, searing whine.

Somewhere above you, his breathing steadies. Measured. Calm.

You try to move. Your arms won't listen. The edges of the room begin to blur, then fade altogether.

Through the narrowing slit of vision, you see him crouch. The red suit fills your view. One hand reaches out, gloved fingers brushing a fallen bell beside your face. He picks it up, turns it once between his fingers, and slips it into his pocket.

Then, softly, almost tender, he says,

"Sleep tight."

Darkness closes over you, heavy and final.

Your last thought before it takes you is that no one will ever find this place.

No one will ever know what you found.

No one will ever find you.

THE END

You died in the loft of the Van Vleet Ski Lodge on Christmas Eve, 2025. Van Vleet struck you once with a blunt object, fracturing your skull. You lost consciousness within seconds and died from head trauma minutes later.

Your body was never found. The official story was that you left Pine Hollow early Christmas morning, heading back to Boston. Your parents received a text from your phone apologizing for leaving so abruptly. They believed it.

The King of Christmas continued his work.

ACCEPT IT

You let it happen.

The warmth is a kindness after all this pain, all this cold, all these years of running. Your body has been trying to tell you something, and finally, finally, you listen.

You think of Sarah, nine years old, running into the backyard in her red mittens. All these years of guilt. All these years of wondering if the bracelet, the lie, the blame you placed on her, if any of it mattered.

Maybe it didn't. Maybe Sarah's disappearance had nothing to do with your childhood cruelty. Maybe there are just places in these mountains where children fall and vanish, hazards left unsealed, corners cut, and no amount of guilt changes that.

Or maybe that's not it at all.

Seven more children after Rachel. All on Christmas Eve. That's not accidents. That's a pattern, and patterns have authors.

But you'll die never knowing the truth.

The uncertainty should hurt, but you're too tired to care anymore. Sarah's face appears behind your closed lids, smiling, nine years old forever. Whatever the truth is, wherever she is, you'll never tell it. The mountain has claimed you both now.

There's a strange peace in surrender, if not in understanding.

You sink into the warmth, let it wrap around you like arms, like forgiveness, like the end you've been running from for thirty years. The mountain's embrace is gentle now, almost loving. The cold has stopped being cruel. It's just… quiet.

Your breathing slows.

Slows.

Stops.

Above, snow falls into the shaft, silent and patient. It settles on your face, your chest, your outstretched hand. The flakes are small and perfect, each one unique, each one melting against your skin until they're not melting anymore because your skin has no more warmth to give.

The sky darkens to black. The wind keeps blowing. The mountain stands, indifferent.

By morning, fresh snow will have filled the opening, smoothing it over, making it look like nothing was ever there. Just another drift on an abandoned slope. Just another secret the Frost Mountains keep.

THE END

You died in an old logging shaft, forty-nine years after it should have been sealed. You discovered that the old logging camp left dangerous, unsealed hazards—places where a child could fall and disappear.

Maybe that's what happened to Rachel Van Vleet in 1976. But how does that explain why seven more children went missing?

The question dies with you. This time.

RACHEL'S BEDROOM

The second bedroom is small. A child's room.

Your torch beam sweeps across walls that still show the ghosts of posters, discoloured rectangles where paper once hung, a few tattered corners still clinging to pushpins. One remains mostly intact: a kitten hanging from a branch, "HANG IN THERE" faded to pale brown letters. The image is bleached nearly white, but you can still make out the shape.

A single bed against one wall. The frame is solid, but the bedding has deteriorated to shreds; what might have been a quilt is now just rotted scraps, stuffing from the pillow spilling out like snow.

On the pillow, arranged carefully: stuffed animals. A bear, a rabbit, something that might have been a dog. The fabric is ragged, eaten by time and moths, fur worn to bare patches. But they're positioned deliberately, facing outward, as if someone still tucks them in.

This was Rachel's room.

And they never cleared it.

Your throat closes.

A bookshelf stands against one wall. Your torch picks out spines: faded, colours shifted, but titles still legible. *Anne of Green Gables, A Wrinkle in Time, Charlotte's Web, The Secret Garden*. Books that an eleven-year-old girl loved in 1976.

Anne of Green Gables. Sarah's favourite.

Your hand reaches for it before you can stop yourself. The cover is faded to a uniform tan, original image barely visible. The binding cracks when you open it, pages brittle yellow. No inscription, no name. Just a book that a child loved once.

You put it back carefully, exactly where it was.

The dresser across from the bed is where all the maintenance has been focused. While everything else in the room shows decades of decay, the dresser top is different.

Dust-free.

A gallery of framed photos, arranged with deliberate care. The glass protects them; you can see the images clearly despite the fading. Colours have shifted strange, blues gone entirely, leaving everything tinted yellow-red like aged film. But the faces remain.

School photos showing Rachel at different ages: missing front teeth, gap-toothed grin, more serious as she got older. A family snapshot, the three of them in front of the lodge, mountains behind. A Polaroid of Rachel on skis, face lit with joy. Another of her holding a stuffed rabbit. You glance back at the bed, at the deteriorated rabbit positioned on the pillow. The same one.

The central photo, largest: Rachel at eleven. Dark hair, bright eyes, smile showing permanent teeth coming in. Taken sometime in 1976, months or weeks before she disappeared.

And surrounding it, arranged in a perfect circle: seven pine cones.

You lean closer. The pine cones aren't decorative scatter, they're deliberately placed. Each one perfectly formed, scales intact. Your torch catches their surfaces: dry but not brittle, brown but not grey with age.

Recent. Weeks old, maybe a month.

Fresh. Someone's been here. Recently.

Not forty-nine years ago. Recently.

Cleaning this specific surface.

Arranging these specific cones.

Something catches your eye behind Rachel's central photo: a frame edge barely visible. You reach out, fingers trembling, and tilt the large photo forward carefully.

Another picture leans against the wall, smaller, half-hidden.

Rachel's mother. Formal portrait, professional. She wears a blouse with a collar, hair styled. No smile, just a direct gaze at the camera.

A single white stone sits on top of this frame. River stone, worn smooth by water, white as bone.

Why separate? Why hidden? Why does Rachel get seven offerings while her mother gets one?

Your torch beam wavers. Your hand is shaking.

The room around you shows fifty years of decay; the posters gone to dust, the bedding rotted, the stuffed animals falling apart. Everything has aged, deteriorated, returned to the mountain.

Except this dresser top. Except these photos. Except these pine cones.

Someone has been coming here. For decades. Letting everything else fall apart while maintaining this one small shrine. Dusting the frames. Placing fresh pine cones. Keeping Rachel's face visible.

Your parents kept Sarah's room for three years before packing it away. Three years of walking past that closed door, of your mother unable to disturb it, of pretending preservation meant something.

This room has been a shrine for forty-nine years.

The Van Vleets left. Everyone knows that. Six months after Rachel disappeared, they packed up and drove away, destroyed by grief.

So, who's been maintaining this?

Your breath comes faster. You need to understand.

You could keep exploring.

Or you could leave. Right now. Get to your car, back to town, tell someone what you've found.

Every instinct screams that something is wrong. This isn't an abandoned building. Someone is using this space.

But you're a journalist. You investigate. You find truth even when it's uncomfortable.

What do you do?
Go to the master bedroom
Leave the apartment now

"It's fine, Dad." You squeeze his hand once, then let go. "I'll be right back."

"Jenny..."

"I'm just showing him the apartment. Ten minutes."

Your father's face is tight with concern, but he nods. "Be careful."

"I will."

You climb out of the cruiser. The cold hits immediately, stealing your breath. The sheriff closes the door behind you, sealing your father inside the warm car.

"Lead the way," the sheriff says.

You walk toward the service entrance, the sheriff's flashlight beam guiding your steps. The broken handle still hangs crooked where you left it. You step through, into the corridor, into the dark.

"Through here," you say, voice echoing. "To the lobby, then upstairs..."

A hand catches your shoulder. Spins you around.

The sheriff's face is different now. Harder. The flashlight beam cuts up from below, casting shadows that make him look skeletal.

"I'm sorry," he says.

"What..."

His radio crackles. He lifts it. "I've got her. Bringing her in now."

A voice responds, scratchy, distant: "Good. I'm in the storage room."

Storage room.

Your blood goes cold.

"No..." You try to pull away. The sheriff's grip tightens.

"My daughter is seven years old," he says quietly. "Emma. She talks back. Gets into trouble. She's on the list." His eyes are dead. "The only way to keep her safe is to follow the rules."

You wrench free and run.

Back toward the service entrance, toward the car, toward your father...

A figure steps into your path. Red parka. White fur trim.

It's Santa Claus.

But it's not.

You know it's not.

It's a twisted, warped version of everything that Santa Claus is not.

"Miss Matthews," he says calmly. Voice like gravel and winter. "Going somewhere?"

You turn. The sheriff blocks the other direction.

Trapped.

The man in red steps closer. In the flashlight beam, his face is ancient, weathered, half-hidden by the hood. But his eyes are clear and cold.

"Your father's waiting in the car," he says. "Wondering where you are. Worried. In about ten minutes, the sheriff will go back out there. He'll tell your father there was an accident. That you fell. That you hit your head." His voice is patient, explaining. "Your father will want to see you. The sheriff will bring him inside. And then..."

He produces rope from his coat.

"No." The word tears from your throat. "No, please..."

"You made your choice when you came here. When you broke into my home. When you tried to expose what shouldn't be exposed."

The sheriff is already behind you, catching your arms, holding them still while the King of Christmas binds your wrists. You scream, but the sound just echoes in the empty lodge, going nowhere.

"Your father will die thinking it was an accident," the old, terrifying man says, almost kindly. "At least he'll have that comfort. He won't know what you know. Won't see what you see."

He gags you with a strip of cloth. The sheriff lifts you surprisingly gently and carries you deeper into the lodge, through passages you didn't see before.

A storage room. Small. Concrete. A drain in the floor.

And your father is still in the car. Still waiting. Still thinking you'll be right back.

The door closes. The lock clicks.

But they don't leave.

You hear the scrape of something metal. The sheriff's footsteps, retreating. Just one set of footsteps.

The King of Christmas remains.

"I'm sorry," he says, and his voice is gentle. Almost paternal. "But you understand, don't you? Rules must be enforced. Order must be maintained."

You try to scream through the gag. Try to thrash. But the ropes hold.

"Your father will never know," he continues, crouching beside you in the dark. "That's a kindness. He'll think it was quick. Painless. He won't see. Won't understand. Won't carry that image."

Hands on your throat. Firm. Certain.

"Naughty children," he whispers. "They all fight at first. But it passes. It always passes."

The pressure increases.

You can't breathe.

Can't scream.

Can't...

The world narrows. Sound becomes distant, muffled, like you're underwater. The cold concrete beneath you fades. The darkness behind your closed eyes deepens from black to something beyond black.

Your last thought isn't of yourself.

It's of your father.

Still sitting in the warm car, heater running, waiting for you to come back. Thinking you'll be right back any minute now.

And he's next.

The realisation crashes through you like ice water. You brought him into this. Your obsession with Sarah, with finding answers, with not letting go. It's the same disease that kept him searching for four decades. The same stubborn refusal to accept what couldn't be changed.

You followed the sheriff without hesitation. Without questioning. Because you wanted so desperately for someone official to finally care, to finally help.

And now you're dying.

And your father will be next.

Because of you.

The darkness takes you before you can finish the thought.

THE END

You died in a storage room at the Van Vleet Ski Lodge on Christmas Eve, 2025. Van Vleet strangled you while Sheriff Larkin held you down. You lost consciousness within two minutes and died from asphyxiation shortly after.

Your father died ten minutes later in the same room. The sheriff told him you'd had an accident, brought him inside to "see you," and Van Vleet killed him the same way. He never knew you'd led him into a trap. He died believing he was coming to help you.

Neither body was ever found. The official story was that you and your father left Pine Hollow together early Christmas morning, heading back to Boston. Your mother received texts from both phones. She was forced to believe them.

The King of Christmas continued his work.

GO TO THE POLICE

"Siobhan's right. This is too dangerous to handle ourselves. We need to go to the police. Let them investigate properly."

You look at Katie.

"Maybe with actual evidence, with all three of us as witnesses…"

Katie's face falls slightly, but she nods.

"You're probably right. I just… I wanted to see it. To know for sure."

"Better to be safe," Siobhan says, standing. Her relief is palpable. "We go through proper channels. That's how this should be done. I'll drive. You're exhausted, and my car handles better in this weather."

You *are* exhausted. The adrenaline from the lodge discoveries is fading, leaving you hollow and shaky.

"Okay. Thank you."

The three of you bundle into coats and head out to Siobhan's SUV. Katie climbs into the back seat with you, settling close, her shoulder warm against yours in the cold car.

"It'll be okay," she says quietly as Siobhan starts the engine. "We'll make them listen."

The Pine Hollow Police Station is only a few minutes away, its brick facade stolid against the falling snow. Lights glow in the windows. Someone's working late on Christmas Eve.

You expect Siobhan to park, but she pulls up to the front entrance instead. "Wait here a moment. Let me see if the sheriff's available."

She disappears inside. Through the glass doors you can see her talking to someone at the front desk. A brief conversation, a nod, then she's coming back out.

"He's here. He'll see us." Siobhan opens your door. "Come on."

The three of you enter together. The station smells of coffee and floor wax, institutional and familiar. The deputy at the desk barely glances up as Siobhan leads you past, down a hallway, toward an office at the back.

Sheriff Larkin emerges before you reach the door. He looks at the three of you. His gaze lingering on Siobhan, then Katie, then you. Something passes across his face. Not surprise. Recognition.

"Ladies," he says. "Come on in."

He leads you into the office and gestures for you to take a seat. You sink into one of the chairs. Katie sits beside you. Siobhan remains standing near the door.

"So," Larkin says, settling behind his desk. "Jenny Matthews…"

"I found evidence," you say before your nerve fails. "At the old ski lodge. Someone's been living there. Maintaining it. I have photos…" You pull out your phone, the screen showing 15%. "…of what I found. Sheriff, someone has been using that building. Recently."

Larkin takes your phone, swipes through the images. His face remains carefully neutral. "When did you take these?"

"Tonight. Maybe two hours ago."

"You went up there alone? In this snow?"

"I had to see for myself. And what I found, it proves someone's been there. Someone who's been keeping that place maintained for decades."

He studies the photos for a long moment. When he looks up, his expression is unreadable. "This is good work, Ms Matthews. Thorough. I can see why they brought you to me."

Something in his phrasing makes your stomach flip. Why they brought you. Not why you came.

"We thought you should see it officially," Siobhan says from her position by the door. "Proper channels."

"Of course." Larkin hands your phone back. "Well. This certainly warrants investigation. Evidence of recent habitation in an abandoned building. That's a concern. Could be squatters, could be something else. Either way, it needs to be checked out."

Relief floods through you. "Thank you."

"I take all credible reports seriously." He stands, reaching for his coat. "Tell you what. Why don't we all go up there right now? You can show me exactly what you found. Better to see it firsthand than rely on photos."

"Now?" Katie's voice is small.

"No time like the present. Snow's only getting worse. If we wait until morning, we might not be able to get up there at all." He pulls on his coat, checks his duty belt. Radio, flashlight, keys. "Plus, if someone is using that building, they might notice things have been disturbed. Better to document everything while it's fresh."

It makes sense. It all makes sense. But something in Katie's face makes you hesitate.

"Katie?" you ask.

She forces a smile. "No, he's right. We should go. All of us."

"My car's got four-wheel drive," Larkin says. "More reliable than an SUV on those mountain roads. We'll take mine."

You follow him out to the parking lot. His cruiser sits under the streetlight, official and reassuring. He opens the back door for you and Katie.

"Procedure," he says, almost apologetically. "Can't have civilians up front during an investigation. Department policy."

You climb in. Katie slides in beside you. The door closes with a heavy chunk. No handles on the inside. You notice but don't question. Police cars are built that way. It's normal.

Siobhan gets in the passenger seat. The sheriff starts the engine, and the heater kicks on, filling the car with warm air.

As he pulls out of the lot, he glances at Siobhan. "Everything ready for tomorrow? Family coming in?"

"Just us this year," Siobhan says. "Lily's excited though. We got her that bike she wanted. She's been so good."

"Emma too. Counting down the hours." He chuckles softly. "They grow up so fast. Have to protect them while we can."

"We do what we have to do," Siobhan agrees quietly.

The conversation seems normal, mundane holiday small talk, but Katie's hand finds your arm in the dark. Her grip is tight, her palm sweaty despite the cold.

"You okay?" you whisper.

She nods but doesn't speak. Her face is turned toward the window, watching the town slide past.

The sheriff's eyes find yours in the rearview mirror.

"So, Jenny. Walk me through exactly what you saw up there. Start from when you entered the building."

You describe it. The service door, the lobby, the stairs to the apartment. The warm air. The preserved rooms. The evidence someone's been maintaining the space.

"Interesting," Larkin murmurs. "Very thorough investigation on your part. Almost like you were building a case."

"I'm a journalist. It's what I do."

"Mmm." He turns onto the mountain road. "And who else knows about this? Besides us?"

"No one. I came straight to Katie after I left the lodge."

"Smart." The word sounds like approval, but something in his tone makes your skin prickle. "Keeping it contained. That's good."

Siobhan's hand rests on the door handle. Relaxed, casual. But her knuckles are white.

The drive feels longer than it should. The dark presses close, trees crowding the narrow road. Snow falls in thick curtains, reducing visibility to just a few feet beyond the headlights.

Katie's grip on your arm tightens with every curve. Her breathing has gone shallow and controlled.

"Katie, what's wrong?" you ask.

"Nothing." But her voice cracks on the word.

The sheriff's eyes are back on the rearview mirror. "Katie's just nervous. Aren't you, Katie? Going back up there. Knowing what might be waiting."

"Yes sir," Katie whispers.

The lodge appears. Dark shape against darker sky. Your car is still in the lot, half-buried now. The sheriff parks beside it and kills the engine.

Silence crashes in.

"All right," he says, turning to face you through the divider. "Here's what's going to happen. You're going to show me everything you found. We're going to document it properly. And then we're going to have a conversation about what comes next. Understood?"

You nod. The doors unlock with a click that sounds too loud.

The four of you walk toward the service door. You leading, Katie close beside you, Siobhan and the sheriff following. The door hangs open where you left it.

"Through here," you say, stepping into the corridor.

The warmth hits immediately. The sheriff notices. You see his face change slightly. "You're right. Definitely warmer than it should be."

You lead them through the lobby, up the stairs. Each step echoes off concrete. Katie's hand stays on your elbow the whole way, her grip never loosening.

At the apartment door, you pause. "This is it. The Van Vleets lived here. And someone's been maintaining it ever since."

The sheriff's flashlight sweeps the living room. Empty corkboard where Rachel's drawing was. Disturbed dust on the table. "Show me."

You take them to the master bedroom first. The dresser with modern clothes. The sheriff photographs them with his phone, methodical and professional.

Then Rachel's room. The shrine. The photographs. The seven pine cones.

The sheriff studies it all in silence. When he finally speaks, his voice is quiet. "You were right. About all of it."

You turn to Katie, relief flooding through you. Finally. Someone believes you. Someone's going to help.

But Katie won't look at you. She's staring at the floor, tears streaming silently down her face.

"Katie?" you say.

She doesn't answer.

You turn to her. She's crying, silent tears sliding down her face. "Katie, what…"

The sheriff's hand closes on your shoulder. Firm. Inescapable.

"Here's the thing, Ms Matthews. What you found here, it is significant. You're right about that. But it's also… complicated. This town has a certain way of handling these complications. A system that's been in place for a very long time."

Your heart hammers. "What are you talking about?"

"Katie and Siobhan did exactly what they were supposed to do. When someone becomes a threat, when someone finds things they shouldn't, asks questions they shouldn't, they report it. They bring that person in. That's the protocol. That's how we keep order."

"You're insane." You try to pull away but his grip tightens.

"No. Just practical." He looks at Siobhan. "Make the call."

Siobhan pulls out her phone. Dials. You watch, frozen, as she lifts it to her ear.

"Don't," you whisper. "Please don't."

Katie is openly sobbing now. "I'm sorry. Lily. I have to protect Lily. I can't let him take her. I can't…"

"It's ringing," Siobhan says.

A voice answers. Scratchy, distant. You can't make out words but you hear the tone. Rough. Male.

"It's Siobhan Wilson," she says calmly. "We have a situation. The journalist. Jenny Matthews. Sarah's sister. She found your rooms at the lodge. She has photos. Sheriff Larkin has her contained at the location now."

A pause. She listens.

"Yes. She came to us first, we followed protocol. Brought her to the sheriff, brought everyone up here."

Another pause.

"Understood. We'll wait."

She hangs up. Looks at the sheriff. "Twenty minutes."

Your stomach drops. "No. No no no…"

"I'm sorry," Katie sobs. "I'm so sorry, Jenny. But I can't lose Lily like I lost Tommy. I can't."

The sheriff guides you out of Rachel's room, back through the apartment. His grip is iron, professional. You try to fight but he's too strong, too practiced at this.

"You're all insane," you gasp. "The whole town. You're all helping him…"

"We're all protecting our children," Siobhan says coldly. "That's what parents do. We make sacrifices. We follow the rules. And the rules say that threats get reported. You became a threat the moment you walked into that lodge."

He takes you down the stairs, through the lobby, to a storage room you hadn't noticed before. Small, concrete, with a heavy door and a single chair.

"Sit," he says.

You don't. He pushes you down.

Zip ties appear from his belt. He secures your wrists to the chair's arms, your ankles to its legs. Professional. Efficient. Like he's done this before.

"For what it's worth," he says, "I am sorry. You seem like a good person. But my daughter is seven years old. And if I don't follow the rules, she'll be next. That's how this works. That's how it's always worked."

He steps back. Katie appears in the doorway, face streaked with tears.

"Say goodbye," the sheriff says to her. "He'll be here soon, and then we need to leave. Can't be here when he arrives."

Katie comes closer. She crouches in front of you, won't meet your eyes.

"I'm sorry," she whispers again. "Lily… She was Amy's friend. I watched Amy get taken last year and I thought… I thought if I just kept following the rules, kept reporting the threats, kept placing the bells… Lily would be safe. That's all I want. Just for her to be safe."

"So you'll let him kill me instead."

"Yes." The word is broken but final.

Siobhan pulls Katie to her feet. "Come on. We need to go."

The sheriff takes one last look at you. "For what it's worth, Ms Matthews, you were right. About everything. The lodge, the maintenance, the identity of the person living there. You solved it. You just didn't realise that solving it would make you a target."

They leave. The door closes. The lock clicks.

You're alone in the dark storage room, wrists and ankles bound, waiting.

Twenty minutes, Siobhan said. You don't have long.

The King of Christmas. The man who's been killing children for forty-nine years.

And you're tied to a chair, unable to run, unable to fight, unable to do anything but wait.

You think about Sarah. About that last glimpse of her red mittens disappearing into the snow. About your thirty-nine years of guilt and distance and unanswered questions.

You think about your parents, still in their house on Evergreen Lane. About the chest full of bells in their hallway. About how they'll never know what happened to you, just like they never knew what happened to Sarah.

You think about Katie, sobbing in the back of the cruiser, choosing Lily over you. About Siobhan's cold calculation. About the sheriff's practiced efficiency.

The whole town. All of them. Complicit. Trapped in a system that demands sacrifices to keep running.

Time passes. You don't know how much. Five minutes? Ten?

Then: footsteps in the lodge. Heavy. Unhurried. Coming closer.

The lock rattles. The door opens.

A figure fills the doorway. Red suit. White fur trim. Hood up, face shadowed.

He steps inside. Closes the door behind him. Pulls back his hood.

The face beneath is weathered, bearded, somewhere between sixty and eighty. The King of Christmas.

"Well," he says quietly. "Sarah's sister. Took you long enough to come home."

You try to speak but only a whisper comes out. "Please…"

"Such a long time," he continues, moving closer. "I've been waiting. Hoping. Knowing that someday, guilt would bring you back. And here you are."

He crouches in front of you, studying your face like you're a puzzle he's finally solved.

"Sarah was innocent. Did you know that? Genuinely innocent. She kept saying 'I didn't do it, I don't know what you mean, please.' Over and over." His voice drops. "She died confused. Scared. Not understanding why."

"I'm sorry," you choke out. "I'm so sorry. I was eleven. I didn't know…"

"But you did know. You stole that bracelet. You blamed your sister. And when she was taken, you stayed silent."

He stands. Produces a knife from his coat. Simple, worn, the blade catching the dim light.

"Please," you sob. "Please, I'll do anything…"

"You already did." He steps behind the chair. "You came back. You found my home. You gave Katie and Siobhan no choice but to bring you to me. This is your fault, just like Sarah's death was your fault. You've always been guilty. Always been the one who deserved punishment."

You feel his hand in your hair, tilting your head back.

"I'll tell them you fought," he says quietly. "I'll tell them you begged. But really, this is mercy. Thirty-nine years late, but mercy all the same. Sarah's been waiting for you. Now you can finally tell her you're sorry."

The blade is cold against your throat.

You close your eyes. Think of Sarah's face. Think of your parents. Think of all the choices that led here, to this room, to this chair, to this moment.

The blade moves.

There's pressure. Warmth. Then nothing.

The darkness is absolute and final.

THE END

You died in a storage room at the ski lodge, betrayed by the women you trusted and delivered to the King of Christmas by the sheriff himself. Katie and Siobhan followed protocol—reporting threats to protect their own children. In Pine Hollow, everyone is complicit. Everyone participates. Everyone survives by sacrificing someone else. Everyone except outsiders.

Sometimes the system isn't broken. Sometimes it's working exactly as designed.

YOU TAKE THE ROAD

You choose the road.

Your feet find the packed snow. Easier here. You can move faster.

But "faster" is relative. You're stumbling. Weaving. Your legs won't go straight.

You try to jog. Your coordination is shot. You nearly fall. Walk instead. Fast as you can.

The world keeps tilting. You put a hand out to the trees at the road's edge. Use them to stay upright.

How long have you been moving? No idea. Time is strange.

The distant lights. Are they closer? You can't tell. Everything is doubling.

You stop. Squeeze your eyes shut. Open them.

A little better. Not much.

Keep moving.

Behind you: silence now. Did you lose them?

Or are you just too drugged to hear properly?

Then: engine sound.

Or are you imagining it?

No. Headlights. Coming around the curve behind you.

You try to run. Your legs tangle. You fall. Get up. Fall again.

The vehicle is slowing.

Spotlight. Blinding white. You throw a hand up to shield your eyes.

Sheriff Larkin's cruiser.

What do you do?

Flag down the cruiser. Turn to page 459
Try to run. Turn to page 301
Hide. Turn to page 453

PULL OPEN THE HATCH

You climb onto the bed. The mattress sinks under your boots, springs groaning. The frame sags, soft from years of damp. You steady yourself with one hand on the wall.

The hatch has no cord, no handle. Just a wooden panel flush with the ceiling. You raise your torch, press the end against it, and push. Nothing. You shift your stance, feel the mattress compress beneath you, and push harder.

The panel jerks. Shifts an inch. Then...

A sharp crack. The hatch swings open.

The ladder drops fast, metal flashing in your beam. You lurch back, boot slipping on the sagging mattress. It slams into the bedframe where your head just was. Metal on wood, loud as a gunshot.

You catch yourself against the wall, pulse hammering. The ladder sways, still intact. Above, darkness yawns: one way up, one way down. You push that thought away.

Just a quick look. Five minutes.

You grab the ladder. The rungs are cold, rust rough beneath your palm. First rung. Second. It holds. You climb.

Your head clears the opening. The loft is bigger than you expected. The full length of the apartment below. Low ceiling, beams slanting down at the sides. You crouch, torch sweeping the space.

Boxes. Dozens of them. Cardboard splitting, stacked in corners. Others (plastic bins) sit newer, out of place. The air is thick with dust; you taste it when you breathe.

You haul yourself up, boots on plywood. Solid. Someone built this to bear weight.

You open a box: papers. Old invoices, maintenance logs from 1975, 1976. The paperwork of a business already dying. Another holds moth-eaten curtains. Another, broken ski gear.

Nothing useful. Just the remnants of a life packed away.

Still, if the Van Vleets really left after Rachel vanished, why leave all this? Files, linens, supplies. You'd expect emptiness. Bare walls, not rooms caught mid-breath, as if someone stepped out one winter and never came back.

The thought sticks as you move deeper into the loft. Your torch catches on something that doesn't belong here: a row of opaque blue bins, snap-lid, modern. The kind you'd buy anywhere. Too new for this place.

You drag one toward you, pop the latches, lift the lid.

Inside: Christmas.

Garlands, strings of lights, ornaments dulled by time. Enough to deck the entire lobby of the lodge.

You brush aside a tangle of tinsel, a cracked glass bauble, a velvet ribbon turned grey with dust. They're old (the originals, from the resort's first winters) but they couldn't have been left here like this. Not packed so neatly, not in boxes that didn't exist fifty years ago.

You shift the top layer aside, and something glints beneath. Bells. Dozens of them. Layer on layer, heavy and silent, their silver dulled but unmistakable.

Every one identical to the bells that haunt your parents' doorstep.

And then the connection hits you. The folded clothes in the dresser downstairs, modern denim, shirts with fresh creases. The same careful hands that placed those drawers have been here, too. The clothes, the decorations, the bells. Not remnants. Preparations.

Someone's been keeping this place.

A sound breaks the stillness.

A door slams below. Hard, sudden, close enough to shake dust from the rafters. You jerk upright, heart in your throat. Silence follows for a beat... and then, faint but unmistakable, comes whistling.

A tune you know too well.

The notes drift up through the cracks in the floorboards, light and careless, echoing through the hollow rooms. A Christmas song, in an empty lodge.

Santa Claus is coming to town.

You kill the torch. Darkness presses close, thick as cloth.

The whistling goes on, unhurried, tuneless between verses.

He's here.

Your thoughts splinter into choices:

Hide. Turn to page 395

Get out of the loft. Now. Turn to page 362

"He comes too." Your voice is firm.

The sheriff frowns. "Really, there's no need…"

"I'm not leaving my father alone in the car." You don't know why you feel this so strongly, but you do. Some instinct. Some certainty. "We stay together."

Your father's hand finds yours, squeezes. "Together," he echoes.

The sheriff's expression flickers then smooths into resignation. "All right. Both of you, then. But stay close and don't touch anything."

You and your father climb out together, hands still linked. The cold bites, but his grip is warm.

The three of you walk toward the service entrance. The sheriff leads, flashlight beam cutting through the dark. You and your father follow, shoulder to shoulder.

"Through here," the sheriff says, pushing through the broken door.

The corridor swallows you. Your father's hand tightens around yours.

Into the lobby. Up the stairs. Your footsteps echo in the silence.

At the apartment landing, the sheriff stops. Pulls out his radio.

"We're here," he says into it.

A crackle of response. You can't make out the words.

Your father goes still beside you. "Who are you talking to?"

The sheriff doesn't answer. Just opens the apartment door.

A figure sits in the middle of the shoddy, faded sofa. Red parka. White fur trim.

It's Santa Claus.

But it's not.

You know it's not.

It's a twisted, warped version of everything Santa Claus is not.

441

"No…" Your father tries to pull you back toward the stairs. But the sheriff is already there, blocking the way, hand on his belt.

"Bill," the figure says, not moving from the sofa. Voice like gravel and bells. "Jenny. I've been waiting."

He spreads his arms wide across the back of the sofa, relaxed, like he's holding court. Like this shabby apartment with its peeling wallpaper and Rachel's shrine is a throne room.

"You brought your little girl to see me," he says, almost delighted. "How thoughtful. It's been so long since a father brought his daughter to visit on Christmas Eve."

Your father's hand tightens around yours. "Let us go. We'll leave. We won't tell anyone. We'll…"

"Sit," the King of Christmas interrupts. His voice is gentle. Patient. "Come sit on my lap, Jenny. Tell me what you want for Christmas."

The words freeze you solid. The childhood ritual. The mall Santas, the photo ops, the "What do you want for Christmas, little girl?"

Except this isn't a mall. This is a tomb. And the man on the sofa has been killing children for forty-nine years.

"She's not going near you." Your father steps in front of you, shielding. "You want someone, take me. Let her go."

"That's very noble, Bill. But you know it doesn't work that way." The King of Christmas tilts his head, studying you both. "She's been naughty. Breaking into my home. Taking pictures. Coming here to destroy what I've built. The rules are clear."

The sheriff's hand closes on your shoulder. Pulls you forward, away from your father's protection.

"No…Dad…"

Your father lunges. The sheriff catches him, twists his arm behind his back. Your father cries out, but the sheriff holds him fast.

"Bring her here," the King of Christmas says, patting his knee. "Let's have our little chat."

The sheriff forces you forward. Across the living room. Past the corkboard with Rachel's faded drawing. Past the Christmas decorations that have rotted in place for half a century.

To the sofa.

To him.

Up close, his face is ancient. Weathered like wood left too long in the elements. But his eyes are bright. Clear. Focused entirely on you.

"Sit," he says again.

The sheriff pushes you down. You land on the King of Christmas's lap with a jolt. His arm comes around your waist, holding you in place. The other hand produces something from his coat pocket.

A knife. Long. Thin. Sharp.

"There we are," he says softly. "Just like when you were small, yes? Sitting on Santa's lap, telling him your wishes."

You can't breathe. Can't move. His arm is iron around your middle.

"Dad…" Your voice comes out strangled.

Your father is still struggling against the sheriff's hold, but it's useless. The sheriff has him pinned, forced to watch.

"What do you want for Christmas, Jenny?" The King of Christmas's voice is right by your ear now. Almost tender. "Tell me. What's your deepest wish?"

"Please…"

"Is it to see your sister again? To know what happened to Sarah?"

Your throat closes.

"She was naughty, you know. Stole a bracelet. Blamed another child. Just like you're naughty now. Just like your father's been naughty for so, so long, asking questions, looking where he shouldn't look."

The knife moves. You feel it against your back, cold through your coat.

"No," your father chokes out. "No, please, she's all I have left..."

"You should have thought of that before." The King of Christmas's voice stays gentle. Kind, even. "Before you taught her not to let things go. Before you passed your disease to her. *Obsession.*"

You see your father's face. See the moment he understands what's about to happen. See his eyes go wide, his mouth open to scream...

The knife slides in.

There's no pain at first. Just pressure. Just the sense of something wrong, something foreign entering your body where it shouldn't be.

Then the pain comes. Sharp. Bright. All-consuming.

You try to scream, but only a choked gasp emerges. Blood fills your mouth. How is there blood in your mouth?

Your father's face. That's all you can focus on. His face as he watches you die. The horror. The anguish. The complete devastation of a man watching his child be murdered and unable to stop it.

"I'm sorry," you try to say. But the words come out as bubbles. Red bubbles.

The King of Christmas holds you almost gently as the strength drains from your limbs. Like a father holding a sleeping child.

"There now," he murmurs. "It's almost over. You'll see Sarah soon."

Your vision is tunnelling. Your father's face blurs at the edges. But you can still see his eyes. Still see him trying to break free, still hear his muffled screams through whatever gag the sheriff has forced into his mouth.

I'm sorry, Dad. I'm so sorry. I brought us here. *My* obsession. *My* need for answers. I killed us both.

The darkness creeps in from the edges. Your father's face fades. The last thing you see is his tears.

The last thing you feel is the King of Christmas stroking your hair.

"Good girl," he whispers. "Such a good girl."

Then nothing.

THE END

You stayed with your father. He stayed with you.

You died on the King of Christmas's lap while your father watched, helpless.

He died moments later, reaching for your hand one last time.

In Pine Hollow, staying together doesn't save you. But at least you were together at the end.

Two more bodies. Two more bells for your mother's doorstep.

The King of Christmas returns to his sofa, and waits for the next visitor.

DRIVE AWAY

Your hand moves. Not to the window button. To the keys.

You twist the ignition. The engine coughs, catches.

The man steps back, startled. His mouth moves, saying something, but you can't hear over the blood roaring in your ears.

You throw the car into drive.

In your rearview mirror, you see him standing in the street, watching you go. Just a shape in the darkness. A man you'll never identify.

Your hands shake on the wheel. Your breath comes in gasps.

You don't stop until you're three blocks away, pulled over on a side street, engine idling, heart still hammering.

Was that smart? Or cowardly?

Was he dangerous? Or was he trying to help?

You'll never know.

You check the time.

The night is far from over. Bells will still be placed. You still have time to make other choices.

What do you do now?

Go to the Wilsons' residence Turn to page 309
Go to your parents' home Turn to page 335

STICK TO THE FOREST EDGE

You turn the wheel, hug the edge of the clearing, keeping the trees to your right.

It's slower. The ground is rougher here. More roots, rocks, uneven terrain. Your car bounces and jolts.

Behind you, Larkin follows. Closer now. His headlights fill your rearview mirror.

But you're near the trees. You can duck back in if you need to. You're not trapped.

The clearing stretches to your left, tempting, wide open - but something stops you. A gut feeling that you have to follow.

Larkin is right behind you now. He could ram you. Force you into a tree. Make you stop.

But he doesn't.

He's following the perimeter. Matching your pace.

You keep driving, hugging the tree line, looking for an opening back into the forest.

There: a gap in the trees ahead.

You swerve toward it, branches scraping your car as you plunge back into the woods.

Larkin follows.

The chase continues, slower now, winding between pines, your headlights carving tunnels through the darkness. You're trying to put distance between you, trying to find a road, a house, anywhere.

Your front tire hits something. A root. A rock. You don't know.

The steering wheel jerks. You overcorrect.

The car slams sideways into a tree.

The impact throws you against the seatbelt. Your head snaps forward. The airbag explodes, punching you in the face.

For a moment, everything is white powder and ringing ears and confusion.

Then Larkin's headlights pin you.

His cruiser stops ten feet away. Door opens. He steps out, flashlight in hand.

You try to restart your car. The engine grinds, coughs, dies. The front end is crumpled. Steam hisses from under the hood.

You're not driving anywhere.

You fumble for your seatbelt, pop it, shove the deflating airbag away. Reach for the door handle.

"Don't." Larkin's voice. Calm. Tired. "Just… don't."

You push the door open anyway. Stumble out into the snow.

"Miss Matthews…"

"Stay away from me!" You back up, hands raised. Your head is pounding. Blood trickles from your nose where the airbag hit.

Larkin stops. Doesn't advance. Just stands there, flashlight pointed down, one hand resting on his belt.

"You should have stopped when I asked," he says quietly.

He pulls his walkie-talkie from his belt. Presses the button. Static crackles.

"Are you there?"

A pause. Then a voice, distorted by static, but calm: "Go ahead."

"I have Matthews. The daughter. Out past Pine Lake. She crashed trying to run." Larkin's eyes don't leave you. "Do you want me to bring her up there or deal with her here?"

Your blood turns to ice.

Silence on the other end. Long enough you can hear your own heartbeat.

Then: "Deal with her."

"Copy that."

The radio clicks off.

Larkin clips it back to his belt.

"I'm sorry," he says. And he sounds like he means it.

He steps towards you before you have time to think.

You try to move but your legs are shaking, your head spinning from the crash. You manage two steps before he catches your arm.

"Don't make this harder," he says quietly.

His hand moves to his holster.

You see him draw his gun and your blood turns to ice.

"Larkin, please…"

"Run," he says quietly.

You stare at him. "What?"

"Run." His voice is flat. Tired. "Just… run. Don't make me do this looking at you."

Your body makes the decision before your mind catches up.

You run.

Into the dark forest, away from the headlights, crashing through underbrush and snow. Your boots slip on ice. Branches whip your face. Your lungs burn with cold air.

Behind you, Larkin's voice: "I'm sorry."

The gunshot cracks through the forest.

You don't feel it at first.

Just a punch between your shoulder blades. Hard. Like someone shoved you.

Your legs stop working.

You're falling.

Snow rushes up to meet you. You hit the ground face-first, can't get your hands up to catch yourself.

Then the pain comes.

Burning. Spreading from your back through your chest. You try to breathe but something's wrong, the air won't come right.

You're on your side now. Don't remember rolling over. You're looking back toward where you came from.

Larkin is walking toward you. Gun still in his hand. Flashlight in the other.

You try to crawl. Your arms won't work. Your legs won't work.

He reaches you. Kneels down. The flashlight beam is too bright. You squint against it.

"I'm sorry," he says again.

You try to speak. To say something. Anything.

But blood fills your mouth instead.

Larkin's face blurs. The flashlight beam halos around him.

"Your parents won't know," Larkin says. "No one will find you out here. I'm sorry about that too."

His voice is getting distant.

Everything is getting distant.

You think of your parents. Waiting for a call.

You think of Sarah. Red mittens in the snow.

And then the thinking stops.

THE END

You were shot in the forest outside Pine Hollow on Christmas Eve, 2025.

Your body was never found. Sheriff Larkin filed a report stating you fled a traffic stop and disappeared into the woods. He organised search parties that found your crashed car but no sign of you.

The official theory was that you wandered into the forest, disoriented from the crash, and succumbed to the elements. Your body would turn up in spring, they said, when the snow melted.

It never did.

Your parents waited for a call that never came. They never learned what happened to you.

Two Matthews daughters lost to Pine Hollow. Both vanished on Christmas Eve. Both never found.

The King of Christmas continued his work.

BACK IN ROOM 12

In Room 12, you close the door behind you, leaning against it until the silence settles back in. You've bought yourself peace for the moment, but it's a lie, one you'll gladly live with. Because no matter what you just told them, you know where you'll be when the bells come tonight.

You spread the folder contents across the faded bedspread. The map draws your eye immediately, your father's careful hand marking the town in blue ink, the four houses circled in red, the ski resort and mountains sketched in at the top of the page.

Four houses. Four families still living with the weight of not knowing what happened to their children.

Henderson. Wilson. Crawford. *Matthews.*

Your finger traces the line of Evergreen Lane, stops at the circle marking your parents' house. You've stayed away for too many Christmases. Too many years of excuses and assignments that kept you conveniently distant. Boston felt safer than here. Easier than facing the empty space where Sarah should be.

But Katie and Siobhan are the only people who've shown any concern for your safety.

And you just lied to them.

Which means your parents are all you have left. They're the only ones you can trust now.

You check your phone. 6:14pm. Hours yet before midnight, before whoever places those bells makes their rounds. Your body aches with exhaustion; you've been going since early this morning, running on coffee and adrenaline and guilt. If you're going to sit in the dark all night watching your parents' house, you need rest first.

You pull off your boots, your heavy sweater. Set an alarm for 9:30pm. That gives you three hours to sleep, then time to get ready and drive to Evergreen Lane before the bells come.

You lie on the bed fully clothed, the folder beside you, the map still visible in the dim light. Your thoughts spiral. Sarah in her red mittens. Your father's spidery handwriting. Katie's fear. Siobhan's anger.

You close your eyes.

This time, you'll be there when the bells come.

Stakeout at your parents, Turn to page 227

YOU HIDE FROM THE VEHICLE

The engine sound is getting louder.

You can't face him. Not like this. Not drugged and frozen and barely able to stand.

You stumble off the road into the tree line. Not far; just out of sight.

Your feet sink in deep snow. You push forward, hands outstretched in the darkness, feeling for trees.

The headlights are getting closer. Sweeping up the road toward you.

You need to get DOWN. Get hidden.

Your foot catches on something. It could be a root. You fall forward, hands hitting snow and...

Nothing. A depression. A hole.

You feel around frantically. It's... some kind of burrow? Animal den? The opening is maybe two feet wide, carved into the hillside beneath a fallen log.

The spotlight beam sweeps across the trees above you.

No time.

You push yourself into the hole headfirst. It's TIGHT. Your shoulders barely fit. You have to exhale completely to squeeze through.

The earth is frozen. Roots dig into your sides. The smell is animal: fur and den and earth.

You pull your legs in, cramming yourself as far back as you can. Curling into a ball in the tiny space.

Your heart hammers so loud you're sure he'll hear it.

The cruiser stops. Right there. On the road maybe twenty feet away.

Through the small opening of the den, you can see the spotlight sweeping. Back and forth. Across the trees.

The engine idles.

Don't move. Don't breathe.

A car door opens.

Footsteps. Crunching in snow.

"Miss Matthews?" Larkin's voice carries through the cold air. "I know you're out here somewhere."

You press yourself deeper into the den. A root digs into your back. You bite down on your tongue to keep from making noise.

The footsteps come closer.

He's OFF the road. In the trees.

The spotlight beam sweeps across the log above your den. The light filters down through gaps, catching on your breath in clouds.

Stop breathing. STOP.

You hold your breath. Lungs burning. Vision starting to spot.

"You're not thinking clearly," Larkin continues. His voice sounds… close. Too close. "The drugs, the cold…you're not going to make it to town like this. Let me help you."

The beam moves away. Then back. Directly across the log above you.

Is he looking AT your hiding spot?

Can he see the opening?

You squeeze your eyes shut. Like that will help.

"Last chance," Larkin says.

Silence.

Long. Terrible.

Then: footsteps. Moving away.

Back toward the road.

You still don't breathe. Don't move.

The car door opens. Closes.

The engine revs. The cruiser starts moving.

Slowly. Barely.

You hear it creep forward down the road. The sound fading.

You count to sixty. Then sixty more.

Silence. Just wind through the pines.

You risk letting out your breath. Gasping. Quiet as you can.

You wait longer. Another sixty count.

Nothing.

Slowly, painfully, you start to extract yourself from the den.

Your shoulders catch. You have to twist, wiggle, pull. The roots scrape your coat. One catches your hair, yanks. You bite back a cry.

Finally, you're OUT. Lying in the snow, gasping, shaking.

You're so cold. The den was cold, but this is WORSE. The air is frozen. Your wet clothes are starting to freeze.

Get up. Have to get UP.

You push yourself to hands and knees. Then to your feet. Stumbling.

The road. Where's the road?

There. A break in the trees. You can see the packed snow.

You make your way back to it. Every step is agony. Your legs are so heavy.

But you're AHEAD of Larkin now. He thinks you're behind him. Or dead. Or gave up.

You're ahead.

The town lights are closer. Much closer. You can see individual buildings now. Street lights.

Pine Hollow.

You're going to make it.

You start walking downhill. Faster now. Urgent.

One foot. Then the other.

The lights get closer.

Closer.

You recognise shapes now. The church steeple. The Inn's sign.

You're at the edge of town.

Houses. Real houses. With lights on. Warm inside.

Your parents' house. Where is…

Evergreen Lane. There.

You turn onto it. Your street. Your childhood street.

The house at the end. White trim. Christmas lights. Home.

You stumble up the walk. Up the porch steps.

Your hand is shaking so hard you can barely knock.

But you do. Three times. Hard.

"Mom?" Your voice is hoarse. Barely there. "Dad?"

Footsteps inside.

The porch light flicks on.

The door opens.

Your father stands there. Face shocked. Then terrified.

"Jenny? Oh my God… JENNY…"

He pulls you inside before you can collapse.

Your mother appears. "Bill, what…JENNY?"

She runs to you. Her hands on your face. "You're freezing. You're…oh God, you're hypothermic. Bill, call 911…"

"No." You grab her arm. "No. We can't. We can't call anyone."

Your parents stare at you.

The front door explodes inward.

Not kicked. RAMMED. The frame splinters. The door slams against the wall so hard it bounces back.

Sheriff Larkin fills the doorway.

He's breathing hard. Snow on his shoulders. His hand rests on his gun belt but he hasn't drawn.

Not yet.

"Evening, folks." His voice is calm. Conversational. Like he's making a social call. "Sorry about the door. Didn't want to waste time knocking."

Your father moves in front of you and your mother. "What the hell do you think you're doing? This is…"

"This is a wellness check, Bill." Larkin steps inside. Closes the broken door behind him as best he can. "Your daughter escaped from my custody while I was trying to help her. She's hypothermic.

Possibly suffering from exposure-induced psychosis. I need to get her to the hospital."

"She said you tried to kill her." Your father's voice is steady despite the fear in his eyes.

"She's confused. Disoriented." Larkin's eyes never leave you. "The cold does that. Makes people paranoid. Aggressive. I was trying to keep her safe and she attacked me. Ran into the woods. I've been searching for her for the past hour."

"That's not..." you start, but your voice is hoarse. Weak.

"Miss Matthews, you need medical attention." Larkin takes a step closer. "Your parents need you to get medical attention. Let's not make this harder than it has to be."

Your mother's hand finds your father's. You can feel her shaking.

"We're not going anywhere with you," your father says.

Larkin's expression doesn't change but something shifts in his eyes. Something cold.

"That's unfortunate," he says quietly. "Because I'm not asking anymore."

His hand moves to his gun. Doesn't draw it. Just rests there. A promise.

"Here's what's going to happen. Jenny's going to come with me to the hospital. You two are going to stay here. You're going to tell anyone who asks that she was confused, disoriented, and I helped her get the medical care she needed. And life goes on."

"And if we don't?" Your father's voice is barely above a whisper.

Larkin's smile doesn't reach his eyes. "Then you won't need to worry about bells anymore. Any of you."

The threat hangs in the air.

Your mother's grip on your father tightens.

You can feel your legs trembling. From cold. From fear. From the drug still in your system.

The back door is through the kitchen. Twenty feet away. Maybe less. If you run, would you make it? Would your parents?

Or maybe you can stall him. Keep him talking. Someone might notice the broken door. A neighbour might call for help. Something might change.

But Larkin's hand is on his gun and his eyes are dead and you know that he'll do it. He'll kill all three of you right here in the living room if you make the wrong choice.

What do you do?

RUN - Make a break for the back door. **Turn to page 405**
TALK - Try to stall, negotiate, buy time. **Turn to page 348**

YOU FLAG DOWN THE CRUISER

Sheriff Larkin pulls to the side of the road and gets out. Says something. You can't quite hear over the ringing in your ears.

"…safe now…got him…hospital…"

Hospital. That sounds good. You're so tired. So cold. Everything hurts.

He's walking toward you.

Wait. Wait, he locked you up. He's not…

But he looks concerned. Genuine.

And you're so tired.

"Come on," he says. Closer now. Reaching for you. "Let's get you warm."

Warm. Yes. The cruiser is warm. You can see heat shimmering from the open door.

You can barely stand. Your legs are shaking: cold or drugs or both.

The cruiser is right there. Warm. Safe.

Larkin is reaching for you. "Come on. You're hypothermic. We need to get you to a hospital."

Hospital. Yes. You need…

Your feet move before you decide. Stumbling toward the cruiser.

He opens the back door. Helps you in.

The warmth hits you immediately. So warm. You sink into the seat.

The door closes.

You slump against the window, eyes closing.

Just for a moment. Just…

The cruiser starts moving.

You force your eyes open. Try to focus.

Through the windshield: the road. Going up. UPHILL.

Wrong direction.

"Wait…" Your voice is slurred. "Town is… down…"

"I know," Larkin says quietly.

You try the door handle. Locked. No handles in the back.

"You're taking me back," you whisper.

"I'm sorry." His eyes find yours in the rearview mirror. "But you knew too much. You saw too much. There's no coming back from that."

You try to stay awake. Try to think. But the warmth, the drugs, the exhaustion…

Your eyes close.

When they open again, you're not in the cruiser anymore.

You're in a different room. Colder than before. Darker.

Your wrists and ankles have been bound again. Tighter this time.

And standing in the doorway, silhouetted against the light:

Someone who looks very much like Father Christmas.

He steps inside. Closes the door.

In the dim light, you can see him properly now. An old man. Red suit; not a costume. A ski suit. Crimson jacket and pants. Dirty white trim.

Your blood turns to ice.

Is this the King of Christmas?

"Welcome back, Miss Matthews," he says.

But his voice is cold. Flat. No warmth. No patience.

He moves closer. Studies you for a moment.

"You ran," he says.

You don't answer. Can't.

"I don't have time for this anymore." He reaches down, grabs your arm. Hauls you upright.

Your legs barely hold you. Still drugged. Still frozen.

"Wait…"

"No."

He starts dragging you toward the door.

You try to pull away. "Please…"

He doesn't respond. Just keeps pulling you into the hallway. Stone walls. Dim lights.

Your mind is racing. This is him? THE person who took your sister. Who took all of them.

And the sheriff? Why isn't he…?

You only have time for so many questions.

"What did you do to Sarah?" you gasp. "Where is she? WHERE ARE THEY?"

He doesn't answer. Just keeps walking. Pulling you with him.

Another door ahead. He opens it.

The room beyond is pitch black. Freezing.

"Please…" you try again. "Just tell me…"

He shoves you inside. Hard.

You hit the floor. Pain explodes in your shoulder, your knees.

"You should have left when you had the chance," he says from the doorway. His voice is emotionless. Matter-of-fact.

"WAIT…"

The door closes.

Lock clicks.

You're alone in the darkness.

Complete darkness. You can't see your hand in front of your face.

The cold seeps in immediately. Worse than before.

Your breath comes in clouds you can't even see.

You pull at the ropes on your wrists. They don't give.

You try to stand. Your legs give out. You collapse back to the floor.

Think. THINK.

But your mind is sluggish. Drugged. Frozen. Exhausted.

You don't know where you are. Don't know who he is. Don't know what happened to Sarah.

You tried so hard to find answers.

And you're going to die knowing nothing.

Time passes. You can't tell how much.

You're shaking violently. The cold is inside you now. Deep. Bone-deep.

Your thoughts are getting slower. Foggier.

That's bad. You know that's bad.

But you can't remember why.

The shaking stops.

That should worry you. You know it should.

But you're so tired.

You close your eyes.

Just for a moment.

Just…

THE END

You died of hypothermia in a locked room at the Van Vleet Ski Lodge on Christmas Eve, 2025.

Your body was never found.

Sheriff Larkin filed a report stating you fled his attempted rescue and disappeared into the forest. The official story was exposure. An accident. A tragedy.

Your parents buried an empty coffin next to Sarah's grave.

Two Matthews daughters lost to Pine Hollow. Both vanished on Christmas Eve. Both never found.

The King of Christmas continued his work.

WHY DID NO ONE STOP YOU?

The question hangs in the air.

Van Vleet just looks at you. Waiting.

And suddenly it clicks. The sheriff's dismissiveness when you arrived. The decades of bells left on doorsteps with no investigation. Your father's forty-two years of being stonewalled, his research ignored, his questions shut down. The way every authority figure in Pine Hollow looked the other way.

"The sheriff," you say slowly. "All these years. The bells, the disappearances. He never really investigated, did he?"

Van Vleet's expression doesn't change.

"He knows." Your voice hardens. "The sheriff knows about you."

"They all knew," your father says. "Didn't they? The town knew you were here."

"Most of them." Van Vleet looks down at his hands. "Not you. Even after your daughter, they still didn't let you into the circle of trust. Must sting."

Your father moves before you can stop him.

He's across the space in two steps, hands reaching for Van Vleet's throat. The chair tips backward as Van Vleet jerks away, but your father catches him by the collar of that red jacket, hauling him up.

"Dad, NO!" You're on your feet, grabbing your father's arms, trying to pull him back.

"You KNEW!" Your father is shaking Van Vleet, his face twisted with rage and grief. "You knew where she was. You knew what happened to her. And every time I came to the sheriff, every time I showed them my research, every time I BEGGED for help..."

"Dad, let go!" You're pulling harder now, your voice urgent. "Let GO!"

Your father's grip loosens. Not because he wants to. Because he has to. Because you're pulling him back and he's eighty-two years old and the adrenaline is fading and suddenly he's shaking.

Van Vleet straightens his jacket, breathing hard. There's a red mark on his throat where your father's hands were. He doesn't look frightened. If anything, he looks... satisfied. Like he proved a point.

"You see?" Van Vleet's voice is rough but steady. "That's what grief does. It makes you violent. It makes you dangerous. Now imagine an entire town living with that fear. Imagine parents terrified that one misstep, one moment of anger, one act of violence might mark their child for punishment."

"But why?" you ask, breathing hard, your hand on your father's chest, holding him back. "Why would they protect you?"

Van Vleet's mouth twists. "Because they were afraid."

"Afraid of what?"

"Of me." He says it simply. "Of what I'd do if they didn't cooperate. Of whose child would be next if they stepped out of line."

The words hang in the air. Your father has gone very still.

"You threatened them," you breathe.

"I didn't have to. Not after the first few." Van Vleet looks up. "They understood. Report me, investigate me, try to stop me...and I'd take their child. Their grandchild. Someone they loved. It was that simple."

Your father's hands clench on the arms of the chair. "You held the entire town hostage."

"I gave them order." Van Vleet's voice hardens. "Before me, Pine Hollow was dying. Crime rising. Young people leaving. Families falling apart. No one respected authority. No one followed rules. And then..." He stops. "And then Rachel died. And I realised something. People don't respond to laws. They respond to fear."

"So you became what they feared," you say quietly.

"I became what they needed." Van Vleet leans forward slightly. "Parents who couldn't control their children? They had a solution. Children who acted out, who stole, who hurt others? They knew there would be consequences. Real consequences. Not juvenile detention or therapy or slaps on the wrist. *Real* consequences."

"You murdered children," your father says. Voice shaking. "You're calling child murder a 'consequence.'"

"I took bad children." Van Vleet's voice is flat. "Children who did wrong. And yes, I made sure they never did wrong again."

"But Sarah..." Your father's voice breaks. "Sarah wasn't bad."

"I was told she stole." Van Vleet looks at you. "A mother told me Sarah took her daughter's bracelet. That Sarah was becoming a thief. That she needed correction before it got worse."

Your blood turns to ice.

Barbara's bracelet. The one you took. The one you were going to plant in Sarah's room.

"Who?" you manage. "Who told you?"

"Helen Warren." Van Vleet says the name like it's nothing. Like it doesn't matter. "She came to me. Told me what Sarah had done. Asked me to... handle it."

The system crystallises in your mind. Parents informing on each other's children. Creating a pecking order. Protecting their own by sacrificing others. And Van Vleet at the centre, judge and executioner.

"And if someone didn't play along?" your father asks quietly. "If they refused to participate?"

"Then their child went on the list." Van Vleet's voice is matter-of-fact. "Simple as that. Cooperate and your family stays safe. Resist, investigate, ask too many questions..." He shrugs. "People learned quickly."

The room tilts.

"But Sarah didn't take it," you whisper. "I did. I took Barbara's bracelet. I was going to frame Sarah for it but I didn't... I never got the chance because that night..."

You can't finish. Can't say it.

Van Vleet stares at you. Really stares.

"You," he says quietly. "It was you."

Your father makes a sound. Grief and shock mixing.

"I was eleven," you choke out. "I was jealous and stupid and I took the bracelet and Helen Warren saw it was missing and she thought... she thought Sarah..." Tears are streaming down your face now. "Sarah died because of me. Because I stole that bracelet. Because Helen Warren thought..."

"No." Your father's hands are on your shoulders, firm. "Sarah died because he murdered her. Because this town let him. Because Helen Warren was so terrified for her own daughter that she sacrificed someone else's. Not because of you."

But you can barely hear him over the roaring in your ears.

Van Vleet is still watching you. His expression is complicated. Guilt. Pity. Something else.

"She was innocent," he says quietly. "I realised that. After. Sarah kept saying she didn't do it, that she didn't understand. She wasn't like the others. She was..." He stops. "Pure. Good. I took the wrong child."

"You took my daughter." Your father's voice shakes with rage. "Because a scared mother lied to protect her own. Because a system you created let you murder children and call it teaching. Because..."

He can't continue. The weight of it, all of it, is too much.

Van Vleet looks between you both. At your tear-streaked face. At your father's barely controlled fury.

"I'm sorry," he says. And he sounds like he means it. "For what it's worth. Sarah... she's the reason I stopped. For fifteen years after her, I took no one. Because she proved the system was flawed. That I was punishing innocents based on lies."

"But you started again," you say. Voice hollow. "Daniel Peak in 2001. Emily Taylor. Amy Crawford last year."

"Daniel... was different. His parents wanted to leave town. Daniel... Sweet kid, blonde-haired..."

"Don't talk about him like that," your father snarls.

Van Vleet waves his hand, dismissively. "The sheriff told me we couldn't let them go. They knew too much, of course. They'd done their share of leaving bells. It was time they got their own."

"Holy shit," you say as it dawns. "You made the parents of the children you'd taken leave bells?"

"Everyone has their turn." He says it as though it's a simple, known fact.

"But they did leave town..." As you say the words, you doubt the truth in them.

"Did they? Everyone has to remember that I am here and that actions have consequences." Van Vleet actually smiles.

"You're not God. You're just some old man in a shitty ski suit that doesn't even look like a Santa outfit." Your father is rising again, and you shake your head, press against his leg. No. That's not the way. You don't know how this ends but it's not with two octogenarians having a fist fight.

Van Vleet just looks at you both. Waiting. Like he's curious to see what you'll do next.

Your hand moves instinctively to your pocket.

Your phone.

Still there. Still recording.

You started the recording the moment you sat down. Every word of his confession captured. Rachel's accident. Marcie's murder. The system. The threats. Sarah. All of it. Documented. Preserved.

Van Vleet doesn't know.

But you do.

Your father is shaking beside you. Rage and grief and decades of helplessness radiating off him like heat. You can feel it building. The same fury that made him lunge at Van Vleet's throat. But worse now. More final.

You have the recording. You have everything you need to expose him, to expose the town, to burn this entire corrupt system to the ground.

You could end this. Right now. Insist on taking him to real authorities outside Pine Hollow. Make him face justice. Stop this before it goes any further.

Or you could let him keep talking. See what else he reveals. Give your father more time to… you don't know. Process. Decide. Whatever he needs.

Take him to real authorities. **Turn to page 477**
Let Van Vleet keep talking. **Turn to page 469**

LET VAN VLEET KEEP TALKING

You don't move. Don't speak. Your mind is racing but your mouth won't form words.

Van Vleet watches you both in the silence. Your father is still trembling with barely contained rage. You should do something. Say something. But you can't seem to make the decision.

The moment stretches. And in that hesitation, Van Vleet seems to relax slightly. Like he's interpreting your silence as uncertainty. As weakness.

"The sheriff won't help us," you finally say, your voice barely above a whisper. "Will he? Even after everything you've told us."

Something flickers across Van Vleet's face. Not quite a smile.

"The sheriff?" The man actually laughs. Short, bitter. "You think I only have the sheriff on my side?"

The casual way he says it makes your blood run cold.

"What does that mean?" your father demands.

"It means you're more alone than you realise. The sheriff. The mayor. Town council. Business owners. Parents." He pauses. "The town tolerated you, Bill, because you already had nothing left to lose. But they never helped you. Because helping you meant becoming targets themselves."

"Jesus Christ," you whisper.

"It's an elegant system, really." Van Vleet sounds almost proud. "Everyone polices everyone else. Everyone protects the order. And I..." He spreads his hands. "I just maintain it. I'm the threat that keeps everyone in line. I find out who's naughty or nice. Turns out the King of Christmas does have a list."

"You're not Santa Claus, you're a terrorist," your father says. Voice hollow. "You've held an entire town hostage for forty-nine years through terrorism."

"I prefer to think of it as guardianship." But Van Vleet's voice wavers slightly. "Someone had to maintain order. Someone had to make sure…" He stops. Starts again. "After Rachel, I couldn't just let chaos win. I couldn't let children keep being bad, keep being reckless, keep dying because no one taught them consequences."

And there it is. The crack in his justification. The grief underneath the monster.

"And Jenny… You only got to leave because you knew nothing. You were innocent. You were. But now…"

Your father moves.

No warning. No hesitation. Just pure, protective fury.

He's on Van Vleet before the old man can finish the sentence, hands closing around his throat. The chair tips backward, crashing to the floor. They go down together in a tangle of limbs and that red jacket.

You stand there.

Watching.

Van Vleet's hands scrabble at your father's wrists. His face is going red. His mouth opens but no sound comes out.

"Don't you DARE." Your father's voice is barely human. "Don't you dare threaten her. Not her. NOT HER."

You should stop this.

You could stop this.

Your father is eighty-two years old, strangling a man in the middle of an abandoned ski resort. This is murder. This is wrong. This is…

Van Vleet's eyes find yours. Pleading. Desperate.

The man who killed Sarah.

The man who just threatened you.

The man who's gotten away with it for forty-nine years.

You don't move.

Van Vleet's struggles are weakening. His hands fall away from your father's wrists. His eyes are still on yours, still pleading, but the light in them is fading.

You watch.

You just… watch.

Your father's hands don't loosen until Van Vleet stops moving entirely. Until the body goes completely slack beneath him.

The silence that follows is absolute.

Your father stays there for a long moment, hands still around Van Vleet's throat, breathing hard. Then he pulls back slowly. Looks down at what he's done.

Looks up at you.

"Jenny," he says. Voice shaking. "I…"

"I know." Your voice sounds far away. Calm. Too calm. "We need to go. We need to get Mom and leave. Right now."

Drive back to Pine Hollow Turn to page 472

DRIVE BACK TO PINE HOLLOW

The drive back to Pine Hollow passes in silence.

Your father's hands are steady on the wheel. Too steady. Like he's concentrating very hard on this one simple task: drive, turn, brake, park. Don't think about anything else.

Your phone with your secret recording is heavy in your pocket. Van Vleet's confession is there. And probably the sounds of what happened after.

Your father parks in front of the house on Evergreen Lane. The porch light is still on. The bell still sits where it was left last night.

Your mother opens the door before you reach it. Takes one look at your faces.

"What happened?" Her voice is thin. Frightened.

"We need to leave," your father says. "Right now. Pack one bag. We're going."

"Bill, what…"

"Now." The word is final. "We can't stay here. Not anymore."

Your mother looks at you. You nod.

She disappears inside. You hear her moving through the house, opening drawers, grabbing things. She doesn't ask again. Forty-two years in Pine Hollow has taught her when not to ask questions.

Fifteen minutes later, you're back in the truck. One suitcase. A box of your father's research that he refuses to leave behind. Your mother in the back seat, silent, watching the town slide past the windows.

No one stops you. No sirens. No sheriff's truck blocking the road.

No one knows yet what you have done.

You. The Matthews. The comer-inners.

The Matthews family left suddenly. Christmas morning. Some emergency back in Boston.

There's no man in a red suit to tell people what to think. Not anymore.

The town limits sign passes. THANK YOU FOR VISITING PINE HOLLOW. DRIVE SAFELY.

Your father's hands finally start to shake on the wheel.

Your mother reaches forward, rests her hand on his shoulder. Says nothing.

You watch the mountains disappear in the rearview mirror. The Frost Mountains. The resort. The apartment where the King of Christmas lies dead on the floor.

THE END

You left Pine Hollow with your parents on Christmas morning, 2025. You never went back.

You don't know what happened after. If someone found Van Vleet's body in that apartment. If the town covered it up.

You never wrote the story. The recording sits on your phone, backed up, encrypted, waiting. Evidence of murder - Van Vleet's and your father's both. You can't use it without destroying your family. So it stays hidden.

Your father doesn't talk about what happened. Your mother doesn't ask

Sometimes you search online for Pine Hollow news. Missing children. Disappearances. You find nothing. But that might just mean they got better at hiding it. Or it might mean that without the King of Christmas, the town finally learned they didn't need him. That they could be better.

You'll never know.

.

SNOOP AROUND

You set down your mug and stand. Just a quick look. Katie will be upstairs for a few more minutes at least.

You move into the kitchen; it's small, neat, the counter clean except for the kettle and a box of tea bags. You open a cupboard quietly. Mugs. Plates. Nothing unusual.

Another cupboard. Spices. Canned goods.

You're about to close it when you see something on the worktop beside the sink.

A small bottle. Blue label.

You reach for it, pull it down.

Rat poison. D-Con. Active ingredient: Brodifacoum.

Warning labels cover the bottle. Skull and crossbones. KEEP OUT OF REACH OF CHILDREN.

Your first thought is practical, almost maternal: Fancy keeping this around with Lily in the house. A child her age could easily reach this shelf. Why would you keep poison somewhere a child could get to it?

You turn the bottle in your hands, reading the warnings.

Then the thought stops.

Katie wouldn't have left it here with Lily around.

She sent Lilly upstairs.

But…

Your gaze drifts to your mug on the coffee table. Half-empty.

The chamomile tea that tasted slightly bitter. That you attributed to the lemon.

The warmth spreading through you. The softness at the edges of your vision that you thought was exhaustion.

Oh.

Oh God.

No. No, you're jumping to conclusions. This is Katie. Tommy's sister. She's been nothing but kind since you got here. She invited you in, made you tea, shared her home. She wouldn't...

Your hands start shaking. The bottle nearly slips from your grip.

You set it back on the counter, push it to where it was. Your fingers are clumsy. Everything feels slightly distant, like you're operating your body from somewhere far away.

You need to sit down. You need to think. You need to...

You turn back toward the living room and the floor tilts.

Your hip catches the edge of the counter. You grab for support, knock over the box of tea bags. They scatter across the counter, the floor.

Damn it.

You bend to pick them up but the movement makes your head swim. You straighten too fast and the room lurches.

Footsteps on the stairs.

Katie appears in the doorway between the kitchen and living room.

She sees you. Sees the scattered tea bags. Sees your face.

"It'll be over soon," she says.

Her voice is soft. Almost kind.

You try to speak. Your tongue feels thick. "Katie... why..."

"I'm sorry." And she sounds like she means it. "I really am. But I can't let you... I can't risk Lily."

You take a step backward, away from her, but your legs won't cooperate. Your hip hits the counter again. You grab for the edge.

"Please," you manage. "Hospital. I need..."

Katie shakes her head slowly. "It's too late for that."

Your phone. Where's your phone?

Your pocket. Your coat pocket.

You reach for it, clumsy, your fingers not working right. You pull it out. The screen is too bright. You can't focus on it.

Katie doesn't try to stop you. She just watches.

"Who are you going to call?" she asks quietly. "Your parents? So they have to watch you die too? The sheriff? He won't come. Not for this."

You try to dial. 9… your finger slips. You try again.

The room tilts violently. You drop the phone. It clatters on the tile floor.

You sink down after it. Can't stay standing. The floor is cold. Hard.

Katie comes closer. Kneels beside you.

"I'm sorry," she says again. "You should have left. When I warned you. When Siobhan warned you. But you wouldn't listen."

"Sarah…" you whisper. "I just wanted… to find…"

"I know." Katie's hand touches your shoulder. "I know. But some things… some things can't be found. Some things have to stay buried. For everyone's safety."

Your vision is tunnelling. The edges going dark.

Katie's face above you. Blurring.

"It'll be over soon," she says. "I promise."

And it is.

THE END

You died in Katie Wilson's kitchen on Christmas Eve, 2025. Your investigation ended here.

Jenny Matthews' body was never found. Her car disappeared from Birch Street. The official story was that she left Pine Hollow suddenly, unable to face the memories. Her parents never learned the truth.

The King of Christmas continued his work.

TAKE HIM TO THE POLICE

"We're taking you to the police. Now."

The words come out harder than you intended. Final.

Van Vleet's expression doesn't change. He just looks at you. Then at your father.

"The sheriff?" he asks. Almost amused.

"State police," you say. "Real police. In the city. Not your corrupt friends in Pine Hollow. We're taking you down this mountain and we're putting you in front of authorities who will actually investigate. Who will actually care about seven dead children."

That gets a reaction. His jaw tightens.

Your father is already moving, pushing himself up from his own chair with a grunt of effort. "You're going to stand up. You're going to walk to our truck. And we're driving you to real justice."

"And if I refuse?" Van Vleet asks. Still sitting. Still too calm.

"Then we make you," you say. Your hand moves to your pocket, feeling the shape of your phone. Still recording. Every word of his confession captured. "You just told us everything. Multiple murders. A conspiracy. We have evidence now. You're done. This whole damn town is done."

Van Vleet looks between you both. Really looks. At your father, eighty-two years old, breathing hard from just standing up. At you, in your early fifties, running on adrenaline and no sleep.

"You think you can force me?" he asks quietly. "I might be old, but look at you two. You think you can make me do anything?"

"We'll do what we have to," your father says. His voice is steady but you can hear the tremor underneath. The fear that Van Vleet is right. That you won't be enough to end this the right way.

Van Vleet stands slowly. Carefully. Like he's considering his options.

For one moment, you think he's actually going to comply. That he's going to walk to the door, accept that it's over, let you take him down the mountain to face what he's done.

Then he moves.

Fast. Impossibly fast for an eighty-four-year-old man.

Not towards you. Towards the apartment door. His hand is on the handle before you can react.

"Stop!" Your father lunges after him but Van Vleet is already through, the door slamming behind him. You hear his footsteps pounding down the stairs.

You're moving. Running. Your father behind you, both of you hitting the doorway at the same time, nearly colliding. Down the stairs. Your feet barely hitting each step. The flashlight beam bouncing wildly.

Through the lobby. The lodge door. Out into the blinding white of Christmas morning.

Van Vleet doesn't head for the parking lot where your father's truck sits. He heads uphill. Directly uphill, toward the ski runs rising into the mountains behind the lodge. For a moment, he looks for the world like Father Christmas out there, red suit against white snow. But he is not. He is the embodiment of everything that is the opposite of Santa Claus. He is living evil, and you have to bring him to justice.

"VAN VLEET!" Your voice rips across the snow. "STOP!"

He doesn't stop.

He doesn't even look back.

You run.

The snow is deep. Deeper than it looked. Each step sinks six inches, sometimes more. Your boots are meant for city sidewalks, not this. Every stride is work. Within thirty seconds your calves are burning.

Van Vleet moves steadily upward. He's not running exactly. More like a fast walk. But he knows where to step. Where the snow is packed. Where the old groomed runs are underneath all this powder. This is his territory. He knows every inch of this mountain.

You don't.

Your foot catches on something hidden beneath the snow. A rock. A piece of old equipment. You pitch forward, catch yourself with your hands, snow burning cold against your palms. Push yourself up. Keep moving.

Your father is behind you. You can hear him. His breathing is laboured, harsh. Too harsh.

"Dad," you gasp. "Dad, go back. Call for help."

"Not leaving you." Each word is a wheeze. "Not losing you too."

The red jacket ahead is the only colour in all this white. You focus on it. Follow it. Your lungs are screaming. The cold air feels like knives every time you breathe in.

The slope gets steeper. Your thighs are cramping. You're not a runner. You haven't trained for this. You write stories sitting at a desk in Boston. You drink too much coffee and not enough water, and you definitely don't climb mountains.

Van Vleet is pulling ahead.

No. No, you can't let that happen.

You push harder. Ignore the pain. Ignore the burning. Ignore the voice in your head saying you can't do this.

Sarah. Think about Sarah. Nine years old. Taken from your garden. Her last moments terrified and alone because Helen Warren lied and you stole a bracelet, and this man decided that was enough reason to murder a child.

You push harder.

The jacket is getting closer. You're gaining on him. He's old. He's fit but he's eighty-four. He has to tire eventually.

You're maybe twenty yards behind him now. Fifteen.

He reaches a plateau. A flat section where the beginner slope used to be. He doesn't stop but he slows slightly, looking around like he's getting his bearings.

You're closing the gap. Ten yards. Eight.

Your father is falling further behind. You can barely hear his footsteps now over your own heartbeat pounding in your ears.

Five yards.

"Van Vleet!" You have just enough breath to shout. "There's nowhere to go! You can't outrun this!"

He stops.

Turns to face you.

You slow, wary. Is this a trap? Is he armed? You don't think he had time to grab anything but you don't know.

He's breathing hard too. Not as hard as you but hard enough. His face is flushed. Sweat on his forehead despite the cold.

"You're right," he says. "I can't outrun it."

You take a careful step closer. Then another. Close enough to grab him if he runs again. "Then stop. Come with us. Face what you've done."

"I have faced it." He looks past you, down the slope. Your father is maybe fifty yards back, struggling through the snow, one hand pressed to his chest. "Every day since I lost my daughter. Every time I looked at her photos. Every time I made someone leave a bell. I've been facing it."

"That's not the same as justice."

"Justice." He says the word like it's foreign. Like he's testing the taste of it. "Is that what you think will happen? You'll take me to the city. Tell them your story. They'll investigate Pine Hollow. Find the truth. Arrest the sheriff, the mayor, all the complicit parents. Take the entire town in? Everyone pays for what they've done?"

"Yes."

He smiles. It's sad. Tired. "Maybe. Maybe that's how it should go. But I won't be there to see it."

He turns and starts walking again. Not running. Just walking. Steady. Purposeful.

Toward a section of the slope that looks… wrong somehow. The snow sits differently there. Lower. Like something underneath is disturbing it.

"Where are you going?" You follow. Not running now. Just matching his pace.

"Home," he says simply.

You're close enough now to see what he's walking toward. A depression in the snow. Long and rectangular. The edges too straight to be natural. Warning signs poke up through the powder, faded and illegible after decades of weather.

Your father's words echo in your memory: *Logging camps have infrastructure. Kiln vents, equipment pits, drainage shafts. Some of it went twenty, thirty feet down.*

"Don't," you say. Because suddenly you know where this is going. What he's about to do.

He stops at the edge of the depression. Looks down at it. Then at you.

"This is where it happened," he says quietly. "Christmas Eve, 1976. Rachel was playing out here in the snow. God, she loved it up here. Loved pretending to ski. She was going to be good, I could tell. Natural athlete."

You're close enough to grab him now. But something in his voice stops you. Makes you listen.

"The snow was deep that year too. Just like this. She didn't see the warning signs. Didn't know about the old kiln vent from when this was the Frost Timber logging camp." He gestures at the depression. At the warning signs barely visible. "We'd covered it with plywood when we were building. Temporary measure. I was going to do it properly. Pour concrete. Make it safe. But we were out of budget. Marcie kept saying we needed to make it safe but…"

Your father has caught up. He's bent over, hands on his knees, gasping for air. But he's listening too.

"I told Rachel not to play up here," Van Vleet continues. "Told her it was dangerous. But she was eleven. Eleven-year-olds don't always listen." His voice cracks. "She fell through. The plywood had rotted. Too much snow weight. Twenty feet straight down onto concrete and rusted metal from the old kiln."

The wind cuts across the plateau. You're shivering but you don't think it's from the cold.

"You could have called for help," your father manages. Still breathing hard. "Could have gotten her out. Gotten her to a hospital."

"I tried." Van Vleet's hands are shaking. "I ran up here. Called down to her. She was crying. Screaming. Saying it hurt, saying she couldn't move her legs. I couldn't reach her."

He stops. Takes a breath.

He doesn't finish. Doesn't need to.

"She died alone," you whisper. "In the dark. In pain."

"Yes." The word is barely audible. "And I couldn't face it. Couldn't face that it was my fault. My negligence. My rush to save money. My daughter died because I cut corners."

Your father straightens slowly. "So you created the King of Christmas."

"I told Marcie we had to lie. Had to say Rachel was taken. Abducted. Some monster who came in the night. She didn't want to. Wanted to tell the truth. Wanted to close the resort, leave Pine Hollow, start over somewhere else. Somewhere we could grieve honestly."

"But you couldn't let Rachel go," you say.

"No one would care. This was my fault. I deserved it." He gestures at the pit.

"Marcie supported me at first," Van Vleet continues. Voice flat now. Matter-of-fact. "Six months later, when they'd given up looking for her, when the town didn't care anymore, she said we should tell the truth. That we were wasting police time. Wasting time! On our little girl!"

"So you killed her too," your father says.

"I couldn't let her tell. Couldn't let her ruin the story." Van Vleet looks at him. "You understand that, don't you, Bill? You understand doing anything to protect your daughter? To make her death mean something?"

"No." Your father's voice is steel. "I understand losing a daughter. I understand grief. I don't understand murder."

Van Vleet's face hardens. "The first child I took was David Drake. Two years after Rachel. Kid who vandalised the resort. Spray-painted graffiti on the lodge. I didn't need anyone to tell me he was bad."

"He was a child," you say.

"He was *bad*. And when I took him, when I made it look like the King of Christmas had come for him... the town changed. Parents started watching their children more carefully. Kids started behaving. And I realised... Rachel's death could save other children. Could teach them consequences before they made fatal mistakes."

"You're insane," your father breathes.

"I'm a father." Van Vleet's voice rises. "A father who failed to protect his daughter. Who killed her through negligence. Who created a system to make sure other children learned to be careful. Learned to follow rules. Learned that actions have consequences."

"You created a system of terror," you say. "You held an entire town hostage. You murdered seven children. You didn't save anyone. You just transferred your guilt onto everyone else."

Van Vleet stares at you. At your father. The wind howls across the plateau.

"Maybe," he says finally. "Maybe you're right. Maybe I am insane. Maybe it was all for nothing." He looks down at the pit.

"But Rachel's been waiting for me. I'm sorry I took so long, baby girl."

He steps forward.

Into the depression. Toward the edge where the snow sits strange and low.

"No!" You lunge forward but your father's hand catches your arm.

"Let him go," your father says.

"We need him alive. For the trial. For…"

"Jenny." Your father's grip tightens. "Let him go."

Van Vleet is at the edge now. The snow beneath his feet shifts. Cracks. The rotted plywood underneath is visible now, dark and broken.

He looks back at you both one last time.

"Tell them," he says. "Tell them everything. The town. The system. The truth about Rachel. Burn it all down. You're the only one who can."

"Van Vleet, don't…"

He steps forward.

The plywood gives way with a crack that echoes across the mountain.

He drops.

Not a jump. Not a dive. Just… drops. Into the darkness.

You hear the impact. The terrible, final sound of a body hitting concrete twenty feet below.

Then silence.

Just the wind. And your breathing. And your father's hand still on your arm.

You're frozen. Staring at the hole in the snow. The broken plywood. The darkness beneath.

"He's gone," your father says quietly.

You nod. Can't speak. Can't process what just happened.

Your father pulls you back. Away from the edge. Away from the pit that took Rachel forty-nine years ago. That took Van Vleet now. That holds them both forever.

"We need to call someone," you manage finally. "Report this. Get authorities up here."

"Not Pine Hollow authorities."

"No. *Real* ones."

Your hand goes to your pocket. Your phone. Van Vleet's full confession. His admission about Rachel. About Marcie. About the system. About everything.

Evidence.

You have everything you need.

"Come on," your father says. His arm around your shoulders. "Let's get back down. Get your mother. Get out of here."

You let him lead you down the slope. Back through the snow. Past the lodge. To the truck.

Continue to page 495

FEEL AROUND FOR AN EXIT

You need to find a way out.

The door is locked. But maybe there's something else. A vent. A loose board. Anything.

You roll onto your side and start inching along the wall, feeling with your shoulder, your legs, any part of you that can reach.

The wall is stone. Cold. Solid.

You reach the corner. Start along the next wall.

Shelves here. Metal shelving units bolted to the wall. You feel behind them with your feet. Nothing. Just wall.

Your ankles ache from the rope. Your wrists are numb.

You keep going.

The third wall has a boarded window, high up near the ceiling. You stare up at it now, trying to judge the height.

Even if you could get your hands free, even if you could stand, it's too high. And boarded from the outside.

No exit there.

You continue around the room.

The fourth wall, the one with the door, offers nothing.

You've made a complete circuit.

There's no other way out.

You slump against the wall, breathing hard, exhausted. How long have you been doing this? Minutes? An hour?

You don't know.

Your shoulder throbs. Your head pounds. The drugs are still in your system, making everything feel distant and heavy.

You close your eyes.

Maybe if you just rest for a moment...

The sound of voices outside gets louder. Closer.

The lock clicks.

The door opens. Turn to page 409

ROLL DOWN THE WINDOW

You press the button. The window descends halfway. Cold air rushes in, sharp and biting.

"Jenny." Katie's face softens. "I thought that was your car. You really did it. You came."

"I told you I would," you say carefully.

Katie nods, glances back at the house, then at you. "Look, I'm sorry about earlier. Siobhan and I... we were scared. For you, I mean. This whole thing is..." She shakes her head. "But I understand why you're doing this. I do."

You wait, trying to read her.

"Come inside," Katie says. "Please. It's freezing out here, and you'll see better from the window anyway. Plus, Lily's still awake and I hate leaving her alone for too long."

"I don't want to impose..."

"You're not." Katie's smile is genuine, warm. "Honestly, I'd feel better knowing you're inside where it's safe. And warm. Come on."

She steps back, gestures toward the house.

You hesitate for only a moment, then unlock the door and climb out. The cold bites at your face. Katie waits for you, arms wrapped around herself.

"Siobhan's out," Katie says as you walk toward the house. "Working late at the Inn. It's just me and Lily tonight."

You think for a moment of how you slipped downstairs, refilled the thermos that you haven't touched. How you were right to be careful; Siobhan was still at the Pine Hollow Inn. That was one confrontation you didn't need. Siobhan and Katie are two very different sisters.

Inside, the warmth is immediate and enveloping. The living room is cosy. An enormous Christmas tree takes up one corner, fully lit and decorated. Stockings on the mantel.

And there, on the couch, a little girl. Maybe seven or eight. Dark hair in a ponytail. She's watching a Christmas special, wrapped in a blanket.

"Lily, honey," Katie says gently. "This is Miss Matthews. She's a friend of mine."

Lily looks up, studies you with dark, serious eyes. "Hi."

"Hi, Lily," you say, smiling. She's so small. So alive. You think of Sarah at that age, and your chest tightens.

"It's almost bedtime," Katie tells her. "Go brush your teeth, okay? I'll come tuck you in in a few minutes."

"Okay, Aunt Katie." Lily slides off the couch, pads past you toward the stairs. You hear her footsteps overhead, the sound of a door closing, water running in the bathroom.

Katie watches her go with obvious affection. Then she turns to you. "Tea? I was just about to make some. And you must be freezing."

"That would be great, actually. Thank you."

"Make yourself comfortable." Katie gestures to the couch as she moves into the small kitchen. "You can see the street from the front window. That's what you're here for, right? To watch?"

You move to the window, pull the curtain back slightly. You have a clear view of the street, the birch trees, your car parked beneath one of them.

"Perfect vantage point," you admit.

"Better than sitting in a cold car," Katie calls from the kitchen. You hear water running, the kettle being filled. "I have chamomile, peppermint, or English breakfast. What's your preference?"

"Chamomile sounds perfect."

The domesticity of it all is disarming. This is Katie's home. Her safe space. And she's letting you in, making you tea, treating you like a guest rather than an intruder.

Maybe you were wrong about her. Maybe she really does want to help.

Katie returns with two steaming mugs. She hands you one and the warmth seeps into your palms immediately.

"Careful, it's hot."

"Thank you." You take a tentative sip. Chamomile, honey, a hint of lemon. It's exactly what you needed.

Katie sits on the armchair, curls her legs under her, cradles her own mug. "So. Tell me the plan. What exactly are you hoping to see tonight?"

You answer, keeping the window in your peripheral vision. "I want to see who places the bells. Who's actually doing it. If I can photograph them, get evidence..."

"You think you'll catch him," Katie says softly. "*The King of Christmas.*"

"No one has so far. But it looks a lot like no one has tried. Despite..." You stop, not wanting to reopen old, or fresh, wounds.

"Despite last year." Katie says, and takes a sip of her tea, considering. "And what will you do? If you see someone?"

"Photograph them. Follow them if I can. Get answers." You lean forward slightly. "Katie, someone out there knows what happened to Sarah. To Tommy. To all of them. And I'm done waiting for the police to do something."

"I understand," Katie says, and her voice is kind. "I really do. You've been carrying this for almost as long as we have. I know what that feels like."

The empathy in her voice catches you off guard. You feel tears prick at your eyes and blink them back.

"I'm sorry I tried to stop you earlier," Katie continues. "That was fear talking. But you're right. Someone should be doing something. And if the police won't..." She trails off, shrugs. "Then I guess it has to be you."

"Thank you," you say quietly. "For understanding."

Katie smiles. "I'm Tommy's sister. I always will be."

Overhead, you hear Lily moving around. Katie glances up. "Let me go tuck her in. Help yourself to more tea if you want. And keep watch. If you see anything, yell for me."

"I will."

Katie sets down her mug and heads upstairs. You hear soft voices, Lily's giggle, Katie's murmur. The sound of a door closing.

You're alone.

Do you

Stay put and watch the window Turn to page 491
Snoop around. Turn to page 474

STAY AT WINDOW

You stay put. You're not here to snoop through Katie's house. You're here to watch for whoever places the bells.

You turn your attention to the window, watching the street. The snow is falling steadily now, covering everything in white. Your car sits beneath the birch tree, already accumulating a layer on the windshield.

You take another sip of tea. The warmth spreads through you, soothing. You feel some of the tension start to ease from your shoulders.

Katie returns a few minutes later, settling back onto the couch. "She's down. Out like a light."

"She's sweet," you say.

"She is." Katie picks up her mug again. "I worry about her, you know. Growing up here. With all this…" She gestures vaguely. "But what can you do? This is home."

You understand exactly what she means. The complicated relationship with Pine Hollow; wanting to leave, unable to leave, trapped by love and fear and history.

"Did you ever think about having kids?" you ask, then immediately regret it. "Sorry, that's personal…"

"It's okay." Katie looks at her tea. "No. I never wanted them. Not here. Not after Tommy." She glances at you. "Does that make sense?"

"It does," you say softly.

"But Lily… she's my niece. Siobhan's daughter. And I love her like she's my own. So I guess…" Katie trails off, smiles sadly. "I guess I got to be a parent anyway. Just in a different way."

The vulnerability in her voice makes her seem so human. So real.

You take another sip of tea. It's cooler now, easier to drink. You finish half the mug.

"So," Katie says, settling deeper into the couch. "What do you think? About the King of Christmas. Do you think he's still out there? Still... doing this?"

You open your mouth to answer, but a wave of dizziness washes over you.

You blink. It passes.

"Sorry," you say. "I'm just... tired. It's been a long few days."

"I bet," Katie says. Her voice sounds slightly distant. Or maybe that's just you.

You shake your head, trying to clear it. Focus on the window. The street. The snow.

But everything is starting to feel... soft. Blurred at the edges.

"Katie," you say, and your voice sounds wrong. "I think I..."

You rub your eyes. The room feels softer somehow. Edges blurred.

Katie is watching you. You can feel her gaze.

"Jenny," she says quietly. "I need to tell you something."

You try to focus on her face. It's becoming harder. "What?"

Katie sets down her mug. Hasn't touched it, you realise distantly. She's been holding it but not drinking.

"I can't let you do this," she says. Her voice is steady. Sad. "I can't let you keep digging. I can't risk Lily."

The words filter through slowly. You're trying to understand but your thoughts are sluggish, tangled.

"What... what are you...?"

"The tea," Katie says simply.

The tea.

You look down at your empty mug. Understanding comes slow, like wading through fog.

"No," you whisper. "Katie, no..."

"I'm sorry." And she sounds like she means it. "I really am. But you wouldn't stop. I warned you. Siobhan warned you. But you

492

came anyway. You told us you were coming, and I…" She trails off.

"I didn't have a choice."

You try to stand. Your legs won't work. You slump against the couch cushions.

"Please…" Your tongue feels thick. "Hospital… you can still…"

"It's too late for that." Katie's voice is gentle. Almost kind. "It'll be over soon. I promise it won't hurt much."

Your phone. You need your phone.

You reach for your pocket but your hand won't cooperate. Everything is so heavy. So slow.

Katie doesn't try to stop you. She just watches.

"Lily," Katie says softly. "Everything I do is for Lily. You understand that, don't you? You'd do the same. For Sarah. If you could have."

Sarah.

Your sister's name pulls at something deep inside you. You wanted to find her. You wanted answers.

"I just… wanted…" you manage.

"I know." Katie reaches out, puts her hand over yours. Her touch is warm. "I know what you wanted. But some things… some people… they can't be found. And looking for them just puts everyone else in danger."

The room is tilting now. Or maybe you're tilting. You can't tell anymore.

Katie's face above you. Blurring. Multiplying into two Katies, then three, then one again.

"I'm sorry about Sarah," Katie whispers. "I'm sorry about Tommy. I'm sorry about all of them. But I can't be sorry about this. Not if it keeps Lily safe."

You want to argue. Want to tell her she's wrong. That Lily will never be safe as long as the King of Christmas exists. That killing you solves nothing.

But the words won't come.

The darkness is coming instead.

"It'll be over soon," Katie says. "I promise."

The last thing you see is her face. Sad. Resolved. Alive.

And then nothing.

THE END

You died in Katie Wilson's living room on Christmas Eve, 2025. The poison worked quickly.

Katie called Siobhan. Together, they moved your body. Your car disappeared from Birch Street. By morning, the snow had covered any trace you'd been there.

The official story was that Jenny Matthews drove out of Pine Hollow late Christmas Eve, unable to face the memories. Her parents waited for a call that never came. They never learned the truth.

The King of Christmas continued his work.

SIX MONTHS LATER

Your apartment in Boston overlooks the Charles River. Eighteenth floor. Too expensive, really, but after everything, you needed windows. Light. A view that goes on forever.

Your parents now live three floors down. Same building. Close enough for Sunday dinners. Close enough that your mother can drop by with leftovers. Close enough that your father can finally stop searching, stop documenting, stop carrying forty years of grief like a weight he can't put down.

He's taken up woodworking. Makes birdhouses in the building's workshop. Donates them to parks around the city.

The story broke four months ago.

THE KING OF CHRISTMAS: How One Man Terrorised a Town for Nearly Half a Century

By Jenny Matthews

Your byline. Your words. Fifteen thousand of them, laid out across six pages of the Sunday Beacon. Every detail. Every victim. Every year. The system exposed like a wound.

It went viral within hours. Networks picked it up by evening. By Monday morning, the FBI was in Pine Hollow.

You'd given them everything. The recording. Van Vleet's full confession. The location of his body. The pit where Rachel died. Where he'd followed her forty-nine years later.

They found him exactly where you said. Twenty feet down in the darkness. The fall had killed him, the coroner said. Massive trauma. Instantaneous.

And then they found the room.

The cold room in the resort's basement. The one you hadn't seen. The one Van Vleet never mentioned.

Seven bodies. Preserved in the mountain cold. David Drake. Claire Henderson. Tommy Wilson. Sarah. Daniel Peak. Emily Taylor. Amy Crawford.

All of them. Waiting.

Your mother cried for three days when they told her. Not grief, exactly. Relief. Sarah was coming home. After thirty-nine years, Sarah was finally coming home.

The trial coverage plays on the TV behind you as you work on your laptop. CNN. The Pine Hollow case. Day thirty-seven of testimony.

Sheriff Larkin on the stand. Looking old. Looking tired. Looking like exactly what he is…a man who chose complicity over courage for twenty-three years.

"Did you know Robert Van Vleet was alive and living at the resort?"

"Yes."

"Did you know he was responsible for the disappearances?"

"Yes."

"Did you investigate?"

A pause. Long enough that the judge prompts him.

"No."

"Why not?"

Another pause. Longer this time.

"Because he threatened my daughter."

The prosecutor doesn't let up. "So instead of protecting eight children who disappeared, you protected your own child by helping cover up their murders?"

"Yes."

That clip will play on every news channel tonight. You've already seen it seventeen times today. It never gets easier to watch.

Fourteen other people are facing charges. Mayor. Town council members. Parents who left bells. Parents who reported other people's children. Parents who knew and stayed silent.

Helen Warren was arrested two weeks after the story broke. Accessory to murder. She knew. Everyone in Pine Hollow knew. When she told Van Vleet that Sarah stole the bracelet, she knew what would happen. She chose her daughter's safety over Sarah's life.

Her trial is still pending.

Barbara Warren changed her name, moved to Oregon, won't speak to her mother.

Katie Wilson did one interview. Today Show. Cried. Said she was terrified for Lily. Said everyone was terrified. Said they had no choice.

The internet tore her apart for it. Chose your own survival over dead children. That was the consensus.

You didn't watch that interview. Couldn't.

Pine Hollow is dying. Not figuratively. Actually dying. Property values collapsed. Businesses closed. The Pine Hollow Inn shut down in March. The café followed in April.

Last week, the town council voted to dissolve Pine Hollow as an incorporated municipality. Let it be absorbed by the county. Let the name disappear.

Some wounds don't heal. Some places can't be saved.

Your editor wants you to go back. Do a follow-up piece. "Ghost town: What's left of Pine Hollow six months later."

You said no.

You're not going back. Not ever.

Your father knocks on your door at six-thirty. Right on time for Sunday dinner.

Your mother is behind him, carrying a casserole dish. Some kind of pasta thing that smells like garlic and cheese.

They come in. Your mother sets the casserole on the counter. Your father heads straight for the windows, like he always does. Stands there looking out at the city. At the river. At the endless sky.

Your mother is setting the table. Three plates. Three forks. Three glasses of water. This ritual you've built together. Sunday dinners.

No TV. No phones. Just the three of you and whatever your mother's cooked and the fact that you're all here, alive, together.

She pauses. Looks at you.

"The cemetery called," she says quietly. "Sarah's headstone is ready. They'll install it next week."

You nod. Can't quite speak.

After they found the bodies, after they brought Sarah home, your parents had a funeral. A real one this time. Not an empty casket. Not hopes and prayers and maybes. A funeral with a body to bury. With closure.

You spoke at it. Told stories about Sarah. About how she loved horses. About how she shared her Halloween candy. About the little sister you lost and spent forty years trying to find.

Two hundred people came. Families of the other victims. People from Boston who'd followed the case. Journalists. Strangers who felt connected to the story.

"What does it say?" you ask. "The headstone."

Your mother's eyes fill. "Sarah Matthews. Beloved daughter and sister. Taken too soon. Found at last."

Your father turns from the window. Comes to the table. Sits. Reaches across and takes your hand. Takes your mother's hand. The three of you connected.

"She's home," he says. Voice rough. "That's what matters. She's home."

After dinner, after your parents leave, you sit at your laptop. The story you're working on now isn't about Pine Hollow. It's about a missing girl in Maine. Cold case from 2003. Nineteen years old. You've been investigating for three months. Following leads the local police gave up on years ago.

You found something last week. Small thing. Credit card transaction. Guy who said he never met the girl, but his Visa shows he bought gas in her hometown the day she disappeared.

Police are following up. Might be nothing. Might be everything.

This is what you do now. The missing. The forgotten. The cases everyone else stopped caring about.

Some wounds never fully heal.

But some truths are worth telling, no matter how long they take to surface.

You told the truth.

And Pine Hollow fell.

And Sarah came home.

And that has to be enough.

THE END

You exposed Robert Van Vleet and the system that protected him. Seven families finally got answers. Justice came to Pine Hollow, even if it came too late.

The story you wrote changed laws about how small-town law enforcement is overseen. It sparked a national conversation about complicity and silence. The Beacon saw a forty percent increase in subscriptions.

Your parents lived three floors down. Sunday dinners. Woodworking. Fresh flowers on Sarah's grave every week.

Pine Hollow dissolved as a municipality in September 2026. The resort was demolished. The land returned to wilderness. The pit was filled with concrete. No one visits.

You kept writing about the missing. Kept finding the ones everyone else stopped looking for.

Some stories end. Some wounds close. Some children come home.

This one did.

A NOTE FROM THE AUTHOR

Thank you for reading *King of Christmas*.

If you enjoyed Jenny's story and want to know which path through Pine Hollow I consider the 'true' version of events, I've created a canonical edition that follows a single timeline from beginning to end. You can find it on my website jerowney.com

If King of Christmas resonated with you, I'd be incredibly grateful if you could leave a review on Amazon, Goodreads, or wherever you like to share your reading experiences. Reviews help other readers discover books they might love, and as an independent author, each one means the world to me.

You can also find me on social media:

Instagram: @jerowneywriter
TikTok: @jerowney
Facebook: @jerowneywriter
Facebook reader group: One More Chapter… JE Rowney Readers

With gratitude,
J.E. Rowney